The Winning of Lady Wisdom

By Sarah Dixon Young

The Winning of Lady Wisdom

By Sarah Dixon Young

The Winning of Lady Wisdom

Published by Incarnation Press.

ISBN 979-8-9875252-0-3 (HC)
ISBN 979-8-9875252-1-0 (PB)
ISBN 979-8-9875252-2-7 (E-book)

To Nick and Colleen Geray,
in whom Wisdom finds a home

To Darius Chaske,
whose journey inspires others to seek the Wisdom of Christ

And in loving memory of
Dusti Goodbird,
who won.

"I do not cease to give thanks for you, remembering you in my prayers, that the God of our Lord Jesus Christ, the Father of glory, may give you the ***Spirit of Wisdom*** and of revelation in the knowledge of Him, having the eyes of your hearts enlightened, that you may know what is the hope to which he has called you, what are the riches of His glorious inheritance in the saints, and what is the immeasurable greatness of His power toward us who believe, according to the working of His great might that He worked in Christ when He raised Him from the dead and seated Him at His right hand…"

Ephesians 1:16-20

"But now I understand a loser's doomed to win
How every dying man is sure to rise again…"
-"Hands in the Air" The Waiting

Table of Contents

Cast of Characters

Hyperon: A villager traveling to the city of Opportunity. Based on Hiram-Abi in 1 Kings 7:13-14 & 2 Chron. 2:13. He was called Hyperon by Clemens of Alexandria in *The Stromata*.

Adam: A man who lives in the city of Opportunity and works for Mr. Specter. Based on the first man, Adam, representative of the flesh, Romans 7:14-19.

Mr. Specter: Adam's employer, a former actor, who professes to be interested in overcoming the injustices of society. Based on "The Scoffer" in Prov. 9:7-8.

Wisdom: The Lady who calls to all in the streets of Opportunity, inviting them into her home. Based on Prov. 8.

Folly: Wisdom's twin and Specter's Associate. An actress at the Megascops Theater. Based on Prov. 9:13-18.

Prudence: An orphan living on the streets of Opportunity who is rescued by Lady Wisdom and adopted by Marv and Obedience Grace. Based on Prov. 8:12.

Horbah: A worker that Hyperon recruits for Mr. Specter. Horbah means destruction. Based on Jer. 44:6

Paideia, a.k.a. Paddy: The proprietress of *The Banquet Bakery*. Based on 2 Tim 3:16. Paideia means instruction that trains someone to reach full development and maturity.

Marv and Obedience Grace: Friends of Wisdom. Parents of Prudence. Based on Rom. 4:3-4, 16-17

Haste: A bully at Prudence's School. Based on Prov. 6:18.

Rocky Loam: The mother of Bene & Sparrow, two of Prudence's friends. Based on Matt. 13:20-21.
Bene: The son of Rocky Loam. A friend to Prudence. Bene means good. Based on Joshua 1:7-9.
Sparrow: The daughter of Rocky Loam. A friend to Prudence. Based on Mat. 10:29
Judas DeCeit: An associate of Mr. Specter's who is able to change his appearance. Based on Psalm 52:1-4.
Lovely, Saul, Pastor, and others: Friends of Wisdom.
The Shadow Children: Orphans in the city, befriended by Prudence.
Malise Dipsuchos: A worker hired by Adam. Dipsuchos means double-minded, wavering, uncertain, and divided in interest. Based on James 1:8.
Haught: A young worker hired by Adam. Haught means high-minded, lofty, and proud. Based on Psalm 101:5.
Cameron: A grouchy, old man who frequents *The Banquet Bakery.* Cameron means crooked nose. Based on Phil. 2:14.

Prologue

The dusty village only had one well[1].

The outcast waited until nearly noon to make the trek there.

Her small son trotted along silently beside her. Because it was the day of rest, they would not be missed for an hour or so. Their usual work grinding grain prevented them from going to the well together on the other days of the week.

Her calloused hands clutched the large earthenware jar and a small handwritten book. The green of the cover had been caressed into grey, and the golden lettering now only sparkled here or there. She also brought their daily allowance of bread[2].

No one greeted them, and she was glad. Mother and son hurried away from the prying, malevolent eyes of the houses, and she squinted against the overwhelming brightness of the noon sun that reflected off the sand.

"Will you read to me today, mother?" her boy panted.

She smiled down at his damp brown curls and nodded. "I think we will have time if we hurry."

The well was deserted, though she could see many footprints in the sand. The boy leaned on it and plopped down in the shimmer of shade that the stones offered. She set her jar on the ground and handed the book to him while she pulled on the rope with all her might.

---

[1] Is. 12:3; Jn. 4:14-15
[2] Mt. 6:11

Her muscles burned with the effort, but she persisted. Her son needed the water[3]. Soon, she saw the bucket attached to the rope emerging from the cool darkness of the deep well.

"Help me," she said.

The boy jumped up and held the end of the rope so that she could reach out one slender hand to grab the bucket. Some water sloshed, but she successfully pulled it toward the side of the well. Being relieved of its burden, the rope went slack, and the boy dropped it. She poured the water from the bucket to her jar, and the boy doused his head in the falling water. She laughed at him. He shook his head, and the water droplets flew from his curls onto her face and arms, sparkling like diamonds.

She watched as he reached into the jar, grabbing at the water. He pouted because it wouldn't stay in his hand. The water ran between his fingers and back out into the jar.

"Come back!" he wailed into the jar.

He looked up at her and laughed, cupping his hands to hold enough of it to satisfy his thirst[4]. She remembered having taught him to do that only three short years before, when he had been a chubby baby. He had cried then at his inability to capture the water in his hand, but she had taught him a better way.

She drank from the water too and bathed her face with her shawl after dipping it in the water. They huddled together in the bright noon sun, and she took out

---

[3] Ps. 63:1
[4] Mt. 11:28-30; Ps. 107:4-6

the hunk of bread she had carried in the bosom of her dress.

She tore it and took the smaller half. The boy gobbled his quickly. She thoughtfully chewed her first bite, trying to savor each grain of wheat that had been sacrificed[5] in its making. The outcast gazed at her chapped hands. The wheat had not been the only thing sacrificed in the making of this bread.

She turned her attention to her son. His cheeks should have been rounded and rosy, but instead, his honey colored eyes were sunk into hollowed cheeks. His thin frame was barely covered by the rags he wore. She had grown up in luxury, and she lamented that her rebellious choices had impoverished her son.

"Will you read now?" he asked around his huge mouthful of bread. She smiled at him tearfully.

"Yes," she said. "I'm full. Why don't you eat my bread while I read?"

He swallowed. "Are you sure?"

She forced a smile. "Quite sure."

He took the bread, studied her for another moment, and then ate her piece as quickly as he had eaten his.

She began the beloved story: "These were desperate times[6]."

She wished she could read the story to the boy every day, but if they lingered at their work, the man who was the boy's father would beat them. The woman knew that if he ever found her copy of the story, he

---

[5] Jn. 12:24
[6] Jn. 1:5

would destroy it. She had secretly carried it with her when the man brought her from her city of Opportunity before the boy was born. She had hidden it, wrapped in a shawl her mother had made, buried deep in her trunk.

"In the darkness and the dirt, a baby was born[7]. Babies don't stay babies forever, so he grew up and became a shepherd[8]," she read.

Once, when the boy was just learning to talk, the man heard the boy talking about the shepherd fighting off the lion and the bear[9].

"Where did he learn such rubbish?" the man looked at her condescendingly.

She shook her head. "It doesn't hurt to teach him the legends of my people," she'd answered.

"Don't be ridiculous," the man had said. "Nothing can make him whole. He was a born a half-breed, and he will stay a half-breed no matter how many silly myths you teach him."

The woman wanted the man to be kind to her son, so she had stopped reading the story. But the boy, who loved the story as he loved his mother, never stopped asking her to read it.

When the man took another wife from the village and had another little son that had no dirty blood from the city of Opportunity, the outcast stopped hoping for his kindness. She gave in to the tender entreaties of her half-blood son and read the story again. However, she

---

[7] Lk 2:7

[8] Jn. 10:14

[9] 1 Sam 17:34-37; Is. 35:8-9

would only read it by the well on rest days so that the man would not hear it.

And she made the little boy promise not to talk about the story in front of others.

He made the solemn vow in order to hear the story again, and he kept it. However, she thought she could tell when he was telling it to himself because his lips would curve into a half-smile even when the work was hard or the beating severe. The story was a door[10] he stepped through, leaving this present life of darkness and suffering.

In this way, the story became more than a legend to the woman, just as it had never been a legend to the boy.

All too soon, she shut the book.

"Mother, I wish the shepherd lived here," he said wistfully, swatting at a fly.

She looked over at the hills. "The shepherd lives far[11] from here, son," she said.

They sat silent for a moment. She wished their hour could stretch into the entire afternoon instead of having to hurry back to the man's unkindness.

"Look at me, my son," she turned to him.

He sat up and looked at her intently, as if waiting for her command.

"When you become a man, I want you to go to the city," she said.

"The city?" he repeated. "What city?"

---

[10] Jn. 10:7

[11] Ps. 38:21; Eph. 2:17

"Opportunity," she said, "the city I came from. You must go back there, and you must look for your shepherd there. This is a true story, and the Shepherd is a true Shepherd."

He scrunched up his nose.

"I don't want to walk that far," he said, in his practical child's voice.

She put her hand on his shoulder. "You must do whatever it takes to get away from here and return there," she said very seriously. "You must find the shepherd[12]."

The shepherd seemed very real to the boy in that moment, and though he did not know the way, the boy supposed it could not be terribly far to the city[13].

"I will go, and I will find him[14]," the boy murmured.

---

12 Jn. 10:16
13 Ps. 107:4
14 Mt. 7:7

Chapter 1

The bus ground to a halt with the shrill screech of brakes.

Hyperon jolted awake in his seat. Darkness shone through his window. He couldn't remember what day it was, much less the time.

"Opportunity!" the driver hollered over his shoulder. "All passengers for Opportunity! You got five minutes!"

Hyperon stood and jarred his head against the low ceiling. It wasn't the first time he'd done that in his two weeks of travel. He rubbed the lump and grabbed his bag. At least he'd never be riding this bus again.

He'd been near the front, so it didn't take long to work his way down the aisle through the mass of sleepily moving bodies. As he reached the stairs to descend, he caught the scent of rain. He turned up the collar on his overcoat. Sure enough, a steamy wetness met him on his first step into his mother's native land.

It was a steady, light rain that surprised Hyperon with its drenching ability. It hung like a fog rising from the hot pavement to cloud his view. There was nothing cleansing about this rain. He trotted to the nearest building and huddled beneath the overhang trying to get his bearings. A man ran past attempting to stay under the overhang. Hyperon unintentionally blocked his way. The man slowed long enough to spit at Hyperon and mutter, "Watch out, villager."

Hyperon suddenly realized that he couldn't just shed his foreign identity[15] like he had his home. His

---

[15] 1 Chron. 29:15

mother had been exiled, and Opportunity just waited to spit him out too. All his longing to be here ran through his fingers like water.

Buildings surrounded him like forbidding sentries and lights flashed everywhere though it was the middle of the night. Cars passed on the road between the buildings and blew horns like no one in the city ever slept. He knew no one. He had no place to go. Yet, he pushed even the hint of memory of home far from his tormented mind. He had no desire to remember the past.

"Hey, buddy, got a light?" came a jovial voice at his elbow.

Hyperon turned to see a young man about his own age staring at him with half a smile. He was blonde and trim. His teeth were perfect, and he held a ready cigarette in his lips.

Hyperon shrugged and reached in his pocket for the cheap lighter he'd found in a rest stop on the second day of his journey. His companion took it and lit the cigarette.

"Beast of a night, isn't it?" he puffed. "I'm just on my way to my place. You look like you could use some soup and a night's sleep."

Hyperon eyed the young man. Was he offended that Hyperon was a half-breed? No one in his hometown had ever offered him anything but scorn. Hyperon pushed his hood back. The other man studied him.

"Are you coming or not?" the stranger asked.

Hyperon's long stride kept an even pace with his new companion as they darted through alleys and across streets. Once, they hurried over a bridge where Hyperon could hear the black water swirling far below. The stranger kept up a constant banter, but Hyperon answered him little. How would it be if this jovial man slit his throat in the night? Certainly, his father's neighbors would say it had been a just end to what never should have been.

"I just roll with the flow, as the saying goes," his companion was saying, "and here we are." He stopped in front of a low, blue building. Hyperon could hear a child crying inside as the man put his key into the lock.

"I never mind the noise of the others because I don't have to pay anything to live here," he said. They hustled up a flight of stairs dimly lit and took the left hand corridor to a second locked door. Again, the key was produced and utilized, and the door swung open to reveal a living room empty except a huge flat screen television and a mattress on the floor in front of it.

"Whatever else it might be, it's home," the stranger said, flinging his coat to the floor. The kitchen was down a hall to the left, and it was to this that the man led him.

"My name is Adam[16], and you're welcome to stay here as long as you like, as long you don't mind me coming and going as I please," he said.

"Thank you," Hyperon managed. Adam rubbed some grease off of a pot, filled it with water, and set it to boil.

The silence prompted Hyperon to offer, "I'm Hyperon, and I've just come to the city."

"No joke," Adam said, reaching into a thin closet. He rustled for a moment before producing a

---

[16] 1 Cor. 15:21-22

package of ramen noodles. As the door swung closed, a mouse ran past Adam's foot. Hyperon said nothing.

"Opportunity's not so bad," Adam said. "We are an open-minded sort that loves to help outsiders become insiders. I grew up here, and I have lots of friends that help me when I need it. I don't have to lift a finger, and the kind people of the city provide all I need[17]."

"That sounds ideal," said Hyperon, skeptical that anyone would be willing to help him for free. He thought of the man who had cursed him at the bus stop.

"It really is," Adam said, getting down a bowl and spoon, "and you look like you could use some kindness in your life as bad as a meal. Why don't you get some sleep, and then we can go see my employer. You didn't have anywhere to be, did you?"

Hyperon shook his head as Adam poured the steaming water over the bowl of dry noodles. "No," Hyperon said grimly. "I didn't have any plans about what I'd do once I got here."

"You need a plan for your life, man," Adam said. "No more aimless wandering."

The water soaked into the noodles as silence fell between them.

"Your employer," Hyperon ventured. "Will he mind about my heritage?"

Adam smiled and shook his head. "Haven't you been listening to me? What matters about a person isn't where he comes from. It's where he's going that counts. Mr. Specter taught me that. I guess you could say it's his motto."

---

17 Ps 10:2-6

Hyperon nodded, taking a slurpy bite of the ramen that burned his lips slightly.

"Mr. Specter will take stock of what you've done in the past and fit you perfectly for how you can be most useful now," Adam shrugged. "No worries."

After finishing his meal, Hyperon followed Adam down the narrow hall to another room. It had a dusty blanket in one corner but nothing else.

"It's dry," said Adam. "I sleep in by the T.V. so you'll have the place to yourself." With a wave of his arm, he disappeared back down the hall. Hyperon heard the T.V. click on and voices from a program laughing and screeching at each other. He shut the door and slumped down against the wall. At least he was out of the rain.

Chapter 2

Every city has people that it pretends aren't there[18].

Even the authorities turned a blind eye to the roaming packs of neglected children who raided the dumpsters, so long as they stayed out of sight.

Several of them leaned on the dumpster while one taller boy hung over the edge with his head inside, searching for edible scraps.

One of the girls watching him carried a two year old baby on her hip. The baby was traded among the girls like a commodity. People were more apt to give food or money if you had a baby to blink up at them. They all called the baby "Precious Baby Girl," and no one could remember where she had come from. She was used to hard knocks and sleeping on the ground, and she hardly ever cried. The grime made it hard to discern what color her hair or skin was.

The girl holding the baby licked one hand and ran it over Precious Baby Girl's sticky head.

"Did you find anything?" the girl demanded impatiently of the boy.

"Give a fellow a chance!" came back the muffled, impatient reply. A few of the younger children pushed back and forth at one another. One little boy watched cars speed by the end of the alley.

The boy in the dumpster let out a low whistle.

"What is it?" demanded the girl. Even Precious Baby Girl looked up expectantly.

---

18 Ps. 102:17

The boy jumped down, cradling a discarded pizza box. "Still got half a pizza in here!" he said exultingly.

The girl set the baby down as they huddled around him, grabbing at the box. The baby crawled toward them, trying to work her way into the circle.

They began shoving, and the boy who had been watching the cars grabbed the box and ran halfway down the alley.

"Hey!" the older ones shouted. They chased him. Soon, the melee had evolved to another alley, and the baby sat up and popped her thumb into her mouth.

She waited patiently for another little transporter to come and put her onto a hip. So she had always been carted around in her memory. The light in the sky grew greyer, and still the baby sat with her thumb in her mouth. Her eyelids grew heavy, and she slid to the dirty cement and slept.

Precious Baby Girl woke in utter darkness[19]. A dog was sniffing at her. She squealed and slapped at it with her grimy hands. It yelped and ran away.

She rubbed her eyes. Where were the children? They had never come back, and she was hungry. Her thumb would not be enough. She whimpered, and no one came.

She began to cry loud wailing cries, and still no one came for her. The sobs shook her dirty body. Her fears, like all childhood fears, revolved around the darkness and the dog, but didn't venture into the future.

Her cries left her deaf to approaching footfalls[20].

---

[19] Ps. 139:12
[20] Jn. 14:18

They were padding, barefooted footfalls.

Soft, grey light spread through the alley, and a woman with auburn hair and smiling green eyes came and stood in front of the crying child.

She knelt down[21] in the grime and patted the baby's emaciated leg. The crying stopped immediately, and the thumb popped into the mouth as the round eyes studied the woman.

"Hello," the woman said.

Precious Baby Girl hiccupped. She reached out one bony hand to touch the woman's beautiful long hair.

The woman held out her hands and the baby held up her arms in surrender[22]. The woman lifted her onto her hip, not seeming to mind the soiled diaper, grimy skin, or sticky hair.

"Will you come with me?" the woman asked.

The baby knew enough to nod.

"I have good plans for you[23]," the woman told her, in a voice like a song.

In a part of the city that did not have alleys, Precious Baby Girl stared up into the leafy green tops of trees. They arched over the road like umbrellas, and she was fascinated. She cooed and chatted with the woman in her own baby speech. The woman laughed and chatted back, as if she understood every word.

Instead of towering buildings, there were houses. The woman carried the baby through a myriad of streets until they reached a house with low shrubbery on the

---

21 Lk. 10:34
22 Jer. 21:9
23 Jer. 29:11

outside. The woman walked up the sidewalk and knocked three times on the wooden door.

A cheerful, plump woman answered the door almost immediately.

"Come in!" she greeted. Precious Baby Girl eyed her suspiciously, but liked the look of her rosy cheeks.

"I have a task for you," the beautiful auburn-haired lady said, smiling down at Precious Baby Girl.

The plump woman came closer. Her eyes welled up with tears. "Really?"

"Really," the first woman said. "You have been asking for the opportunity to show love, and here is one who needs it."

The plump woman covered her mouth with her hand. A man with a mustache stood from a table in another room where he had been reading and came and stood behind the woman, putting his hand on her shoulder.

"Doesn't she belong to anyone?" the man asked.

"Only to me," the woman said, "and I am entrusting her to you."

Tears ran down the plump cheeks. "Oh, Marv! This is what we've been waiting for," she said and held out her arms to Precious Baby Girl.

The baby was hesitant at first, not wanting to leave the embrace of her first Rescuer.

"It's all right," the woman assured her. "This will be your mother now, and she will share my love with you."

The baby smiled and went to the plump woman. She folded her in an ample embrace, showing the same unconcern for the mess and dirt that the first woman had.

"We will get you cleaned up and fed, my little one," she said. She looked at her guest, "What is her name?"

"No one has known her name except for me," the woman answered, "and I will share it with you- It is Prudence[24]."

[24] Prov. 8:12

Chapter 3

A glass window announced a yellow building to be the office of "Specter and Associates." Bells jingled above the door when they entered, and the carpet smelled new. Hyperon sat next to Adam in the waiting area as a blonde secretary informed Mr. Specter of their presence. Hyperon fidgeted in his chair wishing that his clothes were cleaner, his cheeks more smoothly shaven, and his demeanor less prepossessing as one from the villages.

Mr. Specter came down the hall with the secretary as she returned. Hyperon knew it must be him. He wore a dentally altered smile and a brilliant yellow tie. Everything about him screamed sophistication[25].

"Adam," he said, shaking hands with the younger man heartily, "Hope life is treating you well! Ah, I see you've brought company."

Specter held out his hand to Hyperon. Hyperon grasped it in a firm clasp, as his mother had taught him. A mother's hand should be soft in a boy's life, but his mother had provided the firmness that his father had shirked. Hyperon was glad of it now. At least half of his blood throbbed with the memory of this city.

"This is my friend, Hyperon," Adam introduced. "He's just arrived here."

"Welcome to Opportunity. I trust you'll find that we are ready to embrace you with open arms here in the city," Specter said congenially.

Turning back to Adam, Specter said, "What can I do for you boys today?"

---

[25] Jer. 7:24

"Hyperon here didn't have any firm plans when he arrived," Adam explained, "so I told him about how I work for you and live just as I please. I thought perhaps you could talk him into working for you too."

Hyperon heard the word work and raised an eyebrow. What type of 'work' would Mr. Specter expect from him? Adam hadn't mentioned exactly what he did for Mr. Specter, but Hyperon had anticipated some kind of cost. No one gives something for nothing.

"Well, now, come back to my office," Specter was saying as he led them down the hall. The hall was papered with smiling photographs of children alongside thank you notes written in their childish script. The words 'food,' 'education,' and 'shoes,' jumped out at Hyperon as he followed the others. The office was richly furnished, and Hyperon admired a painting on the wall depicting a beautiful tree heavy with multi-colored fruit[26].

"Have a seat," Specter invited. He sat behind his own mahogany desk and clasped his hands behind his head.

"Hyperon, do you have any work experience?" he asked.

"I've done my time at just about every type of labor," Hyperon answered. "Farming, construction, sales."

Specter drummed his fingertips together[27].

"I suspect," he said in a lower, confidential tone, "that you have been treated poorly by those who have

---

[26] Gen. 2:16-17
[27] Mt. 7:15

employed you in the past. Treated you more like a slave, really, I assume. Am I correct?"

Hyperon studied his own feet. He braced himself for the disappointment of not being hirable due to his mixed heritage.

"I suppose they couldn't do any different," Hyperon said shortly, "and I didn't sign on those jobs to be paid in kindness."

Specter nodded and rested his chin on his fingertips.

"I am sorry you have known such a life," he said quietly. "Adam here has worked for me for several years now, and he has seen the benefit of helping those who suffer to find inclusion and peace. It's helping those less fortunate get what they deserve, really, and fighting for the rights of the common man. You saw all the children in the hallway that we have been able to help."

Hyperon nodded as the thought dawned on him that this man might not object to who he was.

Mr. Specter reached for a photo frame which stood next to his computer screen on the desk. Two brown eyed boys had their arms wrapped around one another. The older one held a soccer ball.

"Just take these boys, for example. They grew up with a single mom who had to work long hours. No one was looking out for them or providing opportunities for their education. They just were going without and getting into trouble. I heard about it and jumped in to make a difference! Look at those smiles," Mr. Specter set the frame back on his desk, smiling.

"I can see you share my passion for fighting the injustices[28] of the world, Hyperon," Specter said, "and I would love for you to use your history, your hurt, and your talents to help make this world a better place for others."

Hyperon had never considered that he might be able to help anyone else. He had never even been able to help himself before now.

"What do you say? Adam can show you the ropes. Your work will be fulfilling, and then you will also have lots of leisure time to enjoy yourself here in the city. It won't really be work at all. You won't be a slave but an associate! Will you join us?" Specter asked.

Hyperon looked into the man's flashing eyes. Though Specter remained perfectly calm on the exterior, his eyes betrayed an excitement. Was he that excited about Hyperon working for him?

"I'm not sure if I will be good at furthering the rights of others," Hyperon balked. "I'm not even sure how one would go about doing that. I'm just interested in what concerns me."

Specter smiled. "My dear boy, you are a prime example. You've been treated poorly all your life simply because of your parentage. You couldn't help that, and I could turn a blind eye to the injustice. I could ignore it and just be 'interested in what concerns me,' as you say."

Specter shook his head sadly.

"And where would that leave you? No! Instead, I am leading an active charge, fulfilling my destiny by

---

[28] Ps. 94:20

turning the world right side up for thousands of people. I don't want people like you to suffer all because of misfortunes that are out of their control. I want to give them the resources, lifestyles, and kindness that they deserve. And I would love it if you joined me."

Specter stroked his chin thoughtfully.

"Your passion is what matters most. I can see it in you! Everything else will follow, but in short, you will simply persuade people to let go of the archaic notions that cause them to mistreat their brothers. You may even be able to hint to them that slaving away working for others is really getting them nowhere." He let that thought settle into Hyperon's mind.

"All I require is for you to agree not to be persuaded by those notions. You must be firm in your resolution against injustice. You must actually be unpersuadable when it comes to any other ways of thinking[29]. You must live and breathe the idea of living life to its fullest. Just think how many people like yourself that you will be able to help," Specter said.

Hyperon considered this. He still didn't feel passion welling up inside him exactly, even though Specter said he could see it. Perhaps it was a growing sense of belonging that he felt.

"Your duties will also include visiting those who have made agreements with me and ensuring that they too remain unpersuadable and continue to uphold the rights of those who deserve them," Specter explained.

"What will we do when someone opposes us?" Hyperon asked.

---

[29] Col. 2:8

Specter laughed loudly, startling Hyperon. He noticed that Adam jumped too.

"You are a fellow with a quick working wit!" Specter explained. "It isn't hard to persuade them to join your cause, and I'll give you all the tools you'll need to do it. Let me show you."

At this Specter swiveled around in his desk chair and reached up to unlock the mahogany cabinets above his desk. He withdrew a box that held stacks of money, several books, a six pack of beer, DVDs, food, a laptop computer, brochures about how to get money through assistance programs, and what looked like political activism buttons[30].

"Appealing to people's collective sense of justice works sometimes, but then we can always fall back on reminding them how inclusive behaviors benefit us all. If all else fails, we use these incentives to reinforce the pleasure and agreeableness of our position," Specter explained.

Hyperon studied the items spread before him.

He nodded slowly and glanced at Adam to read his expression. He was smiling at the things on the desk. It was true that Adam seemed happy with the employment. Specter returned to the cabinet and removed a large spiral bound book and pushed it across to Hyperon.

"All you have to do is sign on the top page[31]," he said.

---

[30] Is. 47:8-10

[31] Prov. 29:5-10

Hyperon picked up the book and looked at the paper on the top. It simply read, "I will be unpersuadable when it comes to injustice, and I will advocate for the rights of the common man. I will labor to keep others from being deceived in order to promote an ideal society, and I will do other pleasurable duties at Mr. Specter's discretion."

He had no idea what was in the rest of the agreement, but it would take him too long to read it. He felt the pressure of Mr. Specter's eyes on him.

Hyperon signed.

Specter smiled and held out his hand. "Unpersuadable?"

Hyperon stood and shook it. "Unpersuadable[32]," he nodded.

---

[32] Jn. 12:40; Is. 6:9-12

Chapter 4

Prudence skipped rope on the step of the porch.

Every few minutes, she stopped and looked anxiously down the deserted road. The trees swayed in the breeze. A few cars sauntered past. Her mother's hum floated out of the window.

"When will she be here, mother?" she called through the screen.

She could hear the smile on her mother's face, "Soon."

She skipped and smelled the baking apple pies and listened to the humming and looked down the road.

A sparkling laugh made her drop her rope.

"Prudence!" called the joyful voice.

The Lady with auburn hair stood at the end of the walk with her arms open wide. Prudence ran to her, lifting her own arms as she had when she was a baby.

She was lifted and kissed, and she hugged tightly around the woman's neck.

"I am happy to see you," the Lady said. "Let's tie your shoe, so you won't trip."

Prudence hadn't even noticed the untied shoelace.

The Lady knelt down in front of her and took the blue laces in her expert fingers.

"Watch closely," she said. Prudence studied the deft movements.

"Cross. Wind. Loop. Hug. Pull tight!" the Lady said. Prudence smiled down at the neatly tied shoe[33], but frowned as the Lady undid her neat work.

---

33 Prov. 1:2-7

"Now, you try," the Lady said. Prudence immediately wished she had paid closer attention.

She knelt beside the Lady and took the ends of blue shoelace in her own inexperienced hands. Cross. She was stuck.

"Wind," the Lady said. Prudence wound one lace around the other.

"Not too much winding," the Lady said with a chuckle when Prudence kept winding.

"Loop. Hug. Pull it a little farther in first! You got it," the Lady cheered her on.

Prudence pulled the laces tight, but her loops were not nearly as tight or as neat as the Lady's.

"Keep practicing," she said, "and then you will be an expert!"

"I will," Prudence resolved.

"I have brought you a gift," the Lady said.

Prudence's eyes opened wide. "What is it[34]?"

"Let's go in, and I will show you."

They walked through the door together. Prudence's mother rushed out from the kitchen, with flour on her apron and arms.

"It smells delicious!" the Lady said.

Prudence's mother hugged the Lady. "We are so happy that you could come."

The Lady sat and ate with them, and Prudence waited very patiently for her present. Finally, the Lady took a small parcel from the pocket of her dress. It was a rectangle wrapped in plain brown paper and tied with a string. She smiled and held it out to the little girl.

---

[34] Ps. 68:18

Prudence took it and undid the string carefully. When she unfolded the paper, she found a green book.

"This is the greatest story that has ever been told," the Lady said reverently. "I hope your mother will read it to you, and then, when you are older, you can read it to yourself[35]."

Prudence looked up. "I already know some of my letters." Her excitement was evident. She flipped through the pages of the book and saw one picture of a shepherd carrying a white lamb on his shoulders. The lamb's legs were held in the hands of the shepherd so that it could not fall or struggle[36].

"Will you read it to me, mama?" Prudence asked, turning to her mother.

"Yes," her mother said, "just as soon as our company leaves. Now, where are your manners?"

"Oh!" Prudence looked sheepish. "Thank you! Thank you so much!"

The Lady's smile forgave her oversight in a moment. "You are very welcome." Then, she turned to Prudence's mother.

"Obedience," she said, "it is getting harder for everyone to meet together[37]. There is a new place that I think will be better than where you were meeting. I want you and Marv to come with me there tomorrow, if you can, and see what you think about holding meetings there."

---

35 Ps. 12:6
36 Lk. 15:4-5
37 Prov. 22:2; Heb. 10:25

Prudence's mother listened with a frown of concern on her brow.

"Of course," Obedience said. "Marv will have off work tomorrow, so we can come at any time."

The Lady took a bite of her apple pie– Prudence wondered how she could eat without ever making crumbs– and nodded. She swallowed.

"That's great," she said. "I will tell you the address, and we can meet there just after dark."

"Yes," Obedience agreed.

"The enemy always looks up for me, but it is my greatest tactic to reach those furthest down[38]. I think this place will be just the thing!"

---

[38] Phil. 2:5-8

Chapter 5

Specter had given them a folded slip of paper with a name and address on it. Adam now took it out of his coat pocket as they walked along the crowded street. Hyperon nervously eyed the masses of people going to and fro.

"I guess wherever you came from is not as big as Opportunity," Adam observed.

"No," Hyperon agreed. "More like a village, really."

It didn't take them long to find the address. Run down duplexes lined the street. They were crammed together so close that Hyperon thought they must all be connected to one another. A few children ran past chasing a small dog.

Adam rang the bell at the apartment noted on the paper. The name was Rocky Loam[39]. The door cracked open, and Hyperon could see the chain lock that stayed in place. Beyond it stood a middle aged woman.

"Yes?" she croaked.

"Just stopping by to see how you're doing, Ms. Loam," Adam said, smiling. "Mr. Specter sent us. He knows how hard it is to be a single mother these days."

The woman's shadowed eyes shifted from Adam to Hyperon and back again. The chain stayed in place. Hyperon caught the rueful glint in her eye that challenged Mr. Specter's knowledge of any mother's hardship. He thought of his own mother. What if she had had someone who came knocking on the door to offer help?

---

[39] Mt. 13:5-6

"We're fine," she said quickly.

"Did you read the brochures we brought last time describing how you might qualify for an assistance program?" Adam asked.

"Yes," she said quickly. "Yes, I read them."

"If you'd like, we can help you with an application," Adam replied solicitously. "If you let us in, we can help with that and see if there's anything else you might need."

She looked back for an instant into the dim interior of her home.

"N...now isn't a good time," she stammered. "I've just got supper on the table."

Adam's smile never faltered. "That's fine," he replied. "Maybe we can stop by tomorrow. In the meantime, Mr. Specter sent you these DVDs. He thought you'd like something fun for a family night."

The woman grabbed at the DVDs through the crack, drew them in, and slammed the door without saying anything else.

Adam shrugged and turned back toward the road.

He whistled. "Now there's a worrisome case," he said. "Won't take help even when it's offered to her. It doesn't even make sense to be so independent and headstrong."

"Why would someone want to help her?" Hyperon asked. "I mean, why would someone give her money through any kind of program?" No one had ever offered his mother money, and she had died destitute and alone.

Adam stopped and shook his head at Hyperon.

"She's a poor single mother, Hyperon." He said it as if it was enough explanation. "Don't you think she deserves help? Mr. Specter advocates for the rights of single women."

Hyperon shrugged. He knew firsthand that they needed help, but why would someone want to help them?

"Of course she needs help," he agreed, "but I guess what I'm asking is where does it come from? 'Money doesn't grow on trees,' my father always said."

Adam's smile returned.

"He was right about that," Adam said. "No, the money actually comes from those who have it. Some like to do their part in giving to the less fortunate, like us."

They walked along the sidewalk in silence, surrounded by the blaring horns and the whiz of cars. A cyclist wove between them and passed on.

"So does Mr. Specter get all his money like that? I mean, from benevolence or whatever," Hyperon asked. Mr. Specter's office had clearly boasted of prosperity.

"Specter was a famous actor before this gig, and he made lots of money then. He just wants to share what he has to help the masses enjoy living life to the fullest. I would say that he is extremely philanthropic; wouldn't you?" Adam replied.

"So not everyone just goes out of their way to help others," Hyperon's doubts swam about him. "What about those who don't want to help?"

Adam stopped and turned to face him. He put a hand on Hyperon's shoulder and looked at him pityingly.

"Blathering idiots," Adam shrugged. "Slave drivers and greedy swindlers, that's what they are. You expected to do hard manual labor like a slave, but aren't you happy that you don't have to? Mr. Specter exceeds all our expectations," Adam said firmly.

Hyperon considered this. It hadn't answered his question.

"Look," Adam argued, "don't you care that there are others out there like you who have no one fighting for them? The whole world fights against them. Oughtn't we to stand up to that?"

Hyperon shrugged.

"Besides," Adam added conspiratorially, "Specter's incentives make any effort on our part worth it[40]. What would you like to do now? We have the whole afternoon to ourselves now that we've finished our visit."

"What will we do?" Hyperon asked.

Adam grinned and rubbed his hands together. "Ah, my friend, now we do whatever we want! What strikes your fancy?"

Hyperon thought for a moment. In his life, he'd never had much time to do whatever suited him. There were so many choices in the big city.

"I'd like some coffee," he finally said, "and to see a play on a real stage in a theater. My town didn't have a theater, but my mother told me of one she visited once when she was a girl here in the city."

"Done," Adam said. "You never mentioned that your ma was from these parts. Why didn't you ever come before?"

---

40 Ps. 78:17-19

"She left to live with my father before I was born and just never returned," Hyperon answered.

"Look," Adam pointed, "there's the coffee shop."

Hyperon aimed for the main entrance, but Adam clapped a hand on his shoulder.

The blond man chuckled, "No, no, my friend! These folks are some of the greedy swindler type. We'll go in through the back[41]."

Adam led through a side alley that ended behind the row of buildings. Laundry hung on a line in the space behind. Adam quietly eased the rear door of the coffee shop open. Hyperon could hear indistinct voices and cups clinking together.

"Wait here," Adam whispered and edged down the hall. Hyperon shifted from one foot to the other. Stealing carried heavy penalties in the village. He had seen a man lose a hand over a bag of stolen vegetables. Surely Adam didn't intend to steal anything.

Suddenly Adam appeared again in the hallway holding two steaming mugs and a brown paper sack.

"Let's go," he whispered. Hyperon began to protest, but Adam shushed him.

When they were back out on the street, Adam handed one mug to Hyperon.

"And that, my friend, is how it's done," Adam said, taking a cautious sip from his mug.

"Mr. Specter gave me a long list of places when I first started working for him that he said were not interested in contributing to the cause of justice. You asked about the ones who didn't want to help. Well, here

---

[41] Prov. 26:23-28

they are. The owners of that cafe create this system of injustice that we're all suffering under. It is only right that they finance the fix- whether they will or no."

Hyperon sipped from his mug. The coffee was better than good.

"Here," Adam said, holding the bag open. "I got bagels too."

Hyperon ate his in three bites. It quickly silenced his scruples. The crowds on the sidewalks thinned as the lunch hour passed. Adam shook his head more than once at the hurry and bustle.

"Poor blighters," he said, "slaves to the system. Hurry, hurry, hurry is all they know how to do. Just to get back to work they hate to provide fortunes for their oppressors. It's sad, really."

Hyperon studied the buildings they were passing, trying to get his bearings. Adam seemed to know every nook of the city intimately. Many of the buildings seemed to touch the grey sky. Their windows reflected one another and cast great shadows onto the streets and sidewalks below. No houses or duplexes lined the street here. There was a flashy window display for women's clothing, a business with tinted windows, and a lawyer's office all in a row. Other business were stacked on top of them. Hyperon wondered at the concrete sight, marveling that there wasn't even a single tree on the whole block.

Ahead, a bold, black building stood out among the grey of the others. It had no windows, only glossy black sides. It wasn't as tall as the others either, but was instead the only sprawling building in the downtown area. It took up a large portion of the block it was situated on.

"Here's the theater[42]," Adam said.

As they approached, the marquis became visible, jutting out from the front of the building. It was the same glossy jet black as the walls, but in red, curling letters it proclaimed *The Megascops*. Twin yellow-eyed owls adorned either side of the marquis. The wide eyes blinked as Hyperon looked at them.

He started and stepped back.

Adam laughed.

"Realistic, aren't they?" he said.

The heads on the owls turned as if they watched the two men approaching.

Hyperon felt as much like a mouse as he ever wished to. He doubted that this was the theater that his mother had spoken of fondly.

At the entrance, red spotlights illuminated a revolving door.

"Come on," Adam said, pulling him past the door. "Even here I know a back entrance."

They passed the door and turned into an alley that seemed dark even in midday because of the black building it bordered. The alleyway curved into the back of the building, revealing one slim door. Moths hovered by the dim light above it. The light wavered in the heat reflecting off the building.

Adam held his finger to his lips and slipped in. Hyperon followed.

---

[42] 2 Thess. 2:9-12

The carpet, walls, and furnishings were richer than any Hyperon had ever seen. Ebony and scarlet seemed to be the motif, with owls patterned in the marble of the floor and the mosaics on the walls. Though there weren't any trees in sight, the faint smell of pine woods was pleasant.

An unattended counter ran along one side of the hall. There, Adam picked up bags of popcorn and cold sodas.

"Mr. Specter owns the Megascops now," Adam explained, "and keeps this table well stocked for his associates. He wants us to know we're appreciated."

Hyperon took the snacks and followed Adam down the hallway.

The curious art caught his eye and begged for further study, but he didn't want to lose sight of Adam. He tried to store the images in his mind. A face with the features scrambled. A candelabra lit with black flame. An open door with a staircase leading down into shadow. A child in a white dress holding a blackened flower. All were displayed in gilded frames, and the owls stamped into the gilding didn't escape his notice[43].

The hallway led to a stage door, and the stage door led into an empty theater. Adam walked right to the front row and sat down with a contented sigh. Hyperon followed his example.

Adam munched his popcorn. The lights dimmed. Hyperon wondered who had dimmed them. They hadn't seen a soul since entering the Megascops.

---

[43] 2 Pet. 2:12-17

Hyperon kept his questions to himself, not wanting to disturb the anticipatory hush before the opening act.

A girl dressed in rags appeared in the spotlight. Her beauty wasn't hidden by her poverty. Hyperon felt immersed in her story from the opening scene. He thought once of his mother, who had told him about being transfixed by the stories of the stage. Otherwise, he became one with the girl, outraged at those who abused her, triumphant when she overcame adversity. The orchestra carried her voice along, and Hyperon forgot all else.

All too soon the scarlet curtain of intermission fell. He blinked into the sudden light. Adam stood and stretched.

"Good, isn't she?" Adam smiled down at him.

"Yes," Hyperon said simply. All at once, he remembered the city, his new job, and the bagels and coffee of the morning.

"I suppose it's girls like this, who have been so mistreated, that Mr. Specter helps," Hyperon ventured, waving a hand toward the empty stage.

"Sure, and those that are even worse off," Adam said.

Hyperon looked at him.

"Have you ever been caught when you're taking things?" he asked suddenly.

Adam shrugged and tipped his popcorn bag up so that the kernels would roll into his mouth.

"A few times," Adam said, "but Mr. Specter knows all the right calls to make. He's friends with the mayor of this city, and he knows some fantastic lawyers. I've never had more trouble than I liked."

Silence fell between them. Adam walked up the aisle. Hyperon preferred to walk toward the stage. He reached it and touched it timidly with his fingertips. He heard a soft tapping and caught a glimpse of small shoes walking behind the curtain. He wondered if it was the girl. He didn't think of her as just an actress. Instead, she was the girl in the story facing a world of wrong. She was the first person he had ever cared about, besides his mother. He wanted to be the one who had what it took to save her.

Her footsteps died away, and he returned to his seat when Adam came back. The lights dimmed again. The curtain opened, and there she was. She was leaning on a closed door at the top of a flight of steps. In her hands was a small guitar, and the music that flowed from her fingertips was even sweeter than that of the orchestra.

She sang:

Buried deep beneath houses of splendor
All I work for I never can keep.
That's why my hands remain empty
But I refuse to sit here and weep.
So I'll stand with a shout and a sparkle
My heart's light will finally shine through[44]
I'll conquer this world with my wisdom
Until they give me my due.
Yes, I'll stand with one foot on injustice
And the other will trod upon wrong

[44] Jer. 17:9-10

Until we're all our own masters
And more voices are singing my song.
So I'll stand with a shout and a sparkle
My heart's light will finally show through
I'll conquer this world with my wisdom
Until they give me my due.

Her words echoed off the walls. The first time she sang about standing, she stood and walked down those steps until she seemed to be standing just in front of Hyperon, singing only for him. He shared her plight. He shared her passion. His heart was singing her song when their eyes met.

The play continued, and the girl rose to great heights. When the final curtain fell, Hyperon leaned back in his seat, satisfied. It stirred in him the ferocity to create his own happy endings.

He and Adam left the theater in silence. He memorized the way as they walked back to their apartment so that he could come on his own another time.

Yes, this new life had taken him by surprise, but he liked it.

Chapter 6

"These were desperate times," Obedience read. "In the darkness and the dirt, a baby was born."

Prudence had managed to get her mother to read the story five times by the time that they left their house the next day. She walked securely between her mother and father and thought about the hazy memories she had of the darkness and the dirt.

Those had been desperate times indeed, but she had been born. However, she knew that the story was not about her, but about Someone who knew just what it was like to be born into darkness and dirt[45].

He was the Shepherd. He was the Rescuer[46].

And the Lady He had sent to do the rescuing had also brought His story.

Prudence hugged the green book to her chest and listened to her mother and father talk in soft voices as they walked through the neighborhood. The sidewalk led them through the maze of modest homes surrounded by shrubbery.

"I have invited the man from work that I was telling you about," her father was saying.

"Do you think it's safe?" Obedience replied.

He smiled. "Staying safe isn't our goal[47]," he said.

She smiled too, but Prudence thought it was a wary smile. "I know, but I do hope this will prove to be a more secure meeting place."

---

[45] Gal. 4:4-5
[46] 2 Sam. 22:17-20
[47] Ps. 4:8

They walked on and met a crossroad. An empty bench faced them from across the street. Prudence took her mother's hand as they watched an oncoming car. When it passed, they crossed and sat on the bench. It was twilight, and the shadowy night tucked in around them.

Prudence looked at her book while they waited.

"There she is," her mother whispered.

Prudence looked up and saw a cloaked figure moving quickly from the opposite direction. The figure approached and sat beside them, filling the bench. Even though she didn't look at them from beneath her cloak, Prudence knew it was the Lady.

"The meeting place is beneath our feet!" she said quietly. "There is a manhole cover just behind this bench. When we move it aside, you will find a ladder, Obedience. You must go down with Prudence. I will follow you. Marv, you can wait here for any others."

They moved quickly. The Lady stood and her cloak screened them from view of the road, should anyone look their way in the dark. Marv sat still as a statue. Obedience stood and led Prudence around behind the bench. Prudence smiled. It was an adventure.

Obedience knelt as if to tie Prudence's shoe, but instead, she grunted a little as she moved the manhole cover. It must have been heavier than she anticipated, but she succeeded.

Quicker than Prudence thought her mother could move, she stepped down the ladder and then smiled up.

"Give me your book, Prudence," she said.

Prudence held it out, and she took it and put it in one of her pockets.

"Now," she said, "turn around, grab the sides of the ladder, and step down. That's it!"

Prudence shivered in the descent and couldn't see the bottom from the top, but she trusted her mother and she trusted the Lady[48].

The tunnel was darker than the night, but they found the bottom and stood huddled together as the Lady's bare feet made whispering noises on the rungs of the metal ladder. Then, all of a sudden, there was a glowing silver light that warmed Prudence again and made her forget about darkness[49].

The Lady led them through the tunneled passages. Rivulets of water ran beside their feet, but the way stayed dry enough to walk on. Finally, they reached a turn off. The Lady's light leapt up higher than it had before, revealing an empty but spacious room with stone walls.

"This will be more difficult for the opposition to find," Obedience said.

The Lady nodded. "And just think how our singing will sound echoing off these stones." She paused. "You know they watch me, Obedience, so I may not be able to come often, but you know that wherever two or three of you are gathered together, there am I among you[50]."

Faces that Prudence recognized began to appear, and the Lady led them from the ladder to the room with

---

48 Prov. 3:5-6
49 Ps. 27:1
50 Mt. 18:20

her silver light. Prudence's father came last, and he smiled as he entered, bringing a new face with him.

They smiled at one another in the silver glow of the light.

"Friends," the Lady said, "here I hope you will find rest for your souls[51]."

Then, they began to sing.

[51] Mt. 11:29

Chapter 7

He waited in the shadows by the bus stop. It wasn't raining like it had been when he'd arrived two weeks ago, but the hot steam still rose from the pavement. He drummed the inside of his arm with his fingertips. This was his first assignment without Adam, and he hated his own nervousness. He tried to think of something else.

Hyperon missed the smell of grass[52]. He had a hazy memory of reading with his mother by the town well. He couldn't remember if there had actually been grass there, but he remembered the smell distinctly. Sheep and shepherds played into his memory too, but that must have been a part of the fairy tale because he had never seen live sheep in his village. His mother had died when he was still quite young. He felt her lack like the city lacked the smell of grass, but he smiled at the memory of her reading to him.

The fleeting memory of pleasure brought the girl to his mind. He had tried to reason with himself that she was simply an actress, paid to act the part of the girl he loved. However, his reason was always dominated by his intense desire to free her, to know her, to save her.

He took a scrap of paper from his pocket. On it, Specter had scrawled, "Find a new recruit at the bus station." He reflected on the superior kindness of Mr. Specter, who had looked for him before he ever even knew him. Had Adam had a paper just like this one?

People hurried through the orange glow of the street lamps. Part of the wonder of the city for him was

---

52 Deut. 11:15-16

that he never saw the same face twice. Adam usually came with him to the bus stop, and they found newcomers together. Mr. Specter helped find the newcomers their own apartments and assignments, but his basic schpeal to them was the same. It was an important task to recruit others who would be willing to take a stand against injustice. Perhaps in this way, Hyperon was helping the girl just a little.

The squeal and hiss of the approaching bus broke into his thoughts.

The doors parted, and passengers stepped down into the night.

A young woman came first but went immediately into the waiting arms of an older woman, perhaps her mother. Hyperon's eyes moved on to the next person.

He was a young man, and strode with purpose to a waiting taxi. An old woman, a woman with a boy, and a man all disembarked, clearly having places to go and things to do.

The final two passengers were men who seemed to be traveling alone. One had no luggage. Hyperon chose him as his man to recruit.

The man looked around at the city lights, much as Hyperon had done on his arrival. Hyperon stepped out of the shadows.

"Welcome, stranger," he said, working up what he hoped was a friendly smile. "You look in need of a hot meal." Hyperon offered to shake hands.

The man was shorter than Hyperon with lighter skin and eyes, but he was stocky– made like a square brick. His eyebrows were also somewhat square, and his brown hair fell greasily over his ears. He neither smiled nor held out his hand.

"What are you– a greeting committee?" the man's rasping voice grated like gravel.

Hyperon shrugged. "Just one stranger offering kindness to another."

A plucky grin broke across the newcomer's face. Hyperon immediately distrusted him.

"Well, I need the meal more than the kindness, so lead on," the man said.

Hyperon turned, smiling back over his shoulder. "Can't the one thing be both?"

The man shook his head.

"I'm Hyperon," he introduced himself.

"Sure enough," the man said, without offering his own name.

They walked past closed shops through the downtown district. The only storefronts that were open were a few bars near the river due to the late hour. Hyperon could hear music playing and women laughing. He liked to walk this way after he and Adam did any work at the bus stop because he remembered that his mother had once mentioned the beauty of the river.

The bars blocked the view of it, so the beauty was lost to him; however, he wanted to walk as close as he could so that he could still catch snatches of its sound.

A horrendous crashing noise startled him, and he whirled.

The man from the bus stop had tripped on a cobblestone and lunged into a metal rubbish bin. The lid had flown off, garbage blew across the street, and the onlookers gathered outside the nearest bar hooted and laughed, pointing at the stocky man sprawled across the sidewalk.

The stranger rolled over the lid, bounced up, and launched himself into the crowd.

A woman screamed and shouts of pain echoed before Hyperon could react. He started toward his new friend to help, but by the time he stood on the edge of the crowd, the man had reappeared.

"Let's get out of here," the man said, just as calmly as if nothing had happened.

One woman lay on the sidewalk with blood over one eye, and a man was cursing and holding a few bloody teeth in his hand. These people weren't the enemy, but he also didn't want to be associated with any trouble.

Hyperon wheeled and ran.

After a few blocks, he slowed, looked back to see only the man from the bus, and stopped.

The man caught up to him.

"My name is Horbah," he said, offering no explanation for the destruction of the rubbish bin, his burst of temper, or the scene at the bar[53]. He did, however, extend his hand.

Hyperon shook it.

They slowly made their way to the apartment, and Adam was in his favorite position on his mattress on the floor. Hyperon went to the pantry to get ramen noodles for their guest as he hollered out introductions. Horbah said little, and Hyperon grew weary of trying to win the man over.

---

53 Phil. 3:19

Horbah gulped down the noodles without one word. When he stood from the table, his chair fell backward into the wall, knocking a sizable hole in the plaster. He said nothing but promptly fell asleep by the wall facing the TV.

"Good work," Adam whispered, not taking his eyes off his show. "This guy looks like a winner!"

It felt good to be encouraged. He thought of the girl and remembered how people had belittled her and blamed her. Whatever he had to do to help her, he would do, but he hoped other newcomers wouldn't be quite so surly.

Chapter 8

Hyperon swung up into the rafters of the deserted warehouse. The bobbing flashlight of a uniformed officer followed him. Hyperon could hear the man's heavy breathing echo off pallets of merchandise. The light swung this way and that– everywhere but on him. Hyperon had found that his wiry frame easily lent itself to shape shifting and loping through the shadows of the city.

He pulled his legs up and lay on a rafter. Even when the light shone on him, the guard didn't see him. Hyperon watched as the man passed and proceeded to the far end of the warehouse.

He dropped back to the floor and put his hands in his pockets. He strained his eyes into the dark recesses of the large room. The flashlight had blinded him[54], but his eyes soon readjusted to the darkness.

Mr. Specter had asked him specifically to do this job alone. His prowess and ability had already exceeded Adam's.

Hyperon removed the bag that was strapped to his back and began to fill it with the items Mr. Specter requested. This warehouse had a little of everything that people enjoyed. Hyperon loaded his bag with electronics, food, cosmetics, clothing, and jewelry. He tried to make sure to get the items that cost the most.

He spotted the office in the wall nearest to him, and he left his bag to try the door. It was locked, but Hyperon took a small case from his breast pocket and chose just the right tool for the lock. It clicked open with

---

[54] 2 Cor. 4:4

one twist, giving him a sense of triumph and accomplishment. He'd only been picking locks a short time, and he was a master. Mr. Specter had said so himself.

The desk was littered with papers, but Hyperon soon located a file with schedules and shipments that he thought would be beneficial to his employer. Instead of stealing the file, he snapped a photo of it and returned it back to its original state. No one would know that he had seen it.

Just as he turned to go, he heard the night watchman's footsteps.

He hurried, relocked the door without a sound, and ran to his bag, now heavy with loot.

The flashlight played over the warehouse, and the heaving breaths of the guard told Hyperon that his getaway would not be difficult. He hoisted the bag onto his back and clipped it around his waist so that his hands would be free. The light rested on him.

"Stop!" the watchman called.

Hyperon leapt back from the light and ran to the foot of a truss, where he could access the rafters again. He shimmied up, and the befuddled watchman was left looking right and left but never thought to look up.

The haul was heavy, and Hyperon had to move slowly[55]. He walked along the beams, always keeping one eye on the furious guard who was now calling for backup on his radio.

Hyperon found a skylight that he could nudge open and unstrapped the bag in order to lift it out first. It

[55] Prov. 21:6-7

caught on a lever, and Hyperon didn't stop shoving it before it ripped. Something– perhaps it was one of the pieces of jewelry– fell and clattered to the ground.

The watchman ran to it, but Hyperon was up and out after the bag before anything else fell. He carried the bag in his arms now, holding the hole shut with his hand.

Once he made it down to the street, he loaded his haul into the storage compartment on Mr. Specter's motorcycle and drove off into the anonymity of the city, humming the song that played on constant repeat in his mind.

Mr. Specter smiled cheerily later when he looked over each item scattered across his desk.

"You seem to have been born for this[56]!" Mr. Specter said gleefully.

Hyperon showed him the photograph of the paperwork that he had found on the office desk. "I found these too, sir, but I thought it best to leave the originals so that the owner wouldn't think he needed to change his shipping schedules."

Mr. Specter beamed at him. "You are perhaps the most intelligent of all of my employees, Hyperon. You have a gift!" Mr. Specter said. "You remind me of me."

Hyperon basked in the praise.

"Go home and get some sleep now," Mr. Specter said. "I will be sending you some things as a thank you, and enjoy living life to the fullest!"

"Thank you, sir," Hyperon said. As he left the office, he passed a man sitting glumly in the waiting area. The man stood, twisting his cap in his hands, and

---

56 Jer. 1:5-6

walked past Hyperon toward the hall. Hyperon heard Mr. Specter say, "I hope you've brought enough to make your payment, Saul." Hyperon hoped that Mr. Specter would wring every cent from the man, but he didn't stay long enough to hear the man's reply.

The thought of the empty apartment wasn't appealing, and Hyperon found his footsteps heading toward the Megascops.

It was deserted, but the back entry Adam had shown him was open. Hyperon made his way to the room where they had seen the play before. The lights were already dimmed, and the show was in full swing. The girl, with her guitar, was singing,

So I'll stand with a shout and a sparkle
My heart's light will finally shine through
I'll conquer this world with my wisdom
Until they give me my due.

He watched her lips now as she sang. He stood[57] watching her, not even bothering to find a seat.

At the last curtain call, when she bowed, he surveyed the room. Seeing no one, he called, "Please, can I talk with you?"

Some spell seemed to have broken. The orchestra music stopped. The girl stood abruptly and stared at him. All was silent except the distant hooting of the owl[58].

A slow smile spread over her face. She walked across the stage and down the steps.

Her words blended with the owl's: "Who are you?" It was an invitation.

---

[57] Ps. 1:1
[58] Prov. 21:24

He smiled, cursing himself for the sweat on his palms.

"It doesn't matter," he said. "All that matters is who you are."

When she smiled, a dimple showed in her cheek. "I am what you will make of me," she said, arching her sculpted eyebrows.

"Is the story," he swallowed hard, "...is the story about you? I mean, is it your story?"

She tilted her head to one side. "I suppose[59] it is all of our stories wrapped into one. Don't you think?"

He stepped closer to her. "I hope our story blends into one," he said. He sounded stupid, but he was a man under a spell. He reached up to touch the tendril of her auburn hair playing across her fair cheek.

Instead of feeling her warmth on his fingertips, however, his hand slipped through her as if she were nothing but air. He recoiled. What magic was this?

She laughed and faded as the theater flooded with darkness. Her laughter led him as he groped through the darkness. He stumbled forward, falling out of a doorway, into the light of the hall with the artwork. He gained more by being in the light, but he hated it for her absence. It made him hunger for the darkness where at least her voice hovered.

Her voice echoed even here, as over an intercom, though he couldn't see her anymore.

"Ask Specter," she said, "and perhaps he will put our stories together."

---

[59] Prov. 9:13

Hyperon didn't know whether to be afraid of her or to pursue her. He stalked out of the back door and went home troubled.

Chapter 9

A video game console, a bottle of energy pills, and a pile of steaming pizzas[60] proved that the shipping schedule had been valuable to Mr. Specter.

"I would be jealous of you," Adam said with his mouth full of pizza, "but I think I've got the better end of this. You do all the work, and we split the rewards."

Hyperon laughed uneasily and turned his attention back to the game.

They played until the pizza and pills were used up. It may have been three or four days. Hyperon had lost track of time.

Sometime during a lull, he had asked Adam about the girl.

Adam shrugged. "Mr. Specter took me to see her once when I had just signed on," he said. "She convinced me that it was worth staying, no matter what my family said."

Hyperon tried not to sound too eager. "Was she real? I mean, she wasn't just a figment of your imagination." He couldn't bring himself to say the word *ghost*, and he didn't want to ask if Adam had touched her.

"Sure she was real," Adam said, "but she lives out near the city gate. What you see at the theater is just a picture of her, really[61]."

Hyperon squinted at the screen. "What do you mean, a picture?"

---

[60] Is. 47:12
[61] Is. 41:28-29

Adam leaned forward as his avatar jumped over several large crates to fire a weapon at an unseen enemy.

"They just project her onto the stage," he explained mechanically, "so that she can do her real work at the city gate. It's like she controls it with a game controller, just like we're doing."

"What's her real work?" Hyperon asked.

"Recruiting," Adam said, "same as we do."

Hyperon sensed that Adam was tired of his questions.

Now, through the heavy fog of sleep, he could hear someone pounding on the door. Adam was closer to it. He'd let Adam worry about it. He pulled the blanket up over his head, willing the sound to go away.

It seemed like seconds later that Adam was nudging him with his foot.

"Specter sent us an assignment," Adam said.

Hyperon mumbled something.

"I think we'd better get to it," Adam said.

As Hyperon dressed and splashed water on his face, he realized that it was dark outside. He wished he had saved a few of the energy pills.

Horbah sat at the table eating when Hyperon emerged from the hall. Adam was tying his shoes. Hyperon noticed with alarm that the table was cracked near where Horbah was and the door knob was on the floor. He bent to look through the gaping hole. Could the guy do anything without wreaking havoc?

"So, what is this assignment?" Hyperon asked. His ill humor was evident.

Adam finished with his shoes and stood up.

"You remember that woman, Rocky? Mr. Specter wants us to join her in protesting her employer. It seems she works long hours at a factory with little pay. It really is unfair," Adam said.

Hyperon remembered her. He had barely seen her through the crack in her door, but he remembered that she had children and lived in a slightly nicer duplex apartment. He remembered her reluctance to accept help, though she had accepted entertainment readily enough.

He and Horbah followed Adam away from the suburban part of the city toward the downtown area where the Megascops and skyscrapers were. The city lights darkened the stars until Hyperon couldn't see them at all.

Eventually, the sky grew lighter and the city lights grew dimmer. Adam stopped in front of a sprawling factory that spewed out black smoke and handed poster board to Hyperon and Horbah.

Hyperon heard the click-click-click of a can of spray paint that Adam was shaking.

"Just make them say something about corporate thugs taking food out of the mouths of single mothers," Adam suggested.

He tossed a can to Hyperon and carefully handed the other can to Horbah, lest there be any accident. Hyperon was quite adept at painting and sprayed the words, "Starving mothers and children" above a group of thin, crying figures of people.

Horbah's poster ripped, and the nozzle fell off of his paint can. Hyperon offered to paint his poster for him.

They were ready a few minutes before workers began to appear on the sidewalk, coming to begin their day's work.

"Hey, man," Adam said to the first fellow, "did you know on the south side they pay workers twice what they're paying you here? Help us demand justice[62]."

The man raised his bushy eyebrows. "That's hard to believe," he said. "They seem to be so appreciative of us here."

"Pshaw," Adam replied. "They just need your labor to turn a profit, that's all. They aren't paying you half of what you're worth."

The man appeared to consider this. "I do work long hours here," he admitted.

Adam nodded. "Hours you could be spending with your family or out on your boat," Adam said.

Hyperon couldn't think of any bodies of water near the city that would even be large enough for a boat, but then, Adam knew it better than he did.

A small crowd gathered around. Several took up posters and joined Adam, Hyperon, and Horbah. By the time Rocky hurried up the sidewalk, the sunlight was just beginning to shine directly on the group gathered outside the factory.

She was clearly surprised to see them there.

"We couldn't just let you continue to suffer under these conditions," Adam told her.

She shook her head. "They pay a fair wage here," she argued.

Adam shook his head pityingly.

---

62 Prov. 15:27

"You have fallen for their lines," he said. "Join us, and you can spend more time at home with your kids."

She waffled at this.

"Here," Adam held out a poster to her.

Just then, an official came out of the building.

"What's this about?" he asked. He seemed to be some sort of security guard, but not a policeman, Hyperon decided. He was round and had graying hair and a full mustache.

"Good morning, my good man," Adam called to him. "We are here to demand the rights of the workers of this factory!"

"Rights?" the guard squinted his eyes. "What are you talking about?"

One of the employees who had been among the first to take a poster called, "We demand fair wages, Roddy!"

The man scoffed. "Then you're looking for a decrease in pay, Williams. Mr. Fairbanks pays you much more than a fair wage."

A murmur rustled through the crowd.

"We don't think so!" Horbah shouted angrily.

At once, the crowd broke into shouts and pushed toward Roddy. Hyperon grabbed Rocky's arm to keep her from being trampled. The surge of people carried them forward until they were against the doors.

"I'll get Mr. Fairbanks," Roddy was yelling, but no one paid him any attention now.

He entered the door and locked it behind him. Horbah and a few others pounded on it. A pane of glass shattered.

Hyperon glanced around for an escape route in case a hasty retreat was needed. Rocky clung now to his arm, clearly frightened.

"We don't need higher wages," she shouted into his ear.

He shrugged. She must not be in her right mind. How could higher wages hurt anyone?

Another man appeared at the door. He reached through the broken pane and opened it outward onto the crowd. The crowd surged backward and quieted.

This was clearly Mr. Fairbanks. He had on a blue button up collared shirt and khaki pants that said clearly that he was the owner of the company. He smiled kindly.

"What seems to be the trouble?" he asked calmly.

The protesters seemed less sure of their demands now.

"We want higher wages!" Horbah called from somewhere near the back. "We refuse to work like slaves for you any longer!"

The crowd's murmur surged again.

Fairbanks began to call out the workers by name that he could see.

"Jeff, do you get a fair wage? Dan, didn't I pay you when you were on sick leave? Rocky, haven't I been accommodating when you've needed to care for your children[63]?"

Rocky stammered, and Hyperon could tell that she was trying to disassociate herself from the rabble. Her face blushed crimson as she looked down at the sidewalk.

---

[63] Ps. 37:30

Someone threw something that hit Fairbanks above the right eyebrow. He ducked but not in time, and red blood oozed out of the white cut in his flesh.

He ducked back into the doors, but again, they were locked before any of the protestors could make their way inside.

A siren soon sounded from around the block.

Mr. Fairbanks spoke over a loudspeaker. "I am willing to negotiate a fair wage," he said more calmly still. "Please disperse. We will close for today and meet for negotiations tomorrow. Anyone continuing to congregate here or cause violence tomorrow will be promptly removed from the premises."

The crowd quickly dispersed as the siren grew louder and a police cruiser appeared.

Horbah dropped his poster and beat a hasty retreat in the opposite direction.

Adam trotted up to Hyperon and Rocky. "All in a day's work!" he said jubilantly. "Just think, Rocky, now you will have more money in your pocket! Why don't we come home with you and help you sign up for the assistance program?"

She slapped him.

He looked shocked. Hyperon stifled a laugh.

"If I have more money, I won't need your worthless assistance," she spat. "Keep it for yourself."

Adam rubbed his cheek and watched her walk away.

"Let's get outta here," Hyperon said, spurring Adam to action. They rounded the corner of the building just as the policeman was climbing out of his car. All of the protesters were out of sight.

Adam huffed indignantly as he ran, “That was the greatest success! She doesn’t know what’s good for her!”

Hyperon wondered.

Chapter 10

"Our assignment is at the school today," Adam announced.

Hyperon folded an entire peanut butter sandwich into his mouth. He'd been improving his technique and had made it back to the apartment with several sacks full of groceries the night before. On a billboard, he had seen the slogan, "Think positively." He decided to adopt that slogan as his own[64].

"Does Specter have babies in his employ?" Hyperon said around his sandwich.

"There's no better time to sign them up," Adam said, reaching for a ball cap that he'd left on the floor by the door.

Hyperon nodded. "Then, let's go."

They took a different route, weaving in and out of highrises and apartments. Hyperon's eyes noticed more than just the people and traffic now. He had begun to see the city as Mr. Specter saw it. He noticed the clothing- some well-made and clean, others shabby and soiled. Expressions revealed a lot too. A care-worn woman carrying a crying baby contrasted sharply with the laughing face of a little boy eating a hot pretzel. Hyperon had never noticed faces before, and it opened to him an entire world to explore.

Adam pointed out the school, surrounded by a fence and other buildings that proclaimed their purposes in tall plastic lettering.

A clanging bell announced the end of the school day. Hyperon and Adam stood on the outside of the

---

64 Eph. 4:14

chain link fence and watched as students of all ages poured out of the doors- and a few boys hopped out of the windows.

"There's the one we want," Adam said of a tall, pudgy boy. "His name's Haste[65]."

The boy saw Adam coming and grinned. He threw a wadded up paper lunch bag at another boy and sauntered over to Adam.

"What'd ya bring me?" he said.

"Is that any way to greet your favorite Uncle?" Adam asked.

Haste laughed. "Sure!"

Adam slipped him a packet of gum.

"Don't eat it all at once like you did last time," Adam said.

Haste only stopped long enough to put two sticks in his mouth. He chomped vigorously.

"Look at that girl," the boy said, pointing to a small girl with long braided pigtails.

Haste chomped his gum and continued, "She makes better marks than anyone else here, and I hate her. I pull those stupid braids every chance I get."

Adam patted the boy on the back.

"Now, you don't want to be cruel," he said. "It's unfair that she does better than you. It's good to make her aware of injustice, but you should educate her, not punish. She may cast off the advantages she has if you help her to hate them."

They watched as the girl bent down to tie her shoe. She set a stack of books on the ground beside her.

---

65 Prov. 1:10-16

Hyperon thought about what he would do in that situation. Perhaps Haste wasn't as proficient a reader as the girl was. That disparity could cause him to fall behind. Hyperon joined Adam in training their young recruit.

"Quick!" Hyperon whispered to Haste, "Now's the chance to relieve her of her cumbersome load!"

Haste threw them a grin before running over and kicking dirt into the girl's face. As she rubbed her eyes, he swiped three books from her stack and deposited them in the water fountain. He held down the button and watched to see what the girl would do. Her education had commenced.

Hyperon was surprised that she was neither screaming nor crying. He had found in his work for Specter that most people became sad or angry when they were first being persuaded to give up their wrongful ideals and toilsome way of life. This girl was different[66].

She blinked and stood up before gathering the remaining books. Then, she walked calmly to Haste.

"I'm very sorry you've chosen to ruin my books," she said to him, "especially that green one. It had such a lovely story of a baby born in desperate times that grew to be just what the world needed. May I tell it to you[67]?"

Haste threw the sopping green book at the girl. It caught her just above her temple. She fell backward. Hyperon saw the deep red of blood flow down from her hairline. Adam hissed. The boy was back to punishing.

---

66 1 Cor. 13:4-11

67 Mt. 5:11

Still she did not cry.

"Why do you waste your time with these dumb books?" Haste demanded. "Come with me to the ball field, and I could show you some real fun. There's a whole nest of kittens down there, and they holler like anything when you clip their tails together."

The girl sat up and dabbed at her head with a handkerchief and politely said, "No, thank you."

A teacher raced out of the building, and Haste ran back to Adam, leaving the rest of the books in the water fountain.

"Haste!" the woman called, "What have you done? Oh, Prudence! Your poor head!"

"I'm all right, teacher," Prudence said, as the woman hovered over her.

Hyperon chuckled at the distressed state of the teacher juxtaposed with the calm demeanor of the girl. It was like watching a frantic bee trying to alight on a gently waving flower.

Adam held out his hand to Haste for a high five. "Just a little less violence next time, eh?"

"So, you want to see those kittens, Uncle Adam?" the boy asked.

"Maybe another day, son," Adam replied. "You'd better scoot before the teacher remembers you're still here."

Haste laughed and ran in the direction of the field.

Adam turned to Hyperon, "Looks like we have little to do here. Haste seems to be getting along just fine."

Hyperon nodded.

"Why didn't that girl blub?" Hyperon mused as they walked away.

Adam shrugged. "She's the toughest nut to crack at the school. Haste has been terrible to her, and still she persists in being kind in return. Doesn't make sense to me," he said.

Hyperon watched as the teacher dabbed at the girl's head. Perhaps she was good because she had all the advantages of a good home and money. The girl met his gaze and waved at him. It startled him. He didn't wave back, but he wondered about the story in her green book[68].

---

68 Prov. 1:4

Chapter 11

Hyperon followed Adam down the cement stairs to the apartment where Horbah now stayed with several other employees. Adam knocked loudly and looked at his watch.

Horbah came out, shrugging into a grungy looking grey hoodie, and shoving the last bite of a hotdog into his mouth. The sleeve of the hoodie tore, and one of the drawstrings disappeared inside the hood. Horbah bent over in a feeble attempt to regain the string.

"You're making us late," Adam complained.

Horbah offered no reply and left the string where it was.

They walked in silence through the deserted apartment courtyard and caught the trolley to an office complex.

Hyperon studied the storefronts. One looked like the office of a construction company. Next to it was a bar called "Rumors."

"If the devils insist on slaving away for other people, I do hope they take the time to relax at the end of the day," Adam muttered, as several workers filed out of the construction office.

One of them was still stuffing his wages into his pocket. He seemed a little too old to be working construction, and Hyperon thought it would be merciful to convince him that there were wiser uses of his time and energy. All at once, Hyperon recognized him as the man who had been paying a debt to Specter. The man must continue to work at this job so that he could pay his debt. Apparently, it didn't pay well, if what Hyperon had overheard in Specter's office was true.

"That's our man," Adam pointed to the one Hyperon had been watching.

Hyperon knew that they would follow the man. Apparently, he had not only been persuaded to work for the construction company but was also acting suspiciously with his leisure time. Mr. Specter had asked them to find out what the man did with his meager wages.

Adam motioned for Hyperon and Horbah to fall further behind, and he stayed close behind their target. The man's companions called to him to join them in the bar, but he smiled and waved them on.

"I have other plans, fellas," he said kindly. They shrugged and went on their way.

The man pushed his wages further down into his pocket, tucked his hard hat under his arm, and swung his lunch pail as he walked. Adam followed at a respectable distance, and the man didn't seem to notice.

He crossed the busy streets, and Hyperon had trouble keeping him in view because of the rush hour crowds. Adam stayed in their line of vision, however, and Horbah grunted along beside him without a word.

The man left the busiest district of the city and meandered in and out of the residential area. Hyperon continually chanced glimpses of the homes. Some were old and run down, but others were neat and homey- almost happy. He shrugged off that unfair impression and reminded himself of the effort and money it would have cost someone to keep a house looking that attractive. Of course, the dilapidated ones would be inhabited by those who were treated badly- like him, or Rocky, or Haste. It wasn't fair.

The man they were following stopped abruptly at a bus stop bench and sat down. He plopped his metal lunch pail on the bench beside him and took a book out of it.

Adam turned to look at Hyperon and Horbah and shrugged. He motioned for them to stay out of sight.

Hyperon found that the shadow of a garage hid them well but allowed them to keep watch.

Adam shoved the lunch pail to one side and sat down beside the man to strike up a conversation as cars passed back and forth on the street in front of them.

Hyperon could only hear snitches of it.

"…reading?" Adam asked.

"I enjoy reading. It is a pleasure," the man answered.

"…not as easy as joining your friends in the bar," Adam replied.

At this obvious allusion to familiarity with the man's habits, the man jumped up and became angry.

"Have you been spying on me?" he accused.

"I am just a fellow employee, making sure you are keeping your end of the contract you signed with Mr. Specter," Adam said. Hyperon wasn't sure that they would discover anything more about what the man had been doing now, but he waited tensely for when he would need to enter the scene.

Horbah grunted.

Hyperon turned and saw that his eyes were fixed on something coming down the residential street.

It was the girl from the school, the one named Prudence.

She wore her backpack and walked alongside a bicycle. Hyperon wondered fleetingly if the green storybook was in her bag.

Perhaps if they could question her, they could find out more about what the man was doing here.

She stopped abruptly when she heard Adam and the man shouting. Hyperon turned back and saw that Adam now had the man by the shirt collar. He had raced right past the education and gotten to the punishment, just like Haste had. Too bad to make a scene here in a public place, but Hyperon supposed Adam knew what he was doing.

He decided he had better focus on the girl. Her attention was arrested by the two men arguing, and she wouldn't see him coming.

He motioned for Horbah to follow him and crossed the street. Horbah tripped on an empty soda can. The girl's attention snapped to them, and she got on her bike.

"Wait!" Hyperon called to her. "We just want to ask you some questions[69]!"

She looked over her shoulder and jumped to pedal. Her braids flew out behind her.

The chase was on, and Hyperon jumped forward. Horbah followed closely. His rising anger pushed education out of his mind. He only wanted to punish her now. The growing dusk covered them, and Hyperon rejoiced in the fear he had seen on the girl's face. She

---

[69] Prov. 12:23

should get a taste of what poor Haste experienced every time she exulted in her superior marks at school.

She crossed a street in front of a car, and it barely missed her. Hyperon ran behind it, saving time. He noticed the stares of a few people on the sidewalk and hoped that they wouldn't cause him any trouble.

She turned abruptly into a side street, increasing her lead.

Hyperon outdistanced Horbah and raced after the girl. She took advantage of the shadows and pedaled close to the oak trees lining the street.

All at once, Hyperon tripped[70] over her bike, which she had cast onto the sidewalk. A wheel was still spinning, and he twisted to avoid falling on his face. As it was, he hit on his shoulder, winced as acorns embedded in his arm, and quickly rolled back onto his feet. Horbah cursed from somewhere behind.

Hyperon glanced around.

The only place she could have hidden[71] so quickly was in the front shrubbery of the house nearest to the sidewalk. It had neat steps leading up to the front door. On either side, red mulch surrounded well groomed shrubs.

Hyperon walked softly toward the front steps, though it was harder to muffle his labored breathing.

He leaned around the steps instead of walking up them. No one was looking out of the front windows or door of the house. Hyperon saw her huddled under the tallest step, like a frightened kitten.

---

70 Prov. 3:21-23

71 Prov. 22:3; Prov. 27:12

"Don't be afraid," he said to her. "I just want to ask you something."

She shook her head.

"Please," he pleaded, stifling his anger to try to befriend her, "just come out and talk to me."

"I have nothing to say to strangers," was her prudent reply.

He remembered Haste's dislike of the girl. He sympathized.

Horbah had caught up to him now and reached around and grabbed the girl. She struggled but did not scream.

Horbah slapped her. Hyperon immediately thought of the blood on her forehead at the school. The little fool would avoid a lot of pain if she would just cooperate.

"Were you going to meet the man with the hard hat?" Hyperon asked.

She didn't answer.

Horbah shook her.

"What would you like in exchange for the information you know about that man?" Hyperon asked sweetly.

"We could get you books or a better bicycle," he offered.

She shook her head. "I would rather be a true friend than a gold ring in a pig's snout[72]," she said evenly.

Hyperon felt like joining in the slapping but didn't.

---

[72] Prov. 11:22

"He is your friend, then," Hyperon said slyly.

The girl's cheeks brightened. "I'm friends with anyone who befriends me." She clamped her mouth shut.

"Why aren't you friends with me, then? I am trying to befriend you. What were you going to meet him for?" Hyperon asked, though he sensed that she wouldn't answer any more questions.

After a short silence, Hyperon heard stirring from within the house. "Let her go," he said. "We won't learn anything more."

Horbah drew the girl nearer to his face. "Without even punishing her sass?" Horbah asked.

The girl turned her face away from his.

"She is not in Specter's employ," Hyperon said, gritting his teeth.

The cat and mouse game was wearing on him. He'd much rather be fighting the injustices of big company owners like Fairbanks or the man at the warehouse by robbing from the rich to feed the poor. Spending time frightening little girls and chasing construction workers insulted his capabilities.

Horbah gave her another shake and released her.

She didn't run[73] like Hyperon thought she might. Instead, she walked calmly back to her bicycle and pushed it away up the sidewalk. She didn't even give them a backward glance.

He hated her.

They walked back to where Adam had been and saw that he had dragged the man into the shadow of the

[73] Prov. 28:1

garage where they had hidden. Hyperon could see Adam beating the man, who no longer resisted.

Horbah rushed ahead and joined the beating. Hyperon felt his frustration building. It was guys like this worker who sapped the pleasure from all the good things Specter gave them. Hyperon approached and kicked the man hard in the ribcage to release his frustration.

The man was clearly unconscious.

They left him and walked back to Mr. Specter's office. It took over an hour to get there, but Mr. Specter greeted them heartily, slapping Adam on the back as they entered through the back door.

"Well, how did your appointment with Saul go?" Mr. Specter led them into his office and retrieved cold drinks from a small refrigerator.

Adam popped his can open and took a long drink.

"Great," he said. "We learned that he is not spending his pay at the bar but taking it to the residential area of town. The girl Haste torments at his school was there too. Hyperon chased her down on her bicycle. It appears that she was coming to meet Saul."

Mr. Specter stroked his chin.

"That is most interesting," he said. He turned to Hyperon.

"And she was not cooperative, I take it," he said, almost sympathetically.

"No sir," Hyperon answered, "but we persuaded some information from her."

Mr. Specter clapped Hyperon on the shoulder and laughed loudly.

"Well, boys, with all of that running and walking, I think you need new shoes[74]," Mr. Specter said. He led them from the room back out into the entryway. There, three shoeboxes were stacked on top of one another.

Hyperon recognized the brand name and logo. He had never had shoes like this.

Specter grabbed the box on top and read the label.

"Ah yes, these are Hyperon's," he said. "You have the largest shoe size!"

He handed the box to Hyperon. Hyperon was so engrossed in opening his box that he hardly noticed as Adam and Horbah also received theirs.

He removed the lid and studied the sturdy leather and tough soles of the shoes. They were well made but not too heavy.

"Try them on! Try them on!" Specter seemed almost as happy as if he were the recipient.

Hyperon sat right down on the floor and slid his feet into the shoes. He laced them up and tied them. They fit perfectly.

"How did you know what size to get?" he wondered aloud.

"I make it my job to know everything about you for your pleasure," Mr. Specter said. Then, he added, "That is true love, son. Because I love you, I know what makes you tick[75]."

---

[74] Isa. 28:14-15
[75] 2 Tim. 3:1-5

Mr. Specter shook his head sadly. “It’s too bad that others have to be coerced into allowing me to love and care for them,” he said.

Hyperon stood up and walked a few steps, loving the feel of the shoes. He’d never had anyone who cared if he even had shoes, besides his mother. Now, Mr. Specter cared enough to buy him the best of the best and to ensure that they fit him perfectly.

They were just the solid ground he had been searching for[76].

---

[76] Ps. 82:5

Chapter 12

He wore his new shoes to Rocky's the next night.

They'd waited until she would be home from work. Adam mused about the negotiations with Mr. Fairbanks. Hyperon just enjoyed the springy feel of his shoes on the pavement.

The pedestrian traffic had slowed so that the sidewalks were clear, though the road was still one blaring mass of light and noise. It grew less as they left the tangled center of the city for the suburban area where her duplex was.

Adam slowed as they approached the front of the house. He turned to look at Hyperon. Hyperon raised his eyebrows.

"Now, it might go a little different this time," Adam said. "If she tries to turn us away, we are going to have to use a stronger form of persuasion. Are you in?"

Hyperon shrugged.

"What do you mean?" he asked.

"I mean, if she won't let us in, you hold the door with your foot while I slide my hand in to undo the chain lock on the inside. I don't want to get my hand smashed off," Adam said.

Hyperon thought fleetingly of Adam botching the interaction with Saul, the construction worker. Patience and smooth words won easier than force.

"Let me try to talk to her before you scare her out of her wits," Hyperon said. "She'll never agree to Mr. Specter's help if you ruin it."

"Ruin it?" Adam's usually jovial face tinged red. "What's that supposed to mean?"

"Your temper is going to lose Mr. Specter his employees," Hyperon said. "I thought we won people through logic and pleasure[77], not browbeating and intimidation."

Adam cooled off just as quickly as he had heated up. "I suppose you're right about that," Adam said.

Their arrival at the door silenced all argument, and Adam knocked. Hyperon heard the echo of it inside the house and then rapid footsteps.

She didn't open the door. "Who is it?" was her muffled question.

"Just Adam," he said.

She opened it slightly, but Hyperon could see the chain lock in place.

"I don't care to sign up for the program, and I don't want any more DVDs, but please tell Mr. Specter 'Thank you,'" she said and began to close the door.

"Wait!" Hyperon said, "How can you be so cold to those who have your best interest at heart? Won't you invite us in so we can talk about the benefit this would be to your family?" He spoke quickly, eagerly. "My mom had to be the breadwinner for our family. I know what it's like."

She shook her head. "It's late," she said. "My kids are sleeping."

"We want to know how the negotiations went for higher wages today," Hyperon pleaded. "Let's at least hear about that."

Adam shifted next to him.

---

[77] 2 Cor. 11:14-15

"Look," she snapped, "I don't know how to make it plainer to you, you half-breed foreigner[78], but I don't want anything you've got. I'm done working for Mr. Specter."

White flashed behind Hyperon's eyes, and he jumped with his full weight at the door. Adam moved even more quickly and had the chain lock off at once. Hyperon could feel her weight against the door for an instant, but then it gave way, sending the men plummeting into the room. She screamed and backed up as they rushed into the entryway.

Adam crossed the room and had her by the hair. He forced her back into a dimly lit kitchen and pushed her into a chair.

Hyperon could see polished counters with clean dishes stacked atop them. A rug rested beneath a table and chairs, and a cheery handmade drawing of a rainbow hung on the refrigerator. Hyperon's mind filled with the image of his own sparse, unfurnished room and her words echoed, "You half-breed foreigner!" Why should she have all these things and show contempt for his situation?

"Mr. Specter has shown you such kindness," Adam was saying through his clenched teeth. The woman was crying.

"Who has persuaded you that you don't need him anymore? Who could possibly do more for you than he has?" Adam asked.

Hyperon caught movement from the corner of his eye and saw a young boy peeking around a corner. The

---

[78] Prov. 11:12

woman saw him too. Her eyes flashed, and she attempted to stand from the chair. Adam held her down.

"I don't need him anymore!" she shouted. "His kindness only brought me misery."

"But you signed the agreement," Adam told her mercilessly.

Adam let her go then, and her son ran to her. Adam grabbed another chair and raised it over the glass topped table. It descended with a deafening crash.

"You take the kitchen," Adam said, "and I will work through the hallway."

The woman's slur reverberated through Hyperon's half-blooded brain, but he had locked eyes with the boy. Thin, with wisps of brown hair falling in his eyes, clinging to his mother, yet daring them to hurt her, the boy reminded Hyperon of who he once had been.

War raged within Hyperon.

"I didn't sign on for this," he finally said aloud, still looking into those daring brown eyes.

Adam lunged and pinned Hyperon against the wall. "Oh, but you did. You're not going to let this rob you of the best thing that's ever happened to you, are you? You're living life to its fullest!"

Hyperon could have easily shoved him away, but he switched his gaze to Adam's fierce blue eyes. He certainly didn't want to ruin his record with Mr. Specter or risk his displeasure. He let the woman's words repeat themselves in his mind: "You half-breed foreigner…You half-breed foreigner…I don't want anything you've got."

Adam released his hold. "Let's get on with this," he murmured.

The woman ran at Adam with her fists. He knocked her down easily with one punch.

"Wait there," he said with a laugh, "and when I'm finished you can tell me who's persuaded you that you don't need Mr. Specter."

The boy huddled beside his unconscious mother. Life was emptying from them in order to fill Hyperon, but his rage blinded him. He repeated the woman's words to himself again, drowning out his own mother's voice.

He heard a dish shatter and knew it had come from his own hand. He didn't owe these people anything. He'd been beaten before. He'd been laughed at and betrayed. Worst of all, he'd been rejected by his father. Mr. Specter, though, had cared about him enough to give him happiness. Adam had taken him in when he'd been a half-breed with nowhere to go. He finally was good at something that his friends celebrated. He wasn't going to let one woman take it away.

It only took minutes for the house to be a shambles. Rocky's little girl had awoken and shrieked for her mother from a back bedroom.

Adam came out of the hall and raised the woman to her feet by her arm.

"Now tell me who persuaded you to reject Mr. Specter's kindness?" he demanded.

Tears coursed down her cheeks as she surveyed the damage. Hyperon had made sure to empty the refrigerator of any homemade contents and smear them over the clean counters.

"Wisdom," she whispered.

At the name, a cold sweat broke out on Hyperon's brow. He'd never heard it before, but something in the way the woman said it broke the dam he had constructed within himself and brought the flood of shame coursing down on him.

"Where was she?" Adam asked, and his voice betrayed a tremor of fear[79]. Hyperon was startled by the feminine pronoun 'she.' Wisdom could be a woman's name, he supposed.

The woman remained silent. Adam slapped her and headed toward the door.

"Let's go," he called to Hyperon.

They'd run at least a mile when Adam said, "I wish I could find that cursed woman and put an end to her propaganda."

"Who is she?" Hyperon asked.

"She is the epitome of everything I hate," Adam said. "I'm glad she doesn't come near me. It's almost as if hardship and suffering drip off of her like a disease."

"Surely one woman couldn't do that much harm," Hyperon said.

"She's not just a woman," Adam said. "She is a Lady."

Hyperon heard the word 'Lady' echo in his mind. He had a negative view of the imperiosity ladies possessed.

"She'd never search *me* out, then," he chortled to Adam. "Ladies and half-breeds don't mix." Rocky's slur replayed in his mind.

They slowed to a walk.

---

[79] Prov. 1:7

"Don't be so sure," Adam advised. "She's not your typical Lady. If she thought you'd listen, she'd preach at you about seriousness and gravity and prudishness all day long. She's the very source of injustice, if you ask me."

"You've seen her?" Hyperon asked.

"No," Adam admitted, "but I know all about her. Mr. Specter told me. He met her once and rejected all she had to offer. He'd had enough of her abuses."

The sun was rising when Hyperon settled back on the cold, hard floor of his room to sleep. It cut into his side like the harsh reality that it was. In Rocky's house, he had seen comfortable beds and cushy pillows. Specter might offer forms of entertainment, but they were fleeting, and one just couldn't sleep on a video game. The inconsistencies needled him.

Hyperon's mind raged. He tried to stoke up the repetitious memory of Rocky's cruel words about his race, but the name 'Wisdom' whispered in his dreams.

He dreamt that he was in Rocky's house, spreading the preserves on the kitchen counter and smashing the glass jar, when he heard his own name whispered. *Hyperon.*

He turned to see who it was, but he found that he was blind[80].

He stumbled in darkness, stepping on a sharp shard of glass.

Hyperon.

---

[80] Is. 42:16; Acts 9:9

His skin grew hot, and he covered his face. He was afraid of the woman's voice. All of a sudden, blinding light pierced through his darkness[81].

"Don't kill me!" he shouted. "Don't kill me."

In the light, his blindness melted away. He saw a shepherd kneeling down[82]. He could smell the fresh scent of the grass, but he struggled to look at what the shepherd was kneeling next to. He took a step closer, though the pain in his foot[83] ached.

A lamb, spotless white, had been ripped open by some beast. Its entrails littered the ground[84]. The shepherd was weeping[85].

Now, Hyperon heard his mother's voice, "In the darkness and the dirt, a baby was born."

Now, he heard Specter's voice, "You must kill the shepherd, Hyperon."

Now, he heard his mother again, "You must find the shepherd[86]."

Hyperon.

He knew in that instant that it was Wisdom calling his name. He resolved to hide[87] from her.

The light flashed and consumed him.

"Don't kill me!" he shouted again and sat up. The room was empty but for the lingering scent of grass.

---

81 Jn. 8:12
82 Ps. 23
83 Gen. 3:15
84 Rev. 5:12
85 Is. 53:6
86 Ez. 34:15-23
87 Gen. 3:8

Chapter 13

Adam answered the door with a drink in his hand.

"Come in," he said with a smile to the overweight coed standing on the welcome mat.

She giggled and walked past him into the overcrowded room. Music blared from the speakers Mr. Specter had given them for the occasion. Adam only knew half of the people that had shown up for their party, but the more the merrier.

"Hey, Ted," Adam called waving to an acquaintance sitting on the couch. Ted waved nervously. Adam sauntered over.

"Ted, you've got to lighten up, old man," Adam said. "There's plenty of food in the kitchen, or drinks if you'd rather." Adam emphasized this by sipping from his own glass.

"No thanks," Ted replied nervously.

"How 'bout I introduce you to a few of these girls?" Adam said, looking at the ones nearest to him. Ted was shaking his head no, but Adam turned to the nearest one.

Her lipstick was bright, and her laugh did not grate on one's nerves as much as some others.

"Carla," Adam said. "This is my friend, Ted."

Carla turned and smiled. Ted looked like he'd rather be on a deserted island.

"Nothing wrong with a little fun, Ted," Adam said. Carla walked over and sat beside Ted.

"You from Opportunity, Ted?" she asked. At his nod, Adam decided his work was done in that quarter.

Adam scanned the room for Hyperon. The party was really for him, after all. Even Mr. Specter spoke admiringly of Hyperon's talents for picking the best recruits from the bus stop. He was gifted in this line of business, and performed his work without the troublesome involvement of the authorities. Six months had passed profitably for them.

Adam enjoyed all the benefits that Hyperon's skill flung his way, but he had begun to suspect Hyperon of doubts. Hyperon sometimes sat in his room listlessly instead of joining in the fun when Mr. Specter rewarded them. It threatened Adam's prosperity and security whenever Hyperon acted like that. He would do whatever it took to keep life the way it had become[88].

When Specter had called him in for a private meeting, Adam had been afraid that Hyperon's doubts had incriminated them both in the eyes of their employer.

"Adam," Mr. Specter always wore the same optimistic smile and the same optimistic tie. "Shut the door and take a seat, will you?" Adam had obeyed.

"I'm worried about your colleague, Hyperon," Specter lost no time. "He seems preoccupied with his own thoughts instead of being concerned for the disenfranchised of our society. Has he been asking any questions or voicing any doubts to you? Honestly, I'm concerned for his mental health."

Adam was a good liar. His thoughts flew to the night at Rocky's when Hyperon had hesitated and the questions he had asked about Lady Wisdom. He

---

88 Rom. 7:18

wouldn't mention those or he might lose his position too. Perhaps he could rise in Mr. Specter's estimation if he made himself sound like the good guy.

"I'm worried about him too, sir. He's a serious sort, that's for sure," Adam agreed, "but he's wholly dedicated to our cause. He seems tormented some by his past." Safest to blame Hyperon's gravity on the past instead of the present, Adam reasoned, and he often heard the tormented cries of his nightmares.

"I always remind him of our purpose," Adam added, "and encourage him to think about how good you are to us."

"Ah, I see," said Mr. Specter. A short silence ensued while Specter tapped his fingers together. Perhaps the flattery had been overdone.

"I suggest two things, Adam. Why don't you take whatever resources you need and have a big bash at your place? Invite young people. Let the food and wine flow. Music. Whatever you think sounds fun. Hyperon is sure to delight in a good party."

Adam nodded.

"And second, if you still find him morose, I'll arrange a visit with Folly," Specter said.

Adam beamed. "He'd love that, sir," Adam said enthusiastically. "He's loved her performances."

"Great! Can I rely on you to set these things up for your friend?" Mr. Specter asked.

Adam nodded again. "Certainly, sir."

"Good," Mr. Specter smiled. "There's nothing like helping a friend."

Adam didn't see Hyperon in the crowd. He searched the back bedroom, but none of the groups there included the lanky, dark-haired Hyperon. The kitchen likewise was full of everyone except the man he sought. Finally, on the third pass through the living room, Adam was chuckling at how well Ted and Carla were getting along when he spied Hyperon through the sliding glass doors.

Adam slid the door wide enough to squeeze through to the tiny patio and laughed.

"The party's in there," he pointed his thumb back over his shoulder, "and here you sit."

Hyperon didn't stir.

"You don't know how to have fun," Adam jested.

"I just can't bear to have a temporary fun," Hyperon said quietly, as if speaking might cause the sun to set more quickly[89].

"Temporary? Man, we got our whole lives with this sort of party," Adam said.

Hyperon then turned to look at him, putting both feet on the ground. "And then what?"

Adam rolled his eyes. "What does it matter? Today is all we have[90]. Don't worry about tomorrow," he said.

Hyperon laughed joylessly. "It's hard not to when Specter will be here tomorrow carting off the speakers, the food, and the girls. Then, we'll go back to ramen, sleeping on the floor, and mice in the closet."

Adam hadn't thought of this, but he had a ready answer. "He always brings something better[91]."

---

89 Eccl. 3:11
90 1 Cor. 15:32-34
91 Prov. 5:22

Hyperon studied his friend and shrugged his shoulders.

Adam allowed the silence to hang between them.

"We have a job to do for Specter tomorrow, and then the next day, he wants you to meet a friend of his," he said.

Hyperon raised an eyebrow. Adam knew he had heard about the job but not the friend.

"I'm telling you, man, she's the kind of woman to make you forget your troubles," Adam said laughingly. "It's the girl from the theater."

This got Hyperon's attention. "The real girl or the hologram?"

Adam rolled his eyes. This guy must have a hollow leg to contain so much skepticism.

"Why can't you get it into your head that the hologram is the real girl? Mr. Specter just projects her onto the Megascops screens so that more people will hear her message," Adam argued.

"Well, are we just going to see another projection?" Hyperon pushed him.

Adam smiled. "Nope. You get to meet the real girl."

A car horn blared from below, and an old woman from a downstairs apartment bellowed up, "Turn that music down or I'm reporting you!"

"Go ahead," Adam offered back.

"Are you coming in?" he said to Hyperon.

"Why not?" Hyperon answered.

Chapter 14

The hangover still buzzed in his ears when he followed Adam the next day. He carried a rotisserie chicken under one arm and a bag of French fries in the other. With his free fingers on the arm carrying the chicken, he clutched a bag containing four foil containers of alfredo pasta. Adam's arms were also laden with a feast fit for a king.

Hyperon hadn't eaten since before the party, and the aroma of the chicken teased his senses. All he'd done was drink, and he regretted it now[92]. They joined the throngs of people on the sidewalks, weaving in and out, even passing many other food delivery men. Maybe he only noticed how many of them there were because of how hungry he was.

They weren't far from their own apartment building, but the number of towering apartments between them and home made it seem farther than it was. Hyperon looked up to see a woman beating a rug out on the small concrete porch of a second story apartment. He walked faster so that the dirt wouldn't fall on him.

Adam turned left at the next dilapidated high rise. Hyperon balanced his bags and caught the opaque glass door to the entryway with his elbow. He was glad Horbah hadn't come along.

Adam punched a button on a call panel, and Hyperon couldn't understand the garbled reply.

---

92 Prov. 23:20

"Always talks with his mouth full," Adam grumbled. Another door buzzed and opened for them, and Adam led the way up a flight of old stairs.

Soon, they were standing outside of apartment 206. The hall all around was littered with cans and empty cardboard takeout containers. Adam moved some of the trash aside and knocked. The door buzzed and opened.

A nauseating smell whisked Hyperon's hunger from his mind. He looked down at his feet as he followed Adam down a narrow hall, trying to avoid stepping in whatever was making that smell. Plastic lids, ketchup packets, and empty bags lined the floor. The lights were too dim to see beyond the first layer of refuse.

"I hope you did not pick up those French fries from Frydaddies. They use peanut oil, and I just detest the taste of things fried in peanut oil," came a grumbling voice.

"Mr. Specter loves you and knows what makes you tick. He knows all your dietary needs," Adam answered, "so we made sure to grab your fries from Ole Ole."

Adam's echo of Specter's words made Hyperon glance down at his shoes. They weren't anything like this mess, and he wanted to keep them clean. He wished he could get far away from this place. Instead, Hyperon followed Adam into a small room where sat the most enormous man he had ever seen. He was so fat that Hyperon couldn't see what sort of seat or couch he was sitting on.

"And I am just not feeling like chicken today," the grumble continued. "I wish you had brought Italian instead."

"Ah, Gluto," Adam set some of the food down on a side table and looked down at the man, "Hyperon here has the pasta[93]."

The man called Gluto looked expectantly at Hyperon. His swollen face ran with sweat, and a few crumbs dotted his upper lip like a sparse mustache. Hyperon tried to smile, but the stench was making his eyes water.

"Well," Gluto said expectantly.

Hyperon quickly set the packages of food on the table. Gluto never stood, and Hyperon wondered if he could. He only shifted and lifted the lids off of the pastas, each in turn. He sniffed[94] each one, and Hyperon wondered how he could manage to want to smell anything. It was then that Hyperon noticed that the smell was coming from the man. Running out on the sides of whatever it was he was sitting on was his own excrement[95]. Hyperon realized that the man couldn't move from the spot where he was.

After Gluto lifted the last lid of the pasta dishes, he turned to Adam with flashing eyes.

"They're all the same!" he grumbled.

"But they're all your favorite!" Adam protested, still with a smile.

---

93 Prov. 28:7
94 Eccl. 10:1
95 Jud. 3:22

"I thought one of them would at least have some other toppings, maybe pepperonis or banana peppers," Gluto argued. "Don't you know that the senses need the element of surprise that variety affords?"

"That's why Mr. Specter also had us pick up these fried cheesecakes," Adam said, rummaging through one of the bags.

Gluto looked on eagerly.

Adam pulled a fuchsia conical container from the bag and opened it. Gluto's eyes lit up. Hyperon suppressed a gag.

"You know Mr. Specter cares for your every need," Adam reminded the man. "He sees that you have all you want."

"Of course, of course," the fat man's ire dissipated as he took a few huge mouthfuls of the cheesecake.

"Mr. Specter asked for a photograph of you enjoying yourself," Adam said, producing a camera.

"Sure," Gluto said. He tore a leg off of the chicken and held it up between his teeth. Grease ran off it onto his chin. Hyperon knew then that he would vomit and started backing down the hall. When he reached the door, he ran.

Adam found him sitting on the sidewalk outside the lobby later.

"We've got to work on your weak stomach, man," Adam said. "Can't you enjoy the sight of a man enjoying himself? I'm glad I got some pictures for Mr. Specter."

They returned to their empty apartment to await their meeting with the girl from the theater the next day.

Hyperon opened the pantry but found that even the mice had the sense to move on when the party was over.

"Cupboard's bare," he said. It reminded him of a poem his mother had once sung to him, but he couldn't remember how it began.

"We will make up for it tomorrow," Adam said, rubbing his hands together in anticipation. Nothing seemed to dull his enthusiasm or hunger for the next pleasure. He sank down in front of the T.V. and was lost in the oblivion of thoughtlessness.

Hyperon slunk down the hall and flopped down on the blanket in the corner of his room. He'd come from his village enslaved to the shame of his heredity. He'd been freed from that here in Opportunity and found something he could take pride in. He was a good 'injustice hunter' as Adam called it. Mr. Specter was pleased with his work. Why was he so miserable?

His mother's song haunted his memory now. It had been about a dog that had no bone. Every time its owner went to get it something new, she returned to find the dog amused with something else. Just as he drifted off to sleep, he remembered the ending:

"This wonderful dog
Was Dame Hubbard's delight,
He could read, he could dance,
He could sing, he could write;
She gave him rich dainties
Whenever he fed,
And erected this monument
When he was dead."

Hyperon felt his mother's voice wrap around him. He heard in the silly rhyme a portrait of what he had become. In his dreams, he saw the little schoolgirl's wave and the grease dripping down Gluto's chin. Hyperon hated that grease. He hated the filth. He hated the empty poverty. He hated himself for being a part of it all and for not returning her wave[96].

---

[96] Amos 5:15

Chapter 15

Obedience dabbed at Prudence's bleeding knee and clicked her tongue. Prudence swiped at the tears running down her cheeks.

"I don't know what happened to Mr. Saul," she told her mother.

"Your father has gone to check, honey, and everything will come out right in the end." Obedience concentrated on unscrewing the lid of the antibiotic cream.

"I wish the Lady would come," Prudence said, and she felt like she might start to cry again[97].

Obedience hugged her with one arm and dabbed at her knee with the other. "So do I, but you know, we can live like she would, even when she isn't right here with us."

Prudence considered this. What would the Lady do when the boy ruined her book or when the men chased her down the sidewalk and threatened to hurt her?

Obedience soothed the bandage over her wounded knee. "I am sorry about your bicycle and your book. You must have been so frightened," Obedience said.

Prudence nodded. Obedience sat down next to her. They were silent for a moment.

"I'm frightened too," her mother said matter-of-factly. "And when I'm worried or anxious or frightened, I think about the end of the story[98]."

---

[97] Prov. 7:4
[98] Is. 26:3

Prudence turned to her mother. "What story?" she asked.

"The story about the Shepherd. Do you remember what happens at the end?" Obedience asked.

Prudence nodded and smiled a little. Her dimple shone brighter than the scar above her eyebrow.

"The sheep are safe with the Shepherd," Prudence said.

Obedience nodded, "Yes. But the story wasn't always safe. Do you remember the first time I read it to you? Somewhere in the middle of the story, you covered your ears and said you didn't want to hear any more."

Prudence giggled. "That was because I didn't know the end."

Obedience smiled. "When we know the Lady, we know the end of every story," she said.

Prudence considered this.

"The end of every story is Love[99]. That is why we choose to love no matter what our story may look like in the middle," Obedience explained.

Prudence heard footsteps on the sidewalk outside the front door, and her father's voice called, "Obedience?"

Her mother jumped up and ran to open the door. Her father labored under Saul's broken and bloodied form. Obedience reached out to help, and together they carried the wounded man to the living room and laid him down cautiously on the couch. Prudence jumped aside to make room for him. She barely recognized his face.

"He's hurt," her father said, "but he spoke some."

---

[99] 1 Jn. 4:8

"I will bind up his wounds[100] first," Obedience said and rushed to get more supplies from the kitchen.

Prudence's father smiled reassuringly. "Sometimes, the Lady does the rescuing, but sometimes, she allows us to join her in her work[101]," he said while he removed Saul's shoes.

Marv turned his attention back to Saul as Obedience hurried into the room, tearing strips of cloth from an old sheet. Together, they worked until they had stopped the worst of the bleeding.

"Water," Saul croaked.

Obedience held a cup to his lips.

Saul's eyes searched until they found Prudence. "You are safe," he whispered.

She nodded. "I wish I could've kept them from hurting you," she said.

He shook his head. "The worse hurt would have been if they had persuaded me back into my old ways," his whisper gained strength. "But Wisdom dwells with Prudence[102]. I knew coming to hear more of the Shepherd's story was better and more important than having a few drinks[103]."

Prudence smiled. She wished the Lady really did live at her house.

"I don't know where those men went," Saul said, turning his eyes back to Marv. "I hope they won't hurt any of the others. I think they just came after me because I still owe a debt to Specter that I am having trouble

---

[100] Lk. 10:34
[101] Eph. 2:10
[102] Prov. 8:12
[103] Lk. 14:33

paying." His voice rasped, and he looked ashamed as he said it.

"Wisdom has settled all your debts, Saul!" Marv said soothingly.

Tears trickled out of the wrinkled corners of Saul's swollen eyes and mixed with the blood on his face. "I wish I could believe it," he whispered.

"The Lady may use even this to help Specter's workers hate what is evil and love what is good," Marv said.

"This is just the middle of the story," Prudence said.

Saul nodded and turned his face toward the wall.

Chapter 16

"Maybe one of these days Specter will give us a car," Adam huffed as he ran to catch the trolley. Hyperon jumped up beside him and delighted in the fresh wind blowing through his dark, curly hair. Sleep had eased his self-hatred from the night before, and he risked enjoying the present. *Think positively.*

They sat near the edge and watched the world stream by as they were taken to a different part of town. Adam seemed uncharacteristically fidgety.

A little girl near them held a bag of popcorn. Hyperon could tell by the smell that it was still warm and coated in butter. He hoped the sounds from his stomach[104] didn't carry beyond his own seat. He considered reaching over and taking a handful of it from her, but her father sat nearby.

After awhile, Adam took a paper and a comb from his vest pocket. He ran the comb through his hair while studying the paper.

"It's not far," he said.

Ahead, Hyperon could see the gate of Opportunity. It was the opposite gate from the one he had entered on the bus. He hadn't been here before. The trolley slowed to give the pedestrians and merchants time to clear the street ahead. Hyperon heard a merchant shouting about the quality of his pottery, some women's voices rising over a quarrel, and a dog barking. People thronged together, inspecting the wares at each booth.

---

[104] Mt. 5:6

Just before the gate, the trolley stopped and Adam stood. Hyperon followed his example and stepped off the back.

They were immediately engulfed in the sea of people. Adam stood on tiptoe to see over their heads. Hyperon gazed up at the gate. It spanned the whole city wall from top to bottom. Beside it, in the stonework of the wall, were many windows and smaller doors of the shops and homes built into it. He wondered what it would be like to have one of the top rooms with a view of the entire city.

One voice arrested his attention[105].

"Wouldn't you like to be your own master? Haven't they taken enough of our lives and livelihoods?" The girl's voice sounded sweeter than it did in the theater. Hyperon searched the wall frantically for a glimpse of her. Surely it was too sunny here to be fooled by holograms.

"Join me, and we can make a name for ourselves," she pleaded.

Hyperon finally spied her sitting to the left of the gate on a second-story balcony. She was above the heads of the onlookers but close enough to be seen[106].

"Come into my home. I have everything you could ever need here. We will finally get what's owed to us when we band together," she said. Hyperon wondered whom she was addressing. Adam began walking toward her as a man transfixed.

---

105 Prov. 5:3

106 Prov. 9:13-16

“This world is full of injustice,” she called, and Hyperon admired her raised fist. “You, my girl, how have they wronged you?”

Hyperon tore his gaze from her to look at a young woman in the crowd. Everyone seemed to be staring up at the second story balcony, including the young woman[107].

“All I wanted was to go to medical school,” the young woman replied, “but they wouldn’t even let me apply.”

Hyperon’s attention swiveled back to the girl on the balcony. She was nodding. “They took your dream! Why shouldn’t this young woman be allowed to follow her heart?” she called to the crowd.

Adam, and a few others, yelled out their indignation.

The crowd jostled Hyperon as they surged nearer to the balcony to hear.

“What about you, there? Yes, you in the back?” Hyperon turned along with everyone else to see a person of nondescript gender and clothing.

“They tried to make me fit their patriarchal definitions,” the person said.

“What I say is we should be allowed to make our own definitions! What is a person if we aren’t allowed to even define our own personhood?” the girl announced. “Love is acceptance[108]. Silence is violence!”

The crowd cheered. Hyperon knew that if she called on him, he would tell her all about how his father

---

[107] Prov. 15:21
[108] Rom. 1:32

hated him and the rejection he received because of his mixed heritage.

"Open invitation to you all," she called. "Come tonight for supper, and we can discuss how we can finally get our due!"

Her eyes rested on Adam.

"Adam!" she called. "Long time no see!"

She motioned that she would come down to the street level, and the crowd seemed unwilling to disperse. Hyperon envied Adam's personal acquaintance with the girl.

She disappeared into the drapery of the balcony but quickly reappeared at the street level door. Adam elbowed his way through the people, and Hyperon struggled to keep up with him.

When she opened the door, ten voices spoke at once: "Could you please… If it wouldn't be any trouble… What should I do about… I just love you… What can I do for the cause?"

She smiled, and Hyperon memorized every line of her face.

"Come tonight, my friends, and we can really get acquainted. We can make a plan!" she said. It held so much promise.

They were close enough now to draw her attention.

"Welcome," she said. Adam smiled and bowed to her.

"It's been too long," he said.

"Specter only sends those who need a little pick-me-up," she mused, "and who's your dish of a friend? I'd be glad to pick him up."

Hyperon met the girl's bold gaze. Her blue eyes and auburn hair captivated him. She wore a velvet dress of crimson. Its hem rested above her slender ankle. Her feet were bare but for an anklet of bells on her left foot. The garment's three-quarter sleeves covered most of her arms but not her lily-white throat. He had memorized her hologram in the theater, but it didn't hold a candle to seeing her in person.

"This is Hyperon," Adam introduced. "May we come in? I have a message from Mr. Specter."

"I'm Folly," she said, and reached out one lily white hand.

Hyperon extended his hand and shook it. This was no hologram.

"Finally," she said, "our stories can blend into one. Do you want to come in too, Hyperon?"

Hyperon answered her nothing. Her beauty and the allure of her song beckoned to him. She poised like an ornate spider, inviting them like flies into her web[109]. Another of his mother's songs flitted through his mind: *Come into my parlor, said the spider to the fly...* It made him hesitate.

At Hyperon's hesitancy, she produced an alluring pout and said, "Oh, you wouldn't want me to have to eat all alone, would you? I'm sure you would like a nice meal. We can plan all the things we can do together to make this world a better place." She opened the door behind her and brought out a covered tray. He began salivating before she uncovered the warm, crusty loaf of bread.

---

[109] Isa. 59:5-13

"Come," she whispered. "Come and eat with me. I can erase the pain of all the hurt you've ever known. We could conquer the world together[110]."

He fully intended to follow her wherever she led. Nothing could have taken his eyes from her alluring face.

The aroma of the bread faded, and it was replaced by the smell of bright green grass. His vision was clouded by the scene in his mind's eye of the little girl waving, clutching her green book. His hearing seemed to hone in on the screams and tormented groans of the construction worker. He seemed to taste the air of Gluto's hotel. He felt the glass jar hurtling out of his hand to shatter on the floor. Folly was swallowed up by his sensory torments.

At that instant, over the rumble of his stomach, Hyperon heard another voice smoothly ringing, like a bell beside the shrill whistle of Folly: "All who are simple, I invite you. Come. Come to my house[111]."

His palms grew sweaty. It was also a voice he knew, though only from a dream. He poised to run.

Hyperon turned and stared in surprise. Just across the street stood the mirror image of Folly. Her hair cascaded down her shoulders in the same way. Her dress rested at her ankles and covered her modestly. Her feet were bare, but she wore no belled anklet. Though her eyes were exactly the same shade of blue, the second woman's weren't calculating but had a joyful sparkle and enchanting allure.

---

[110] Prov. 9:17

[111] Prov. 9:4-5

In that moment, Hyperon knew he must be looking at Wisdom[112].

Folly hissed, "Hyperon, you don't want to keep company with the likes of her. She is the epitome of injustice. She'll take everything you have and entice you to feast on delicacies where the money would have been better spent on bettering yourself and others. Besides, she's a prude."

Hyperon turned back to Folly. He could hear and see her clearly again now. Adam knelt at her side, but she stood to approach Hyperon. She put her hand on the back of his neck and drew him closer to her so that he could no longer see Wisdom. Her fragrance dulled the smell of grass. He had dreamed about this moment when he would be able to touch her and feel her skin. Those dreams had been more pleasant than the nightmares running from Wisdom, but they faded just like the hologram.

"Stolen water is sweet, and bread eaten in secret is pleasant[113]," she whispered. "You will not have to work for what I give you, and everyone needs bread and water to survive. You deserve to have someone take care of you after all you've been through," Folly pulled back slightly.

"Come on," she invited, "come and enjoy yourself with me. We could right all of the world's wrongs together."

It would be easy to give in, but would it be good? All at once, Hyperon thought of Rocky's little boy. He

---

112 Prov. 8:1-3

113 Prov. 9:17

knew that he had just pretended to fight injustice by doing evil in secret. Folly's song was a lie. It didn't make life better for anyone. It was as if his eyes had been scabbed over for far too long, but now, truth was healing them and tearing the scabs away[114].

Hyperon turned back for another glimpse of Wisdom. She had come closer. He was terrified. She spoke to everyone who walked by, encouraging and inviting them to come home with her[115]. However, instead of addressing them as a crowd, she stopped and spoke with each individual. It seemed that she was a friend to each one, though few followed her. Her eyes locked with Hyperon's. They were separated only by a street.

Hyperon thought about Rocky and the night she had staunchly defended working for Wisdom. He remembered her slur too. He thought about the food that had been in her refrigerator, and he knew he had deserved every slur she could throw at him. He saw again the blood dripping down the forehead of the little girl called Prudence as she waved to him. He thought about Gluto and Specter's kind of fleeting enjoyment and cheap justice. Then, the mental image of his father struck him just as his father's hand had struck him years ago, pouring contempt onto his head. What was he thinking? Wisdom was a lady. She would not really invite a half-breed to sit as an equal at her table.

She never took her gaze from his. As he watched, she stretched out her arms to him.

---

[114] Acts 9:18

[115] Prov. 3:7-8

"Come if you are hungry and thirsty, Hyperon, and I will fill you[116]," she said.

Just then, Adam clapped a hand on his shoulder. "I wouldn't waste time with that mute woman. I've watched her charades a million times, and they never make sense to me. Better to keep your attention on Folly. She has more to offer," he said.

A funny thing happened when Adam's hand rested on Hyperon's shoulder. Though Wisdom's mouth continued moving, he could no longer hear her words[117]. Adam's touch had muted her voice. She did not cross the street, but stood at the very edge of her side motioning to him and calling with her silent voice[118].

Adam steered Hyperon away from Wisdom. Folly met his eyes. He doubted now that she would be able to keep her promises. Hyperon turned his back to Folly to whisper to Adam.

"That was Wisdom," he whispered. Color drained from Adam's face as he looked back at the silent woman.

"That?" he said incredulously.

"I could hear her until you came near me," Hyperon was speaking almost to himself.

Adam shook him. "Who cares? Didn't you come to spend time with Folly?" he snapped.

Hyperon stared at the ground, perplexed. Now that he had met Folly, his questions drowned out all the answers she gave.

---

116 Is. 55:1-3
117 Prov. 38:13
118 Prov. 1:20-26

"I can't think straight," he finally said to Adam.

Adam turned back to Folly. "We have to go, but we'll be back," he said.

"Oh, I know you'll be back," she said in her honeyed voice. "We have a lot to do together, Hyperon."

Adam dragged Hyperon back to the trolley. The poor fool. It was like he'd been shot by that woman Wisdom. He stumbled and mumbled to himself like one in a trance. Adam punched him hard in the shoulder after the trolley was safely underway.

"Snap out of it man! You're embarrassing me," Adam said. "What are you, some lovesick puppy?"

Hyperon looked at him and seemed to focus for the first time.

"I thought you said she was evil," he said.

Adam had said as little as possible about her. True, he hated her, but what she really was, he had no way of knowing.

"I've seen her many times, but I didn't know who she was. I do know one thing: she is evil," he retorted. "Did she tell you how much it would cost to come to her table? Folly's meals are free, but Wisdom's are not. Ask Specter next time you see him."

Hyperon looked down at his folded hands in his lap. Adam congratulated himself on presenting a good, logical case against Wisdom.

Hyperon looked up again. "But you didn't even know it was her until I told you," he argued.

Adam nodded. "I didn't have to know what she looked like to know what her offers cost[119]. Specter told

---

[119] Lk. 14:28

me she charges more than the highest priced harlot but gives nothing," he replied.

"Specter!" Hyperon shouted and stood from his seat. He grasped the hand bar above him for balance and looked down at Adam. "Why is he the authority on everything?"

"Because he has everything in the palm of his hand." Adam remained cool. It wouldn't do to lose his temper now.

"Just think about his office. Think about everything he's done for us," Adam reasoned.

"I'm thinking about my empty belly and that fellow Gluto," said Hyperon. "I'm thinking about right and wrong. I'm thinking about justice and injustice. I'm thinking about draining the life out of good people while I'm enjoying a life of ease and a parade of entertainments that leave my soul as abandoned as my childhood."

"Just put your childhood behind you and live for today," Adam said.

"Easy enough for you to say," Hyperon accused. "You who grew up with two loving parents in a world that accepted you as one of its own. I'll bet you never went without until you worked for Specter."

"I don't go without now," Adam lied.

"Ah yes, and your belly isn't as empty as mine either, I suppose," Hyperon said. "I'm done threatening and accusing women and little kids. Tell Mr. Specter I quit."

"It's not as simple as that," Adam pleaded. "Once you work for him, you can't get out of the agreement. I thought you said you were unpersuadable."

"That's when I was a stupid fool[120]," Hyperon said.

"You were a stupid fool until you worked for Mr. Specter. Think of all you've earned and worked for," Adam argued.

Hyperon backed down the aisle away from Adam. Adam stood and reached out his hand, but he was too late.

"Starting today, I'm hating evil- real evil[121]," Hyperon said, "and I guess I'll be persuaded by anything else." He stepped off the trolley into the swirling masses of people.

---

[120] Ps. 14:1; Ps. 107:17-19
[121] Ps. 97:10

Chapter 17

The bell above the door couldn't even lighten Adam's step as he entered the office of Specter and Associates. The secretary didn't stop him when he led himself down the hallway to Mr. Specter's office. He knocked twice and was bid to enter.

Mr. Specter loomed behind his desk.

"Adam," he said questioningly, "you are the last person I expected today. I thought you would be enjoying your time with Folly."

Adam sank into a chair facing Specter. He sighed and related all that happened. Mr. Specter's face grew angrier the longer Adam talked, so he made the rest of the story as succinct as possible.

Specter stood abruptly and took his fedora from the hooks on the wall. "I suppose we'll find him down on the corner that Wisdom works," he said.

Adam shrugged, "I guess so."

"Well, no use in wasting any more time. Let's go," Specter said, holding the office door open for Adam to follow.

"I don't see how we can prevent him, sir," Adam said piteously.

"Just as you prevent all those other poor fools," Specter snapped. "We'll entice him. Oh!" he stopped and whirled around. "I almost forgot his agreement. If all else fails, I'll present it to Wisdom."

Mr. Specter seemed to know how to get around the city with as few delays as possible. Adam watched as Specter encouraged a bus driver to skip four of his normal stops and wheedled the trolley man out of his fare. Adam could see Folly still sitting in her place by the gate when they approached. It was evening now, and Adam hoped they'd be staying for supper.

The trolley turned and made its way back toward downtown, but Adam followed Mr. Specter to Folly. She stood.

"Oh, Mr. Specter! What a surprise!" she called. People turned to look, and Adam felt proud to be seen with people such as Mr. Specter and Folly. Specter was smiling and kissed Folly right on the mouth.

"My dear," he said immediately, "have you seen that blasted fool Hyperon? He's one of my finest employees, and he's gotten himself mixed up with Wisdom."

Folly rested both hands on her right hip and gave the pretense of deep thought. She shook her head, "I couldn't believe he left, but he'll come back. They always do."

Specter cursed under his breath.

"Have you seen Wisdom?" Adam asked. "Maybe if we find her, Hyperon won't be far."

Specter nodded appreciatively at the question. Folly scowled.

"That pretender is never far from here. We work the same corner, you know," she said, glancing past them to the other side of the street. "Ah, there she comes. Pity she looks so much like me."

They turned, and there Wisdom stood on the steps of some tall building opposite the gate attempting to gain followers. Hardly anyone listened to her compared to Folly's audience, however. One or two stragglers stopped to hear what Wisdom had to say.

Folly regularly attracted a crowd, especially when her rhetoric pitted factions against one another.

"Thank you, my dear," Mr. Specter said. "We'll be back to dine with you. Plan for three of us to join you."

She laughed. "Oh, Mr. Specter, you always have your way."

Adam had once seen a mime with a white painted face and white gloves putting on a performance near his apartment. He had laughed then at the crazy antics of the man who said nothing all the while pretending there was an invisible wall in front of him. No laughter came now as he watched the gesticulating and the soundless words of the poor woman in front of him. The wall still seemed to be a part of the show, but he wasn't sure who had put it there or why[122].

Mr. Specter stopped at the bottom of the stairs and leaned against a pillar. Adam followed suit. Wisdom's gaze swept over them and on to the next passerby. She had as little use for them as they had for her.

"We shall see if he comes," Specter said.

It had not been three quarters of an hour before Adam spied the familiar lanky, dark-haired form in his turned up collar. He came along the way slowly and never took his eyes from Wisdom as she worked.

Adam tugged on Specter's elbow.

"Yesss," Specter hissed, "I see him."

Folly's shrill cries had stirred Adam as they waited. There was a girl with the right priorities. She

---

[122] Is. 59:2

seemed to be able to make all the wrongs of the world right. His mouth watered at the thought of the bread and water they would eat there in secret later tonight. Hyperon drew Adam's attention from her momentarily now. Folly's attention was also drawn.

"Hyperon!" she called. "You have worked so hard and yet have never even tasted the delights I have here. It isn't fair," He didn't glance at her. Adam heard a tinge of jealousy in her voice when she called again, "Why go to a prudish woman with nothing to offer when you see that I would freely give you all I have?" Folly began singing her song.

Adam turned to see how Wisdom bore this insult. She seemed unchanged except that her focus zeroed in on Hyperon. She seemed to be talking to him, but Adam still couldn't hear any sound. Hyperon's face flushed red, as though angry, but he walked slowly toward his Lady.

"Hyperon," Mr. Specter slid out of the shadows.

This drew his former roommate's attention. Hyperon's ascent stopped.

"Don't let this nonsense persuade your unpersuadable mind," Mr. Specter said in his most congenial tone. "You have a future with me. You are good at what you do. I am proud of your accomplishments. You're like a son to me[123]."

At the top of the stairs, Wisdom opened a door. The light that came out blinded Adam so that he had to look away. Specter took a step back into the shadows,

---

123 Mt. 23:15

but inched up onto the next stair. Wisdom seemed to be speaking again.

"Ask her the cost, Hyperon," Specter commanded.

Hyperon stepped up another step toward the Lady. "What is the cost[124]?" he asked.

Wisdom stepped down toward him. Again, she answered soundlessly. Adam laughed.

"Don't tell me you believe words you can't even hear," Adam called to Hyperon. "Sounds like a fairy tale to me."

Across the street, Folly abandoned her song. "Hyperon," she called, "you can't afford her price. You're nothing but a half-breed foreigner. She doesn't really want anything to do with you."

Hyperon took off his coat and laid it down on the steps. He bent and removed his shoes as well. Adam remembered the day Specter had given them the name brand shoes. He wouldn't cast his aside that easily.

Specter inched up another couple of steps, careful to keep out of the light streaming from the open door[125]. The crowd in the street seemed oblivious to the struggle happening above them.

"Wisdom," Specter called, "I have here his signed agreement that he is one of mine." Specter held up the thick document with Hyperon's signature on the bottom. Adam saw Wisdom smile at Specter. She held her hand out to Hyperon[126].

---

124 Prov. 4:5-7; Prov. 16:16
125 Jn. 3:19
126 Col. 2:13-14

Hyperon stepped up one, two, three steps. So did Specter. Hyperon began to run and lunged himself at the woman's feet. Specter grabbed for him but succeeded only in tearing his shirt. The light caused Specter to back away, but not before Wisdom reached out and took the document. It disappeared the moment it touched her hand.

"Look at you, Hyperon," Folly called, "acting like some big milksop, tied to a woman's apron strings."

"This isn't over!" Mr. Specter yelled from the shadow to the side. "I will have you back yet, Hyperon!"

As for Hyperon, he held on to Wisdom's feet, lying on his face, and Adam could hear him weeping.

Chapter 18

Folly's catchy song warred with the ringing voice of Wisdom in Hyperon's mind. First one and then the other played. At first, he wished that he could just dispense with both[127]. As he wandered the crowded streets of the city, he bumped against first one and then another person. They were real. They had real hopes and fears. Hyperon couldn't get any of them to look him in the eye, but he began to see them differently than he had only that morning.

A hologram hadn't satisfied him, and as he bumped against countless flesh-and-blood people in the city, he began to realize that even the flesh-and-blood Folly was only as good to them as a hologram. Mr. Specter's justice was an empty charade. And who knew it better than he did?

He heard Wisdom's call echoing.

Hyperon made up his mind to return to Wisdom. He had questions. He had a hunger that had never really been sated. His need rose up and threatened to choke him as he walked. He couldn't even put a name on it, but it seemed he would be consumed by need before he ever made it back to Wisdom. The city's bumbling twists and turns made the journey much longer on foot than it had been on the trolley.

His hunger plagued him, and he decided to steal a loaf of bread to sustain him on his way. He snuck into the back of a cafe and almost fainted at the heavenly smells surrounding him, though it was not as heartening or honest as the smell of fresh, green grass. He waited

---

[127] Eccl. 1:17

until the plump proprietress had gone to the counter to serve a customer and then snuck into the kitchen.

Three big ovens lined the far wall. All of them contained something delicious. He peered into each one and had finally decided to nab a few crescent rolls from the middle one when she unexpectedly returned.

She stared at him wide-eyed. He stared back. It was the first time he'd been caught.

"Well," she said as she tried to subdue her surprise, "you must be wanting something to eat. Am I right?"

Hyperon turned to go.

"Wait!" she called. "I will pack it so that you can take it with you."

He turned and looked at her. "But I was going to steal it from you."

"And now you're not," she answered with forcefulness as she opened the middle oven.

When she was through, she had stuffed a large sack full of crescent rolls, butter, sliced turkey, and cupcakes. The cupcakes sported maraschino cherries on top. The work she must have poured into each one shamed Hyperon[128].

"That should tide you over until tomorrow," she said pleasantly. "Then just you come back and eat supper with us if you find yourself in this predicament."

He nodded. She handed him the sack.

"Why are you doing this?" he asked. "I don't deserve it."

---

[128] Prov. 6:21-28

She reached up and patted his cheek. "You're too skinny, honey. And you look like you could use some kindness, even if you don't deserve it," she said. "Besides, I know Someone who gives us all what none of us deserve[129]."

"No one offers kindness without strings attached," he said.

She shrugged, "Someone does."

The contents of his bag filled more than just his stomach as he walked along. By the time he made it to the city gate, it was evening time, and for the first time in his life, he was thankful for the good meal he'd had. He could hear Folly issuing her empty promises, but he didn't see Wisdom anywhere.

Walking a little further, he caught the sonorous tone of her voice echoing like a great bell off of a tall building[130]. She stood in front of it like a beacon. Stone stairs lifted her above him. *Where she belongs*, he thought. In contrast, Folly's whistling voice was drawing a crowd. She spoke to first one and then another. The crowd waited to see what magic she would do next, salivating over her promises to right their wrongs.

Wisdom was speaking to an old man, placing a comforting hand on his shoulder. She was imploring him to come in and rest. He didn't think he could afford to stay. Hyperon wished she'd rest her hand on his shoulder like that.

He set one foot on the bottom step. Even if she was too good for him, he wanted to be close to her.

---

129 Heb. 10:29-36

130 Prov. 1:20-21

Folly's high pitched voice grated on his nerves when he heard her call his name. He decided that he wouldn't even turn around. He was finished with holograms. He knew her crowd would be looking to see who she addressed. Better to ignore her.

"Why go to a prudish woman with nothing to offer when you see that I would freely give you all I have?" Folly taunted. She began her haunting song, and he cursed himself for having memorized it so well. He wished he could expunge it from the recesses of his memory so it wouldn't cloud his thinking[131].

"Hyperon," Wisdom called him by name, "Folly's words bear no truth, and so bear her no response. Come to me."

Anger rose in him against Folly, but he continued on to Lady Wisdom. The thought that she knew his name mesmerized him[132]. One step closer. Two steps. Three. He was afraid of her, but he didn't really care if she killed him. He only knew he needed her more than he had needed the meal he had just eaten.

Then he heard the voice he dreaded. "Hyperon," Mr. Specter said, "don't let this nonsense persuade your unpersuadable mind. You have a future with me. You are good at what you do. I am proud of your accomplishments. You are like a son to me." Hyperon turned from Wisdom to glance at Specter. The man had offered him the approval and validation that he had

---

131 2 Cor. 10:4

132 Is. 43:1

hungered for[133]. Hyperon was good at what they did. That much was true.

Hyperon noticed that Mr. Specter was inching his way closer to the top as well. He feared for Wisdom's safety. He knew how much Specter hated her.

As if she had been waiting for his attention, Wisdom spoke to him again. "No mind remains unpersuadable that I persuade," she said.

At the top of the stair, behind her, she turned a latch and a door opened. Light spilled out that was brighter than day. Hyperon could hear birds singing and smell the flavorful aroma of roasted meat and baking bread beyond it. The pleasant memories that had before made him miserable now strengthened him. The smell of green grass, the wind in his hair, the girl's storybook all called to him from beyond the door. How could such beauty be here right in the midst of the turbulent, harried city?

It was then that he remembered the story his mother read to him in secret. "In the darkness and the dirt, a baby was born." How could he have forgotten about the Shepherd? He had forgotten his childish promise to her.

"Come with me, Hyperon, and be persuaded," she said with a smile. "Don't just eat of my food and drink of my wine. Know me. Talk with me. Play with me. Love me. Those who love me, I will love. Those who seek me, I will find. Together, we will bring true help and healing to these streets[134]."

---

133 Gal. 1:10

134 Jn. 7:37-38

"Ask her the cost, Hyperon!" commanded Specter. "It might as well be slavery[135]. You will have to pay her to work!"

Hyperon looked up at the Lady and stepped toward her. The hunger he felt for all that she offered far outweighed any desire he had had before. In comparison, it didn't seem like desire at all, but rather a recognition of something he had been lacking his whole life.

"What is the cost?" he asked, hoping that she would say it would cost him nothing to be with her[136].

"Everything[137]," she replied, stepping down toward him, "My dear Hyperon, I will cost you your life, but what is that to you if you lose this life and gain your soul[138]?"

Hyperon believed her. His life lay motionless, dead beside her vibrant beauty.

"Don't tell me you believe words you can't even hear," Adam called to Hyperon. "Sounds like a fairy tale to me."

Folly laughed loudly from across the street. "Hyperon," she called, "you can't afford her price. You're nothing but a half-breed foreigner. She doesn't really want anything to do with you." Hyperon remembered those words on Rocky's lips. Did Wisdom and her followers feel the same?

Wisdom never wavered in her smile or her outstretched hand. "I know who and what you are,

---

135 Rom. 6:16-19
136 Lk. 14:28
137 Mt. 13:44
138 Mt. 16:24-26

Hyperon," she said. "I know all about your search for the Shepherd. I will help you if you come."

Hyperon took off his coat and laid it down on the steps. He bent and removed his shoes as well. Specter had given him those shoes, and what good had they done him? He'd kicked in doors, eluded police, and ruined lives with those shoes. He wouldn't need them in Wisdom's house.

"Wisdom," Specter called, "I have here his signed agreement that he is one of mine." Specter held up the document with Hyperon's signature on the bottom.

Hyperon grimaced. He had forgotten about that agreement! What would Lady Wisdom think of him now?

He didn't dare take his eyes from her face. His only hope, she seemed always to smile. He focused on her hand this time.

"Don't wait, Hyperon," she said. "Come to Me."

Hyperon stepped up one, two, three more steps. He could hear Specter's steps hastening up the staircase too, and he felt the man's presence in the hair on the back of his neck. He'd have Wisdom even if it meant his death. He began to run, barefooted, empty handed to her, and she came down to him and stood in the light of the door. Hyperon felt Specter grab at his shirt from behind. Just a few more steps and he would reach her. He fell at her feet and looked up.

Specter stumbled backward, but not before Wisdom grasped the agreement[139]. It crumbled and fell

---

[139] Prov. 2:10-12

in particles around Hyperon. He reached out and put his palms on her Achilles tendons and his face on the tops of her feet. Her skin was smooth. Her feet smelled like the dew on grass, and her skin did not burn him as the light in his dream had.

"Look at you, Hyperon," Folly called, "acting like some big milksop, tied to a woman's apron strings."

Wisdom said quietly, "You have chosen to fear my Father, Hyperon, and now, you have the beginning of Wisdom[140]."

"I do not know Who your Father is, my Lady," Hyperon admitted.

"You will know Him better hereafter, but let it suffice to say that you began to know Him at the same moment you began to hate evil[141]."

"This isn't over!" came Specter's voice from far away. "I will have you back yet, Hyperon!"

Hyperon bent his head over Wisdom's feet. "Don't let them take me back," he pleaded.

"No one can take you from the palm of my hand," she promised, and he wept[142].

---

140 Prov. 1:7

141 Prov. 3:7

142 Jn. 17:12; Rom. 8:37-39; Is. 49:15-16

Chapter 18

Adam chuckled as Mr. Specter turned back to him on the steps.

"Hyperon's a fool," he said, and hoped Mr. Specter would agree. Specter snarled and headed straight for Folly. Adam, astonished, trotted along behind.

Folly stood in the doorway of her home in the wall of the city. She held the door open for them as they approached. The loss of Hyperon had aged her noticeably. She held her wrinkled mouth in a grim, determined line. But, Adam mused, what was one man lost when they had thousands in their employ? Adam could easily find someone else at the bus stop to replace him.

Scarlet drapery dimmed the room. A table in the center was laden with loaves of bread and pitchers of icy water. A large king sized bed stood draped in scarlet, and the pungent scent of cinnamon hung about[143]. Adam had noticed it the time he'd been here before, but this time it seemed stronger. Perhaps it even covered another smell he couldn't quite name[144].

A black hall gaped toward the back of the room, and Adam could see a staircase winding down and away from the first floor. He hadn't been down that stair the time before, and truthfully, he had no desire to go down it now. He thought it should have had a flight going up to where Folly had been calling out from the second story balcony, but he didn't see any.

---

143 Prov. 7:16-23

144 Prov. 7:27

Specter cursed and slammed a fist on the table as he sat down. Folly poured him a glass of water. Adam claimed a seat next to Mr. Specter.

"You should have done more," Specter said to Folly. She produced a pretty pout.

"I do all I can," she said. "I don't know what happened. Some men require extra persuasion."

"No amount of persuasion will bring him back," Specter said, staring at his glass.

Adam let the silence hang momentarily and then felt proud to be included in this enclave.

"I can just recruit another worker," he said, expecting to be congratulated for thinking of it.

Specter whirled from his seat so quickly that the chair fell backward. He clenched Adam's collar in his fist.

"You don't recruit a quarter of the men that Hyperon will now recruit for Wisdom," Specter snarled. "While you laze away the days achieving nothing, he will give every waking moment to the spread of her propaganda. Think what a terrible place Opportunity will be!"

Adam's pride lay like a wounded dog at his feet. He shrugged, "I thought you said we could just coast through life, take it easy, once we got what was due to us. Surely one man won't stop that."

Specter loosened his hold and straightened Adam's collar. "You know, you're right. I think we all just need a nice getaway so that we'll be able to enjoy life more when we return. We'll center our thinking and get back on track with our life's philosophy. We'll be better able to bring justice to the masses then."

Folly stood and began slicing the bread with a serrated knife. “Sounds like my yoga routine. Stay for supper, will you, gents?”

Specter agreed and went to a drawer in the wall. He removed several pamphlets.

“Adam, why don’t you choose our getaway locale?” he suggested, holding a fistful of the papers out to Adam.

Adam took them joyfully and spread them on the table before him. Lush tropical isles and lavish skiing lodges greeted him from the pages. Smiling people adorned each page. One held the promise of a weeklong stay on the coast complete with fishing, historical tours, and rich dining experiences. Another advertised a twenty-four hour buffet and pool.

“Take your time choosing, honey,” Folly said, “and have another slice of bread.”

Adam’s bread soaked up all the saliva in his mouth. Without butter or jam, it was frightfully dry, but he hardly noticed as he perused the pamphlets. On the bottom of the stack, he came to one with a photo of a man and a woman sharing a tankard of ale. Snow peaked mountains adorned the landscape that was visible through the window behind them. The tour promised a taste of over two hundred and forty varieties of beer and an evening in each of ten craft breweries.

Specter and Folly leaned close, with their heads almost touching, whispering to one another.

“I’ve got the very one,” Adam said, holding up the pamphlet. “Entertaining and educational!”

Mr. Specter smiled and stood from his chair beside Folly. “Ah,” he said, “I’ve always said you were a snappy chooser." Specter snatched the pamphlet from Adam's hand.

"We'll begin tomorrow whenever we wake up," Specter said.

Adam raised an eyebrow. "How will we get to the location so quickly?" he asked.

Folly now stood from her chair. "Have I ever sent you away dissatisfied? All those places are here within my walls. I will take you anywhere you want to go[145]."

Adam sat back in his chair, rubbing his hands together.

"Good. Avoid all the mess of travel," he said. "I'm ready."

Specter laughed. "That's my boy. Just a few things we want to clear up with you about Wisdom."

Adam thought it strange that Mr. Specter would want to talk about that cursed woman again.

"Could you hear her?" Folly asked, draping an arm around his shoulders.

Adam chortled. "No! Could you?"

Folly's laugh tinkled like the bells around her ankle.

"Certainly not," she answered.

"Do you think Hyperon heard her?" Mr. Specter asked.

Now here was a troubling question for Adam. He'd wondered about this since the first time Hyperon had pointed Wisdom out to him. Hyperon always pretended that he could hear her, and the episode on the

---

145 Is. 5:18-23

stairs earlier had been no different. He puzzled over it for a moment.

"I suppose Hyperon heard whatever he wanted her to be saying," Adam answered. "It's like all the other folks I've run into that say they don't want to demand what's rightfully theirs, or who decline the entertainment you've sent them, Mr. Specter. I suppose all those people just claim to hear Wisdom when really they're following their own foolish ideas."

Mr. Specter nodded. "I quite agree with you, Adam. You have it all figured out," he said. "Sometimes, we believe things because they make us look good to the people we care about, not necessarily because they are true."

Adam nodded and looked back at the pamphlet.

"Let's not delay a moment longer," Specter said. "I'm going to turn in for the night, but you kids enjoy yourselves, and then in the morning, we'll enjoy ourselves into oblivion with the delights Adam has chosen."

Folly giggled.

"Sounds like my kind of party," she said. "More bread or water?"

Adam declined. Specter exited, and so did all the thoughts in Adam's mind. Tonight, he wouldn't think. He would just enjoy.

Chapter 19

Wisdom reached down and lifted Hyperon's chin.

"They are gone for now, my friend," she said. He looked down the stairs only to see the road deserted. Folly had even forsaken her post at the gate. He sighed and forced himself to stand and look into Wisdom's eyes.

"I hardly know what to think or do," he said. The truth was, he was still afraid.

She laughed. It made him smile.

"Let's start by going in," she said, motioning to the door that still stood open at the top of the steps.

Hyperon found that the light pouring out of the door warmed him and filled him with the desire to sprint as fast as he could[146]. It made him think of times when he had been a young child and his mother had taken him to the well near their home. That bottled happiness overflowed now and made him laugh aloud. Beyond the door, perhaps he would even find his mother's legendary Shepherd. How could he have forgotten about that for so long?

Wisdom stepped through ahead of him, and Hyperon followed her. Her dress flowed like water around her bare feet. His feet were bare too, and as soon as they were through the door, the cold stone of the steps was replaced with the warmth of a sand trail. Green grass lined either side, and the city vanished behind them. It seemed that instead of going inside, he had stepped into more of another outside. Wisdom ran ahead

---

[146] Is. 40:30-31

of him, and he began to run too. A stream came into view, and beside it, a table groaned beneath a rainbow of fruits, vegetables, delicacies, and wine. Seven pillars supported a vine-covered canopy that shaded the table[147].

Wisdom slowed and looked back at him. He smiled at her as he came up beside her.

"How did you know I would come?" he asked.

"My Father told me," she said, "and I prepared it all myself to celebrate your coming."

He walked slowly to the table and eyed the richness before him.

"Who is your Father," he asked, "and how does he know me?"

Wisdom motioned to him to be seated at the table, and she gracefully took a seat across from him. She lifted the empty crystal glass which rested before him and filled it slowly from a decanter full of rich scarlet wine. She handed it to Hyperon, and he took it and drank.

"Would you not agree that the older the wine is, the better the flavor?" she asked.

One swallow of the wine filled him with warmth and alerted all of his senses so that he seemed to see clearer, hear sharper, and taste to the fullest extent of his being.

"Yes," he said, "and if that is so, this wine must be very old."

"Indeed," she smiled. "This wine is old enough to be ageless[148]."

---

[147] Prov. 9:1-2
[148] Dan. 7:9

He drank from it again and set it down before him. Its richness kept him from drinking too much at a time. Hyperon focused on Wisdom's words. He was puzzled by them just as he was puzzled by the place he was in.

"This wine is like my Father. He is ageless. He is not bound by time, but because His love is from of old, it is the purest love. He has loved you, Hyperon, before you even came to be[149]," she said, never taking her eyes from his face.

He lowered his gaze and shook his head. "He must be mistaken. I cannot be who he means," he said.

"He has seen your birth. He has been close to you as an outcast huddling in the shade of the well. He traveled beside you from your village those many long nights on the bus. He even wept as you took part in the defilement and torture of his people," her words cut into him, "and yet His love remains pure. He still invites you to drink."

At the mention of his misdeeds, Hyperon's memory raced with images from his time in Opportunity. The debauchery, the intimidation, the theft, and the violence crowded back into his consciousness, and they had all been in the name of Justice. He saw the wicked lie behind it all, and simultaneously realized that he had known it was a lie all along. On the steps, at Wisdom's feet, he had felt new, but now he realized he could never be undone and remade.

Only now did Wisdom's smile falter slightly. "Hyperon," she said.

---

[149] Ps. 139:16

He looked at her and beheld a grave seriousness.

"You decided to leave that behind," she reminded. "Don't rob yourself of the truth by allowing the lie to live again. My Father wants to offer you forgiveness[150]."

"Forgiveness," Hyperon repeated. "I was born cursed. Why would he forgive me?"

"To bring Himself glory," she said.

His brow wrinkled. "I do not understand," he said sadly.

"When you were young, your mother took you to a well. Why did she take you there?" Wisdom asked.

"For a drink of water," he replied.

Wisdom nodded and smiled. "You were thirsty, but she couldn't quench your thirst with an empty jar. She would come to the well, fill the jar full, and help you get what you needed. You have been trying to quench the thirst of the masses out there," she motioned back the way they had come, "with emptiness. You have been empty, and the fixes you offered them were empty[151]."

Hyperon took this in. He knew all about emptiness.

"My Father invites you to come and be filled so that you can pour out His goodness to everyone you encounter," she said. "He will be glorified before everyone that you share Him with, and His well never runs dry."

---

150 1 John 1:9

151 Ps. 107:9

"I am not worthy to be filled. I am a broken vessel[152]," he said quietly.

She smiled. "He has already begun to heal you. I think you understand more than most," she said. "Why don't you eat while I tell you of my Father?"

He nodded. She passed him the laden dishes and he took enough to satisfy his hunger. Roasted lamb. Fresh bread. Potatoes. Greens. He imagined her toiling over her garden, cleaning the produce, and kneading the bread. He wondered if she had wept when she slaughtered the lamb[153]. It was a meal fit for a king, yet here he sat being served by her perfect hands. It seemed like a dream, but the nourishment of the food felt real in his belly.

She stood, walked to a tree nearby, and plucked a harp from its branches. The meat was sweeter because she had prepared it for him. Each spoonful of food nourished his body and comforted his aching soul. While she sang[154], he wrestled with the underlying question, "What will her Father require of me?"

My Father drew a circle on the deep
Dispelling darkness, banishing despair,
Awakening mountains, carving out seas.
His finger planted sure foundations there.
His light and line, dimension and time[155]
Define the ancient paths where He leads us
To lean not on our own understanding[156]

---

152 Jer. 19:10-11
153 Rev. 5:12
154 Prov. 8:27
155 Prov. 8:22-26
156 Prov. 3:5-6

But daily depend on His goodness to feed us.
I've learned to delight in all of His ways
Rejoicing in the works of His hands,
Exulting before Him to bring Him praise,
Inviting all to obey His commands.
A pebble ripples water disturbing[157]
Smooth surfaces, and I cannot refrain
From rescuing simple, lost travelers
Til their ripples all whisper His name.

Her voice flowed around him like the water of her song until he saw the scenes she described. The last scene depicted him on the steps walking toward her outstretched hand. It had been worth the cost to be free from the evil and emptiness of his previous life. Hyperon's stomach was comfortably full. Wisdom hung her harp back in the branches of the tree.

He stood and walked to her, taking her hand in his own.

"What must I do?" he asked.

"It's not a question of what there is to do, but what has already been done. Obey my Father; Abide in Him[158]," she replied.

He nodded. Her blue eyes pierced his soul until his former deeds drained from his memory.

"You have already died to yourself," she said. "That is all that is required. Now, you must allow Him to live through you[159]."

Hyperon stared at the ground between them.

---

157 Prov. 8:30-31
158 1 Jn. 2:27-28
159 Gal. 2:20

"I have nothing," he admitted. "No place to live. No money. No name. How can I be the one the Father wants to live through?"

"You are empty so that you can be filled[160]," she said. "Come. I will show you what you must do."

Hyperon followed her.

[160] 2 Cor. 5:17

Chapter 20

Adam woke around noon. His surroundings confused him momentarily. When he looked out the window, he found that he was looking at the same snow-covered mountain range he had seen in the pamphlet the night before.

He threw off the bedclothes and walked to the window. He considered opening it to better inhale the scent of the mountains. At the corner of the window however, a spot of glue dripped down. The scene had been glued on recently. Adam shrugged. So what if it was fake? It was a pleasant enough picture. He'd enjoy it all the same.

He found his clothes and dressed hurriedly. A bar lined the opposite side of the room. Adam strode to it and admired the tap and the decorative writing on a chalkboard proclaiming the variety of drinks available.

Just then, the door opened and noise swelled in. Folly and Specter walked arm in arm leading a crowd of people.

"Ah, Adam!" Specter called. "Suppose we get this show on the road!"

Adam waved and laughed. Folly dressed in her best for the occasion. She wore a white, low-cut dress with a pleated skirt. She came and kissed him on the cheek.

"We brought along some company since no one wants to drink alone," she said.

Mr. Specter jumped up on the bar and clinked a spoon against a glass. "Today is Adam's day to enjoy himself," he said as soon as he had the attention of everyone in the room. "We'll let him choose the flavor of the day."

The crowd cheered. Adam perused the board again.

All the choices had names like "Siren's Lullaby," "Medusa," and "Delilah's Hot Guava." Adam only had an inkling of flavors and types but didn't want to appear a fool.

His eyes rested on one name. "Sweet Sin," he said. "Let's try that one[161]."

Mr. Specter laughed loudly. "Excellent choice, Adam," he commended.

Folly hopped over the bar and filled a glass with the amber liquid. She smiled at him as she handed him the glass. After the first draught, lights, sounds, and movement blended into one throbbing mass. He slightly remembered an animated conversation nearby between two men he'd never seen before about the superiority of artisan beer above beer brewed in mass quantities by factories. Adam drank enough of both to be past caring.

A disco ball hung stationary while the room spun around. Adam could hardly keep his feet. Bodies pressed against him, pulsing in time to the loud music. He'd lost count of the women he'd met and definitely couldn't recall one name. If this was the first of ten stops, he had a lot to look forward to.

All of a sudden, he realized that Folly had her arms around his neck. Her face pressed in close to his.

"Having fun?" she yelled over the music.

---

[161] 1 Cor. 6:9-11

Her breath was as fermented as the whiskey he'd just drank, but that made her all the sweeter to him. He nodded and took a long swig from the bottle to prove his point.

"Mr. Specter wants to speak to you before you pass out," she said. She had to repeat herself twice before he heard the message.

"Where?" he motioned.

She pointed to a door to the left of the bar. A vague memory of the dark stair pushed forward and caused him to be reluctant.

He fumbled his way to the bar and used it to support himself to the door. It had been left ajar, and he was proud of himself for managing to not have to turn a doorknob- which seemed like an impossible task at the moment[162].

It was hot inside, and Adam followed a short staircase down to a room that had plush red carpet[163]. Mr. Specter lay on a black leather couch with his arm draped over his eyes.

Adam fell over and knocked a vase off of a pedestal.

"Curse you[164]," Mr. Specter whispered. He stood and walked over to Adam.

Adam looked up at him and didn't make an effort to get up. It was the first time he'd seen Specter's yellow tie askew.

"There's the small matter of cost," Specter said.

---

[162] Prov. 20:1
[163] Prov. 7:24-27
[164] Rom. 3:14

"Cost?" Adam repeated.

"This trip is expensive, and we have to come to some sort of agreement on your part of the cost," he said.

Adam's spinning mind was incapable of forming the word 'warning' but he felt that he should be doing or saying something.

"Folly and I have decided that the only thing you'll have to do is go on a little trip after this one is over," Mr. Specter explained as he walked back to his couch.

"Your task is to convince Hyperon to return to us," Mr. Specter explained, "and so, we've decided to let you take anything you think will help you."

Adam felt himself nodding inebriously.

"Why Hyperon? I could get anyone else you wanted," he whined.

"No!" Specter yelled. Then, more serenely, he added, "We need Hyperon. If he works for Wisdom, it will only cause us trouble. Just think what fun you two had together before he deserted you."

Adam remembered. He wondered how he could get into Wisdom's building.

"Oh, you won't have to worry about that," said Specter. Adam wondered if he had spoken his thoughts aloud.

"Wisdom won't let Hyperon stay in there forever." Specter sat down on his couch. "You'll find him out on the streets of Opportunity soon enough, and I have several other associates who will help you."

Adam struggled into a sitting position.

“By all means though, finish your pleasure trip first,” Specter said, and fell asleep. Adam had much to think about as he crawled back up the stairs.

Chapter 21

Wisdom led Hyperon around the table, weaving through the seven pillars supporting the canopy. There were four pillars to the back of the canopy and three to the front. When she reached a corner pillar on the row of three, she stopped.

"To win me, you must complete seven tasks. Indeed, three of them are already finished," Wisdom explained.

Hyperon followed her gaze to the ornate work on the pillar. Scrolling pomegranates hung on vines intricately woven together in the woodwork. In the middle of the pillar, a smooth cylindrical area depicted none other than Gluto. In the carving, Hyperon and Adam were giving him the gift of food from Specter. Hyperon started in surprise and took a step backward.

"Did you carve this?" he asked.

"Yes," she assented and continued to look at the carving.

Hyperon knelt down. "How can you bear my presence?" he asked. "I have done far worse things than this. Yet you know them all."

"Your abhorrence of evil is what is shown here, Hyperon," she said. "This visit made you hate evil in others as well as the deep evil within yourself. The first task has already been won, and that is the task of hating evil[165]."

---

165 Rom. 8:13

She knelt beside him. "You still hate the evil inside of you. I can bear to be in your presence because you have died to that evil[166]."

Her calming eyes took effect. He mirrored her smile slightly.

"You give me hope," he said.

She rose, and he followed her to the next pillar.

Here, in the bare cylinder that adorned the center, was a carving of her Father. It was one of the many images he had seen during his meal and her song. Her Father walked on water, and she was emerging from the ripples. Hyperon loved that image. Her Father had not only shaped her and given her all of the things she delighted in, He had also fashioned Hyperon with the same hand. Hyperon knew that Wisdom belonged to the Father, but in the same moment, he realized that he also belonged to the Father[167].

"Your second task is to fear my Father," she explained. "Just as a coin has two sides, so fearing my Father is the opposite side of hating evil. When you began to hate evil, you began to fear the One Who is Good."

"I feared my father," Hyperon said quietly. "He was a harsh man with a heavy hand, but I do not feel that kind of fear toward your Father- anymore."

Wisdom slipped her hand around his elbow and drew him close to her side. He inhaled the freshness of her hair.

---

166 Rom. 6:6

167 Rom. 8:22-31

"Indeed not," she said solemnly. "Though the One who made us has the power to destroy us, we know that He is the embodiment of Goodness and Love. If He destroyed us, we would not cringe in terror as you did at the hand of your father. Instead, I believe we would kiss His hand and trust in His reviving love. Don't you[168]?"

He nodded. "Yes, it seems that way. It is a fear I've never felt before. It is an odd thing to be afraid and trust in the same heart. I was afraid of you when you first called to me."

"But perfect love casts out terror[169]. Your second task is complete. You fear my Father, and it will grow into love," she said.

She did not remove her arm from his as she led him to the other corner pillar- the third in the row. Here, the depiction made him smile. In the carving, she stood with her hand in his. He admired the intricate detail of her hair and dress. The curve of her cheek mirrored what he saw when he looked at her. Wisdom smiled.

"It wasn't until the third task that you learned to seek me," she said. "You forsook all to find me. I called to you, and you answered. You sought Wisdom, and the third task is complete[170]."

"Anything I forsook is not worth a fraction of your value, my lady," he said.

"And yet, it is difficult to leave behind the familiar," she said.

---

168 Gen. 22"4-5
169 1 Jn. 4:18-19
170 Prov. 1:23

The sun was setting behind the four remaining pillars. A doe grazed beyond them in the meadow. He wished his whole existence was bottled up in that moment.

"Come. We cannot delay," she said. "Soon, you must return to Opportunity, and you must receive instruction and strength for the four tasks ahead of you[171]."

He stopped and drew his arm from hers.

"Go back?" he asked incredulously.

Her sympathetic look only made him feel worse.

"I cannot take you out of the world," she said. "I can only help you live inside of it."

Hyperon turned his back to her. He couldn't quite get enough oxygen. Thoughts of the dirty apartment, honking cars, and angry people crowded out the peaceful scene surrounding him. He'd thought that when he sacrificed everything for her, he'd at least get to leave it all behind. Now, he was surprised to find that he had to sacrifice everything in addition to wallowing in the very nothingness of it all.

Warmth still emanated from beneath his bare feet. He felt the grass between his toes. He looked down at it. Then he knelt and plucked a blade. Standing again, he rubbed it on his cheek. He turned back to Wisdom. She studied him. Her creased brow suggested worry, but her joy still radiated from her eyes.

"Will you be there with me?" he asked.

---

171 Jn. 17:15-19

"I will be there every moment, but you may not see me[172]," she said. "I will give you the tools you need to complete your tasks. We will be doing them together, though it may often seem that you are doing them alone."

He nodded and swallowed. Any amount of time away from her presence seemed too long.

"The fear of my Father is only half of my winning," she explained. "The other half is ability. If you'll let Him, my Father will live through you to complete your tasks[173]."

"I'm ready," he said with sudden resolve. He knew he wasn't going back to his old way of living. He loved Wisdom, and he would do what it took to win her.

She led him to the fourth pillar. The carving on it showed a wood with a divergent path. A compass hung above it.

"You must always remember to hate evil and choose the way of righteousness[174]. Back in Opportunity, it will not always be a clear choice like the one shown on this pillar," she said.

He pointed to it. "It doesn't look clear even here. Both paths look fine. How am I supposed to know the difference between good and evil?" Even as he said the words, he knew that he had always known the difference. He'd just not always acted on it. And as he watched, the carving changed until one path was overtaken by all manner of hideous creatures. The other

---

172 Mt. 28:20
173 Ex. 31:3-6
174 Prov. 8:15-21

path grew lighter- as poplar or spruce wood- and led to a building very much like the one he was in now.

Wisdom reached out and took the wooden compass. Instead of remaining a part of the carving, it came off in her hand. When Hyperon looked at it there, it was an actual functioning compass. It had the cardinal directions, and the needle hovered near the North[175].

"Take this compass as your tool for your fourth task," she said. He seemed inundated by his own questions about how cardinal directions had anything to do with morality, but they stifled him all at once. He didn't ask any of them before they were moving on to the fifth pillar.

In this ornate carving, Hyperon viewed himself in hand-to-hand combat against another. He couldn't quite tell who the cloaked figure was.

"For your fifth task, you will meet an adversary that you cannot overcome by relying on your strength or your wit. You will have to defeat him[176]," she said.

She stooped and picked up a rusted sword hilt from the ground. "This will be your help for this task."

It seemed so insufficient. Hyperon's mind raced back to sleeping on the floor and mice in the cupboard. Could fighting an adversary with a useless weapon[177] bring him to the same vexatious conclusion? Yet, here he stood with the woman he loved. He'd simply trust and try to memorize the instructions she was giving him.

---

175 Prov. 11:5
176 Prov. 19:20
177 Eccl. 9:18

The sixth pillar showed a house in various stages of construction. Wisdom smiled even more brightly at this one. "Your sixth task will be to prepare our home. You will have to build it with your own hands. And Hyperon, don't build in vain[178]."

Her strong hand reached into the carving and withdrew a hammer. She handed it to him as she had done with the compass and the sword hilt. It was surprisingly light. He stored it in his belt beside the hilt.

The final pillar stood in the last rays of sunlight. The day faded fast. On this carving, he could see her Father. Far below Him was a naked man being tortured to death. It was not a pleasant sight. Hyperon looked to Wisdom to see how she bore it.

She leaned forward and caressed the scene tenderly.

"My Father's Son, the Shepherd," she said. "Your final task will be to become a living sacrifice as He did, obeying the Father's will in all things[179]."

It was his mother's Shepherd. In finding Wisdom, he had fulfilled his youthful promise to his mother.

"The Shepherd doesn't have a happy ending, if I remember correctly," Hyperon observed.

Wisdom's attention snapped to him. She leaned forward and kissed him on the mouth. He returned her kiss, but it ended as soon as it began.

"You have forgotten the ending. You will need to ask to read the little girl's green book. You know the girl

---

178 Prov. 24:3-4

179 Lk. 22:42; Jn. 19:28-37

I mean. Find it, and study it. You will find that what you have thought of as the ending is really still the middle of the story. Though it will be your final task, it is far from the ending, Hyperon," she said. "Your final tool is this." From a pocket in her dress she pulled an old fashioned spyglass. She held it out to him. Hyperon stretched it out and held it to his eye.

He could see beyond the horizon into a place of glimmering brightness[180]. There, seated high above all, Hyperon caught his first real glimpse of Wisdom's Father. He was not exactly like a man, and yet he had some semblance of the greatest of all Kings. A rainbow encircled him, but it was a rainbow made up of many shades of green[181]. It gave Hyperon the impression of the golden type of green that shines from a midsummer sun through the greenest leaf. A multitude of people surrounded Him. They sang, but every note they sang was like the final chord of a song. It made each note complete in itself. Wisdom put forth her hand and lowered the glass.

"That, my love, is hope. Whenever you experience despair in suffering or setback, the spyglass will give you a glimpse of the real ending, that is actually not an ending at all but instead, a completeness. My Father drew a circle that has no beginning or ending, and He invites you to step into His circle. That is not mere happiness. That is complete joy," she said.

---

180 Jn. 14:8-9
181 Rev. 4:2-11

He smiled at her. "I don't know how, or where, or when, but I will win you, Wisdom. And then, we will come one day to your Father's land," he promised.

"I love you, Hyperon," she replied. "In all your tasks remember that you have no ability in your own strength. My Father must give you every ability. And that is how Wisdom is won."

She kissed him again. They embraced, and Hyperon found himself standing on the cold, colorless stair alone with his tools. As he turned to begin his tasks, he felt his sorrow melting away into the assurance of her abiding presence[182].

He put the compass in his pocket and resolved to find the girl with the green book.

---

182 1 Jn. 4:16

Chapter 22

The task of finding Hyperon hung over Adam's head with more intensity than any hangover he had the entire trip. Smooth ale tasted like ashes in his mouth. From one tavern to another- though he never left Folly's dwelling- Adam carried the heavy weight of the trip's cost.

At the end of two weeks' time, he found himself alone on a sidewalk in an unknown part of the city. Folly and Specter were nowhere to be seen, and Adam couldn't recall most of what had happened for the previous ten days.

He found a seat on the trolley, and the old woman near him moved away to a different part of the car. Adam shrugged it off. If he offended her high and mighty sensibilities, so be it.

The apartment continued much the same. He was glad to see his T.V. in the same place and his favorite bean bag chair positioned in front of it. Tonight he would relax. Tomorrow he could turn his mind to finding that fool Hyperon. Adam knew that Mr. Specter wouldn't want to be kept waiting.

It was near midnight when the interruption of the T.V. banter woke Adam. Mr. Specter stood before him with the remote in hand.

"Did you think I was joking, Adam?" he asked.

Adam glanced toward the door. He was almost certain that it had been locked.

"No, sir," he stammered, attempting to sit up. "I planned to start in the morning."

Specter nodded. "That's my boy," he encouraged. "Always living life to the fullest and looking out for the less fortunate. You pull this off, Adam, and I think we're going to have to look at a promotion."

"Yes, sir," Adam said.

Mr. Specter set the remote down and strode to the door. He stopped and held it open.

Adam reluctantly followed.

"No time like the present," Mr. Specter said gleefully.

As they walked down the dimly lit flight of stairs, Specter pulled something from his inner coat pocket.

"Hyperon always did enjoy a friendly game," he said. Adam recognized the video game controllers.

"Yeah," he said, perking up a little. "We love that game! I remember this one time we stayed up all night and beat every level."

Mr. Specter stopped at the foot of the stairs.

"Hyperon may not be willing to come here anymore, but there's no rule against taking the game to his place."

Adam nodded.

"If this doesn't work, come see me at the office," Mr. Specter said.

Before Adam could say "Yes, sir," Specter faded into the night.

Chapter 23

Outside Wisdom's door, Hyperon found a new pair of shoes, a new coat[183], and the leftovers of the meal given to him by the baker woman. He smiled when he remembered her kind, round face. As he laced the shoes, he decided to retrace his steps to her shop in order to thank her properly. She was also the only person he knew that had told him about a Someone "who gives us all what none of us deserves." Then, he could collect his thoughts about how to find the girl with the green book and complete his tasks.

The shop was not hard to find, and the aroma pouring from the door came close to the richness of Wisdom's banquet.

A small bell jingled as he entered through the front door. Two customers dallied at a table in the corner, but the rest of the tables were expectantly empty.

The woman huffed and puffed out of the back room to the counter. Her hands were full, and a deep, throaty humming rose from behind her sealed lips. On seeing him, she smiled, causing laugh lines around her deep brown eyes to crinkle. Hyperon thought it was a cautious smile. He returned it and strode to the counter purposefully.

He leaned toward her so that his conversation might not reach the ears of the other two in the room.

"I was in here yesterday," he said.

She nodded, "Hmmmmm?"

"I've come to work off what I owe," he said. "Can I be of any help to you?"

---

[183] Col. 3:9-14

Her smile broadened. "You don't look like the baking type, but you do look teachable," she said.

"My mother always taught me that good cooks don't lick their fingers," he said.

She slapped her hand on the counter and laughed long and pleasantly. The two strangers turned to stare.

One of them hollered, "Paddy, you're the laughingest gal I ever heard of."

She ignored him. "S'pose that's as good a place to start as any," she said. "Hang your coat here and follow me back. I think I've got an apron somewhere that will fit you, or maybe we can just turn one of mine sideways! You're about as tall as I am wide!" She laughed again. He smiled.

Paddy bustled about. Her plumpness carried a different connotation than that of Gluto. This wasn't the obesity born of gluttonous eating but of a healthful stoutness. She finally found the apron and held it out to him.

"What's your name?" she asked.

"Hyperon," he answered.

"You look different than you did yesterday[184]," she remarked. "Something about your eyes is different."

He merely smiled.

"I'm Paideia[185], but everybody just calls me Paddy. Here," she said, gesturing to the counter running the length of the back wall, "you can slice veggies for the stew."

---

[184] Eccl. 8:1
[185] 2 Tim. 3:16

She gave him a cutting board and showed him the barrels of potatoes, carrots, and onions. He felt slightly like the girl in the story who is told to spin a whole room of straw into gold in one night.

Paddy laughed again.

"I'm right glad to have a hand here with all this," she said and bustled back to the front room.

Hyperon eyed the mountains of vegetables. Wisdom had given him tasks, but none so menial as this. However, he could think of no other course of action. Nothing else seemed to fit in with his new way of life, and he didn't even know how to start looking for the little girl. Besides, he owed Paddy at least one full day's worth of work for the food she had so willingly given. He wanted to learn more about her and the Someone she had mentioned in their first meeting.

He listened to her throughout the day as she greeted customers and laughed. Her laugh, instead of grating his nerves, soothed and cheered him. It coaxed a smile to his face.

Once, when she had come to retrieve a needed item, he saw beads of sweat on her brow from her continual labor, but instead of the resentful attitude toward effort that he had seen in so many others, joy shone from her countenance.

"Still at it, I see," she'd said to him on her way past. "Well, you're worth your salt."

Long after the evening meal, he heard her locking the front door. He'd made considerable progress on the vegetables, but the barrels weren't empty.

"Whew!" she said as she came into the back room, "I've never had a better day."

"Did you make that much then?" he inquired politely.

Paddy laughed. "Oh, no. I didn't mean the money, my dear boy. I meant serving the folks that pass through. I live for it."

He focused on the carrot before him. What could she care about the raggle-tag group that came in and out of the bakery? Old men, drifters, scoundrels like himself, women with nothing better to do, and kids out from school had benefited from the work of Paddy's hands all day[186]. The work and love she put into each one filled them up, and she didn't have to steal it from anyone else to give it, either. Love wasn't empty words in her mouth, but full bowls in her hands. She was willing to pour herself out for them. Even Specter had required some return from those that he helped. Hyperon had never met anyone like Paddy before- except for Wisdom. The more he troubled over Paddy's fixation with selfless work, the harder he pushed the knife into the carrot until it slipped into the flesh of his other hand[187].

He dropped the knife and hissed over the pain.

Without a word, Paddy snatched up a towel and wrapped it around his injured hand. The blood stained it right away.

"Here now. Let's get a look at it," she said, easing the towel back to survey the damage.

"No severed fingers," she announced, "but looks like it may need a stitch. Would you like me to stitch it?"

---

[186] 1 Cor. 13:4; Gal. 5:22-23

[187] Eccl. 10:10

He'd rather not, but Hyperon said, "Sure." He couldn't think of any alternatives.

He applied pressure to the blood-soaked towel while Paddy left to fetch her tools.

"I just live across the alley in the back," she said and was gone.

He sat down on a stool, and true to her word, she was back quickly. She carried an antiseptic, a needle that Hyperon judged to be too long, and thread.

Paddy pulled up a stool beside his and set to work immediately.

"Why did you come here today?" she asked as she threaded the needle.

He didn't know how to answer her immediately, so he let the silence hang.

"I owed a debt I could not pay[188]," he said finally.

"You've more than worked it off," she said. "Why were you so willing to get into debt yesterday?"

He remembered the scene with shame. He had been persuaded yesterday that because of the injustices in his life, everyone owed it to him to give him whatever he wanted. Now, he looked at the sweat on Paddy's forehead and thought about how his own emptiness had emptied everyone around him. He wanted to be full, like Paddy, like Wisdom.

"I met Wisdom," he said. Hyperon thought that the admission might have come with sheepishness, but instead, when he thought of his lady, he had only a steady sense of duty.

---

[188] Rom. 8:12

Paddy stopped sewing and looked into his eyes.

"I see," she said slowly.

"And I want to know the Someone who gives what I do not deserve," Hyperon blurted. "You said you knew about that, and I don't know anyone else who does."

She resumed her stitching. Silence covered them like a comforting blanket.

"How did you cut your hand, Hyperon?" Paddy asked.

He wrinkled his brow. "You saw me. I cut it with a knife," he answered.

She laughed. "Yes, but why?" she pushed him further.

"Well, I suppose because my thoughts were occupied with something else and the knife was dull," he said.

She nodded. "The first thing I will tell you about the Someone who gives what we do not deserve is that when we try to get to Him without Wisdom, it is like throwing all of our effort behind a dull knife. In the end, what we deserve is the self-inflicted injury we bring upon ourselves."

He nodded and winced as the needle pulled through his flesh. He definitely wouldn't choose that.

"But working with Wisdom is the best and sharpest of knives. Not only do we prevent injury to ourselves, but the work is done quicker and more efficiently," she said.

She finished her job and cut the thread between her teeth.

"Where will you stay tonight?" she asked.

He shrugged.

"There is a small apartment here above the bakery," she said. "I live in the house next door, so no one lives here now. You are welcome to stay as long as you have need of it and as long as you work in the bakery. I could use the extra set of hands."

He considered the offer and agreed. Where else was he to go anyway?

She stood and stretched her back. "I'll also pay you a fair wage," she said, "and tomorrow, Hyperon, we'll start your growing lessons."

"Growing lessons?" he asked as he surveyed his injured hand. She'd done a tidy job of the mending.

"You've met Wisdom, and you want to know more about the Someone who gives what you do not deserve. Tomorrow, I'll give you a sharper knife, and you can begin to know Him more fully," Paddy explained.

"How can I know Him more fully when I don't know Him at all?" Hyperon asked.

"Oh," Paddy said with a laugh, "I thought you knew that He is Wisdom's Father."

She now had Hyperon's full attention.

"I did not know, but I am anxious to hear whatever you can tell me," Hyperon said. "I love Wisdom, and though I don't deserve her, I am glad to know that her Father can give what I don't deserve. Do you know Him, Paddy?"

Paddy laughed. "You are a different creature than you were yesterday. That's for sure. Yes, I know Him, and I have long known her as well. Get some sleep now. It's late, and bakeries open early."

She showed him the stair leading to the apartment above the shop. The steps creaked, but the door at the top opened to reveal a small yet tidy space. There was a bed laid out with attractive brown linens, a desk and chair, and a washroom. In the far end, there was a small kitchen with a stove top and refrigerator. Hyperon set his bag on the desk and walked the length of the room to the kitchen. There, he realized, was a large window above the sink that looked out on the city. Lights twinkled and cars raced by. He could not see the stars in the inky sky, but he knew they were there blinking back at the city. He smiled. It was simple, but it was the closest to home he'd ever felt. Somewhere out there, Wisdom worked to bring others in to know her Father.

He returned to the desk and looked through the four items she'd given him for his tasks. He wondered if working at the bakery so many hours would keep him from doing what he had to do. Yet, how could he set about doing Wisdom's tasks unless he knew more about her Father? He needed to find the little girl too, but maybe he could do that in his time off.

Yes, he'd stay and learn from Paddy. Then he'd set about his tasks. He picked up the spyglass. On the night's horizon he saw Wisdom's Father shining just as if night never touched Him. It was a hopeful view. Tomorrow would bring better things.

Chapter 24

Prudence ate half of the sandwich, half of the apple, and half of the cookie that her mother had packed in her lunch pail. She stowed the uneaten halves back in the folded napkin at the bottom of the pail.

She leaned against the only tree in the school yard and watched some of the other students as they kicked a red ball. Haste was louder than any of the others.

"Prudence?" came a voice as small as a baby bird's. "Will you read to us today?"

Prudence turned to smile at the little girl and saw that there were two others, a boy about her own age, and another girl from the youngest class.

"Yes. Where did we leave off?" she asked, fishing her book out of her pail. The pages had dried from Haste's wetting, though the book did not look as crisp now as when the Lady had given it to her.

Haste and the others were consumed by their game, so Prudence read undisturbed for the last ten minutes of the lunch recess. The three listeners smiled and sighed in turn but never once turned their rapt attention away. Just before the teacher rang the bell, Prudence softly sang the Lady's song. The little girls hummed along.

I've learned to delight in all of His ways
Rejoicing in all the works of His hands,
Exulting before Him to bring Him praise,
Inviting others to obey His commands.

"Prudence," the teacher's voice startled her, and the song stopped abruptly, "how many times must I tell you that that song is not allowed in this school?"

Prudence looked at her teacher with pity. "Against such things there can be no law[189]," she said.

"I asked her to sing it, teacher," the little girl named Sparrow said in her baby bird voice.

The teacher's eyes darted back and forth between them. "This could get me in trouble, Prudence. I know you don't mean any harm, but great harm may come if I let you spread propaganda to the other students. What will their parents say?" the teacher said.

Prudence didn't have an answer, so she said nothing.

"It would be better for you and all of the other children if you would just join in their games," the teacher said. "Real help can't come from books or songs. We must get our hands dirty and be friends even with those who disagree with us. That is the way to change their minds and right the wrongs of this world."

The teacher hurried away to ring the bell before Haste's game got out of control.

"Thank you for reading," said the boy, who was Sparrow's brother, "and for singing. I learn more from you than I ever do in class."

At the end of the day, Prudence hurriedly gathered her things and left the schoolyard at a brisk walk. Instead of heading straight home, she turned toward the tall buildings in the city's center. Her two braids bounced in rhythm on her back as she walked on the insides of the sidewalks, closest to the buildings and farthest from the roads. Most of the adults walking there ignored her. Once, she had to venture out into the middle

---

189 Gal. 5:23

of the sidewalk because of a woman carrying an umbrella who wasn't watching where she was going.

Finally, Prudence found the alley she was looking for in the darkest shadow of the tallest high rise. There were no trees, no birds, and hardly any people in the alley. She looked across the street and saw the black theater with the fake owls on the outside. How she hated those beady, false eyes!

She turned her back to it and darted into the alley. A cat rushed away from her. A black dumpster was half open. A thin little boy sat against the side of it with his eyes closed. Another child, Prudence couldn't tell if it was a boy or a girl, hung inside the dumpster by its feet.

"Hello," she said.

The boy's eyes flew open, and she saw his fear.

"It's okay," she said. "I'm a friend."

The child in the dumpster scurried to climb out. Its scrawny limbs and stiff hair were dirty. The hair would have been black, except malnutrition had tinged it red on the ends.

"I brought you something," she said, and she dug into her lunch pail.

She divided the half sandwich into two pieces and held them out. The children didn't hesitate but took them greedily.

Prudence said down next to them. "I was once here myself."

They stared at her.

Prudence smiled. "Someone cared and gave me what I did not deserve. Do you want me to read you a story while you eat?" she said.

They nodded and ate a little slower while she opened the green book. "In the darkness and the dirt, a baby was born."

On her way home, Prudence wondered if she could ask her mother to pack more sandwiches. She thought often of the children who lived the life she would have lived if it hadn't been for the Lady. She knew the Lady would want her to rescue them too, as much as she was able. Prudence thought of them as "the Shadow Children," and she resolved to ask the Lady how she could help them more the next time she saw her. She wondered if she would be allowed to invite them to their meetings.

Prudence skipped up the front steps of her home.

"I'm home," she said, setting the empty pail and her book on the table.

"How was school?" her mother asked, coming from the kitchen.

"Fine," Prudence smiled. "How was home?"

Her mother laughed and kissed her. "Fine. Your father said that Saul is going to be just fine. We'll have to be more careful about meetings though," she said.

"I am glad that he is getting better," Prudence replied.

How could they be careful about the meetings while inviting more people to them all the time? Prudence's musings stayed with her for the remainder of the evening.

Chapter 25

Adam roamed the streets until daybreak. Finding Hyperon was like looking for a needle in a haystack. What if that fool had left the city entirely?

A fleeting fear of Mr. Specter vanished even as it appeared. Surely, if they were really making the world a better place for the less fortunate, one incomplete assignment wouldn't matter. Maybe Mr. Specter would take pity on him since he had been up all night. He had tried his best, hadn't he?

The sidewalk began to fill with workers getting an early start on their day. Adam pitied the poor fools. They walked down the same sidewalk to the same job everyday just so the same boss could take what was best of their lives and livelihoods. Adam was thankful for Mr. Specter and the meaningful work they did together.

Adam's thoughts cheered him and bolstered him for his task. He was on top of the world living the high life. When he grew old, he could look back on all the fun times he'd managed to grab in his youth, in addition to the way he had bettered the world.

The smell of coffee lured him as he walked past a café. He snuck around the back through an alley, managed to secure a steaming cup of the hot, brown liquid, and sat down at one of their tables without attracting the attention of the proprietors. As he enjoyed his well-earned delight, a conversation at a nearby table attracted his attention.

Two old men were enjoying breakfast together. Adam could see enough of them in his periphery to know that one wore a green golfer's cap and the other wore a brown vest.

"We should have gone to Paideia's," said the one in green. "No one makes muffins like she does."

The other one chuckled, "I even miss her laugh."

"But, I just don't trust the half-breed she had working with her yesterday. Why would she hire such a fellow when there are plenty of other young folks right here in Opportunity looking for work?" asked the first.

His companion shook his head solemnly, "You never know about Paddy. She's always taking in strays. Maybe the guy isn't so bad. I've never known her to make an error in judgment."

"Well, all the same, I might visit the other eating establishments until I hear this guy's gone," said the first one.

The one in the brown vest shrugged. Adam wished they would continue their conversation and reveal the name of Paddy's place. However, the two old men sat in silence. He could just ask them, but he didn't want to draw attention to himself, especially after stealing the coffee. His cup was now empty, but he waited until they stood from their table.

Then he followed them out to the street. They parted ways. Adam chose to follow the one in the green cap. He easily caught up to the man.

"Good morning to you, sir," he said, coming beside the man.

The old man was startled. "Good morning," he grumbled.

"I couldn't help but hear you mention that a different restaurant had better muffins than the one you were just in," Adam said. "Do you mind telling me the name of the better place?"

The man smiled. "Of course, lad. It's the *Banquet Bakery* run by a gal named Paddy."

"Much obliged." Adam tipped his hat and faded away from the old man into the crowd. He now remembered hearing of Paddy and her bakery. Paddy had never been in the employ of Mr. Specter, but many of those who signed on with Mr. Specter had to be persuaded to stay away from her. She was almost as much of a trouble maker as Wisdom.

Chapter 26

"Hold that light a little higher, son," said Father's muffled voice.

Alexander stood on tiptoe to hold the light higher under the hood of the automobile. His father was the only auto mechanic in Opportunity. He spent long hours under the hood.

"Thanks," Father said. The boy heard a few clanks of metal on metal. Suddenly, sparks flew out. Father rolled out from underneath the car.

"Whew," he said. "Solved that one! They're just like a puzzle, my boy."

Alexander resented the grime on his father's smiling face. He resented the fact that of all the automobiles in Opportunity, theirs was the oldest. Half the time it wouldn't crank. He even resented the fact that his father found pleasure in fixing the old pieces of junk.

He blew out the lamp. When he grew up, he would never be a mechanic.

"Let's see what your mother has for supper, eh?" his father said.

Alexander followed him to the washtub in the corner where father washed his hands, face, and neck. Alexander merely washed his hands.

When the door opened, the aroma of mom's biscuits made him realize how hungry he was.

"I was just getting ready to send a search party to the garage!" said Mom.

Father laughed. Three younger brothers sat at the table talking or whining or crying.

As they joined hands around the table, Alexander wondered why they thanked someone other than themselves. They did all the work, didn't they? He resented the bowed heads even though he could still convince himself that he loved the heads. Even though they were fools, Mom and Father cared for him and his brothers. They did the best they knew how. Alexander just wished there was a better way.

In bed that night, he pondered the meaning of life. It was a big subject for thirteen, but his resentment built up until he felt he must either define life or leave it behind.

Mom cracked the door. When she saw his eyes still open, she came and sat beside him on the bed.

"I just came to tuck you in," she smiled.

"I'm too old to need that," he said.

Her smile never wavered, but he had to look away from the hurt that sprang to her eyes.

"Is something bothering you, dear?" she asked.

"No."

She sat silent for some time. Then she began to pray out loud. It was embarrassing, even though there was no one else present to hear. Perhaps that's why it was embarrassing. Her quiet voice folded the words around him just as her hands sat folded in her lap. One word tumbled amongst the rest and rose to the top as she repeated it frequently. Even after she left and he was alone again in the darkness that word hung like a specter over his bed. He awoke in the morning with it still hanging about him like a cloak.

Wisdom.

His father had requested his help immediately after school. Alexander carried his few books under his arm and watched as his friends went to football practice or stood around talking to one another. None of them seemed to have anywhere to be. Why was it that he had to hurry home?

As he turned his back on the school, he heard a voice calling his name.

"Hey, Alexander!" someone shouted.

He turned and saw the tall lanky form of Judas DeCeit hurrying toward him. Judas was a full two years older, and Alexander knew he was involved with a lot of the activities at the school.

"We're just beginning play practice today for the spring school play," he said. "Maybe you should give it a shot instead of hurrying home."

Alexander thought about his father working in the stuffy garage. He thought about all the other boys and girls that were a part of the theater group. He hadn't thought much about acting until that moment.

"I'm supposed to work with my old man today," he said.

"Ahh," Judas waved his hand, "you're man enough to make your own plans. What'll it hurt for just one season? You're always helping your dad."

Alexander longed to be man enough to make his own decisions. He tired of taking orders from his parents. He knew that his father would discipline him, but it wasn't anything he couldn't handle. Besides, what harm was there in taking part in an after school activity? It wasn't like he was joining his buddies at the bar or anything.

He turned back toward the school.

"Fine," he said to Judas. "I'd like to see what it's all about."

Judas laughed and clapped him on the back.

"Good," he said. "You won't be disappointed."

They began to walk together, stride by stride, back to the school. Just ahead, Alexander noticed the slim figure of a girl sitting beneath a towering oak tree in the courtyard. She stood as they approached.

Judas seemed not to see her, and Alexander would have continued right past her had she not spoken to him. He'd never noticed her before.

"Alexander," she said, and her look pierced his very soul, "you know your father would let you be a part of any activity so long as you asked him first."

Her eyes seemed akin to his mother's- searching, compassionate, kind.

"Who are you? How do you know me?" he asked. Judas continued on to the drama room without him, taking no notice of the girl.

"I am Wisdom," she said.

A shudder ran through him. The very spirit of his mother's prayer stood before him. How strange. He had thought the prayer empty, a vapor that rose to the ceiling but no further. Yet, here she stood. His fascination mingled with a strange desire to prove her wrong.

"I'm my own boss," he said, in a vain attempt to convince himself.

"If you claim that, we both know that you're just acting the part," she replied quietly. "Go home today and ask your father about staying tomorrow."

He considered the suggestion.

"Why do you care?" he asked.

"I call to all wanderers," she said, "hoping that some may cease their wandering and put their roots deep into the streams of living water, lest they dry up[190]."

He debated what action to take. She was right about his father, but the lure of answering only to his own authority held sway over him.

"Alexander!" called Judas from the doorway, "What's holding you up?"

Alexander shook his head as if to clear it from the conflict.

"Look," he said, "I don't know who you are, and I don't care. I'm going to do what I want to do." He turned his back to her and didn't look back.

---

[190] Ps. 1:3-4; Jer. 17:5-8

Chapter 27

"If you had wanted to be a part of the school play," his father was saying, "why didn't you just ask?"

Alexander had no reply. His mother's muffled sobbing flowed through the wall and tore at his already sensitive ego.

"If that is what you want, your mother and I will be your biggest supporters. We will come to every play you invite us to. However, you must first ask our permission," his father said. Instead of anger, the voice was tinged with sadness.

He sat down beside his son. Alexander tensed as the muscular arm slid around his shoulders.

"Why must you harbor this resentment against us?" he asked quietly.

Alexander debated about answering at all. What good would it do? But, finally, he formed his response.

"Your life makes as much sense as praying to no one. You work long hours for little pay and no notice. You live in Opportunity because you were born here. You never seem to want to live life on your own terms. Don't you ever get tired of taking direction from your customers, or mom, or whoever-it-is-that-you-pray-to? Everyone else has better stuff than us, and it's not fair," he spat.

His father was clearly taken aback at his words. Alexander knew that they would shock him. But instead of remorse, he felt proud to be enlightening his father after a lifetime of living in the darkness of submission.

"Is that how you see things?" Father asked.

Alexander nodded.

Father studied the oil stain on his work pants.

"Do you still want to do the school play?" It was not what Alexander had expected.

"Yes," he said.

"Fine," his father replied, "just let us know when it will be so that your mother and I can make plans to attend."

Alexander went to his room bewildered. His father had neither questioned nor berated. In fact, it was as if he took no notice of his enlightenment speech. On top of it all, they would let him continue in the drama. He stretched out on his bed.

Yes. He liked being his own boss.

Spotlight shone on the red velvet curtain, and Alexander trembled just behind it. His first audience sat beyond it, expectantly waiting for his performance. He yearned to make them laugh or cry or fear with his words and actions. The stage gave him power. He held sway over their emotions until the final closing of the curtain, if he could play his part well.

The curtain parted. The light nearly blinded him but it also sparked in him the ability to be who he was not.

He, and not the tall, favored Judas, had been cast as the lead role. He played a rich young man who ruled an entire town.

"And yet, I would want you to listen to me because of my honor, because of my valor. If I had Aladdin's lamp, I would instantly wish away my wealth so that I could know you loved me for what I am, not what I have," he said to his female counterpart.

It was a valiant sentiment, but so lost was Alexander in his role that he never stopped to think that the words were the opposite of his own ideals.

The girl came closer on the stage. He triumphed in the anticipatory silence of the crowd.

"But I do love you for what you are," she said her lines almost as well as he did, "and I would follow you anywhere."

When the final curtain closed, the spell ended. Alexander came to himself and peeked beyond the curtain to the mass of moving people in the audience. He saw his father escorting his mother to the back of the auditorium. They would be enthusiastic. He could already hear their praise. He knew he had done well.

Just before he turned to go to the changing room, he spotted her in the front row. She was the only one still seated. Her eyes seemed fixed on his face, though he was certain she could not see him. He studied her brow, her chin, the way she sat in the swinging auditorium chair. He resented the fact that she had been right that day. His arguments had won his parents over, and he clearly had the devotion of the drama teacher, the other students, and the audience. Why not hers?

Wisdom remained a lock he could not pick. In a sea of smiling faces, hers seemed to only frown on him. What would it take to meet her approval? Alexander cursed under his breath. He had no desire to meet her approval, he realized. He simply wanted her to lower her standards and approve of him as he was.

"Alexander," she said his name, and if he had not been looking at her lips, he would not have heard it.

He let the curtain down and rushed away to change.

His entrance stopped the whole room when he came through the hall to the place where refreshments were being served. They all turned to look at him and applaud. Alexander grinned and bowed. He had donned his dress clothes and a bright yellow tie that he thought would befit the lead actor of the play.

His father beamed at him and clapped him on the back. His mother offered him a plate of cookies like it was an offering to a god. His teacher complimented him so profusely, that she nearly ran out of breath. Judas DeCeit laughed with some of the other boys, and the girls took turns at his side. He decided not to let Wisdom's absence ruin his moment in the spotlight.

His parents agreed to allow him to go out to eat with his drama friends. The group was loud in the restaurant and even louder out on the street afterward. The girls laughed, and the boys shoved one another.

"Hey Alexander," Judas called, "what say we liven up this bunch by finding something for us all to drink?"

Alexander had no desire for alcohol, but he knew its uses for controlling the mob. He knew it made for a more level playing field for all the partakers and a hand up for the possessor who did not partake.

"Well, you look older," he challenged Judas. "You buy it."

Judas smiled, "If you front the money."

Alexander dug in his pocket. His mother had given him thirty dollars for supper. He had only spent six.

Judas's fingers closed around it quickly. "I'll be right back," he said.

Alexander could hear one of the girls asking to be taken home.

"What's that, Carissa?" he said, turning to her. "Don't go now!"

She was instantly by his side.

"But my mum would be furious," she said, "and we're all underage."

"We'll just *act* older," Alexander retorted. Everyone laughed. "Besides, it isn't fair to base a law on the age of a person. Why shouldn't we be respected for our maturity instead of censured for our age?"

Alexander watched Carissa's forehead wrinkle in disagreement. It wouldn't take much more prompting from him to sway her.

"Would you let some old fashioned rules dictate your actions?" he asked. "Your parents drink alcohol anyway. They don't really believe that you shouldn't. Plus, we'll be making memories together."

Alexander found immense satisfaction in the way her shoulders went back and she stood a little taller.

"You're right," were the best words he'd ever heard. He rode on that high all night.

"We can go to the docks by the lake. No one's there at night," a boy suggested.

Judas was not long in obtaining the evening's entertainment, and the whole party jumped in the few vehicles they had and sped toward the docks.

In the old red jalopy that Alexander chose, there were six people crammed into four seats. The laughter never died the whole seven miles. The lights of the city swirled behind them, and the stars shone overhead.

They parked in a deserted gravel lot and made for the two docks that stretched out into the tranquil lake. Alexander swam here often as a child with his cousins. It was familiar to him.

Suddenly, he caught sight of a more familiar form sitting on one of the docks.

The others saw her too. She had put on a sweater since the play, but now she sat dangling her bare feet over the edge of the dock without a care in the world. Alexander hated the disapproval emanating from her.

"What are you doing here?" Carissa called to her.

"Perhaps I should ask the same," Wisdom said as she stood up.

Carissa's stunned silence hung over them.

Alexander took the lead role. He wasn't about to let her keep him from something he wanted to do.

He approached her, leaving the rest of the party on the shore.

"I was hoping you'd join us," he said suavely. Perhaps this was the chance he'd been waiting for.

"Why?" she asked.

He raised his eyebrows. "I had hoped to see you after the play, but you disappeared. I want to get to know you better," he said.

Her eyes, so like his mother's, penetrated further than he wanted them to.

"But you did see me after the play," she said.

He did not know how to respond.

"If I told you that if you stay here, it will only cause you pain, would you listen?" she asked.

“Stay with me, and I will listen to every word you say,” he pleaded.

“But you haven’t listened yet,” she argued.

His frustration mounted.

“I have listened, but I know a better way. Come with me, and I will do as you say,” he whispered. “You could keep harm from happening.”

She turned away from him and looked into the face of the stars.

“You cannot have me on your own terms, Alexander,” she said, “but I will ask only once more, please leave this place.”

He chuckled.

“I get everything I want on my own terms,” he said and took her hand.

Judas yelled from the beach, “Is she staying or what? Let’s get this party started.” A murmur of assent rushed through the young people, and Alexander heard their footsteps on the dock. He smelled the alcohol and knew that DeCeit had already started.

Wisdom pulled at her hand, but he dared not let her go. He would show her what a good time she could have if only she’d leave her inhibitions behind. While keeping an iron grip around her wrist, he put his arm around her shoulders and herded her to the group.

“Meet my girl, Wisdom,” he said to them.

Some called their hellos while others were too absorbed in their own conversations to notice. Judas passed a bottle to him.

No one was listening to their conversation now. Alexander put his mouth close to her ear.

"See how many people we could win together? We could sway the whole world," he said. "Just think of the good you might do with an audience like that."

She pulled again at her wrist.

"I do not need an audience because my good is not merely an act," she said between clenched teeth.

"Just leave behind your judgmental attitude and your high-handed ways," he persuaded.

He held the bottle up to her lips.

"Wait," she breathed. "If you do not listen now, you won't hear my voice any more. I will be mute to you. Don't give in, Alexander. Don't give in to yourself!"

He laughed again. "It's not me that I want to give in. It's you," he teased.

Just then, Judas stumbled backward and knocked into them. Alexander momentarily released his hold in order to keep his balance.

Wisdom took the opportunity. She dove into the icy water beneath the dock.

Carissa screamed. The noise of the party sucked into a collective gasp. Wisdom's head appeared as she swam for shore.

She finally stood in hip deep water.

"Flee[191]," she yelled back to them and ran into the woods.

All was silent.

"Weird dame," Judas slurred to Alexander.

Alexander fumed. Wisdom possessed something that he did not. She was the only one in all of his life

---

[191] 2 Tim. 2:22

who could elude his grasp and disapprove of his actions. Right then, he began to hate her for it.

"I will bend her will to my own," he hissed. "You will see."

Judas laughed. "It just isn't going to happen tonight," he said. "Come, forget about her for a while."

Alexander took the offered bottle even though he already held another in his hand. Just as he turned back to the crowd, he heard another splash.

"Carissa!" Judas called. "You're as much a fool as that crazy woman!"

Carissa swam to shore and also disappeared into the trees.

By the time the alcohol was gone, none of them was sober. The cars sat waiting in the parking lot and seemed to be spinning around them. Neither Wisdom nor Carissa was anywhere to be seen.

They helped each other until the cars were still enough to climb into. Alexander's female counterpart from the play, Eve, landed in his lap in the front passenger seat. She giggled. Judas got behind the wheel.

"You sure you can drive?" Eve asked Judas.

"Sure," was all he said.

They raced behind the others, careening through the darkness. Posts, trees, lights all blurred into one dark mass swirling around them like the universe. In their present state, they could neither define it nor did they care to.

Alexander later could only recall the girl's scream of terror and the immense heat as he was ejected from the airborne vehicle and it burst into flame.

Chapter 28

From the moment he awoke to his mother's face in the hospital until graduation day, he lived for one purpose. He would kill Wisdom for abandoning them that night, and he would persuade as many people as he could not to follow her lead. She made the world one pulsing migraine of injustice.

He looked for her everywhere.

He found Carissa weeping at the memorial service held at the school for their nine classmates who had perished in the accident.

"Carissa," he said, and she turned. "Do you know where Wisdom is?"

She blotted at her tears with a tissue. "Even if I did, you would not listen to her," she said.

"Don't you want her to be held responsible for all she has done?" His voice betrayed his anger.

"She is responsible for all she's done. Just look at me. She saved me," Carissa replied calmly.

His disgust wound tightly within him. "If she had stayed like I told her to, none of this would have happened. She never cared about any of them. She just let them die. You saved yourself."

No amount of cajoling could persuade Carissa to betray Wisdom's whereabouts. There were times when he thought he saw her, but she seemed a mirage fading just ahead of his grasp.

The lead thespian group of Opportunity contacted him just after graduation with an invite to pursue acting as a career.

"You would rehearse three days a week, perform on the weekend, have plenty of money in your pocket, and live however you like," the recruiter said over the phone. "In the meantime, you would be interpreting truth and justice to the masses through your acting. Just think what a difference you could make."

It was a deal he couldn't turn down.

A city bus hissed away after dropping him in front of the Megascops Theater. It towered above him, gray against the evening sky. The towering owl statues made the theater the most exquisite building in the city.

He stood staring up at it until someone came out of the revolving door. He didn't want to look like a tourist, so he strode with confidence to the door and entered.

A large wooden desk stood to the left of the entry. Black carpet with specks of gold in it adorned the floors. The centerpiece of the entry was a large mahogany owl statue stretching from floor to ceiling.

"Welcome to the Megascops," said a clerk behind the desk. "May I direct you to one of our seventy auditoriums?"

Alexander removed a business card from his suit pocket and adjusted his yellow tie.

"I'm looking for the Thalia and Melpomene Troop," he said, handing the card to the clerk.

"They always meet in the Mousai Auditorium," the clerk said, returning the card. "Would you like me to show you the way?"

Alexander followed him through winding stairs, halls adorned with modern art, and onto a large elevator.

"The Mousai Auditorium is our largest," the clerk explained. "Will you be joining Thalia and Melpomene?"

"Yes," Alexander answered simply.

They didn't pass anyone in the halls, and the auditorium was empty when they arrived- Alexander had wanted to arrive early- and he sat in one of the balconies to view the stage.

After ten minutes, someone turned the lights on, and Alexander saw that he wasn't alone.

A woman wearing a gaudy hat stood from her seat in the front row and ran her hand slowly along the edge of the stage. Her form and figure drew him and played with his memory. Silently, he crept down the stairs and along the aisle. He was but ten steps from her when she turned to him.

They stared at one another.

"How did you come to be here?" he hissed through clenched teeth.

Her eyes widened. "Do you greet everyone in the same amiable way?" she laughed, dismissing his hate.

"I have been searching for you for three years," he said, coming closer.

She removed her hat and faced him unflinchingly. Alexander took note of the low neckline and pearl earrings. Both adornments were new to Wisdom's appearance.

"You look older," he said. "Beautiful, as always, but I'm sure you're still in the business of ruining people's lives."

She put her gloved hand on his shoulder and threw her head back in a long, loud laugh. Not at all like Wisdom's laugh.

"I can see you have met my twin," the woman said.

"Twin?" Alexander's thoughts rushed behind his eyes.

"Wisdom ruins lives, but I liven ruins[192]," she said. A dimple near the corner of her mouth drew him. "I guess you could say I am her antithesis."

"Are you a part of Thalia and Melpomene?" he asked.

"For now," she sighed and sat back in her seat on the front row, motioning for him to sit beside her, "until I can find better ways to entertain the minds of men."

He raised his eyebrows as he sat beside her.

"I'm pleased to make your acquaintance," he said, holding out his hand.

She took it. "So is everyone else who does," she said, "but you are quick to accept me as a friend."

"Anyone so desperately opposed to Wisdom is a friend of mine," he said. "I want to see the world rid of her idiotic ethics. Her prudishness cost me a lot of friends, and I am plagued daily by the poor wretches who fall prey to her deception."

"It is true that the most alluring call to action is the call to be one's own master," Folly said. "Wisdom's call to action is to forsake self. It is frustrating. I can see why you harbor such just resentment."

"Maybe this acting gig will give me the platform I need to warn others not to follow her. Maybe people will look to me to be their freedom fighter," he said.

"You are exactly right," she said, "and I can't wait to see all you accomplish."

---

192 Prov. 14:1; Prov. 15:21

They sat staring at the stage together. Years would come when they would entrance audiences and spellbind them together. They would make quite a pair for the town to buzz about. For now though, they sat staring at the edge of what might be.

"Do you know why they decorate this place with owls?" she asked, looking at the large circle on the curtain that bore an owl emblem.

"Megascops- it means screech owl," he explained. He'd done his homework.

She chuckled. "Well, what do owls have to do with acting?"

He smiled. "Nothing," he replied, "it's just an attractive theme. But then, if you really dove into their artistic plot, perhaps it would have something to do with how screech owls shy from the light."

"Do they?" she was entranced.

"Indeed," he said, "they hunt nocturnally, and if you were to shine a light at them, they veer away just on the edge of it. Perhaps that is what we do when we act: dance on the edge of the truth."

They sat in silence until they could hear other footsteps approaching. The rehearsal time had come.

"Well, I like you- right down to your yellow tie," she said. "What is your name?"

He smiled at her. "Alexander Specter."

"Mmmmm," she rolled the name over her tongue, "Alexander Specter. I think we could have quite a future together."

He nodded. "And may I ask your name?"

She leaned over and kissed his cheek. He couldn't name the smell that was disguised by the mint on her breath when she said, "Folly."

Chapter 29

Hyperon's knife sliced through more vegetables than he cared to count. The wound on his finger healed quickly, and the *Banquet Bakery* stayed busy. He was careful to keep his knife sharp for its work.

The night before, he had held the compass and relived the scene with Wisdom as she told him about his tasks. The paths had looked so similar, but she'd assured him that he would know which one to choose[193]. He wondered if she meant for him to travel away from Opportunity or if it was a different sort of journey she'd set him on. It was true that there wasn't much chance to hate evil when he was stuck slicing vegetables all day.

"I see that half-smile," Paddy said as she carried in a tray of empty dishes. "Slicing up those veggies suits you."

He chose not to respond, and she laughed as she went out the door.

Later, she locked the door of the bakery and came to the kitchen to wash all the evening dishes, as she did every night.

"Why don't you take some of this soup up to your rooms for your supper?" she suggested. "You didn't get a moment to eat all day."

Hyperon knew that she hadn't either.

"After I get these washed up, I'm going out for a while," she said.

Hyperon's curiosity had been awakened on these occasions when Paddy hurried off to some unknown, late-night destination. He wondered if she had family

---

193 Prov. 3:5-6

that she visited or something of that nature, but he'd never asked her. She let him have his space without questioning his motives or his actions, so he did the same for her.

The dishes clinked and splashed. Paddy hummed. He finished the potatoes for the next day.

"Wisdom gave me tasks," he said.

The humming stopped, but she gave him no other indication that she'd heard. Now that the words were out, he kept speaking. His eyes rested on the knife as he cleaned it and put it away for the next day.

"I don't know how to do what she asked while I'm working here," he confessed. "I don't want to leave, but I must if that's what it takes. I mean to finish what she gave me to do. Also, there is a little girl she told me to visit, and I'll need time to look for her."

Paddy's arms sloshed in suds up to her elbows. She never slowed her pace on the dishes.

"You feel able to do what she's asked?" Paddy asked.

Hyperon hesitated. Wisdom's words flowed back to him.

"No," he answered, "but she said that her Father would give me the ability."

Paddy wiped her hands and arms on her apron and turned to him. She rested her ebony hands on the counter behind her.

"I think He will too," she said thoughtfully, "and why would you need to visit a little girl?"

"There's a little girl that I tormented before," he hesitated, "before I met Wisdom. One of the times, I saw that she had a green book that was so similar to a book my mother had. Wisdom said I would need to find the girl and ask to read the book so that I would understand my tasks better. I don't know. This probably sounds crazy to you."

She shrugged. "It would only be crazy if you didn't do what Wisdom said," she replied.

Hyperon looked at her. "So what should I do?"

Paddy laughed her long, musical laugh. Hyperon smiled, though he felt that the joke was on him.

"Why do you ask me?" she wanted to know. "I don't even know what your tasks are."

"Because I trust you," he said. It was the first time he'd ever said that aloud to anyone, and it felt awkward. He hurried on.

"Well, for the first one, I must choose the right path. It had something to do with hating evil and choosing good," he said, wrinkling his brow, "but the only evil in this kitchen is in my own heart when I get here in the morning."

Her laugh softened into a solemn gaze. "I would say that you're well on your way," she said.

She began stacking the dishes, and Hyperon was disappointed that she wouldn't say any more about his tasks. He began to package up the soup to take upstairs.

"Tomorrow, I will cut the vegetables," she said as he started to walk out. "You will serve the patrons."

He looked at her. The smile she wore led him to believe that she knew something he did not.

"Your mother told you that good cooks never lick their fingers," she wagged her fingers in front of him. "My mother always told me to stay out of the food service industry." Her laugh floated back to him as she removed her apron and gathered her things by the door.

"It may be just the place for you to learn the path of righteousness," she said.

He smiled as the door slammed behind her and wondered again where she was headed.

Chapter 30

Prudence sat between her mother and father on a makeshift bench in the underground stone room. Marv spoke in whispers to Saul, who was smiling despite his black eye. Prudence waved at Paddy and Lovely when they came in. One candle reflected off their faces from the center of their circle, and Prudence thought it grew a little brighter as each person entered the room.

When most of them were seated, Paddy started humming deep in her throat. Other voices blended in, and then they began to sing the words of the Lady's song. Prudence loved how their voices sounded so different yet united in harmony. On the last verse, they heard more footsteps coming down the damp corridor. Prudence felt her father look at her mother over her head.

An uncertain woman with brown hair ducked into the room. A little girl clutched tightly to her skirt on one side, and a boy stood uncertainly on the other. Prudence immediately recognized Sparrow and Bene.

"Come in, honey, and welcome," said Paddy, in her rich voice.

Prudence jumped up and ran to Sparrow. "Come. You can sit by me, if you want to," she said. Sparrow smiled, but her mother was still frowning.

"We don't really know what to expect," the mother said aloud to the group, not daring to meet any of their eyes.

"Then you won't be disappointed," Paddy said with a laugh.

Sparrow tugged at her mother's hand. Marv and Obedience shifted so that the woman and her children could sit next to Prudence. Prudence was so happy that her friends had come.

"I'm Obedience," Prudence's mother whispered over her head.

"I'm Rocky," the woman replied, "and I guess your daughter is friends with my kids at school."

Obedience smiled at Prudence. "We are so glad you've come," she said to Rocky.

Paddy began her deep throated hum again, and their united voices vibrated into the stone walls. Prudence wished that the Lady and the Shadow Children could be there too.

One of the men, named Pastor, spoke about Wisdom, and Prudence loved the stories he told about the Lady.

"I wish I could meet her," Sparrow whispered.

Prudence nodded encouragingly. "Oh, you will!"

They left in small groups of two or three so that they wouldn't attract attention emerging from the manhole cover in the middle of the night. Rocky and her children had been the first to leave, but Prudence hugged Sparrow as they made plans to meet at school the next day.

Paddy crossed the room to where Obedience waited with Prudence.

"Prudence, honey," Paddy said.

Prudence smiled at her.

"Do you remember a tall man with dark, curly hair who used to work for the enemy?" Paddy asked.

Prudence frowned. She did remember the man.

"Yes," she said.

Paddy's eyes softened. "I believe he has changed sides," Paddy explained, "and he is working in my bakery."

Prudence wanted to scrunch up her nose and tell Paddy that a man that bad couldn't change overnight, but she knew those were just her feelings and not the truth.

"Did he see you sometime when you had your green book?" Paddy probed.

Prudence felt Obedience's protective arm around her shoulder.

"Yes," she said, "when he came to the school one day."

Paddy nodded. "I think Lady Wisdom has told him to look for you again, and she wants you to read the book to him," she said.

Prudence looked down at the green book clutched tightly to her chest.

"Did he hurt you, Prudence?" Obedience asked.

Prudence shook her head.

"I thought that he would, but he didn't," Prudence said and told her mother the story of the school yard and the day Saul had been beaten.

"Would Wisdom really ask this of her, Paddy?" Obedience asked.

Paddy chewed her lower lip. "Sometimes the work we must do is not the work we would choose, but only Wisdom knows what the outcome of it will be[194]," Paddy said seriously.

---

194 Eph. 2:10

Obedience's eyes filled with tears. Prudence slipped her slender arm behind her mother and gave her a squeeze.

"Why don't you come to the bakery in the morning before school? His name is Hyperon, and he will be working at the counter. I will be right there, and I will help you," Paddy suggested.

Prudence nodded. "I will," she decided.

Prudence smiled and thought immediately of the Shadow Children and Haste. She would take some of her allowance and buy muffins for them. Perhaps her kindness could help them all[195].

"That's a brave girl," Paddy said, hugging her. She put her hand on Obedience's shoulder. "And a brave mama."

Prudence was glad that Paddy would be there but felt butterflies in her stomach at the thought of meeting her enemy.

---

195 Gal. 5:22-23

Chapter 31

The bell above the door tinkled immediately after Hyperon turned the lock the next morning. An elderly man in a green cap followed him up to the counter. Hyperon began writing the day's menu offerings on a large board. The man cleared his throat.

"Got any muffins?" he asked.

Hyperon smiled, "Plenty. What kind would you like?"

"Swamp," the old man said. Hyperon turned and saw Paddy's special spinach and applesauce muffins in the bin behind him. Their green color made them easy to spot, though perhaps not as appealing as some others.

Hyperon got the man's muffin, took the change offered as payment, and returned to writing as the man shuffled to a seat. Five more patrons entered, were served, and left again in the next ten minutes. The old man still perched on his chair.

"Paddy always talks to me," he said when there was a lull in the foot traffic.

Hyperon wondered what she found to talk about and where she found the time in between all the other things she did.

"I'm Hyperon," he introduced himself.

"Sounds foreign," the old man said.

Hyperon waited for the old man to state his name, but he didn't.

"I've been in Opportunity a while," he said. "My mother was from here."

"Well, why'd she leave? Too good for the likes of us? Obviously had a taste for those of other blood," the man remarked.

Hyperon's half-blood boiled, and he wished he could slice vegetables instead of converse with this crank. He remembered Wisdom then and wondered how she would treat this old man.

"What brings you out so early?" he tried a different tactic.

"Don't you know old people never sleep?" the man demanded.

The bell above the door sounded, and a school girl came in. Her familiar brown braids swayed in time with her plaid skirt. Hyperon felt panic rising as he studied the white scar on her forehead. He desperately remembered how he had chased her down and harassed her. He hated himself. He wondered if she would recognize him and considered ducking under the counter. She smiled at him through the mist of freckles on her nose.

"Hi," she said. "Where's Paddy?"

"She's letting me try working the counter," he replied.

Paddy's voice drifted out from the back, "Good morning!" The girl smiled and called back a greeting.

"And a sorry mess he's making of it," said the old man.

The girl turned to him. "Well, he's got you your swamp muffin, Mr. Cameron. He can't be all bad," she said and smiled.

The old man harrumphed.

The girl laughed. "I'll take four blueberry muffins today," she said, "and I think you'll do a fine job of choosing them."

Hyperon stared at her. He couldn't tell if she recognized him or not. She smiled encouragingly to snap him out of his thoughts, and he turned to get what she asked for. He found the blueberry bin, selected four with the tongs, and handed her the bag.

She reached in her pocket and pulled out just enough to pay. Her wistful glance at the coins made him wonder how she'd come by them.

"I'd best hurry to school so I can get there before Haste," she said. "I want him to have time to eat his muffins before class begins."

"Why would you buy them for him?" Hyperon asked before he could stop himself.

Her cheeks flushed pink. "Well, you saw the things he does. Someone needs to show him what kindness is, and it isn't going to be you or that other guy."

Hyperon didn't have time to reply before she was out the door.

"Always saves up her pennies to buy muffins for the meanest kid in the school," the old man grumbled. "Two when he's been extra nasty, according to Paddy."

"What's her name?" Hyperon asked, watching through the window as she skipped down the sidewalk.

"Prudence," the man said.

Hyperon reflected that he could learn a thing or two from Prudence as he watched her skip toward the school. He regretted that he had not waved to her that day. He regretted that he had not apologized to her today. He slapped his hand to his forehead. He hadn't even asked her about the book. He felt like a fool.

He hit the door to the kitchen.

"Paddy," he said in a mumbled hurry, "she was here, and I didn't even ask her about the book!"

Paddy smiled, and her hands never slowed. "She'll be back," Paddy said.

Shortly past noon, another familiar form came through the door. Hyperon knew before their eyes met who it was, and he was afraid of what her reaction might be.

There were several people ahead of her in the line. Hyperon worked through their orders. When it was her turn, she looked up from digging through her purse and gasped.

"I don't mean to frighten you," Hyperon said apologetically. "Please, I'm working for Paddy now."

Rocky's eyes filled with tears. His mind filled with scenes from the night he had helped to ransack her home and terrorize her children. He knew now that her harsh words had arisen from her fear and not from Wisdom. He wished he could go back in time.

She didn't place an order, just walked straight through to the kitchen. Hyperon hoped that Paddy could persuade her of the change in him. Other patrons had taken notice of their interchange and stared.

Hyperon proceeded to the next in line. Rocky never emerged from the kitchen. Hyperon wondered if she would tell Paddy about who he used to be. His deep regret for his past weighed him down all afternoon[196]. The crotchety old man had departed sometime before the lunch rush began, but at suppertime, he returned.

---

[196] Phil. 3:13-14

As Hyperon carried the potato soup and stewed greens to the man's table, the compass rubbed his leg from within his pocket. He'd almost forgotten about it today. He'd been so busy. He'd put it there just in case the time came for choosing a path. She'd said the compass would help.

"Good to see you back so soon," Hyperon said to the man, setting down his meal in front of him.

"Nowhere else was open," the man said.

The evening sped by, and Hyperon wondered if this was the last night he'd work at the *Banquet Bakery.*

He locked the door and retired to the kitchen to wash the dishes. To his amazement, Paddy had finished the cutting, washed the dishes, and put all in its place. She stood leaning against the counter with her arms crossed. Her smile barely stayed hidden behind her pursed lips.

"Well, I think we both had an education in evil today," she said.

"If you want me to pack my things and go, I will," he told her. He felt like a little boy being scolded- not so much because of her demeanor towards him as the sense of shame he felt at having her think less of him because she now knew some of his past.

"Cameron didn't complain loudly enough for me to fire you," she laughed.

"What happened to Rocky?" he asked.

"Poor soul," Paddy replied, shaking her head. "I let her out the back door. You gave her a terrible fright."

"I thought I was doing well, but seeing her only confirmed that I can never get away from what I was," he said.

"Hyperon," she said, putting a hand on his shoulder, "you already are far away from what you were. Now, straighten up. I have a mission for you tonight."

He looked at her curiously. "A mission?" he questioned.

"You once walked in darkness[197] that destroyed trust," Paddy said, "but tonight, you go to Rocky's house to see if you can build that trust up again."

He shook his head. "She won't let me in the door," he argued.

"Then you better think of a way to earn her trust outside," Paddy said, glancing out the window. "Good thing it's a clear night. Wouldn't want you out in the rain."

Hyperon laughed. "There's no arguing with you, Paddy."

He hurried upstairs to change clothes, but he kept the compass with him. By the time he left, it was late. He racked his brain for ways to apologize and make up for the things he'd done. He remembered the way better than he expected. It didn't take him long to cross town. There sat the home of Rocky Loam just as he remembered it.

Hyperon couldn't bring himself to knock on the door. It brought back too many memories for him. He was sure it would for her as well. All the same, he walked up the walkway. He tripped on something in the darkness and fell. His elbows hit hard, but he congratulated himself on not injuring his head.

As he turned back to see what he had fallen over, he found a hedge clipper. The duplexes would need

---

[197] Is. 9:2

much more than landscaping to make them attractive, but he admired the effort. He thought about Rocky's son-the little boy that had huddled near his battered mother. Perhaps the boy had tried to keep the yard looking nice.

Even in the darkness, Hyperon could see that the vegetation grew wild, making cracks in the sidewalk and covering the windows. He held the clipper in his hand. The long day wore on him, but here, he had found what he could do. Hyperon got to work, and his fatigue faded.

Chapter 32

Adam watched the bakery for days before he saw Hyperon. He managed to be busy enough at it that Specter quit breathing down his neck. Adam positioned himself on the fire escape of the adjoining building just in time to see Hyperon venture outside to dump a bowl full of something- maybe grease- out behind the building in the alley. Watching the building had only served to increase Adam's dislike of his former friend. What did the sorry sap do all the time? It seemed that all he did was work to turn a profit by taking the hard won cash of those who had been victims of injustice. Adam despised him.

Adam grabbed the opportunity to follow Hyperon the night he left. It'd been the first time he managed to be there when Hyperon ventured out, and Adam wasn't alone. Mr. Specter had allowed Horbah and a new guy to tag along. Adam motioned for them to follow at a distance.

As the streets curved away behind them, Adam realized where Hyperon was heading. Not only was he going to exact revenge for his wasted time on that louse, but he might get the opportunity to persuade Rocky to see sense and sign up for the assistance program. Mr. Specter would be so pleased.

Hyperon fell just as he approached the door. Adam snickered into his collar. His accomplices went across the street to wait in the shadows of the front porch of the duplex directly across. Adam slid up beside a tree near the road.

Hyperon got up with an object in his hand. It took Adam several minutes to realize that he had set to work trimming the hedges.

"He's lost his mind," he muttered under his breath.

Hyperon worked without interruption[198]. Adam waited for him to go to the door so that he could brag to Rocky about all the work he'd done. Hyperon never went to the door. One hour passed, and then two. The thugs across the street had most likely fallen asleep. Surely, when he was finished, Hyperon would go to the door to draw her attention to the seeming kindness he had done. He must remember that it was barely a drop in the bucket compared with the amount of money she would have had from the assistance program. Rocky could have hired a whole army of landscapers then.

Finally, Hyperon finished his task and strode up to the front door. He set the clippers on a windowsill, and then he simply walked away. He passed just inches from Adam as he made his way back onto the street.

Adam trailed him, motioning to the other two to stay close behind.

Suddenly Hyperon stopped and turned. Adam wheeled and began walking the opposite direction. The others followed suit. Hyperon lost interest and continued on his way. Adam turned as soon as he could and trotted to catch up. More cars were out now as dawn loomed near. Sounds crowded out the night.

---

[198] Prov. 11:27

Hyperon began to take alleyways and side streets strange to Adam. He must have realized that he was being followed.

Adam motioned for the other men to catch up, and they ran up behind Hyperon just as he entered an alley near the Megascops.

Adam grabbed a plank from an abandoned pallet. Hyperon hurried ahead without turning. Just as Adam raised the plank to hit him, Hyperon turned and flung something at him. It hit him square between the eyes, and he stumbled backward. Horbah ran ahead to catch their prey. The other stopped to help Adam up.

"What happened?" the man was asking.

"He hit me with something!" Adam put his hand to his forehead and felt blood. "Felt like a rock! Catch him!"

They ran to catch up. Just ahead, they saw Hyperon run across a busy road. A bus passed between them, and he was gone.

"I lost him," said Horbah.

"I know where he lives," Adam growled.

Hyperon hung his head as he sat on the edge of his bed. He'd lost the compass. It was all he'd had to protect himself with. Perhaps he should have just fought whoever it was with his fists. A beating would have been better than this sense of failure. His muscles ached and fatigue pinched the corners of his eyes. It would only be two hours before Paddy would be tinkering about in the kitchen below.

He couldn't sleep anyway. He'd failed the first task before it even began. How would he find his way on the right path after he'd lost the only thing directing his steps? Had he lost Lady Wisdom because of this blunder[199]? He didn't know who had pursued him. He wondered if it was Specter's men. Perhaps they kept a watch on Rocky's house now. It had been as dark as the space behind one's eyes just after the light goes out. In any case, he'd lost them before he reached the bakery. They wouldn't know where to find him.

When Paddy came in, he'd been slicing vegetables for forty-five minutes. The grocery boy brought in several boxes of supplies for the day. Paddy focused on him before coming to stand beside Hyperon.

"Something is wrong," she said.

He didn't know whether to feel anger or sorrow.

"It's me," he said.

"I know something's wrong with you. That's why I said it," she replied.

"No," he replied quietly. "I *am* what's wrong. I failed."

"Could you not find Rocky's place?" Paddy asked.

He couldn't speak about it anymore.

Paddy went to get her apron. The bell above the door announced Cameron's presence before his throat clearing did.

"Well, he's waiting for you," Paddy said.

Hyperon looked up from his cutting.

"I can't," he said.

---

[199] Heb. 13:5-6

"Then perhaps you'll have to look elsewhere for the ability because you have to[200]," Paddy took the knife from him and raised her eyebrows.

Hyperon contemplated quitting. Paddy's bouncy black curls were tinged with gray. Who would help her here if he did?

"I'm sorry I took so long," he said as he went to the counter. "Will it be one swamp muffin or two?"

Cameron ordered all of the same things at all of the same times and had all of the same complaints. Anytime Hyperon was tempted to snap at the old man, he remembered his own failures and held his tongue.

The bell tinkled, and Prudence strode right up to the counter.

She smiled slightly and stood on tiptoe to lean across it.

"You forgot to ask me if you could borrow the green book," she said quietly.

He swallowed hard. Perhaps it was his fatigue that made him feel the lump of tears in his throat.

"You shouldn't be willing to lend me anything," he said.

She smiled. "The Lady helps me to will and to work for her good pleasure[201]," she said, and she slid the green book across the counter to him.

He took it carefully, as if it were a living thing.

"Thank you," was all he could say.

"I will be happy to talk to you about it after you read it," she said.

---

200 Ex. 31:3; Rom. 7:18-25

201 Eph. 2:10

He nodded.

She turned and left without buying anything. He tucked the treasured volume in his apron pocket. It was only then that he wondered how she had known that he was supposed to ask about the book.

The only noticeable difference in the rest of the day was that Rocky didn't show up. Hyperon hoped the improved appearance of her yard had brightened her day. He couldn't quite tell in the dark, but he hoped he had improved it.

Supper customers had gradually filtered out, so Hyperon was surprised when the door opened. He functioned in somewhat of a trance due to his lack of sleep. He wished the customer would go away so that he could close on time and get to bed.

When he turned, he saw Adam. A small red cut ran across the very top of the bridge of his nose. There was no trace of his former genial smile. He sat in a booth and scowled over his menu at Hyperon.

Hyperon took the seat across from him.

"Nice to see you too. Did you come to eat or seethe?" Hyperon asked.

"What could possibly attract you to a place like this?" Adam snarled. "I think Wisdom has addled your brain."

Hyperon's solemnity returned at the mention of his lady.

"I wondered what happened to you after you went with her," Adam said. "I've been looking for you everywhere."

"Why?" Hyperon asked.

"I thought maybe you were in trouble. Maybe they were exploiting you or taking advantage of you because of your history… and you made parties more fun," Adam said.

The bell jingled as someone went out.

"Thank you," the lady called over her shoulder. Hyperon half waved.

"You're lying, and I'm not going back," Hyperon said. "It's not what we thought."

Adam rolled his eyes. "Now you're spouting nonsense," he said angrily. "Didn't I warn you about Wisdom?"

"What do you really know about her, Adam? Only what Mr. Specter tells you," Hyperon argued.

"Mr. Specter knows far more than she ever will," Adam said, "and besides, he takes care of his employees. Better than you can say. You're stuck here with some old, fat woman who works you like a slave. You'll regret it, Hyperon. Mr. Specter provided for you before, but you'd better watch your back now."

Hyperon leaned across the table.

"What do you mean?" he asked.

"You know how he'll persuade you to come back," Adam said.

Hyperon sat silent.

"And you would still be willing to carry out his 'persuasion'?" Hyperon asked.

"In a heartbeat," Adam replied. Hyperon didn't miss the shift of his eyes. "It's the least I can do in return for all the trips and the pleasures he's given me. You'd do better to remember the pleasures you had, too. Think of Folly and her song at the Megascops."

"I think you should go," Hyperon struggled to keep his temper in check, "because I am still unpersuadable."

"One more thing," Adam said, laying down the menu, "stay away from Rocky."

Hyperon narrowed his eyes. Again, the red cut on Adam's face came into focus.

"Was it *you?"* he asked.

"Next time, you'll be the worse for wear," Adam swore under his breath. Hyperon watched him storm out. Paddy emerged from the back, crossed the room, and locked the door.

"A friend of yours?" she asked.

"Not anymore," he said.

"You should take a page from Prudence's book then and get him a muffin next time," she said.

Hyperon looked at her standing there, soapy hands on wide hips, and felt the girl's book in his apron pocket.

"He'd as soon kill you as look at you, Paddy," Hyperon said. "You shouldn't let him in here if I'm away."

"There's worse things than killing a body[202]," Paddy pulled her left sleeve down to reveal her shoulder and turned around. Hyperon could see hideous scars across her shoulder. It made him think of his father. He had scars too, but he winced to see it on the shoulders of his friend.

---

[202] Mt. 10:28-36

"What happened?" he asked. He started to ask her who would do such a thing, but he knew that he had once done such things. Adam still did such things.

"They can kill a body, but they can't tame a soul, and that's that," she said. "I always have to think that someday, he might be persuaded too."

Hyperon hung his head. "Maybe we should give Prudence the job. She's got pluck! But, it's no use. He's unpersuadable."

"Weren't we all[203]?" she asked.

He followed her back to the kitchen to wash dishes. Again, the work was completed.

"I think you need rest," she said, "and we can talk tomorrow about your next mission."

Hyperon was too tired to argue.

Hyperon ascended the stairs to his apartment, contemplating the next thing he could do for Rocky. He still hadn't seen or heard from her. It wasn't that he really expected to. If she had noticed the work he'd done in her yard, she wouldn't have known it was him.

He shut the door and sat down at the desk where his treasure lay. He set the green book among them, vowing to read it as soon as he could. He'd lost the compass and failed Wisdom's first task, but he looked at the sword hilt and vowed not to miss the second.

---

[203] Rom. 5:10

Chapter 33

Several nights later, loud steps banged up the stairway. Knocking followed.

"Hyperon," Paddy called. He hoped nothing was wrong.

He pulled open the door.

"Do you have plans tonight?" she asked.

He raised his eyebrows.

"Why don't you come with me on my weekly outing? We can consider it your second mission."

He shrugged. "Sure," he said. She turned to walk back down the stairs. He glanced over to the desk at the sword hilt. He threw it in a shoulder bag and hurried after her.

She put her finger to her lips before opening the door.

"You mustn't tell anyone about where I take you, who you see, or what we do there," Paddy patted his cheek. "I know you can be trusted[204]."

He shook his head.

"Sometimes I question your judgment," he said.

"Now, in case we're watched, I will go first. You come five minutes behind. Follow me to the bus stop. You know, the one near Prudence's school," she explained.

He didn't have time to agree before she had slipped out the door, but he knew just the bus stop she meant. He shamefully remembered the last time he had been there.

---

[204] Acts 9:26-27

He followed her instructions and arrived at the bus stop. The bench was empty. He hoped no harm had come to Paddy. His curiosity was aroused. Mr. Specter would love to know what he was about to find out. What could Paddy possibly do out so late every week? He turned and gazed up the road behind him. It seemed as if he was alone. He sat down on the bench to wait.

Several cars passed and then the night watchman. Still, there was no Paddy.

Suddenly, the manhole cover in front of him lifted several inches. He jumped up.

"Shhh," came a hiss. It opened slightly wider, and there were Paddy's chocolate eyes laughing at him. He looked both ways, lifted the cover and climbed down the ladder after carefully replacing it.

"This is bizarre," he said.

Paddy hummed. She carried a light, and he followed her down a short passageway and into a room. Dark, damp bricks lined the walls. Boxes, packing crates, and pallets were the only furniture.

Twenty faces gathered around a small lamp. He recognized some of them. It was like a gathering of everyone Specter hated.

"You do have a knack for finding the worst misfits, Paideia," one man said. Hyperon turned and recognized him as one whom he and Adam had persuaded to stay in Specter's employ. He thought he remembered that his name was Saul. Rocky, also, was there with her two children. They clung to her now, cowering in his presence. Prudence was the only face that offered a smile.

"Please," he said as he stood before them, "I have been changed by Lady Wisdom[205], as you all have." His words surprised even himself.

"How do you know that about us?" asked another woman.

"Seeing you almost brings her here," he said, inhaling. His exhale was more of a sigh. "I can see her light in your eyes."

"How do we know it isn't a trick?" the first man demanded.

"You don't," Paddy said, coming to stand beside Hyperon. "He is a risk, as were you, Saul. The time has come, though, for Hyperon to learn that there's more to being on the right path than staying off of the wrong one."

Hyperon looked at her. He didn't understand.

She looked in the eyes of everyone present, then back at him.

"To be on the right path, you must do what is right. To use a compass correctly, you must follow[206] its direction at every step, every twist and turn. You can't just look at it once and forget about it," she said.

Suddenly, the memory of his midnight work in Rocky's yard came behind his eyes. He glanced toward her. Yes. If he kept walking the right way, doing what was right, then each step must take him closer to his final destination. Life with Lady Wisdom would be won one step at a time, not in a momentary decision. But, he had lost the compass.

---

[205] Ps. 22:19-24

[206] Mt. 4:19-20

He took a seat next to Prudence on a crate. The little girl smiled at him. Paddy sat also. Her humming returned and grew louder. Suddenly, Prudence started to sing. Their voices all blended, and the song pulsed through the sewer, though it should have been free to fly to the heavens. Hyperon wished he knew the words, and then he realized that he did.

It was Wisdom's song about her Father.

Every note was like the notes he heard when he looked through Wisdom's spyglass. Each one was complete and finished, not lacking anything. Though, when it ended, he felt that he himself was the one who lacked. When they finished singing, Prudence stood up and walked near to the lamp.

"Wisdom helped me overcome fear and anger this week," she said, "at school. She helped me see beyond the hate of my classmates to their needs. I still have a long way to go, but I think I helped them see Wisdom's kindness." Prudence looked right at Hyperon.

"She is our compass," the little girl said.

Hyperon fought the emotion rising in his chest. It wouldn't do to bawl like a baby in front of these people. Had he lost his mind? When he looked into Prudence's clear, shining eyes and heard her exultant testimony, he knew for sure that Wisdom lived and moved and had her being in and among these people[207].

A man named Pastor stood as Prudence sat down.

"Instead of working late last Tuesday, I went home and listened to my wife as she made supper. I

---

[207] Acts 17:28

haven't really listened in too long, but Wisdom helped me to see that it was needed," he said.

Rocky stood and took his place. "It's been two months since the kids and I have refused to be entertained by Specter's DVDs. Instead, we've decided to work together to repaint the inside of our home. Also, someone took the time to touch up our landscaping. We were thankful."

When she sat down, Hyperon noticed the little boy pat his mother on the back. He seemed proud that she'd spoken.

Paddy stood. "Hyperon was nice to Cameron two days in a row, with no sleep!" Those in the room turned and smiled at him. He felt suddenly shy and conscious.

"Everything I am now I owe to Wisdom, and to you, Paddy, for being willing to take me in," he said from his seat.

"You see," Paddy said, "walking the right way is more than just not going the wrong way."

Hyperon smiled. The whole meeting made him uncomfortable. It had an otherworldly feel. However, it had to do with his Lady. Wasn't it that other world that he longed to get back to? And yet, how sharply this sewer contrasted to the world where he had walked, and dined, and dreamed with Wisdom.

Pastor stood. "Specter is still hard at work, though. Let's remember to help each other this week when his employees come to call, and let us remember to repay them with kindness[208]," Pastor eyed Hyperon.

---

[208] Lk. 6:27-31

Hyperon's gaze swept the room. They'd all felt the effect of Specter's hatred. Even Paddy's scars were somehow connected with him. He thought about Adam, about being unpersuadable. Wisdom made a big difference. How could he make Adam hear her?

Just then, the lamp went out[209].

---

209 Mt. 4:16

Chapter 34

Adam nursed his wounds on his way to Mr. Specter's office. If it were up to him, he'd forget about the fool entirely. Specter had plenty of others. Maybe he'd just suggest that.

Mr. Specter must have been expecting him. The secretary ushered him back to the office immediately.

His yellow tie gleaming, Specter smiled at Adam when he entered.

"Adam," he said, "please have a seat." He walked over and closed the door as Adam took the indicated chair.

"You look a little worse for wear," Specter said. "Perhaps I can spare a few comforts for you this evening. I'll send them to your apartment directly." He made a phone call, ordering pizza, people, and beer. Adam congratulated himself on his good fortune.

"Now," Specter sat in his desk chair and spun to face him, "what can you tell me about Hyperon?"

"He's working at the Banquet Bakery," Adam related. Specter grew serious, then pale.

"Paideia," he muttered. "I know her."

Adam kept speaking without taking much notice. "I followed him one night and saw him work in Rocky Loam's yard for hours without pay or thanks. He works like a slave at the bakery. When I spoke with him…"

"You spoke with him?" Specter interrupted.

Adam shrugged. "Why not?"

"He is dangerous, I tell you," Specter said, with concern edging his voice. "Don't let his words into your ears, my boy, or you'll end up a sorrier mess than he."

Adam nodded.

"What did you tell him about your assignment?" Specter asked.

"Nothing," Adam said. "I just told him if he didn't get back to the way things were, you'd have to persuade him."

Specter chuckled. "And what did he say to that?"

Adam looked into Specter's eyes. "That he was unpersuadable."

Again, the mirth drained from his face. Anger replaced it. Specter brought his fist down on the desk. An uncomfortable silence followed.

Adam shifted in his chair and cleared his throat.

"So, perhaps we can look for new recruits," Adam suggested. "That is how I found Hyperon, after all."

Specter reached for a red stress ball and kneaded it within his fist. He stood up and paced to a large calendar on the wall.

"All investments require a certain amount of risk," Specter muttered, almost to himself.

Then, turning to Adam, he said, "Go home and enjoy yourself for tonight. When you come back tomorrow, I'll have a new assignment for you."

Back out on the street, Adam heaved a sigh of relief and congratulated himself on having dumped Hyperon for something easier. He emptied his mind of all his cares and dwelt on the pleasures that lay before him.

Specter pushed the call button on his desk.

When his secretary answered, he said, "Call DeCeit[210] and tell him to get here as quickly as he can."

When the secretary announced DeCeit's arrival through the intercom an hour later, Specter hurried out to the waiting area. There was no one there but some young punk with blue hair and nose piercings.

He started to turn and ask the secretary where his guest had gone when the punk stood up.

"You called, Specter?" he said in an adolescent voice that matched his appearance.

Specter laughed. "I didn't recognize you," he said, clapping him on the back. "Why, you're older than I am, and here you have me convinced that you're still wet behind the ears."

DeCeit simply smiled and led the way to Specter's office.

"Where'd you find blue hair dye?" Specter was saying as he shut the door.

DeCeit shrugged, plopped in a chair, and propped his high tops on Specter's desk.

"I don't even remember what color it is naturally," he said with nonchalance.

Specter sat in his desk chair and spun to face his co-worker.

"I have a job I need some help with," he said.

DeCeit licked his lips and smiled. "Working together is a beautiful thing," he said.

"You see," Specter hesitated, "I've lost one to Wisdom."

---

[210] Prov. 12:20

DeCeit was already shaking his head. “You know I can’t get them back from her,” he said. “Remember what happened before?”

Specter nodded solemnly. A vision of DeCeit crawling on the floor like a worm at the feet of Wisdom filled his mind’s eye.

“But I’m not asking you to get him back,” Specter explained. “I have an agent who will. He just needs a little help.”

The smile appeared again on DeCeit’s face. “I see,” he said.

Specter drummed his fingers on the desk, somewhat nervously. “Also, I need you to make sure that my agent isn’t taken in by any of their filth,” he said.

“It’ll cost double,” DeCeit said.

“Done,” Specter agreed. DeCeit stood and extended his hand. They shook.

“He’ll be here tomorrow- my agent,” Specter explained. “Can you come at any time after noon?”

“Your wish is my command,” DeCeit hissed and walked out the door.

Specter watched him go loathingly. He hated working with the fellow. However, he was growing desperate. If Hyperon was indeed working for Paideia then it wouldn’t be long before he was wreaking havoc on the whole town and all those in Specter’s employ.

He massaged the red stress ball as he thought about it now. Toward the end of his stage acting days, Specter found Paideia homeless, shivering outside the Megascops late one night. He knew Folly would be able to turn Paideia’s plight into money in their pockets. Hadn’t they worked together seamlessly before?

Specter had taken Paideia in, given her food and a bed for the night. He remembered with disgust how she had swept the floor of the office and cleaned the restrooms. She wanted to work for the food, she'd said. He had meant to educate her on all the ways she had been unjustly treated and persuade her to join his cause against injustice. With her willingness to do the menial labor, she would be a valuable tool in his hand. She seemed pliable, but when he brought the agreement for her to sign the next morning, her eyes flashed. Even alone in his office now, he could hear her rage.

"I don't work for nobody but Wisdom," she'd said through clenched teeth, "and I won't do any work such as what you're suggesting."

Specter hadn't heard Wisdom's name in years. He had wondered if she'd left Opportunity entirely.

"How do you know her?" he'd asked incredulously.

"How can I not?" the woman asked.

"She left you homeless and alone," he argued. "Why would you still want to work for her?"

"She has her own reasons for what she does, and I have never been alone," Paideia answered.

He sneered at her. "You look alone to me."

"No one can snatch me from her hand[211]," Paideia said, "and maybe it's her hand that you need. Maybe that's why I'm here."

Specter knew that he had no chance to persuade Paideia then. When he looked at her, all he could see

---

[211] Heb. 13:5-6

was Wisdom. His rage took over, and he'd beat her senseless. He left her laying a pool of blood on the floor.

She was not softened by the beatings. She was unpersuadable, and Specter took out all his rage against Wisdom on her. He attempted to have others persuade Paideia, but even that had no effect.

"Where does Wisdom live?" he'd asked.

"Near the gate of the city," Paideia answered. "She calls out to everyone who passes by there."

Specter knew just where to set Folly up in business. The very next day he purchased the two-story home built into the wall of the city. He rode the trolley there early in the morning and there she was. She seemed to have matured, but he could tell she hadn't changed.

She looked at him through doleful eyes but said nothing.

"You could've been mine," he said, "but now I have everyone who was meant to be yours."

She shook her head sadly. He triumphed.

When he returned to his buildings, Specter discovered that Paideia was gone. No one could tell him where or how.

Several months later, Folly lost one of her best customers and informed Specter that the man frequented a bakery run by none other than Paideia. He'd lost another one to Wisdom, but he vowed to exact his revenge on Paideia.

Specter had waited many years for his revenge. Now, Hyperon's presence made it ideal to kill two birds with one stone. It wouldn't be long now before he plucked his birds out of Wisdom's hand.

Chapter 35

Hyperon smiled when Paddy rapped on his door first thing the next morning. They'd only gotten four hours of sleep after the mysterious sewer meeting, but it had been restful.

"I'll be down soon," he growled through the door. Paddy's humming retreated, accompanied by the creaking of the stairs.

Something about the meeting stuck with him as he worked throughout the day. He'd been afraid of the sudden darkness until Paddy's laugh echoed through it.

"Well, our time's up already," she'd said. After they'd held hands and stumbled and laughed their way back to the manhole, Paddy explained that the lamp oil had run out. Usually, they kept extra on hand, but the store keeper had raised prices on the oil recently and none of them could afford it.

But the feeling that shadowed him wasn't fear. It was a pleasant sensation of camaraderie, almost as if he had a secret that would change all that was evil in the world to good. Being with others who had been changed by Wisdom awoke in him again the love that he had for her. Being with them helped him realize that the evil men he knew did not understand justice at all. The people he had just been with- they understood it completely[212].

Prudence came in.

"I didn't ask you last night, but did you read the book?" she asked conspiratorially.

[212] Ps. 37:30; Prov. 8:20; Prov. 21:15; Prov. 28:5

He smiled. Every page had brought the smell of fresh, green grass and the cool, refreshing taste of water from the deep part of the well[213]. He could hear his mother's laughter when he read that book. He could feel Wisdom's kiss.

"Yes," he said, withdrawing it from his apron pocket.

"I was afraid to come here at first," she told him, "but Paddy said it would be alright."

Hyperon blinked at her. "Paddy asked you to come?" he asked.

Prudence smiled. "Yes. She said that the Lady said you needed to read my book. Doing what the Lady says is better than muffins, isn't it?" she answered.

He laughed.

Cameron coughed from the corner. "Paddy's laugh must be contagious," he said. "Is there any cure? I hope it doesn't kill you."

Prudence rolled her eyes and giggled.

Hyperon smiled. "Have you always known her-the Lady, I mean?" he asked.

Prudence shook her head.

"I was once a baby born in the darkness and the dirt," she said. "I was a baby with no real name and no real home who managed to survive in the alleys. The Lady found me and gave me a name and a home."

Hyperon was startled.

"So, you're adopted?" he ventured.

---

[213] Ps. 23; Jn. 4:14

She nodded. "Aren't you?" she asked, blinking up at him[214].

He had thought that she was so good because of all the advantages that came with a good home and family. However, that was far from the truth. She was so good because Wisdom had saved her, adopted her. Yes, in that sense, he had been adopted too.

He winked as she left, and considered the accumulating pile of money that Paddy was paying him. He'd been saving what he could for his tasks. He knew he'd have to save a lot in order to build the house. But surely he could spare what was needed for oil. It'd be worth it to gather with the others again[215]. He had so much to learn.

When Adam walked through the door of the Banquet Bakery, Hyperon's pleasant thoughts seemed to walk out. Adam wasn't alone, but Hyperon didn't recognize the blue-haired punk with him.

"Hyperon," Adam said, leaning on the counter. "I just stopped by to apologize for yesterday. I can see that you've changed, and I respect that."

Hyperon distrusted the offered smile. A quick glance at the blue-haired fellow revealed nothing. Dark sunglasses masked his eyes.

Paddy emerged from the back, wiping her hands on a blue dishrag. "Well, gentlemen, how about a croissant on the house?" she said.

Adam slapped the other guy on the back. "Never turn down free food, right Judas?" he said.

---

214 Gal 4:4-6

215 Heb. 10:24-25

"An adage I live by," agreed the other man.

"I'll have blueberry," said Adam, taking a seat in one of the booths. Hyperon would have much preferred to package the croissants to go. Judas followed Adam and sat across from him.

"Chocolate chip," he said.

Hyperon looked at Paddy, expecting her to serve them since she made the free offer.

"Well, don't just stand there gawking like a school girl," Paddy said under her breath. "Give them those croissants prudently."

Hyperon couldn't help but smile. Paddy returned to the kitchen as he grabbed the tongs and put croissants on plates.

He served Adam and Judas.

Before Hyperon could hide himself under the mound of dishes in the kitchen, Adam invited him to sit down. Even in Paddy's absence, Hyperon could hear her admonition to "prudently." He sat.

"Hyperon, you know I couldn't hear Wisdom before," Adam began, "but since I've seen the change she's made in you, I want to see her again. I need to hear what she has to say."

It was the last thing Hyperon expected.

"What about Specter?" he asked.

"I'm a free man, aren't I?" Adam said. "I'm no slave[216]."

"Well, you know where she works," Hyperon said. "I can't take you there, though, until I complete my tasks."

---

216 Rom. 6:20

Adam raised his eyebrows.

"Tasks?" he asked. "What? She gave you work to do before allowing you to see her again?"

Hyperon regretted mentioning it. He didn't answer the question. Adam's companion had polished off his croissant and was licking his finger to pick up all the crumbs left on the plate.

"That's rich," Judas said, not even bothering to look up from his task. "Find a dame willing to marry you, and she sets you right to the work she should be doing herself."

Hyperon's anger bubbled up behind his eyes.

"I chose to work[217]," he said, as calmly as he could.

Adam reached out a hand and placed it gently on Judas's shoulder. His eyes though, he kept on Hyperon.

"Don't you think you could at least go with us to find Wisdom?" Adam pleaded. "Just think how happy she'll be to see you."

Hyperon stood and walked to the large storefront window. Staring out at the passersby, he contemplated seeing Wisdom again. He'd drink in the sight of her, but he knew he couldn't stand to see disappointment in her eyes when he confessed his failure to complete even one of his tasks.

He glanced down, and on the windowsill lay a single blade of grass. He picked it up and smiled. Rubbing it against his cheek, he remembered those moments in Wisdom's house. He knew he should not trust Adam.

---

[217] Eph. 2:8-10

"No," he said, turning around. "I can't go with you."

Adam rolled his eyes and stood from the table.

"Oh come on! Is it your- what did you call it again?- tasks?" he said.

"Yes," Hyperon answered.

"Maybe we could help you with them so that we could know Wisdom better," Adam suggested. "What are they?"

Hyperon remembered them. He thought about what would happen if Specter knew his plans.

"You should look for Wisdom, Adam," he said, "but I cannot help you. She's so much better than the life I had. We didn't even know what justice and injustice meant then. We had it all confused. Don't you ever get tired of the running and every pleasure never being quite enough?"

A shattering sound brought their attention to Judas who had dropped his plate on the counter.

"Oh," he said. "I'm so sorry. Butterfingers. Let's go, Adam."

He left the fragments of the plate there and headed for the door.

Adam shrugged. "Well, maybe you'll change your mind. We'll be back tomorrow," he said and trotted after his friend.

Paddy emerged again from the kitchen. Hyperon held up one of the shards of glass.

"Went that well, huh?" she said.

He rolled his eyes.

"What'd they want?" she asked.

Hyperon didn't look at her but focused on his task of cleaning up the broken plate.

"Adam said he wants to meet Wisdom," he said.

"You believe him?" she asked.

"No."

Other customers began coming about that hour, and they were busy until closing. Paddy turned the lock in the door, and they cleaned the kitchen together.

"He asked me about my tasks," Hyperon told her.

"You hadn't even told me about them," she said.

"I didn't tell him either," he replied. "I don't trust him."

"Neither do I," she said. "All the more reason to be prudent."

He laughed, and so did she.

"Paddy," he asked, "how much does oil cost?"

She looked at him. "Seems to me the price was up to what I pay you for a whole week of work," she said, "but no matter. I bought some last night."

He smiled. "You can't fund every meeting," he said.

"Try and stop me," she said.

He knew better and went up to bed with a full mind.

Chapter 36

Adam never was one for rising early, but Hyperon's tasks intrigued him. It seemed that his former friend was heaping work on top of work in the name of supposed justice.

And all Adam could do was wonder why.

DeCeit took one last drag from a cigarette and was crushing it on the sidewalk beneath his high top sneaker when Adam met him there the next morning.

"Let me do the talking today," DeCeit said.

"Fine," Adam agreed. It hadn't gone so well the day before. He could tell that Hyperon didn't trust him. He was used to his family or his enemies distrusting him, but this was the first time he'd had a friend for an enemy. It made him realize that Hyperon was his friend.

The bell above the door jingled as they walked in, and Adam could see Hyperon's displeasure at their appearance first thing in the morning. He was bent over clearing a table.

"Good morning, my good man," DeCeit said. "The baked goods were so delicious yesterday that we determined to come back."

DeCeit led the way to the table Hyperon had just cleared.

"Good," Hyperon said. "What kind would you like?" Both men ordered muffins this time and added coffee.

Adam watched Hyperon as he set muffins on plates and poured coffee. He glanced at DeCeit who sat comfortably in the booth opposite him. For the first time, he wondered why Specter had teamed him with this guy.

Business picked up as soon as Hyperon served them, and they had no chance to speak with him while the line at the counter remained long. Adam watched as the little brown haired girl wearing braids came in and talked with Hyperon. He wondered why the man would waste time on a little girl who always seemed to bring trouble with her. He could overhear snippets of their conversation.

"Paddy bought oil," he was saying. The girl's face lit up.

"In that case, I'll take two muffins," she said, digging in the pocket of her plaid jumper for some change.

Hyperon reached in his pocket as well and laid extra change on the counter. Adam couldn't quite hear what he said because someone walked through his line of vision and the bell above the door jangled.

"Oh, thank you," the girl was saying as Hyperon put three muffins into the bag, "I've only ever tasted one of Paddy's muffins[218]."

Hyperon smiled at her and waved as she bounced out the door.

DeCeit sipped his coffee, and Adam knew he was just waiting for the bakery traffic to settle down.

"Remember, we agreed I'd talk today," he hissed as the last group of old men sidled out the door.

Hyperon wiped down the table they'd just deserted and returned behind the counter to arrange pastries and set out midday items. DeCeit stood and sauntered to the counter. Adam followed.

---

[218] Ps. 34:8

"Busy morning," DeCeit said.

"Indeed," Hyperon answered.

"My name is Judas," he offered his hand.

Hyperon shook it.

"Hyperon," he answered.

"Adam and I are intrigued by your escape from Specter," DeCeit said.

Adam watched as Hyperon's eyelids fluttered slightly. Other than that slight motion, he concealed his thoughts.

"I know it has to do with Wisdom, but how does one find her?" DeCeit asked.

Hyperon picked up a broom and began sweeping.

"What would you do if you did find her?" Hyperon asked, looking at Adam.

Adam had no answer. He directed his gaze to DeCeit.

"Why, get to know her as you have," DeCeit said quickly. "Specter's demands are so hard to meet. It seems we are just signing people up to demand justice but never getting it. It's more profitable for Specter to have more people convinced that they are misused victims. And one does get tired of harassing other unfortunate souls. I thought Wisdom's way might be easier."

Hyperon fixed his eyes on his broom. An uncomfortable silence settled over them.

"It is not easier," Hyperon finally said.

Adam could see that fact as plainly as he could see the nose on his face. The occasional persuasion he did for Specter was nothing like the slavery Hyperon was bound to in his life with Wisdom.

"Then why do it?" DeCeit asked.

"Because I love her[219]," came the ready reply.

"How do you know she returns your love?" DeCeit pressed him.

Silence, except for the bristles of the broom scraping the hard stone floor, hung over them.

"She told me so," Hyperon said.

"Ah! A Woman's words are so often fickle," DeCeit laughed. "She can't love only you."

"She doesn't love only me. She loves all," Hyperon said, "but she promised to be mine one day, and I believe her promise[220]."

"I knew a dame like that once," DeCeit laughed and looked at Adam. "Adam, you remember Folly?" Judas turned back to Hyperon. He started humming the song Hyperon knew all too well. The words flitted just behind his eyes as he saw again the beautiful hologram demanding her due.

"Promises at her place are stacked as high as the ceiling, but she loves all too," DeCeit raised his eyebrows. "She'd give her love to anyone who came within twenty yards."

"You don't know the love I speak of. Wisdom isn't like Folly," Hyperon said. "I've met them both."

"But they look alike," DeCeit pointed out.

"But one day, I will complete my tasks and Wisdom will be mine," Hyperon's words were measured and strained.

---

219 Jn. 14:15

220 Prov. 4:5-9

DeCeit leaned his back against the counter to face Hyperon, who was now sweeping out under the tables.

"Like a fairy tale," he mused.

"Except true," Hyperon amended.

"Your mother thought it all a legend," DeCeit said. "Wisdom is certainly legendary, but that is all."

Adam shifted on his feet nervously. He felt anger emanating from Hyperon, and yet the man maintained a cool, steady calm[221].

"So, when is the happy event planned? Have you picked a wedding date?" DeCeit asked.

"No," Hyperon said. "I must first finish my tasks."

"You must earn her favor[222]?" Judas pushed.

"No," Hyperon wrinkled his brow. "I must make her my own. I already have her favor. I have to learn to let her Father work through me[223]."

DeCeit flinched. Adam threw his own arm up as if to block a projectile, yet he didn't know why. He felt as if an electric shock had coursed through him.

"Under her Daddy's thumb, then?" DeCeit composed himself quickly.

Hyperon dropped the broom and it hit the stone with a loud crack. In two strides, he had crossed the room and taken DeCeit by the collar.

"Listen," he commanded, his blue eyes flashing, "I don't know who you are or why you're asking me

221 James 1:19-20
222 Gal. 2:16
223 Titus 3:4-8

these questions, but I'm done with this conversation. You have nothing to do with Wisdom!" Two shakes of DeCeit and Hyperon shoved him toward the door.

"Hasty, hasty!" DeCeit said, shaking the wrinkles from his shirt. "I'll be back. Come on, Adam." He walked out the door.

"Don't hurry," Hyperon shouted after him. Adam could see the vein in his neck pumping hot blood.

"Adam, you need to choose which path you're on and get on it. There's no middle road[224]," Hyperon said to him.

"Sorry about that guy, man," Adam said. "I'd better go." He strode toward the door, but all of a sudden, an image of the little girl filled his mind.

"One more thing, though," he said, whirling around. "Why did you buy that little girl a third muffin?"

Hyperon stared at him. His anger had put it out of his mind momentarily.

"It isn't just anyone who gives all they have to someone who hates them," Hyperon said, as his anger melted away. "She spends all her allowance on muffins for others. I thought I would return her kindness."

"Does she really deserve it, though? Surely her parents could give her whatever she wants," Adam wondered.

"Who deserves kindness, Adam?" Hyperon asked.

Adam shrugged. "I do," he said. "It's karma, man." Hyperon stared at him.

---

[224] Rev. 3:16

Adam shrugged again and walked out the door. He spotted DeCeit in the crowd across the street. Adam caught up and fell into stride beside him.

"Well, that was brilliant," Adam said sarcastically.

DeCeit smiled and kept walking. He seemed not to notice the colossal failure they'd just had in Specter's employ.

"Aren't you worried about how to explain this to Mr. Specter?" Adam asked.

"Specter might as well work for me," Judas muttered. Then, louder, he said, "Our work is done with Hyperon for a week or so. The words I said will swim around in his mind until he loses sight of his idealist truths."

Adam shook his head. He didn't understand.

"How will mere words make Hyperon forget about Wisdom?" he asked.

DeCeit rubbed his hands together. "Oh, he won't forget her. He'll begin to doubt her[225]," he explained.

Adam began to doubt Specter. He wondered if Wisdom could offer him a better deal.

---

225 Jude 1:22

Chapter 37

Prudence carefully unwrapped the sticky muffins as the little Shadow Children hovered near her.

"These are the best muffins in the whole city," she told them.

The two children never spoke to her, and Prudence didn't know whether it was because they were still fearful or because they couldn't speak. When they communicated with one another, it was by nudges, clicks, and grunts- at least, in her presence.

The younger one, who Prudence now assumed to be a girl, dove into her muffin right away, smacking her lips loudly in appreciation. However, the older one, a boy, studied Prudence with thoughtful eyes.

"What is it?" she asked.

The child ran into the darker part of the alley. When Prudence took a step to follow, the smaller one grabbed onto her dress. When she looked at her, she shook her head. Prudence stood still and waited.

The older child came back carrying something and held it out to her.

Prudence took it and held it up to the light. It was a wooden compass. The needle still pointed north.

"You want me to have this?" she asked. The child nodded and started on his muffin.

Prudence tucked the compass into her pocket. "Thank you. It is very nice. Well, I'd better get to school quickly," she said.

The Shadow Children smiled at her. The younger one waved with her free hand while she licked the fingers of the other.

She wove through the city, careful to stay on the insides of the sidewalks when she could.

"Hey!" came a familiar voice when she only had one block left to go.

She turned and smiled. She remembered what Paddy had told Hyperon about a compass. You don't just look at it once, but you use it to guide you continually as you travel. Prudence thought about the Lady. She hadn't just rescued Prudence that one time, but she was Prudence's guide all the time, at every time. This made Prudence smile wider, even though it was Haste running to catch up to her.

He ran as fast as he could toward her and jumped up as he pulled one of her braids.

"Where's my muffin today?" Haste said as he turned to look at her.

She shrugged. "None today," she said.

His forehead creased in a frown.

"Ah," he moaned, "why not?"

Her smile stayed intact. "You know, whenever you eat these muffins, you get hungry again later. Maybe you could join us when I read the book, and you will find something that satisfies forever."

He rolled his eyes.

"According to you, everything is about that book, and I'm sick of it," he said.

"Well, then, you will be hungry," she told him.

Prudence looked ahead and saw that the crossing guard was occupied on the far side of the street. They would have to wait awhile before they could cross. She hoped they would not be late for school. Cars, trucks, and bicycles sped past. A few other children were already gathered at the corner, waiting for their turn. She recognized Bene and Sparrow. Sparrow turned and waved.

"Let's race!" Haste said to her. "If you win, I will listen to your stupid book. If I win, you have to bring me two muffins!"

"Wait!" she said. "Stop! We can't cross yet." She tried to grab his arm. He dodged her grasp and ran ahead. She ran after him, calling his name.

The children at the corner turned to look at them.

Haste spun around Sparrow, and Prudence could see the oncoming car that would plow into him. The driver hadn't seen him yet. It was about three bus lengths away.

Haste ran right past the corner and into the street. Prudence took the compass out of her pocket and hurled it as hard as she could at the car. One of the girls shrieked. The crossing guard was yelling. The brakes screeched, and there was a sound of breaking glass. The car slowed but still slid right into Haste, and he bounced to the ground. A truck behind the car swerved and oncoming traffic came to a standstill.

The crossing guard ran to the boy. The driver of the car was opening his door and looking from the children on the corner to the spidery cracks on his windshield.

"Which one of you threw this?" he shouted, picking up her compass from where it had landed between the windshield and the hood.

Prudence recognized his blue hair from having seen him at the bakery.

She wanted to cry, but she stepped forward.

"It was me," she said. "I didn't know how else to stop you from hitting my friend."

"You were traveling at too fast a speed," the crossing guard called to the driver.

"That's no reason to get my windshield knocked out," the driver said.

The truck driver was out in the street now too, and he was calling for the police. Somewhere in the distance, a siren announced that someone was on the way.

Prudence heard Haste mumbling something to the crossing guard, and she couldn't see any blood. At least he was alive. Sparrow slipped her hand into Prudence's and gave it a squeeze.

The blue-haired driver crossed the road and took hold of her shoulder. "Where did you get this?" he demanded, waving the compass under her nose. He seemed to have forgotten his windshield.

"From a friend," she answered quietly.

She couldn't read his eyes behind his sunglasses, but she hoped he would understand her reasoning.

The policeman came on an old motorbike, and the siren grated Prudence's nerves. He ran to help the crossing guard with Haste.

The man with the blue hair bent down to speak to her more quietly. She disliked his quiet more than his noise.

"Let's say you tell me who the friend is who gave you this compass, and I will make sure you don't get into any trouble for this little incident. How does that sound?" he said.

Prudence knew she couldn't give the name or address of the child. The Shadow Children belonged nowhere and everywhere in the city.

"I hope you don't get in trouble," Sparrow whispered, "because tonight is the meeting night. You don't want to miss it."

Prudence looked at Haste. The policeman was helping him sit up. Haste protested loudly. Prudence felt sure that he would be fine.

"How about you, little one?" the blue haired man was speaking to Sparrow. "Do you know where your friend got this? Maybe it was at meeting night?"

Sparrow shook her head. "We don't get things at meeting night. We just sing," Sparrow said.

"And where is meeting night?" he asked.

Prudence squeezed Sparrow's hand. This man did not need to know any more than he did.

"Maybe you should move your car," Prudence suggested.

The policeman was helping Haste limp to the school. The crossing guard was hurrying towards them. One of the waiting vehicles honked.

"Too fast in a school zone," the crossing guard started talking even before she reached them.

Prudence looked back to the blue haired man to see if he would argue, but he was gone. Just she and Sparrow, Bene, and the other children were gathered there. However, standing near her was a black haired boy who had not been there before.

"Where did that fellow get to?" the crossing guard asked Prudence.

"I," she began, and looked at the boy, "I'm not sure."

The crossing guard set her hands on her hips and sighed. "Well, you children better cross with me now. What a ruckus! I always tell Haste that he must wait for me before jumping out into traffic. He's just no good at waiting, and it nearly got him killed[226]."

The guard turned, blew her whistle, and held up her stop sign while the huddle of children followed her across the street. The cars waited impatiently.

Prudence stared at the blue haired man's car with the busted windshield. She was glad she had thrown the compass because Haste was not as seriously injured as he could have been; however, she was sorry she had lost it.

Just as she stepped onto the street to follow the others, the black haired boy said, "I will give this back to you if you tell me where the meetings are."

He held up the compass.

Sparrow tugged at her hand, saying, "Let's go."

Prudence was bewildered. Could the man have turned into a boy? How could he do that? She thought of the Lady and knew that this man couldn't be trusted.

"That sounds like a bad trade to me. Why don't you just keep it?" Prudence said, turning her back to him. The blue haired man watched them go.

"I'll find you and your little friend," he said to her back.

[226] Ps. 70:1-5

Chapter 38

"Hyperon."

He knew her voice, and he sat up in bed. His eyes scanned the gray recesses of his room, but she was not there.

Instead, all that met him were the words of that scoundrel Judas: "Like a fairy tale…"

He swung his legs off the bed and sat on the edge rubbing his face. Was that all she was? A fairy tale? All he had of her were these whispers of his name and the fading memory of a pleasant afternoon.

He eyed his remaining tools as he ate his simple breakfast. The rusted sword hilt, the hammer, and the spyglass weighed heavy on him. He crossed the room and picked up the spyglass. Her Father shone through, but did He ever do anything but sit there?

All of a sudden, the words of Her song, the song he had sung with the others in the sewer that night, floated through His mind. Her Father had created. He could see her being born from the ripples of the Father's feet in his mind's eye. As if in response to his thoughts, the spyglass shook and became too hot for him to hold. He dropped it and jumped back. It rolled under the table. Hyperon left it there, too afraid to touch it again.

Paddy had given him the day off. He thought of his tasks. It was all so strange. Doubt filled his mind. He'd failed the first task. He wondered who the enemy would be that he could not defeat by power or wit. The whisper of his name had seemed to denote danger and warning.

He stuffed the sword hilt into a shoulder bag and set off. His steps carried him to Rocky's. The scene that met him plunged his spirits even more. Garbage littered the path to her front door- worse now than before his midnight effort to clean her yard. Plants had been uprooted. Branches were torn off trees. He hurried up the sidewalk and knocked on her door.

Her muffled voice came from the inside.

"Go away," she said. "Oh please, go away."

"Rocky," he called, "it's Hyperon."

Silence met him. Then he heard her boy.

"Hyperon," he chirped. "Those other men have been here."

"Open the door, son," Hyperon urged.

Something bumped against the inside of the door, and Hyperon could hear the mother pleading with the son to just leave the door locked and closed against any who would enter. Rocky's sobbing pierced Hyperon.

He sat down on the pavement, leaning back against the door. He would not force his way in. If she were to trust him, she'd have to open it.

He looked up at the sound of quickly padding footsteps approaching from the corner of the house. It was her boy.

"I came out a back window," he explained. Dried blood caked his hair.

"What happened?" Hyperon asked, standing quickly and reaching out a hand to the boy's shoulder[227].

The boy studied him solemnly with his brown eyes. "I thought you might know before I even told you," he said.

---

227 Is. 8:11

"I could hazard a good guess," Hyperon replied, shame filling him.

"Men came, just like you did that night. They broke the door open. Mama fought them at first, but they hurt her so she fainted. They wrecked everything, even my head," the boy put a hand tenderly up to the wound.

"When was it?" Hyperon asked, studying the wound.

"Two nights after our last meeting," the boy answered. "They knew about it, but I don't know how."

Hyperon studied his hands. He'd done the same, and worse, to people in the past. Yet now, he fought the desire to kill the men who tortured others so.

"Is your sister okay?" he inquired about the little girl.

"They took her," the boy said.

Hyperon snapped his attention to the boy's face.

"What?"

"The men took her, and we haven't any idea where she is. That's the last I remember. They were carrying Sparrow out. She was flailing and screaming, and there I was trying to knock that guy's block off. Somebody hit me from behind, and when I woke up, they were all gone, and there I was with a gash in my head[228]," the boy recounted.

Hyperon hardly trusted himself to speak without betraying his emotion.

"What is your name?" he asked finally.

"Bene," he said.

---

[228] Mt. 10:28-31

"Bene," Hyperon said, resting a hand on the boy's shoulder, "you are a brave boy."

"I'd rather be known as a wise boy," Bene confided, "but then, it is so hard to be wise in the moment like that."

Bene sat beside Hyperon.

"Your mama," Hyperon asked, "is she hurt?"

"I can't hardly tell," the boy confessed. "She's done nothing but cry since they took Sparrow away. But I don't think she'll let you in. She's been saying that she's not trusting anybody but herself from now on."

"Why do you trust me, Bene? You've seen how horrible I really am," Hyperon asked. The boy would be right to doubt him and hate him.

"But I've also seen how wonderful Wisdom is, and she's your lady. If she can love you, then I don't see how I couldn't love you too," he said.

Hyperon felt like weeping.

"What should we do?" Bene asked.

"I'm going to get Sparrow back," Hyperon said quietly with sudden resolve.

Bene stood before him.

"You shouldn't go without Her, sir," Bene said seriously.

Hyperon studied the boy.

"But there may not be time to find Wisdom before Sparrow is hurt or sold or anything," Hyperon explained.

"Take the time," Bene pleaded. "If you go find Wisdom, I will go and call Paddy. Mama will be okay here until I get back. Those men won't come back unless we go to another meeting. That's what they said, anyway. And we'll need help to find my sister."

"I still wonder how they discovered our meeting," Hyperon wondered aloud.

He took three strides toward the road and then turned back to Bene.

"Did you recognize any of the men?" Hyperon asked.

The boy shook his head. "They were all strangers to me," he answered, "but one had blue hair."

Bene ran off in the direction of the bakery, and Hyperon climbed aboard the first trolley heading south to the city gate where he had found Wisdom before. Along the way, he thought about the sword hilt in his bag. He had considered going straight into Specter's office, but he remembered her words, "Neither power nor wit." He knew he possessed too little of either.

He hopped off the trolley before it even stopped and spotted Folly sitting on her side of the street. Apparently, she saw him as well.

"Hyperon!" She seemed excited to see him. "I have been looking for you. Come, why don't we talk about how we can make this world a better place for everyone? People are dying and being used by others every day, and we could stop it. Come and talk with me."

He ignored her and the gawking crowd that was gathered around her, and cast his gaze up the steps on the opposite side of the street. She didn't know anything about how to keep others from being used. She didn't understand his desires anymore.

Specter sat on the very step where he had thrown himself at Wisdom's feet. Judas stood beside him. Anger rose in Hyperon, and he wondered what these two brutes had done with the child and his lady.

He strode boldly up the steps and faced them squarely. He wished that Wisdom would open the door, come striding out, and put an end to their evil once and for all. But the door stayed closed.

Specter smiled. Judas wore his sunglasses as usual, and Hyperon couldn't read his emotions.

"Hyperon, don't you think it's time you stopped this madness and came back to work?" Specter said. "Just think of all I could do for you."

"Where's the girl?" Hyperon demanded.

"Girl?" Specter said, taken aback. "Whatever are you talking about?"

"Don't play dumb," Hyperon threatened. "I want the little girl your men took, and I want her now."

Specter laughed. "Touchy, aren't you! I don't know about any little girl. You're just angry that your game is over."

His words confused Hyperon. "Game?" he asked.

"You pretend as much as all of the children you've befriended," Judas said. He came forward a few paces in order to be immediately in front of Hyperon.

Hyperon resisted the urge to place a square undercut right on the lower part of his jaw.

"This lady you're always speaking of- she isn't here, is she? The girl you're alluding to. No one else seems concerned. If she were really missing, don't you think her mother would be the one searching for her?" Judas said.

Hyperon glanced toward the street. Folly's crowd stood staring up at him. Folly gave him a playful smile. He wondered if he sent someone for the police if it would do any good. He wondered where Wisdom was.

"It's all a game you've been playing with yourself," Judas said. "If you call the police, they'll just lock you up in the loony bin because you are out of your mind."

More likely than not, they'd take the bribe Specter slipped them and beat me as soon as we were out of sight, Hyperon thought.

Specter stood.

"You should just come back to work," Specter patronized him. "Remember the carefree hours you had? And the parties? And the women? What did you lack[229]?"

Hyperon remembered all of those things, and he still felt shame over them. He also remembered the broken bits of humanity he helped Specter to crush. An image of Rocky cowering on the floor filled his mind.

"Everything," he spat.

Judas held something up for him to see. It was the compass.

Hyperon wavered. Could there be two? It was the exact replica of the compass the Lady had given him. It was supposed to lead him away from evil, and here it was, right in evil's palm.

"That belongs to me," Hyperon said quietly.

---

229 Ez. 28:4-5

"But it is in my grasp, and it helped me learn all about your meetings[230]," Judas said. "You all get together and talk about a lady and her father who aren't even there. Seems more like a funeral than a celebration. Is it really worth losing your lives over? Couldn't you just sing your songs and tell your stories to yourselves in the darkness of your own homes? It would be so much…" Judas paused, "safer."

"Is that a threat?" Hyperon tried to sound calm.

"Little girls wouldn't need to go missing if you would just do as you're told," Judas said.

Specter smirked and crossed his arms. "Persuadable yet?"

Hyperon's fingers reached for the sword hilt in his bag. He had a growing awareness that this was it. This was the second task. He couldn't think of a single word to answer their arguments, and they had him outnumbered too. How had they known he would come here? Power and wit weren't on his side. He knew he couldn't fight them alone. He needed Wisdom, and he couldn't find her.

Specter slipped down the stairs toward him noiselessly, calculatingly. Hyperon pulled the hilt out of his bag and held it in front of him. Though it made no sense[231], it was all he had of Wisdom, and he knew now that she was no imaginary friend. The burn from the red hot spyglass still pricked his palm. He held up the hilt and looked at it.

---

230 Gen. 3:1

231 Eccl. 9:18

Judas laughed as he stood in front of Wisdom's door.

"And now you're going to fight with a broken sword?" he shook his head. "Oh, Hyperon! How delusional[232]!"

Specter stood three steps above him now, close enough for Folly's onlookers not to hear his words.

"If you don't come back now, I will kill the little girl," he said.

In that moment, Hyperon's doubt sloughed off like old skin. His vision sharpened, and he could see that because Wisdom loved him, he was a threat to Specter's work. He knew now that he would never give in. He could hear her voice in his mind, guiding him, urging him.

"Hyperon," she whispered, "abide in me[233]."

"You will have to kill me first," Hyperon said to Specter through clenched teeth and lunged forward with the hilt.

Specter dodged and fled back several stairs while shrieking, "DeCeit! Do something!"

Hyperon's only thought was to get to them before they got to Sparrow.

Judas DeCeit ran down to meet Hyperon, calling "He can't hurt us," back at Specter. His sunglasses fell off and shattered on the concrete. He dropped the compass, and it bounced down the steps toward the road. He rushed to engage Hyperon in a fight. His arms were raised as if to squeeze the life from Hyperon's jugular.

---

232 1 Cor. 1:25-31

233 1 Jn. 3:24

Hyperon stood still, gripping the hilt tightly with both hands and waiting[234].

Just as DeCeit's fingers closed around Hyperon's throat, there was a brilliant flash of light. From the sword hilt, a golden-green blade shone[235]. Hyperon felt the slight pressure of another hand on his hand and could see a few inches of the blade on this side of Judas's body and several inches showing through behind his back. The fingers that had one moment before begun choking the life out of him were now growing slack and cold.

A sickening gurgle came from the lips of DeCeit. Hyperon, watching his face, saw it pass from the likeness of the blue-haired punk to the annoyed look of a disgruntled businessman to the disenchanted grimace of a bitter old man. The blade disappeared, and DeCeit fell on the stone steps as the pallor of death became the last mask he would ever wear.

A breeze lifted Hyperon's brown curls as he stared at the sword hilt in his hand. Tremors wracked his body. Someone from Folly's side of the street was yelling, "Someone call a constable!"

Hyperon knelt shakily on the stairs and looked up at Specter. Specter was uncharacteristically discomposed, huddled in the shadow of the roof's overhang and looking aghast on the dead form of his former friend. Disbelief morphed into anger on his face.

"Murderer!" he shrieked and rose to point his finger down at Hyperon. The crowd on the street buzzed. Hyperon could hear running feet coming nearer.

---

234 Ps. 37:7; Ps. 34:11-13
235 Heb. 4:12-13

"Even now, if you come back to work for me, I will get you out of this trouble," Specter hissed. "You don't need this level of stress all the time. Just say the word, and I will talk with the police."

Hyperon laid the sword hilt beside the body. "I'd rather rot in prison," he said.

"Have it your way," Specter shrugged.

Just as the policeman came into view, Bene came from the opposite direction and bounded up the steps to kneel beside Hyperon. A winded Paddy jogged behind him.

Folly's mob all began talking at once, each vociferously telling a different version of what had happened. The policeman jotted notes on a pocket notebook but exasperatedly made his way as quickly as he could up to Hyperon.

"Where's the dead man?" the policeman asked. "All these people claimed they saw a murder."

Hyperon looked down at the body of Judas DeCeit, but to his surprise, nothing remained. No glasses. No clothing. No body. Not even a blood splotch on the concrete.

"I don't know," Hyperon could hardly speak above a whisper.

Hyperon offered no other explanation. Why defend himself when Specter had stacked the odds against him? Had Wisdom really meant for him to kill a man? Wisdom- all goodness and compassion- had seemed to be there with him. He couldn't have triumphed in his own strength or wit, but he was unsure if he had passed his second task.

Paddy finally caught her breath.

"This man works for me. I will vouch for his character," she told the officer.

The officer nodded.

"Well," he turned back to Hyperon, "was there another man here?"

"Yes, and his name was Judas DeCeit," Hyperon said.

"A friend of yours?" the officer asked.

"An acquaintance," Hyperon replied.

Folly yelled from the other side of the street, "We all saw him plunge the sword right into him!"

The officer nodded again. "Well, where is the sword?"

Hyperon motioned to the hilt, which had assumed its antique look. No blade remained. Hyperon stooped and picked it up.

The officer laughed.

"You must be joking," he said.

He took the hilt from Hyperon and turned it over one way and then another.

"A man's been stabbed, but there's no body. And there's no blade on this here," he said.

Hyperon nodded. "I don't really understand it myself, sir," he admitted.

"Hyperon heard that this Judas DeCeit had kidnapped a girl, and he was trying to help find her," Paddy explained.

The officer raised his eyebrows. "Is that so? What is the girl's name?"

Paddy gave the name and address, and Bene confirmed the story of Sparrow's kidnapping.

Specter came out of the shadows.

"Officer, this man is a murderer and needs to be taken in right away. He's a danger to the public if he can murder with some mysterious weapon and then make the bodies disintegrate completely," Specter said.

The officer nodded. "Of course, Mr. Specter," he said, putting his notepad away.

"You'll have to come with me," he said to Hyperon, grabbing his arm to turn him around. The officer began to clasp his wrists in handcuffs.

"Why handcuff him? Why take him at all? You have no proof that there even was such a person as Judas DeCeit," Paddy said, moving Bene farther from Specter.

The officer shook his head. "Well, he has been disturbing the peace," he told her at last.

Paddy patted Hyperon on the shoulder as the officer led him past.

"It'll come out all right," she told him. "Remember your Lady and her Father."

"We'll want to question you about Mr. DeCeit, Mr. Specter," the officer told Specter. "I will send an investigator to your office directly."

"That sounds fine," Specter replied. Then, to Paddy, he said, "Harboring this murderer won't win you any friends, Paideia."

Paddy didn't reply to him, but guided Bene back down the steps toward the trolley.

"Don't listen to their lies, Hyperon," she said.

"I don't care about what happens to me, but we must get Sparrow back," he said. Then to the officer, he said, "The little girl! Specter had men kidnap her. You should question him about where she is."

"Just come with me," the officer said.

“We’ll find her,” Paddy reassured him. The officer led him away down the street past the onlookers.

“You’re still welcome here, Hyperon,” Folly called out. “I’m not one to judge.”

Chapter 39

Adam jabbed the volume button on his remote. Anything to drown out the clamor that child was making. He'd done a lot of unsavory things while in Specter's employ, but this was the worst.

Horbah had brought the little devil in the night before. It appeared as if they'd tried to drown her. Her wet hair clung to her cheek, and her clothes dripped on his floor. She had been crying then, and she still hadn't stopped[236].

He'd offered her a doughnut this morning, but she'd pushed it back at him from inside the dog kennel he'd locked her in.

Adam had no use for children. He didn't have any of his own that he knew of, and whenever they were around, he felt uncomfortably exposed. It was like they could see through him to all the things he had forgotten about himself.

Even the TV couldn't keep his mind from wandering back to the bakery where Hyperon had bought the muffin for the little peacemaker. Her swinging brown braids annoyed Adam, even in memory, almost as much as the little howler's noise did now.

"Just keep her there until the investigation is over," Specter had ordered over the phone last night. "My office is crawling with policemen, but I'll relocate her when they've been satisfied."

Adam hoped their satisfaction came at a quicker, lower price rather than one that would prolong his misery.

---

[236] Mt. 19:14

As a crime scene investigation thriller played on the screen in front of his eyes, he replayed the details he'd been told about how Hyperon killed DeCeit.

Specter was furious.

The other employees were afraid.

"It was a green light that came out of nowhere- like a science fiction movie or something," his colleague Horbah had told him when he brought the girl. "DeCeit was even bolder than Specter, and what I'm wondering is, if this bloke has the power to kill him, what's he got up his sleeve for the rest of us?"

"Surely he doesn't mean to simply murder us in our beds," Adam reasoned.

"I don't know what he means to do, but I do know I'll be steering clear of him[237]," Horbah said, "and if I were you, I'd watch my back. He's out to find this little girl."

"He lived here for almost a year. I know this guy," Adam explained. "He didn't seem out of the ordinary then. It's not like he has super powers or anything."

Horbah shook his head and raised his eyebrows. "Killing a man- an intelligent man- with some kind of hocus pocus sounds like a superpower to me[238]."

Adam secretly reveled in the fact that he wouldn't have to work with DeCeit any longer. Now that the guy was dead, Adam realized that he never had trusted him. He wondered again about Wisdom and the life she offered. Perhaps he should make another trip to

---

237 2 Cor. 2:14-16

238 2 Cor. 10:4-6

the bakery- without Specter's knowledge- and find out what he could from Hyperon.

"They're letting you go, fella," the jailer said, jangling through his keys on the other side of the bars.

Hyperon looked up at him without comment.

"You're free to go[239]," the jailer repeated.

"Why?" Hyperon couldn't wrap his mind around why they would let him go after keeping him a week.

"I guess the guy everyone says you murdered didn't even exist," the jailer told him. "They couldn't find his name in the phone book. He had no residence. He had no next-of-kin to be notified. There weren't any photographs of him. Not even Mr. Specter could prove that there had been such a person."

Hyperon stood and followed the man to the door that opened to the outside. The sun shone in a brilliant sky of blue. He walked away and found himself on the familiar sidewalk to *The Banquet Bakery.*

Paddy was elbow deep in the dishwater when he came through the back door.

"Cameron's missed you," she said over her shoulder.

Hyperon smiled for the first time since he'd had the day off over a week before.

"I missed him too," he said sincerely. "How'd you know it was me coming in your back door?"

"No one has the big step you have except you," she turned to look at him. "And I asked the Father for

[239] Lk. 4:18

you. Don't you know that's the only reason you're walking free?"

His smile deepened.

"Paddy, besides Wisdom, you understand the Father better than anyone I know," he said.

"Well, that's a mighty high compliment," she said. "I'll take it. You get to Cameron's swamp muffin now, and we'll chat later."

Hyperon enjoyed being busy at his ordinary bakery tasks after having contemplated a lifetime of inactivity in prison. He'd had plenty of time for thinking, but he still hadn't formed a firm grasp on Judas DeCeit or how he had completed the second task. What stuck out in his mind most was the whisper of her hand on his when the green light flashed. It was her voice in his mind telling him that she was not a fairy tale but a real, living, breathing love who would always be found when sought[240]. He could trust her. His doubt had died on the steps alongside DeCeit.

Adam came into the bakery just before closing time. He came to the counter and waited until Hyperon met his gaze.

"Tell me more about her," Adam pleaded. "Tell me why you're willing to work like a slave."

The last customers had already gone, so Hyperon crossed to the door and turned the lock before turning back to face Adam.

Hyperon took his broom in hand- Adam remembered it well from the time before- and began furiously sweeping.

---

[240] Mt. 7:7

"I will tell you about her," Hyperon said. "I will tell you everything. But, will you promise to look for her? And if you find her, will you promise to really listen?"

"If I can hear anything she says, I will listen," Adam promised.

Hyperon began at his meeting Wisdom, which Adam remembered, and proceeded to tell him everything about the banquet, the wine, her words, and his tasks. He told Adam about helping Rocky and his desire to help others hurt by Specter's schemes. He told him of his resolve to find Sparrow. The only thing he did not tell Adam was about the meetings. He could risk everything of his own, but he wasn't willing to risk the well-being of those brave souls who followed Wisdom.

When Hyperon finished his tale, he was seated across from Adam in one of the booths, and the street outside was empty.

Adam nodded and rubbed the few days' stubble growth on his chin.

He thought of his own "vacation" with Folly. He thought of Folly herself. What had Wisdom actually given Hyperon? A mere kiss or two, uncertain promises? Folly may not have been as high and mighty, but she certainly was an immediate rewarder of his seeking.

"I want to learn more about her," Adam said finally. "I will come again soon." With that, Hyperon let him out the front door and locked it behind him[241].

Paddy had already headed for home, so Hyperon wearily climbed the stairs to his apartment. He replayed

---

241 Acts 17:18-21

all of his conversation with Adam. He remembered DeCeit's dying gurgle. He asked the Father for Sparrow. Only the Father knew where she was. He thought about his third task. Tomorrow, he'd make plans for Wisdom's house. He may have failed the first sign and corrupted the second, but he was sure he could accomplish the third.

He opened his door and sat on the couch. It felt good to be here instead of in jail. He smiled as he pictured himself and Wisdom sitting before an inviting fire of an evening.

He crossed the room and picked up the hammer. He flipped it in his hand.

Distinctly, he heard her voice, "My Father must give you every ability."

He knew she was right.

Chapter 40

Horbah knocked early the next morning. Adam had stayed late with Hyperon and had too much on his mind to fall asleep immediately. Plus, that kid was still making a horrible racket. His last thought as he drifted off had been to hope that the neighbors couldn't hear her. Horbah was beating on the door before it finally roused him.

"Specter sent you some things last night, but you weren't here," he began as soon as Adam swung the door open.

"I had to get away from that tiresome crier," Adam responded irritably.

"Only a few more days, and we can move her," Horbah said, "or dispose of her." He laughed. Adam shrugged as nonchalantly as possible. He wondered what Hyperon's response would be if they did kill the little beast. Somewhere in the back of his mind, he also wondered what that fiendish Wisdom would do to him. He knew that the girl's mother, Rocky, was a friend of hers.

Adam walked away from the door and flopped down on the couch. He picked up the remote and flipped through the channels as Horbah helped himself to the meager refrigerator contents in the kitchen.

"So, where did you go?" Horbah asked around the bite of sandwich that was in his mouth. The question seemed nonchalant. Adam's mind sprang suddenly alert at Horbah's lack of eye contact and his persistence in knowing where Adam had been the night before. Adam knew that Specter had sent him.

"Just walked around," he mimicked the nonchalance and added a shoulder shrug for effect.

The little girl picked that moment to commence her wailing, and Horbah seemed anxious to leave.

"I'll come by tomorrow," he said. "Let's go shoot some pool."

Adam dared not take his eyes from the screen.

"Sounds good, man," he said.

The door slammed behind his departing guest. Adam gave him five minutes then glanced out the window to be sure he was truly leaving.

He walked back to the kennel with the girl in it. She stank, and he abhorred the sight of her red rimmed eyes. Her cries had dwindled to whimpers.

"You want your mama?" he asked her. She nodded.

"You remember Hyperon? He's a tall, curly haired guy," Adam asked again.

"I saw him in the underground," came the timid reply.

"The what?" Adam prodded, with renewed interest.

"The underground, in the sewer where we meet others who know Wisdom and sing her song," the little girl explained.

"And Hyperon was there?" Adam questioned.

"Yes," she answered.

Now, here was valuable information.

"I will take you to him tonight," Adam said.

A shadow of a smile played across her face.

"But first," Adam coaxed, "you have to tell me all about the underground."

"Okay," she squeaked.

As she spoke, he made mental notes of the names and places she didn't even know she was betraying. He'd satisfy both sides by returning the girl tonight and making it up to Specter with the information on the morrow. He rubbed his hands together and smiled at her. It was going to work out perfectly.

"When I got there, it was too late," Pastor's rather gruff voice lost its edge.

Hyperon studied the faces gathered around the lamp. Paddy was able to afford extra oil this time, so there was little chance of it going out. Their grim faces reflected his own disgust at the things which had happened to Rocky and her children. Bene sat beside him stoically. Rocky had refused to come.

Pastor had heard about Specter's visit to Rocky and had rushed over there only to find a bleeding Bene, an inconsolable mother, and that Sparrow had been kidnapped.

"Well, we all know what happened," Paddy sighed, "but the question is: how will we get her back?"

Silence answered her. Each appeared deep in thought.

"Hyperon worked for him recently," Pastor suggested at length. "Where did he keep his spoils?"

"He would move her around," Hyperon answered quietly, "not keep her in one place."

"Could we come up with enough ransom money?" a woman named Lovely proposed.

"Hmm," Paddy said. "There's a thought, but why did they take her in the first place? If we could answer that conundrum, then we could come up with the best plan to find her. Maybe they don't want money."

"We've also got to think about mom," Bene ventured solemnly. "She's so ate up with fear she can't do anything or go anywhere."

Prudence wrinkled her nose, as if she were thinking very hard. "I might know why they took her," she said and proceeded to tell them the story of Haste, the blue-haired man, and the compass. "He seemed very interested in Sparrow mentioning our meetings."

"Where did you get the compass?" Hyperon wanted to know.

Prudence hesitated. "From some children in an alley," she said.

"Oh, Prudence!" Obedience admonished, but Marv said, "You know that Prudence never takes unnecessary risks, dear." He hugged his daughter.

"I had a compass from Wisdom, but I lost it in an alley," Hyperon said.

"And you had the sword hilt to help with DeCeit too. Did Wisdom give you other things to help you? Could any of those help find Sparrow?" Prudence asked. Marv smiled at his daughter.

Hyperon shrugged. "I am supposed to build a house next," he said and pulled the hammer from his bag. They all looked at it.

"I don't see that a hammer will help us much," Saul said.

Hyperon shook his head. "It won't do much good for Sparrow," he said, "but maybe I can repair some of Rocky's furniture or home."

"It'd be a shame to have to delay your house," Paddy said sympathetically.

Hyperon grinned at her. "Isn't it you who always says, 'Walking the right way is more than just not walking the wrong way'? And as far as that goes, I have a little savings set aside we could use as ransom if that is what they're after."

Prudence rewarded him with a smile.

"I'm in construction," Saul ventured, "and I could help with the mending too."

"We could all help with that," Marv said.

"But we have to find Sparrow first," Obedience pointed out.

"I wish the Lady was here," Prudence sighed.

"We all wish that," Pastor said.

"She hasn't left us as orphans though[242]," Paddy said. "She's given us her guidance and one another. And we can take this matter to her Father."

The dank walls dripped in the shadows cast by the lamp light. From somewhere far away, they heard the echo of a manhole cover falling back into place.

Bene raised his eyebrows. Paddy extinguished the lamp. Everyone hardly dared to breathe. Hyperon crept toward the open doorway of the little room where they hid. If someone came in, he or she would meet Hyperon first.

Footsteps passed by the room on the stone pavement of the sewer. They paused just past the doorway. The stranger carried a dim light, not as bright as their own lamp. In the brief second that he had passed

242 Jn. 14:18

the doorway, Hyperon had not been able to get a clear glimpse of his face.

The footsteps retreated. Everyone remained silent. They heard another manhole cover fall into place. Paddy relit the lamp.

"Now who was that?" she wondered aloud.

They continued their plans in nervous whispers. Hyperon would front the ransom money. Lovely, who had no prior dealings with Specter, would make a casual visit to his office and leave a note with the secretary. In the meantime, Saul, Pastor, Marv, and Hyperon would work on repairing the damage done to Rocky's home. Paddy, with Bene's help, would repair what she could of the poor woman's soul. Prudence would keep her ears open at school and see if she heard anything of interest. All of them would seek Wisdom's Father.

Just before they parted, Hyperon brought forth the spyglass. He held it with an oven mitt now, even though it had never grown hot again like it had when it burnt his hand. He stood and held it out so they could all see it.

"Times seem discouraging," he said, "but Wisdom told me that to keep up my hope, I needed to keep my eyes fixed on her Father. She gave me this device with which to see Him. I want to share it with all of you[243]."

One by one, they drew near and put one eye up to the viewing glass. Some became silent and tearful. Others, like Paddy, let out whoops of joy, forgetting the danger that had passed not long before. All went away

---

[243] Jn. 16:13-15

changed by the good hope Hyperon spurred them to remember. Over all, the Father sat sovereign. He knew where Sparrow was. He knew Rocky's heart. And He knew each of them. With that, they left, steeled for the tasks Wisdom's Father had given them, that they might help bring about the joyful ending that would one day be theirs[244].

Hyperon watched Paddy enter her house as he fumbled with the doorknob of the bakery. Morning hovered nearby, and his thoughts turned toward his bed.

Just as the door swung open, a firm hand grasped his shoulder and shoved him through the opening. Hyperon spun to attack whoever was behind him.

"Wait, wait," came the gruff whisper.

Hyperon hesitated. Then he realized that it was Adam.

"You're lucky I didn't sock you," Hyperon said, putting his hand on Adam's shoulder. "What do you think you're doing sneaking around here?"

"Can we go up to your place?" Adam said, out of breath.

Hyperon debated with himself for a moment before turning and leading Adam up the stairs.

He lit the lamp in his apartment and sat on the couch. Adam paced nervously in front of him.

"Well, what is it?" Hyperon asked.

Adam held his hands out helplessly in front of him.

"I have the little girl," he said finally.

---

244 Jn. 16:33

Hyperon stood.

"Where is she?" he demanded.

"I left her in the alley outside," Adam said.

Hyperon had the door open and took the stairs two at a time as he rushed out the door again. His eyes adjusted quickly to the darkness of the alley.

"Sparrow?" he called quietly. It was only at that moment that he wondered if he'd walked into a trap. He glanced wildly around him, like an animal in a corner.

"Here I am," came her small voice.

Adam was behind him now.

"But wait, you didn't listen to my deal," he was saying.

Hyperon ignored him. He followed the little voice and knelt down by the kennel secreted between two dumpsters. Her smell hit him then, and he found it locked.

He whirled back to Adam, who stood behind him.

"Unlock it," he demanded.

"Not until you listen," Adam whined.

Hyperon took two steps toward him and grabbed his collar as he had done to DeCeit in the bakery.

"Unlock it, I said," he hissed between clenched teeth, "and we can talk later."

Adam wrenched himself free from Hyperon's grasp and removed a key from his pocket. He knelt down and opened the door. The little girl flew into Hyperon's arms. He lifted her effortlessly and ran to Paddy's.

He beat on the door with his foot. It didn't take her long to answer.

"Hyperon?" she wondered. "Oh my!" escaped her lips when she saw Sparrow.

"Oh, child," she crooned as she took the tiny bundle from his arms. "Come with me now. You're safe. You're safe." Sparrow's sobs seemed to ebb out of Hyperon's own soul.

"Lock your door, Paddy," Hyperon said. "I will come for you at opening time."

All Paddy said was, "Sure," as the door closed on the pair.

Hyperon turned to Adam and motioned him to follow. Soon, they were back in the apartment. Hyperon had no appetite, and Adam asked for nothing. So, they sat without food or drink at the table.

"I was not supposed to bring her here," Adam said, "but I knew how much you cared about her."

"You kept her like an animal," Hyperon said, raking his hands through his hair. "How could you treat another human being that way?"

Adam shrugged.

"She's just a child. She might not even remember it by tomorrow," he reasoned.

Hyperon seethed.

"What happened to giving a voice to the voiceless? For making sure everyone gets their due? Some cause, huh?" Hyperon demanded.

"Anyway, you must promise not to tell anyone that I brought her," Adam said, "or I will tell Specter all I know about the Underground."

Hyperon stared intently at Adam.

"What do you know?" he asked in a half-whisper.

"Names, place, dates, and times," Adam said. "She even sang me this baby's lullaby about Wisdom having a father. Its simplicity made me question if you could really believe all this, Hyperon[245]."

"I'd rather believe what seems foolish to you than do what is despicable," Hyperon said.

"I do what I have to," Adam replied.

"What did they want with the girl?" Hyperon questioned.

"How should I know?" came the reply. "Did Specter ever tell us the whys? Doesn't he rather give orders and keep his motives to himself? Seemed ready to do away with her."

Hyperon studied him. "There is no truth or justice on your side, Adam. You must change sides," Hyperon counseled.

Adam shook his head. "I can't change sides yet," he said simply. "I have a signed contract with Mr. Specter."

"Well, what will you tell him?" Hyperon asked.

"That you came for her," Adam replied.

Hyperon shook his head.

"I thought you wanted to learn more about Wisdom," he said.

"I do," Adam said. "Can't you see that I'm trying to help you?"

Hyperon silently studied his hands.

"I have to go," Adam said. "Just watch your back."

---

[245] 1 Cor. 3:18-20

Hyperon said nothing as Adam let himself out. An hour went by as he pondered Adam's words and what course of action he should take. Of course, his pondering finally rested on Wisdom. He would build her house, and he would rebuild Rocky's. Wisdom would care for Bene and Sparrow, and so that's what he would do. And he'd keep his eye out for Specter.

He knocked at Paddy's later. She let him in and led him to a back room where a bathed Sparrow lay asleep on a down mattress with a white quilt wrapped around her. The wet tendrils of her nut brown hair clung to her face. He reached out and lightly pushed them away.

Paddy motioned him to follow her to the outer room.

"Look what happens when we ask Wisdom's Father," Paddy said. Then she questioned, "Why did they bring her now?"

"They know about the underground meetings from her, Paddy," Hyperon said. "I'm not sure what they've done to her, but she told them everything. We have to get word to the others that it isn't safe to meet there anymore."

Paddy pursed her lips and nodded.

"We can get Prudence to help spread the word," she said.

"I'll go to visit Marv and Obedience, and then see if I can talk to Rocky before the bakery opens in a bit," Hyperon said, "but don't you go anywhere. Don't let anyone in here for any reason, Paddy."

"All right," she agreed.

"I will be back as soon as I can," he promised.

“May Wisdom go with you,” she said.

He rested his hand lightly over his heart. “She does.”

Chapter 41

Obedience let him in right away, even though it was obvious that she and Marv had both been asleep.

"Sparrow is safe at Paddy's," he told them, declining to sit down or even come too far into the house.

"Thank the Father!" Obedience said, hugging Marv.

"But Specter knows everything about the underground. He was even able to learn all of our names from her," Hyperon told them.

Marv nodded. "We'll need to be careful," he said.

Hyperon nodded.

"I'm off to Rocky's," he said, with his hand on the doorknob. "We have to let everyone know that it isn't safe to meet there anymore. Perhaps the Lady will think of another place."

"Yes," Obedience said, "she always does."

To his surprise, Rocky's door swung open before he even knocked.

Bene stood there.

"Heard you comin'," the boy said.

"You didn't know it was me," Hyperon chastised lightly. "You've got to be careful."

Bene grinned.

"Oh," he shrugged, "your steps are that of an honest man. You don't skulk or tread lightly like someone who's got something to hide or a fight to pick."

"Where's your mom?" Hyperon demanded.

"Sleeping," came the reply.

Hyperon followed the boy into the house, and pain filled him at the sight. He barely recognized the dining room or kitchen. It had been clean and proper when he had been here under Specter's employ, and it had angered him. Now, looking at the filth and unkemptness of it all, his sorrow outweighed the indignation he felt then.

"I found Sparrow," Hyperon told the boy. "We've got to get your mom out of here in case they come looking for her."

The boy turned away and leaned against the wall. Hyperon's confusion melted as he saw the young shoulders shake beneath the sobs.

"She's okay," he comforted. "She's had a rough time, but when I left her, she was bathed and sleeping at Paddy's."

The boy wiped at his eyes.

"It's not that," he said. "It's just that….mom, she….she won't even know to be happy about it."

The sobs continued. A new curiosity about Rocky's condition led Hyperon down the hall to the bedrooms. The first one he peeked in was clearly the boy's. He crossed the hall and pushed another door open.

The unmade bed was unoccupied. Trash littered the floor. The TV was on and turned up loud. Hyperon scanned the room. There, just on the other side of the bed, he saw her arm.

He walked carefully, attempting not to step on the cans and bags strewn across the floor. She was passed out, and in her hand she held an empty bottle of sleeping pills.

He knelt beside her and took in the resemblance to Sparrow's sleeping form- the same nut brown hair, the same eyelashes. But Rocky's sleep was far from natural.

Hyperon heard Bene sniffle in the doorway behind him.

"How long has she been like this?" he asked the boy.

Bene shrugged. "A week," he replied. "I can't even get her up to eat or anything. I got her pajamas on her, and I tried to give her some water."

Hyperon stood and lifted her in his arms. She was still alive.

"Well, we can't leave her here," he told Bene.

"Where can we take her? We can't just walk down the street carrying her like that," Bene protested.

"I'll hire a cab," Hyperon said.

Hyperon carried Rocky down the block and turned left to reach a main street. He set her feet down and supported her with one arm while he hailed a cab with his other. Bene trotted behind him, carrying Rocky's worn out shoes.

Thankfully, the cabbie didn't act as if an unconscious woman in his car concerned him, and they arrived at Paddy's without incident. Bene knocked on the door.

"Paddy, it's me," Hyperon called.

He heard her sliding the lock from the other side.

"What's happened?" she demanded as soon as she saw Rocky.

"Sleeping pills," Hyperon answered, pushing past her.

"Set her on my bed," Paddy was saying from behind him.

After Paddy and Hyperon got Rocky situated, Paddy asked, "Now where did that Bene go?"

They left the room in search of him and found him sitting beside the sleeping Sparrow.

He showed no emotion now, just stroked his sister's hand.

"You're going to stay with me, now, son," Paddy said.

"You ain't got the money for that, Paddy," he told her.

"We'll make it work," she said.

Hyperon approached and set his hand on the boy's shoulder.

"I'll help too," Hyperon told him, "and since Paddy will be busy here with Sparrow and your mom, you could pitch in by helping in the bakery after school."

Bene never took his eyes from Sparrow's face. He was quiet for a moment.

"All right," he said finally. "We'll stay if I can pay our way."

Hyperon nodded. "It never hurts to receive kindness either," he said. "Paddy's kindness to me- even when I would have stolen from her- helped me to know Wisdom."

Bene's attention snapped to Hyperon.

"You would have stolen from her?" he asked incredulously.

"I would have, if she'd let me, but instead, she packed up more than I would have taken in a bag and gave it to me with a blessing," Hyperon smiled.

Bene looked at Paddy.

"That was Wisdom working in you," he said.

Paddy nodded, "Mmhhmm."

"And to think, Hyperon, now you are Wisdom's man," Bene said.

Hyperon was glad that the boy's attention had turned back to his sister, for a lump formed in his throat and tears sprung to his eyes. Wisdom's man, indeed. He'd come a long way from the half-breed, half-starved, evil man that he had been. Because of Wisdom, he had no desire to go back. But he still had a long way to go to ever be worthy of her. He marveled that she had chosen him even when he was not worthy.

"Cameron will be wanting his swamp muffin," Hyperon said quietly. "I'll open up the bakery."

Chapter 42

Adam went directly to Specter.

"They came for the girl, sir," he began.

Specter's nonchalance fell away for a moment, and he stared across the desk at Adam.

"You let them take her?" was his first cautious question.

"I'd heard what they did to DeCeit," Adam said. "I don't want any part of that."

"That was a freak chance," Specter said dismissively. "They have no real power. Well, who was it?"

"Hyperon," Adam said.

Specter drummed his fingertips on the desk.

"I learned something from the girl before they took her," Adam said.

Specter raised his eyebrows.

Adam proceeded to tell him all that he'd learned about the underground meetings.

Silence ensued after he'd finished, and a gnawing feeling ate at Adam's stomach.

"And what would you say their next move would be, Adam?" Specter asked sweetly.

Panic rose in Adam as he scrambled to think of a response.

"Think for a moment," Specter said, "and you will realize what it is."

"They will meet together to, um, talk about what they will, uh, do next?" Adam stuttered.

"Half right," Specter said, swiveling in his chair and standing up. "They will find a new place to meet and then they will discuss what to do next."

"They wouldn't necessarily look for a new place," Adam contradicted.

Specter slammed his fist on the desk. "The girl will tell them all she told," Specter said through a wicked smile.

Adam began to nod slowly. He hadn't thought of that.

"And you will build them a place to meet," Specter instructed.

"Me?" Adam whined. Building a place sounded like a lot of work.

"I don't know how," he protested. "It would be hard, long work. I'm not used to that. These people don't need our charity… your charity. They could rather give you something."

Specter chuckled.

"My dear boy," he said, "I will take all that they have. And I didn't say you'd have to build it with your own two hands. All of my resources are at your disposal. I'm sure you can find some laborers."

Adam's panic settled within him. He smiled. Of course, he'd hire other people to do the work for him.

"But how will I persuade them to meet in my building? I mean, why wouldn't they just meet somewhere else? They've avoided buildings in the past to stay under the radar of detection," Adam wondered.

"Make it worth their while," Specter grinned.

As Adam stood to leave, Specter stopped him.

"One more thing," Specter said. "Try again to make friends with Rocky, the girl's mother."

Adam nodded, put his hat on his head, and walked out.

Prudence hurried to the alley after school. She had a few other visits she was supposed to make for Hyperon and didn't want to be too late getting home.

The alley looked dark and abandoned, even in the sunny afternoon. The dumpster was empty. Prudence kicked an empty can and walked further back.

The little children were sleeping in one another's arms, covered with an old curtain. She smiled at them.

Quick footsteps made her whirl around.

"Why do you always come here?" Haste's voice asked.

Prudence wondered why he would bother to follow her. She hoped he wouldn't learn about the Shadow Children. She couldn't bear for them to be tormented, so she walked toward Haste, trying to keep him from being able to see the sleeping forms in the dark end of the alley.

"What are you doing here?" she asked.

He shrugged. "I'm supposed to follow you," he said.

He ran up to her and shoved her. Prudence stumbled back a few steps but didn't fall. Haste looked past her, but his eyes glanced over the children.

She hoped his loud voice wouldn't awaken or startle them.

"It's none of your business where I go," she said.

"Oooo," he taunted, "tart! I won't have any sass. What do you have in your bag?"

He shoved her again and tried to take her bag. She clung to it but said nothing.

All of a sudden, his eyes focused on something behind her. She tried to turn and warn the boys, but he was holding onto her shoulder. His grip relaxed, however, and he let go as he stepped away from her. He backpedalled toward the street opening of the alley, and finally, turned and ran away at full speed.

She turned to see what had frightened him and saw the Lady. She smiled at Prudence. Then, she bent and woke the sleepers.

"Hello," the Lady said to them. "Wake up now. I have something for you to do."

It was Prudence's turn to smile. She knew what it was like to be given a task by the Lady. The children sat up and rubbed their eyes. The younger one stood immediately and held her arms up to be held by the Lady. She stooped and picked her up.

"Did you know about Sparrow?" Prudence asked.

"Yes," the Lady said.

"Did you know that we can't meet in your secret place anymore?" Prudence asked.

"Yes," the Lady said, smiling at the little girl in her arms.

"What do you think we should do?" Prudence asked. Even in her perplexity, she still smiled watching the Lady with the two unkempt babies. Now, the older boy was standing and holding onto the Lady's hand.

"Trust," the Lady said, "like a little child."

Prudence smiled. "What are their names?" she asked.

The Lady smiled wider. "Truth and Justice[246]."

---

[246] Ps. 111:7-9; Ps. 45:4; Ps. 89:14; Zech. 8:16-17

Chapter 43

Saul clapped Hyperon on the back as they surveyed the new kitchen cabinets.

"I've been doing this all my life, but you have already surpassed my skill," he said admiringly.

Hyperon smiled.

"We did it together. I couldn't have learned so quickly if you hadn't helped me," he said.

Marv and Pastor walked past, carrying out the bags of trash and an irreparable coffee table. Their evening work was starting to make a difference in Rocky's home. Hyperon hoped it would be even nicer than before he had helped to destroy it.

When Marv came back in, he whistled.

"This is fine work. Did you do this kind of carpentry in the villages?" Marv asked Hyperon.

"No," Hyperon had never even seen fine woodworking in the villages.

The four men stood in silence.

"I finished the dining room table, and all we have left is the back rooms," Hyperon said.

"The table sure is a nice one. You've never made one before?" Pastor asked.

"No," Hyperon answered. Pastor whistled.

Saul nodded. "Hyperon has learned more quickly than anyone I ever saw," he said.

Marv smiled. "The Lady helps him," he said.

Hyperon locked up after the others left one by one out the back door. Specter's men were surely keeping a close eye on the place, but Hyperon hadn't noticed any sign of them.

He tossed his hammer up and caught it again with a smile. He would sleep well this night.

He walked down the sidewalk toward the busy street, but before he could make the right hand turn toward the downtown and the bakery, a movement in the shadow caught his eye.

He looked, but he couldn't see anything distinctly. He turned his back and began to walk. A car drove by. A dog barked.

Suddenly, he heard the soft padding of hurried footsteps, and before he could whirl around, something had grabbed the back of his shirt. He raised the hammer to strike whoever it was, but he hesitated.

The grey eyes of a filthy child looked up at him imploringly. The child's hair was matted, and the one shirt he wore was like a tattered robe over the slender frame.

Hyperon swallowed in a vain attempt to control his rapid breathing and heart rate.

The child pulled at his shirt, but it was the opposite way than he had intended to go.

"I'm going this way," Hyperon said.

The child- he thought it was a boy- shook his head, pulled Hyperon's shirt again, and pointed in the direction of the city wall. Hyperon gazed down the street. He knew that Specter employed children. Was this one to be trusted? He had a vain, momentary wish for the lost compass.

He turned toward the child and cast one look back at the city. He would have to wait a little longer for sleep.

The child smiled and clapped its hands when he turned to follow.

The houses became sparser. Cars didn't travel this far from the city. In fact, Hyperon was surprised when the pavement gave way to gravel. Then, the gravel gave way to a dirt path. Hyperon noticed that the child was barefooted. Still the child led to the city wall. It loomed tall and black on the horizon. Hyperon had come through one gate. He had met Wisdom near the other. He had never heard if there were other openings or if people sometimes tried to scale the walls.

"Who are you?" Hyperon asked quietly.

The child turned back to him only long enough to nod and smile and then continued at an even quicker pace. Hyperon lengthened his strides. He scanned the shadows for enemies.

There were no houses now. The grass was tall. The smell of it hit him all at once, and tears sprang to his eyes. The path they followed ran right along the edge of the wall. There were no lights, but the distant glow of the city illuminated their steps, even while it darkened the starlight.

Suddenly, the child stopped. Hyperon almost bumped into him.

There, fixed to the city wall, was an advertisement. The boy pointed to it.

"Land for sale. Inquire at --," and it listed an address.

Hyperon read it twice. He looked at the boy.

"Why do I need land?" he asked.

The boy pointed at the hammer.

Hyperon studied the hammer.

Flashes of pictures came to him: Prudence, the underground, Wisdom's song, the carving of Wisdom's house, Paddy laughing, and the oil lamp going out.

This land would make a beautiful place for Wisdom's house, and once he built the house, he could help her people meet together without fear. Specter had never sent any of his men this far from the city, at least not that Hyperon knew of.

The soft padding of the boy's footsteps made Hyperon look back at him. He was running away.

"Wait!" Hyperon called. In answer, the boy only laughed and kept running.

Hyperon looked back at the sign and memorized the address. He would work to build a house for Wisdom.

The bakery was busy the next morning, so he didn't look up when he heard the bell above the door announcing a new customer. However, when he heard the shattering of glass as the door slammed, he knew who he would see when he looked up.

Horbah stood there, absently looking down at the piles of glass that had just been knocked out of the door. All of the other customers stared in silence. Hyperon reached for the broom and dustpan.

The hum of conversation resumed as he knelt and began sweeping up the particles of glass. Horbah didn't move but stood in the doorway watching him.

"They just don't make doors like they used to," he said.

Hyperon looked up at him.

"What do you want?" Hyperon wanted him to leave.

Horbah shrugged. "A muffin. Isn't this a bakery?"

Hyperon nodded and carried the first dustpan of glass to the trash can. He dumped it and kept sweeping while the line at the counter grew longer. Horbah meandered to the back of the line.

Hyperon finished sweeping up most of the glass and returned to the counter. He helped three people, and then noticed that Lovely was next. She ordered a chocolate muffin, and he wanted to ask how her visit to Specter's office had gone, but he didn't. She half-smiled, and he hoped she understood that it wasn't safe to talk.

Horbah was next, and he only ordered a glass of water. Hyperon filled a Styrofoam cup and handed it to him[247].

"I need to ask you some questions," Horbah said.

All of Hyperon's rage about Sparrow's kidnapping bubbled just beneath the surface of his cool exterior, but he said, "You'll have to wait a minute until I serve the rest of the line. Why don't you sit over there[248]?"

Hyperon pointed to a padded booth. He hoped it was more indestructible than the door.

Horbah took his seat, but his Styrofoam cup sprang a leak. Hyperon ran another to him and returned to the counter[249].

---

247 Rom. 12:16-21
248 Deut. 32:35
249 Josh. 6:21

Obedience came in with Prudence. Hyperon shook his head slightly, and Obedience's smile faded. Prudence continued to smile, but said to her mother, "Oh, they must be out of sparkleberry muffins today."

Hyperon almost laughed.

When he had served the line, he walked to Horbah's booth, but he didn't sit down. He brought the broom so that he could continue sweeping up any glass he had missed, but also so he would have a weapon should he need one. The sword hilt was in his apartment.

"Isn't it ironic that you don't trust me even though you trained me?" Horbah had a self-satisfied smile.

Hyperon didn't trust himself to answer.

"You used to be the best of the best, the epitome of the rags to riches story," Horbah said.

Hyperon kept sweeping.

"You were the mixed-blood poster boy for Mr. Specter's program. He could take even you and make you a mastermind at working the system," Horbah continued.

Hyperon's mind flashed back to the work he had done with Marv, Saul, and Pastor the night before. Wisdom's people rarely mentioned his heritage now, but Specter's people always did. Folly had. Adam had. Horbah had. They wanted him to feel like a spat upon victim.

He said nothing.

Hyperon sipped his water and looked at Hyperon over the rim of his cup.

"I need to know if Adam has been here," he said finally.

Adam came every day. Hyperon distrusted him as much as ever, and silently raged at Adam for his inhumane treatment of Sparrow, but he talked to Adam about Wisdom. He wanted Adam to know her and to be changed by her.

It wouldn't do for Horbah to know that Adam was coming.

So, Hyperon still didn't answer[250].

"What? Have they made you such a stupid fool that you've forgotten how to talk?" Horbah said.

Hyperon stopped and looked at him. "Talk can't help you or answer your questions," Hyperon said.

Horbah rolled his eyes and crumpled the Styrofoam cup in his hand. Water ran out onto the table and floor. Horbah didn't seem to notice that it dripped onto his pants and shoes. He stood up.

"Tell me if that fool has been here[251]," Horbah demanded.

Hyperon didn't back away but stood his ground.

"The only fools that frequent here are the ones who stay in Specter's employ[252]," Hyperon said calmly.

The other customers were staring now.

"Well," Horbah seemed to reconsider bodily harm to Hyperon, "there's more than one way to skin a cat."

He stormed back out the door, but there was no more glass to break. Hyperon sighed.

Bene came in soon after.

---

250 Prov. 17:28
251 Prov. 19:3
252 Prov. 26:11

"What happened?" he asked, pulling the door open cautiously.

"One of Specter's men," Hyperon told him.

Bene nodded solemnly.

They worked together through the supper hour. Hyperon sent Bene to tell Paddy about the door, and she sent word back that she would order a new one. Bene told Hyperon that his mom and sister were doing fine.

Just as he was preparing to nail a board over the door and clean up, Hyperon saw Adam ambling up the sidewalk. He waved to Hyperon, and Hyperon opened the door for him.

Bene scowled from where he was sweeping behind the counter. Hyperon crossed to him and led him to the kitchen while Adam took off his coat and sat at one of the booths.

"Why don't you clean up the kitchen while we talk?" Hyperon suggested to the boy.

The boy's shoulders slumped, and Hyperon could tell he was fighting for control.

"It's okay, son," Hyperon said. "I'll be over to Paddy's in just a bit."

"I won't let you go back," Bene said. "You're Wisdom's man now. You can't go back to being what you were."

Hyperon raised his eyebrows in surprise.

"I wouldn't consider it, Bene," Hyperon said. "I would rather be killed than deny Wisdom."

The boy nodded. "But then, why are you talking with him?"

Hyperon replayed that awful night at Rocky's house when he had helped to make this boy's life a nightmare. Bene still feared Adam.

"If I could change, I have to believe that he could too," Hyperon said.

The boy looked away.

"Yeah," he said. "I guess so. I'll clean up in here."

Hyperon put a hand on his shoulder.

"That's it," he said. "I'll be over soon." Bene nodded.

Adam waited at the corner booth where he had once sat with DeCeit. Hyperon thought about the sword hilt as he walked toward Adam. He didn't need that kind of weapon with Adam.

"I have an idea," Adam was saying.

Hyperon sat down across from him and leaned back, slouching against the booth cushion.

"Horbah was here today," Hyperon said.

Adam raised his eyebrows. "No wonder the door is busted," he said.

"He was asking about you," Hyperon added.

Adam studied his hands.

"I think Mr. Specter is worried about me," Adam said.

Hyperon nodded and rested his chin on his hands.

"So, what's your grand idea?" Hyperon asked.

"You have to meet somewhere, and I just found a piece of property by the city gate. No one would suspect you there, and I have some friends who could build a nice little house for meeting in. It would still be secret, and it's out of the hustle and bustle." Adam's excitement found release in the torrent of words.

Hyperon's attention was arrested.

"On the west side of town?" he asked.

"Yeah," Adam replied. "It's the perfect set up. No more hiding in other people's waste. It's clean and pretty there- you would like it."

Hyperon already knew he liked it there.

"Have you already spoken with the owner?" he asked carefully.

"No," Adam admitted, "I wanted to talk to you about it first."

Hyperon studied his hands.

"Why would you do this, Adam?" Hyperon asked forthrightly.

"After listening to you talk, I've decided that the way to get to know Wisdom is to get to know her people," Adam shrugged. "It's the least I can do for hurting them."

After Adam left, Hyperon rushed through his cleaning and went to Paddy's. Paddy's laugh floated out to him as he entered the back door. The two children sat with her over a game at the dining room table.

"You keep playing," Paddy told them, "while I give Hyperon his marching orders."

Sparrow giggled.

"Hyperon doesn't march, Paddy," she said. "He shlumps because he's so tall."

Bene laughed too, so Hyperon 'shlumped' over to the table and back to Paddy again. They all laughed uproariously.

The children were still chuckling when he and Paddy went into a back room. He told her about Adam's offer.

"I wouldn't trust him farther than I could throw him. You need to buy your place soon," Paddy agreed, "but I've got some news for you."

He listened.

"Rocky left," she said.

"What?" he asked. "Where did she go?"

"She didn't tell me where she was going, just said she didn't feel safe here[253]," Paddy related. "I tried every way I knew of to stop her, but she was determined. She is letting her hurt blind her. I haven't told the children yet. She didn't want them to know."

"I'm going to her house to work tonight," he said. "Maybe she'll be there."

"She has no other place to go," Paddy agreed. She put her calloused hand on Hyperon's shoulder. "What a different man you've become! Instead of sacrificing people for some false ideal, you're setting aside all your ideals to show love to people. That's wise," she smiled. "I wish I could help you build your house while you're off building for others."

He grew embarrassed.

"You've done more for me than I could ever do for the others," he told her.

"Oh posh," she said, swatting at him with the towel she was holding. "Off with you, now."

He hurried to Rocky's and found the woman sitting at the mended dining room table.

---

[253] Mt. 13:5, 20-21

"Why did you do this for me?" she asked without turning toward him. Her voice was flat, broken.

"Wisdom's work heals Specter's hurts," he told her. "I needed to make amends."

"What a joke," she said. "Nothing can make up for my pain."

Hyperon decided not to address her bitterness[254].

"I still have to finish the back rooms," he told her, "and then I'll work on the roof a bit."

"Why bother? It all gets ruined."

He fought the temptation to be angry with her.

"Rocky," he said, moving in front of her to make eye contact, "you have a safe, stable place at Paddy's. Why not stay there?"

She stood up shaking with rage. He could see that she was pale and drawn. She measured out her words between lips tightened by anger.

"Why trust you? Why trust anyone? I tried that. I trusted Specter. I trusted Wisdom. I trusted you. I'm done with disappointment. Done with trust. From now on, I'll just listen to my heart," she ranted. "I'll live each moment. I'll make my own life the way I want it[255]."

He stared at her. One question surfaced above all the others.

"When did Wisdom disappoint you?" he asked softly.

Rocky laughed bitterly. "Did she keep my child from brutal kidnapping and who knows what else? How

---

[254] Prov. 15:1

[255] Prov. 28:26

do I know she won't allow worse to happen in the future? You'll see when it happens to you."

"Surely you can't say that Wisdom is responsible for Specter's actions," he pointed out, "and Wisdom saved your child."

"If she's so good and powerful, she could stop Specter," Rocky argued, "and *you* saved my child."

"Not without Wisdom," he said. "Besides, she was brought to me."

"Who brought her?" This was news to Rocky.

"Adam."

Rocky leaned back in her seat.

"Then maybe I should trust him," she said.

"I thought you were done with trust, and here you are ready to trust this guy willy-nilly," Hyperon's anger threatened, "when he's the same one who destroyed what you had!" He swallowed it and crossed the room to sit beside her.

She turned her back to him. "You destroyed what I had!"

Silence hung between them. Echoes of her angry slur returned to his mind, but instead of making him angry, he had the dawning awareness that she still needed to know Wisdom. She hadn't really met the Lady at all. Rocky had only come close through hearing other people's stories. The ache he had for her grew as he contemplated her poverty- living without the Lady was lonely and bleak, and he knew that better than most.

"Listen, why don't you come back to Paddy's until you get this all figured out," he said. "It's safer for you there. Wisdom is offering you the safe solution this time. You'd be a fool not to take it."

She reached out and slapped him. He fought the urge to react.

"You're the fool! Leave my house," she demanded, "and don't come back."

He stood, suddenly very tired.

"Come with me," he pleaded once more.

"I don't need you, or anyone," she spat.

"What about the kids?" he asked.

At this, she hesitated. "I hope they have more opportunity to trust than I ever had. Keep them. I just need some time for myself."

He nodded and turned toward the door.

"It's never too late," he told her. "Even in the middle of the night, Paddy will let you in."

He turned west out of her driveway and let the starlight guide him to the grassy place by the city wall. All the way out of the city, Hyperon thought of the way Rocky had once defied Specter and fixed up her house. He remembered her refusal to accept the cheap imitations of justice and charity that Specter offered. He remembered the whispered name, Wisdom's name, as he had first heard it from her bloodied lips. He had hated and admired her then, even though he hadn't understood. Adam had told him about Wisdom because of the things Rocky had done. His frustration mounted as he asked himself what he could have done to help her. How could he show her that Wisdom could still be trusted?

It was midnight when he reached the spot. He sat down on a tree stump beside the road and stared into the darkness that rested over the land. He could still hear the distant hustle of the city- even at night- and the glow of street lights was visible. But just above him, one bright star blinked. The trees swayed in the wind. He laid his hammer across his knees and inhaled deeply.

Suddenly, there were footsteps shuffling along the road. Hyperon strained his eyes in the darkness. They were slow footsteps, not the quick padding footsteps of the child. He thought briefly about Specter. This would be just the place he'd be most vulnerable. At least he had the hammer.

The form coming through the darkness was small and limping. As his eyes adjusted, he beheld the form of an old woman.

He rose from where he sat and approached her.

"You certainly are out late, mother," he said. "Can I help you back to the city where you'll be safe?"

"What does it mean to be safe, my son[256]?" asked her creaking voice.

He smiled. "I guess it means to be near help," he said.

The hood nodded.

"Safe doesn't mean the absence of danger then[257]?" she questioned.

"I suppose not, if help is at hand," he replied, taking her elbow. She hobbled beside him.

"One who had help at hand would always be safe," she said.

He nodded, perplexed.

She laughed then, and he knew her.

---

[256] Ps. 3

[257] Ps. 23:5

"Wisdom," he said breathlessly, and the old woman faded to reveal Wisdom in her scarlet cloak. Now, Hyperon was laughing, and he embraced her.

He tried to take her in all at once- the sight and smell of her, the sound of her laughter- and found that he was overwhelmed. But he also found that the heaviness of his former thoughts was gone.

"This is a beautiful spot," she said.

"Do you like it?" he wondered. He was eager to please her.

"Certainly," she said. "You have done well, Hyperon."

"I often feel that I would do better with you by my side," he said. "I've even looked for you where I saw you at first, but I never find you there." He wanted to tell her everything that had happened since he had last seen her, and his words tumbled over one another.

"Now that I am yours, you might not see me," she said. "I go with you through the city, to Rocky's house, at Paddy's. I live through you. You have help always at hand[258]."

"It is so much better to see you," he confessed.

She squeezed his hand and led him to sit back on the tree stump. She settled down close beside him.

"I am more hurt over Rocky's rejection than you can know," Wisdom said, "and so, I wanted to comfort you in your grief. Also, I wanted to tell you about the hedge[259]."

He laughed.

---

258 1 Jn. 4:9-21

259 Job 1:10

"Does the landscaping matter more than the house?" he asked.

She laughed too.

"Not that kind of hedge," she said.

He listened intently while staring into her eyes. She was beautiful, perhaps more beautiful than she had been the last time he had seen her.

"I will be your hedge of protection," she told him. "I live through you, but I will also guard you during what is to come."

"Will it be difficult?" he asked.

"Terribly difficult," she said with gravity.

"But you will protect me?" he asked.

"I may not protect you from harm," she admitted, "but I will protect you from being snatched out of my hand."

"If I am in your hand, then what harm can befall me?" he asked.

"Perhaps physical harm, but that will be all," she said. "There is nothing further they can do to you[260]."

"Thank you for telling me this," he said. "I think I can do whatever you give me to do if you are my hedge[261]."

She kissed him then.

"One day, we will meet never to part," she said.

"I live for that day," he said.

"As do I."

---

260 Lk. 12:4

261 Phil. 4:13

She was gone. Her words still hung on the breeze, and her scent lingered around him. He went home and slept soundly.

Chapter 44

Adam strode confidently on the familiar walkway. This assignment from Specter would be a breeze, and possibly pleasurable to him as well. He raised his fist and knocked on the front door.

"Who is it?" came the muffled voice.

"Adam," he said honestly.

To his surprise, she unlocked the door and swung it open. Rocky seemed thinner than he remembered, but she wore a low cut shirt that reminded him of Folly.

"Adam," she said pleasantly, "come in. I have some things I'd like to discuss with you."

He walked past her into the dining room. The floors and table were patched and attractive again. He wondered if it was Hyperon's work or Rocky's.

"Have a seat while I get us some cold drinks," she was saying. He watched her as she entered the kitchen. She was an attractive woman. No wonder Specter used so much of his resources on her.

She returned carrying two beers. She sat next to him and crossed her legs.

"Hyperon tells me that you rescued my little girl," she began.

Adam thought back to what he had done to the little girl, the form of her sobbing, lying in her own waste. Rescue seemed a bit much.

"Why, yes," he said, "though I don't like to mention it. It was something anyone with a heart would do."

"Well, I wanted to thank you," she said, sipping from her bottle.

"It must have been terrible for you while she was missing," he said solicitously, placing his hand over hers that lay on the table.

"It was," she said, "and Wisdom did nothing[262]."

He duly noted the bitterness in her voice.

"I've been trying to learn as much as I can about Wisdom," he said, "and I'm still confused. Anytime I see her out and about, I can't hear a thing she's saying."

Rocky shook her head. "Even if you could hear her, you'd drown out her words," Rocky said. "I wish I had."

"It hurts to be betrayed," he agreed. This was going to be easier than he thought.

She nodded. Silence hung between them for a time.

"Where are your children now?" he asked. He'd seen the boy in the bakery and wondered if they were still staying at the home of the bakery owner.

"It's probably better for them if they stay at Paddy's," she admitted. "I need time to myself to sort this out."

"You're staying here alone, then?" he questioned.

"Yes," she replied.

He stood and walked to the sliding glass door that looked out into the alley behind her house.

"I don't know what I'm about," he said aloud. "I'd rather not work for Specter any more, but if I quit, he'll evict me from my place."

He paused for effect.

---

[262] Lam. 3:5-6

"And I'm not sure I'm ready to follow Wisdom either. It seems so mystical and surreal when Hyperon speaks of her, like a fairy tale," he said.

"That's exactly what I think, too," she consented.

"Hey," he said, "you and I should team up. Us against the world." He chuckled.

She smiled, but he noted that it did not reach her eyes.

"Sounds intriguing," she said, "and if you need a place in the meantime, you can stay here."

"Well, that's kind of you," he said, sitting back down to be closer to her.

"What will you do if you quit your job?" she asked.

"Well, I know some folks I can work with in the construction business," he said with a shrug. "In fact, I told Hyperon that our first job can be building a new place for you all to meet to talk about Wisdom."

Her eyes opened wide.

"I thought you weren't sure about her," she said, "and how did you know about the meetings?"

"Your little girl told me about them," he said, "and even though I don't want to commit personally to being a Wisdom follower, I can still be a philanthropist. Most of her people are good folks who mean well."

Rocky sat silently, rolling her empty bottle in her hands. Adam wondered if she believed all that he told her. On the surface, she seemed like the skeptical sort. However, deep down, he felt that if he played his cards right, she would fall for him hook, line, and sinker.

"Perhaps I can help you," she said finally, "then I can see my kids enjoying meeting with the others again."

“That would be wonderful,” he agreed, “and I would get to see more of you.”

She smiled and looked away.

“It’s been a long time since anyone thought much of me,” she said.

“Then, you’re due,” he replied.

The sizzle of hot pan on skin brought Hyperon fully awake as he pulled the first batch of muffins from the oven. He howled and shook the injured hand in the air.

“I don’t think that will help,” Paddy said calmly as she entered the kitchen with Sparrow in tow.

Sparrow giggled. Hyperon smiled and held out his finger for her to kiss.

“You think this is funny?” he teased her. She stood on tiptoe and kissed the injury, giggling more.

“Think I’ll help you today,” Paddy said, tying on her apron, “and Sparrow wants to see what you’re doing in here all the time.”

“Maybe she’ll get a smile out of Cameron,” he said.

“Doubt it,” Paddy replied.

Hyperon poured more flour into a large mixing bowl. The delivery boy had been around even earlier that morning carrying the heavy bags of flour. Hyperon didn’t envy him his job. The flour made him think about the place where he had come from. He no longer thought of it as home, but he could remember the brown, waving wheat just before the harvest. He remembered walking along a field with his mother as she pulled heads of grain from the stalks and rubbed them in her hands to show him the kernels.

"See, Hyperon," she had said, "it's bread seeds. When you get enough of them together, you can grind them into flour and then bake it into bread[263]."

He smiled sadly as he remembered her. He wished he could introduce her to Wisdom.

"You're thinking so hard you've forgotten the yeast," Paddy said.

"Just thinking about this flour," he told her, "about all the wheat it takes to make one bag of flour."

"Isn't it funny that the wheat must die in order to give us life?" Paddy mused. "For we all need our daily bread[264]."

The picture of the wheat kernels resting in his mother's hand lingered in his mind's eye.

"If I close for you, you can go buy your land today," Paddy said. Her words startled him, and he stared at her a moment before understanding dawned.

"You've got yourself a deal," Hyperon said.

The address he had for the man selling the property turned out to be a residential place. It was in a long row of two-story homes that leaned on one another for support. Cars raced by on the busy street, and Hyperon climbed a few steps to knock at the door.

Cameron, wearing his familiar green cap, answered.

"It's you, is it?" he said unceremoniously. "Come in."

---

263 Jn. 12:24-26
264 Mt. 6:11

He turned and left the door agape, and Hyperon hesitated only a moment before following the man and closing the door. A tripod globe, a large vase, and a bronze peacock crowded the front hall. The smell of shoe polish and dill made his nose itch slightly.

"Are you the owner of that parcel of land, sir?" Hyperon asked.

"Well, isn't this the address from the letter you sent to inquire about it?" Cameron answered.

"Yes, but," Hyperon hesitated.

The old man gave a grisly smile. "But you didn't expect to find me here?" he suggested.

Hyperon shook his head and returned the smile.

The man led into a thickly carpeted room with mahogany panels on the wall below a chair rail. He sat in an overstuffed chair. "Truth is, this parcel belonged to my late wife," Cameron said with a sigh.

The man's gruff exterior melted as he spoke about his wife. Hyperon wondered why he had never thought to ask Cameron if he had any family. His kindness had been very shallow, it seemed.

"She loved that spot. Anyway, I heard that you are planning to build a house for the woman you love. Is that right?" Cameron asked, peering over the top of his spectacles.

Hyperon could only nod, dumbfounded.

"Well, I want to do this in memory of my wife," he said hurriedly. Hyperon thought he was avoiding the show of too much emotion.

"I have the papers right here," Cameron said. "All we have to do is sign." He led the way to a small, round kitchen table. A paper and pen were set neatly on top. Cameron picked up the pen and offered it to Hyperon.

Hyperon took the pen but lowered it to his side. "Meaning no disrespect, sir, but how did you learn of my plans? Why would you sell to me?"

"Because you have the money, boy," he replied, "and because the time to sell is when someone's buying. I have watched you at work. You are the one who should have the place."

Hyperon nodded slowly, raised the pen, and signed on the line.

Cameron signed and then held his hand out to shake Hyperon's. Hyperon shook it.

"I do have to tell you, son," Cameron said as they walked back to the front door, "I own the parcel next to this one and another young fella came asking to purchase it today. I have a mind to sell it to him, but I thought it'd be fair to give you some forewarning." The words were as gruff as ever, but Hyperon could now hear the kindness beneath.

Hyperon laughed, "Forewarning is good! It shouldn't interfere with my parcel, but thank you for the heads up."

Cameron handed Hyperon the deed, and Hyperon folded it and stuck it in the inner pocket of his jacket.

"You're a harder worker than the other guy, that's for sure," Cameron said. "I bet you get more return for your labor than he will. Hard work pays in the end."

"I plan to at least test that theory," Hyperon said. He started off down the steps and across the busy street. He was already drawing the plans for Wisdom's house in his mind.

Though the sun was setting, he went directly to the new purchase. He'd have a year or two of payment before it was completely his, but this was a start.

Hyperon studied the trees and paced off the section where he'd like to place the house. He calculated the square footage and the days until he'd be ready to pour concrete for the foundation. By the time he returned home, he fell into bed and slept the sound sleep of contentment.

Having a land deed in his hand made Adam stand tall as he walked down the street, away from the old man's home. The fact that he'd had to convince the old codger about his ability to work on the land didn't needle him now that it was his. He could do whatever he wanted. Even Specter would be second in command for this project.

If he played his cards right, Adam could manage to pull things together for himself for once. He could make a gradual break with Specter and set up his own business. Staying at Rocky's would allow him to save up the money he'd been spending on his own upkeep. He might help her some, but surely she wouldn't expect a lot.

He would need about five men to finish the construction in the amount of time he had. He would relish being the boss. Perhaps he'd pay Folly a visit and get the names of five likely candidates. In the meantime, he headed back to Rocky's.

Chapter 45

"Forty-seven, forty-eight, forty-nine, fifty," Obedience counted as Prudence skipped rope.

Prudence tripped on fifty, and set the rope down. She caught her breath and watched her mother shelling peas.

"I think you set a record that time," Obedience said.

Prudence nodded. "It's good that the Lady showed me how to tie my shoes. I've been a lot better since then," she said.

Prudence sat down by Obedience and grabbed a pea pod.

"No matter how good I get, I will always trip up at some point," Prudence said.

Obedience nodded with a smile. "That's true," she answered.

Prudence thought about Truth and Justice in the alley.

"Mother, I've been thinking about the end of the story," Prudence said.

Obedience's brows creased in concentration, and though her eyes were fixed on the peas in her lap, Prudence knew that her thoughts were fixed on the conversation.

"The Shepherd becomes king, the book says, and reigns forever with truth and justice," Prudence paused. "Do you think when the Shepherd is King that I will be able to go on and on skipping my rope without missing a step[265]?"

---

[265] Is. 25:8-9

Obedience thought for a moment.

"Yes," she said. "I think we will be able to go on and on doing the right things for as long as we want to do them."

Prudence used her thumb to strip the peas from the pod and put them in the bowl.

"Then, the Shepherd's sacrifice was worth it," Prudence said, thinking through the beloved story in the green book.

Obedience nodded, "Yes."

"I wish the Lady would tell us all she knows about the Shepherd and the sacrifice and the forever now," Prudence said wistfully.

Obedience laughed. "Shelling one pea at a time makes a meal eventually," she said, "and there's a lot to be learned in the process."

Prudence smiled. She focused on the pea in her hand and hoped to be like the Lady in each moment that came, even if some of her questions remained unanswered.

Chapter 46

Folly didn't have to call his name. She just smiled from her perch near her front door as Adam approached.

"Well, I thought you'd forgotten about me," she said.

He knew better. Her acting skills were superb.

"I need a favor," he said.

"Well, then, I'm your lady," she replied. "Come on in, and we'll talk."

The sparse interior never ceased to shock him. He remembered the trip he'd taken here, where the bar had been, all the bodies crammed in one small space. None of that was here now. Now, it was just the scarlet draped bed, the table with the bread and water, the black hallway in the back, cinnamon and clove covering that other elusive smell.

As she poured the icy water, Adam's mind involuntarily went to Hyperon's hand pouring rich, hot coffee into a mug. He pushed the thought away and focused on the business at hand.

"I need the names of five men who can do construction work," Adam got right to the point. "It's for Specter."

"Funny," she said, sitting down next to him, swinging her bare foot just above the floor, "he never mentioned it to me."

"Well, he mentioned it to me," Adam said.

"No need to get cranky," she pouted. "I'll give you the names. It'll be good for them."

She crossed the room and rummaged through a gilded box. It was full of wallets. Adam instinctively felt for his own. It was still in his pocket.

Folly picked up first one and then another, flipping glibly through the contents and tossing it back in the box again.

Finally, she chose a plain black leather wallet and said, "This is the one."

She came to the table where Adam sat.

"You need Malise Dipsuchos," she said.

Adam grunted, "That's a mouthful."

"He'll get your other four guys," Folly said. "He bosses a whole crew of likely fellows. They'll suit your purpose."

Folly opened the wallet and showed Adam the photo ID. Even from just the head shot, Adam could see that the man was short and stocky with thinning black hair. His lips protruded, and he did not smile.

"He's not a bad guy," Folly said, reflecting on the photograph. "I always like to see him come around."

"Where do I find him?" Adam asked. He knew better than to expect her to give up the wallet.

"He and his crew have been working on the south side of town. If you take the trolley to the lumberyard, you should find him," Folly explained, "but don't make them work so hard that they forget to come here to join the cause and have a little fun."

"I doubt that they'd forget," Adam said ruefully.

"Obviously you haven't," she said provocatively.

Adam thought it wouldn't hurt to stay awhile.

"I don't want to serve her," Bene said.

"Your reluctance to serve her shows that you're harboring bitterness, Bene. Bitterness is no good. Trust me; I know," Hyperon whispered to him in the kitchen.

The boy stood resolutely refusing to serve his mother who had come to the bakery for the first time in the month since she'd been gone.

"What kind of a mother deserts her own kids?" Bene whispered fiercely. "Just think of how poor Sparrow cries herself to sleep."

Hyperon nodded sadly.

"That hurts me too," he admitted, "but what kind of children hold back forgiveness from their mother, even an undeserving mother? She's been through a lot too, you know[266]."

The boy hung his head.

Paddy smiled from across the kitchen and nodded at Hyperon as if to say, "That used to be you!"

Bene took the bowl of hot soup and pushed through the door to the dining room of the bakery.

Hyperon followed him through the door but stopped at the counter to wait on another customer. Out of the corner of his eye, he watched as the young boy set the soup down in front of Rocky.

She looked as though she hadn't slept in days, but she'd tried to cover that up with dark eye makeup. Her clothing clung to her in a way that Hyperon had never seen her dress before. She'd lost weight.

But in that moment, as she looked up through the sheen of tears at her son, Rocky looked like the woman she had been when she stood against him in her own

---

[266] Mt. 7:12-14

home. She'd defended her children and followed Wisdom's way. How he longed to see her back on that path again!

Her lips were moving slightly. Bene bowed his head and reached for her hand. He raised his mother's hand to his lips and kissed it for all the world to see.

Hyperon's own tears threatened to spill over. If one could see forgiveness, he had just witnessed it[267].

Bene returned without looking at Hyperon and retreated to the kitchen. Rocky sat stirring her soup without eating it.

Customers ebbed, so Hyperon went to her table. He sat down as gingerly as if she'd been a bird.

"Hello," he said quietly.

She said nothing.

"I'd still like to work on your roof, if you're willing," he said.

She looked at him then. Her eyes seemed like dead seas- devoid of life.

"You're crazy," she said, "but I do need the help."

"I'll come this evening after work," he offered.

"What I really need is some groceries," she said.

He looked at her thin frame. "All right," he agreed.

"My boy seems well," she said, stirring her spoon around her soup bowl again.

"Both children worry for you," he ventured.

The bell above the door announced another customer.

---

[267] Mt. 6:14-15

"I'll come about seven," he told her. She simply nodded.

When he looked up, he saw that the customer was one of Specter's men. He wasn't sure of the man's name, but he'd seen him with Adam before.

The man ordered a coffee and sat down.

Lovely came in with Prudence. They were laughing together, and Hyperon thought of Wisdom. Her joy was so evident on their faces.

"How was school, Prudence?" he asked.

"I think the muffins are working," she said with a wink. He laughed.

As Lovely ordered a hot chocolate for each of them, she said quietly to Hyperon, "Specter's men hit Saul's house last night. He could use your hammer."

Hyperon nodded, but didn't venture a reply. He felt the eyes of Specter's man on him.

When he brought the steaming mugs to the table where the ladies were sitting, he had written on a napkin, "Tomorrow. 4:00."

She smiled and said, "Thank you."

Bene and Sparrow swept up the dining area after closing and Hyperon hurried through the dishes with Paddy.

"Why you in such a hurry?" she asked.

"I told Rocky I'd work on her roof tonight," he explained. "I want to get there before it is fully dark."

Paddy smiled.

"Also, would it be possible for Bene to work in my place tomorrow? Lovely said Saul's house got hit by Specter last night and he could use some help fixing things up," Hyperon said.

Paddy laughed.

"When are you going to build Wisdom's house?" she demanded.

"As soon as I can," Hyperon said, "but I can't just let these other things go. They need help."

"They sure do," Paddy said, "and who's paying for it?"

Hyperon shrugged.

Paddy dug deep into her apron pocket.

"Take the money from the bakery today," she said. He began to protest.

"Take it, I say!" she said seriously. "Why else would this place be called 'The Banquet Bakery' unless all were invited to partake[268]?"

It was his turn to smile.

"Paddy, why can't everyone see all that Wisdom does for her people? Why aren't they just coming out of the woodwork to belong to her?"

Paddy placed the roll of bills in his hand, and he pocketed it. Not so long ago, he would have been tempted to steal it and never return. There was no such temptation now.

"Was it easy for you?" Paddy asked him.

He remembered the struggle, the months of torment, the selfish pride, and the fear of Specter. He thought of Folly's wiles and Adam's pleadings.

"No," he said finally. "No, it wasn't easy. But it was worth it."

"Well, you live like She's worth it, and others will follow you over that difficult path. Perhaps because

---

268 Song of Sol. 2:4; Lk. 14:17

your footprints are there to step in, the way won't be as hard for others as it was for you."

Hyperon finished his dishes and made it to the hardware store in time to buy several bundles of shingles and some other roofing supplies. Then, he went to the grocery store and spent all but a few coins of the day's earnings. Hyperon hoped Saul's repairs wouldn't require too many additional materials. Maybe the older man would have some supplies on hand or get permission to use the cast offs from the job sites where he worked.

When he came up the walk at Rocky's, he noticed how the landscaping had fallen into disrepair again. How quickly it had happened! Someone was sitting on the front porch.

When he got close enough, he saw that it was Adam. Instinctively, he glanced over his shoulder to see if any of Specter's other men were around.

"It's just me," Adam said nonchalantly. "I'm living here."

Hyperon was stunned.

"But where's Rocky?" he asked.

"She's inside," Adam replied. Then, louder, he called, "Babe, someone's here!"

The door opened, and Rocky appeared in the same clothes he'd seen her in at the bakery.

Hyperon looked from Rocky to Adam. Awareness washed over him, and he felt he might drown in it.

"There's a ladder in the back," she said simply, offering no explanation.

Hyperon fought nausea. It wasn't jealousy, but he did care that she had joined herself to a man he knew to be dishonest. It could only increase Rocky's misery. He wondered if Adam was merely following Specter's orders.

Hyperon nodded, woodenly set the bags of groceries on the porch, and went to the back. He climbed the ladder with one load of shingles on his shoulder. The leaky parts of the roof were not extensive. He thought he could manage the job in a few hours. It would take longer than that to sort out what to do about Adam living with Rocky.

He worked long after darkness descended. If he finished her roof, he'd have time for Saul tomorrow and after that, Wisdom's house.

When he finally came down the ladder, hammer in hand, the roof was no longer leaky and Rocky sat alone on the front porch.

"It is finished[269]," Hyperon said.

"Great," she said, lacking enthusiasm.

"Where is Adam?" he asked.

"Sleeping," the simple reply.

Hyperon wished Wisdom was there to speak for him. He considered his options. He decided to speak the truth in love[270].

"I am afraid you will be hurt by Adam living here, Rocky," Hyperon said. "He works for Specter, and if you belong to Wisdom, you don't belong with him."

"He doesn't work for Specter anymore," she defended, "and you should mind your own business

---

[269] Jn. 19:30
[270] Eph. 4:15, 25-32

instead of passing judgment on me for living with a man."

He came and stood immediately before her.

"I am not passing judgment," he said. "I am offering Wisdom."

She stood and turned to the door.

"And I am declining the offer," Rocky said. "I've accepted a better one."

The door slammed, and he was standing alone, hammer in hand. He remembered the day she had rejected their attempts to help her get higher wages. Did she just see him as an interfering dolt?

Somehow, the thought that came into his mind's eye was of little Sparrow, huddling in her dirty cage. She could not come to live with Rocky while Adam was here. Under Paddy's capable hand, Sparrow had thrived and become the smiling, joyful little child that she should have been all along. Coming here would destroy all of that, but he also knew that a child needed her mother. He resolved to talk to Paddy about it. He was sure Wisdom already knew about Sparrow.

When Hyperon reached Saul's the next day, much of the damage had been cleaned up. Several items of furniture needed his attention, as did the man and his family[271].

"What did they want?" Hyperon asked.

Saul shrugged. Hyperon remembered when it had been him attempting to force Saul back into Specter's employ.

---

271 Is. 58:6-12

"I am not going back," Saul muttered. "I am not going back."

His wife came and put her arms around him.

"They offered me alcohol," he proceeded, "because that always worked in the past. But, Wisdom helps me say no every time now. It's then that they turn on the furniture."

"I am so glad you were not killed, Saul," his wife said quietly.

"I'm glad you were safe in the back room," he said. They looked at one another. Hyperon smiled a quiet kind of smile and set about fixing the two chairs, one door frame, and the table that had been broken. Marv and Pastor had stopped by and fixed the locks and the door before Hyperon had come.

As Hyperon was leaving, Saul said, "Aren't you working on a house?"

"Yes, sir," Hyperon said. "Well, I will be. I have the property and the plans. Now, I just need to get started!"

"And yet you took the time to help me?" Saul questioned.

"Of course," Hyperon said. "I am not who I once was[272]."

The man was silent for a moment.

"Neither am I," he replied.

He shook hands with Hyperon.

"Tomorrow, I will come help you with your house," Saul said. "A house for Wisdom! Can you

---

272 Jn. 9:25

imagine, dear?" he called back to his wife from the doorway, "having Wisdom as a neighbor?"

Hyperon slid the hammer into the belt he wore and bid them a good night.

Chapter 47

Adam leaned against the fence at the entrance to the lumberyard. Men passed wearing hard hats. A crane busily unloaded large metal beams from a shipping container. A train sounded in the distance, a long, lonely wail that echoed over the city.

After Rocky told him about Hyperon's words, Adam was content to put all his effort into opposing the half-breed. The injustice of being labeled a ne'er-do-well rankled him. Even if it required work, Adam was game.

Finally, he spotted the man he was looking for. Malise Dipsuchos appeared as if he had walked out of the photograph Folly possessed. The only difference was the hard hat covering his thinning hair and the big metal lunch pail in his hand.

"Dipsuchos," Adam said as the man passed.

He turned to Adam. "Do I know you?" he inquired.

"No," Adam said, "but we have a mutual friend."

The man was a full head shorter than Adam. He squinted at Adam and approached. Adam could tell that Dipsuchos did not want anyone to overhear who the mutual acquaintance might be. He filed away the ability to control Dipsuchos with his own guilty conscience and his desire to hide his past actions[273].

"Folly gave me your name," Adam said, "because I'm looking to hire a work crew of about five men. Can you help me?"

Dipsuchos stroked his chin with his empty hand. His eyebrows had shot up at the mention of Folly.

---

[273] Ps. 32:5

"What is the project, sir?" he asked. "My men and I, we are honorable men. The works we do must be honorable works[274]."

Adam smiled reassuringly. "We will be building a community center where all members of the community will be welcome. The followers of Wisdom will even hold their meetings in this building," he explained.

The man's face lit up. "Yes. Yes, we will work for you, sir," he said. "Whenever I can work for Wisdom's cause, I do it gladly. It is like gold coins in my spiritual coffers, yes?"

"Exactly," Adam said. Then, "How soon do you think you can get your crew in order?"

"We can be on the job tomorrow," Dipsuchos replied.

They shook hands, and Adam decided to go to the bakery. It was busy because it was so close to noon. He ordered a simple soup and sandwich from Paddy and took his seat. Rocky's boy brought it to him without comment, and he was left to his own thoughts. When he was almost finished, Hyperon emerged from the kitchen and came to his table.

"How are you today, Adam?" he inquired, sliding into the booth seat across from him.

"Great," Adam replied around the last bite of sandwich, "how are you?"

"Fine. Busy in here today," Hyperon said.

---

[274] Gal. 3:10

Adam finished chewing and pushed his plate away. "If you want your day to stay fine, then stay away from Rocky," Adam said in a low voice.

Hyperon looked surprised.

"I am concerned about her, Adam," he said honestly. "I am afraid you are using her."

Adam was a little surprised at Hyperon's blunt truthfulness, but he didn't let it register on his face.

"I wouldn't do that," Adam lied.

"But Specter would," Hyperon countered.

"I care about her," Adam said.

"Like you cared about all the women that came by our apartment," Hyperon replied. "Don't forget I lived there and did those things too."

Adam stood to go, so Hyperon stood as well.

"Stay away from her, or you'll be sorry," Adam wanted to communicate that Hyperon had crossed the line.

"What happened to the philanthropist who was interested in Wisdom's ways?" Hyperon challenged.

"He is standing before you," Adam said suavely. "It's you that has left Wisdom's way. You go around heaping guilt on the head of a defenseless woman and trying to break apart a loving relationship. How can you claim that as Wisdom's work?"

Adam left the bakery, smugly glad about the shock on Hyperon's face. He hoped that his words twisted like a knife in Hyperon's belly for the remainder of the day. He couldn't afford for Hyperon to throw a wrench in his well laid plans.

Paddy and Hyperon sat at her kitchen table later that evening. Hyperon had just read a fairy tale to Sparrow. Bene had listened from across the room, trying to pretend nonchalance when Hyperon could plainly see that the boy was as enthralled with the tale as his sister.

When the princess had been rescued at the end of the story, and everyone lived happily ever after, Sparrow asked him, "Did your mother read stories to you, Hyperon?"

"Yes, she did," he answered.

"Where is your mother?" the little girl asked.

"Far away from here," he said.

"Why did you leave her?"

He could not think of a suitable answer that would adequately summarize all the reasons he had come to Opportunity.

"She wanted me to come here, to have a chance at the life she forsook," he said finally.

The little girl changed tracks: "Can we talk to Wisdom, Hyperon[275]?"

"Yes," he said, "I suppose we can."

"Wisdom," she said aloud, "you love us. Please let our mommies come here so they can know you. You love them too- ours and Hyperon's. And help Hyperon build your house, so that you can come soon. I hope that I can have a dress like yours and a love like Hyperon's. It's going to be happily ever after."

She stopped speaking, and the room was silent. Hyperon stroked her brown curls. Wisdom's laughter

---

[275] Ps. 66:19; Mt. 21:22

echoed in his heart. The little girl's words had brought her so near.

"Can I help with the house?" Bene asked.

"As long as Paddy can spare both of us," Hyperon replied.

"That's enough questions," Paddy said, rising from her easy chair. "You children get into bed."

After they had been tucked in, Hyperon had come back to Paddy's table and sat down. He told Paddy about helping Saul that day and about Adam's visit to the bakery.

"Do you think I've spoken wrongly, Paddy?" he asked. "Have I stumbled out of Wisdom's path?"

Paddy took a sip of coffee and peered at him over the rim of her large ceramic mug.

"What were your tasks, Hyperon?" she asked.

He was taken off guard momentarily. He organized his thoughts then recited the tasks: "There were seven, but three I'd already completed. The first was hating evil. The second was fearing Wisdom's father, and the third was seeking Wisdom. The fourth was to choose righteousness, and she gave me the compass I later lost. The fifth was to defeat an impossible adversary, and she gave me the sword hilt that killed DeCeit. The sixth was to build her house, but not to build in vain, and she gave me the hammer. And the last was to be a living sacrifice[276], as her Father's Son did. For that, she gave me the spyglass."

"And you've used the spyglass all along," Paddy pointed out.

---

[276] Rom. 12:1-2

"Well, yes," Hyperon said.

"So do you think that just because hating evil was the first task that you quit doing it or forget about it just because you're on to a different task? It's like the galloping legs of a horse. You can hardly tell which one comes first and which is next. Perhaps all the tasks work together," Paddy said.

Hyperon grinned with half his mouth. "You're clever, Paddy," he said.

"I'd rather be wise," she said.

He chuckled, and so did she.

"You see, Hyperon, the things you said were not unkind. They simply manifested the fact that you hate evil. They stirred up the evil you see in others," Paddy explained, "and because you belong to Wisdom, that evil angers you just as it does her because it results in hurt."

He nodded.

"I was so sure I had failed the fourth and fifth tasks," he admitted, "and I've been slow in even getting to the sixth one."

"Look at all you've been doing," Paddy said loudly. She glanced over her shoulder at the hall where the children were sleeping. More quietly, she said, "You think helping your neighbors is not choosing the way of righteousness? I don't even need a compass to tell me that."

He nodded again. "But Paddy, it just doesn't seem like what I thought it would be when She gave me the tasks. It's dirtier, and more," he hesitated for the right word, "commonplace and down to earth than I thought it would be. It is downright ordinary."

"Did you expect to be like the prince in the story you just read to Sparrow and Bene? Riding in on a Pegasus and slaying a dragon to win your woman? That's a fairy tale, Hyperon. Wisdom's is a true, down and dirty, ordinary story about how the Father of lights[277] sent Light into the world of darkness to bring life to all men[278]. Life is dark, but she is the spark of hope in all the ordinary dirtiness we see[279]. It's the dirty story of a prince of thieves who used to make his living breaking heads and hearts but who is now becoming a baker who mends furniture of an evening and reads stories to little children."

Paddy leaned forward in her chair, and the strain of importance was on her brow.

"One day, Hyperon, because of Wisdom living in us, there won't be no more darkness. No more dirty. No more common place. One day, it will be brighter than happily ever after. One day, it will be the beginning of no more ends[280]."

Later, in his own bed, those words echoed in his mind and heart. He was living for that very day. In the meantime, he had work to do.

---

277 James 1:17
278 Jn. 1:9
279 Isa. 9:2
280 Zeph. 3:14-20; Is. 25:8-9; Rev. 21:3-4

Chapter 48

Dipsuchos arrived promptly with his crew at ten. Adam was at the job site to meet them. He quickly unrolled the plans and discussed them with the foreman.

"It's a simple one story structure," he said, motioning to the plan, "and it shouldn't take long to build. As we discussed yesterday, I will pay you well, and there will be a bonus for finishing early."

Dipsuchos's eyes combed the plan.

"Do you think it wise, sir, to use only beams for the foundation?" he questioned.

Though Adam's sensibilities rankled at the use of the word "wise," he remained calm.

"I don't see the need for a poured slab," he said, referring to a concrete foundation. "It will just use up time and money needlessly. I'd rather get right to the construction[281]."

"As you wish," Dipsuchos answered. He explained the plan and process to the four other men. Adam watched their faces as they received orders. Three of them looked similar to Dipsuchos. The fourth man, one called Haught, was a very young man. His curly blond beard was perhaps the first to ever adorn his young face. He seemed eager to prove himself.

They set to work, and Adam supervised from a shady spot on the perimeter of the property. The trees and the distance from the city made him slightly uncomfortable, but in the daylight, with these workers nearby, he had nothing to fear.

---

281 Mt. 7:26-27

The beams were laid in the shape of a rectangle, and the workers went to work on the framed walls. Building progressed so speedily, Adam fantasized about painting the interior by the next week.

Just before quitting time, he noticed a lone man walking up the road from the direction of Opportunity. As he drew closer, Adam recognized Saul.

Even before Saul had left Speceter's emply, they'd also enjoyed a beer or two after their work was done, and Adam knew Saul to drink more than was good for him. He'd seen Saul do things while drunk that the man probably wouldn't want reported to his wife or his new friends.

Adam remembered following him to the bus stop with Hyperon. He remembered well the beating he had given him. Adam was glad he had given that beating. The man's fake superiority was infuriating. Besides, Saul still owed on his debt to Specter. In the past, whenever Saul's debt had become too much of a burden, Adam had taken him to the bar himself. A few times, he had even bought. He hated Saul now because he wouldn't even accept those comforts or offers of friendship from Adam.

He waited until Saul was near enough.

"Saul," he said from under his shade tree, "what brings you so far from the city?"

Saul started. He was obviously not expecting to meet any in Specter's employ out here.

"I am meeting someone," he answered evasively.

Adam's curiosity was piqued.

"Oh!" he said slyly. "A rendezvous?"

“I’m a different man, now,” Saul said gruffly. “I’m about Wisdom’s business.”

Dipsuchos and his workers had not stopped their labor, but Adam was sure they’d overheard. He needed to make clear that Wisdom could be revered and appeased with works such as they were doing, but that she should not be followed.

“These fine men here are about Wisdom’s business,” Adam said, motioning to his crew, “but you and your friends who persuade people out of their work and their happiness- what does such fanaticism have to do with Wisdom?”

Saul looked troubled and seemed about to reply. Adam interrupted him. “I would pay you a fair wage. I know you still have obligations to meet.”

Saul’s shoulders slumped. Adam smiled. “It will be like old times,” he coaxed.

Adam thought that Saul was contemplating his offer when he suddenly realized that Saul’s gaze was fixed on something behind him. Adam turned to see what Saul was staring at.

Two ragged children were running toward them from the wall. There was no exit or entry here, so they must have come out of the city.

Their unkempt hair ran wild, but Adam guessed them to be about five or six years old. They were throwing something back and forth to one another and laughing. Adam chanced a look at Saul to see if he recognized them.

Saul still stared bewilderingly. Adam looked at his workers, but even then, they didn’t look up from their labor.

As the children ran closer, Adam saw that they were throwing a wrapped package back and forth like a ball. He smiled smugly, hoping that whatever was inside was not fragile.

They ran up to Saul, who backed up a step or two. They smiled and laughed and chattered, but Adam couldn't make heads or tails of their clicking or grunts.

The taller child held the package out to Saul. He took it tentatively. The shorter child clapped its hands and danced wildly.

They looked on anxiously until Saul began to tear the wrappings away. The box looked very ordinary, but now, Adam had a burning curiosity to know what would be inside such a uniquely delivered package.

Saul removed his pocket knife to cut away the last remnants of tape that held the flaps of the box shut. The younger child squealed with glee.

Adam leaned in to get a better glimpse, but he didn't see anything. He looked at Saul.

The man had been transformed from bewilderment to ecstatic joy. The contents of the box illuminated his face until he looked as gloriously happy as the wild children. Then, his face contorted, and he began to sob. He fell to his knees, and scooped a piece of paper out of the box.

He held it tenderly. His sobs subsided as the taller child ran and embraced him. Then, the children ran away toward the city.

"Who was that?" Adam demanded.

Saul didn't reply.

Adam took a step closer and spoke louder, "Who was that?"

Saul shook himself and stood up, still clutching the paper.

"I don't know," Saul said.

Adam rolled his eyes.

"Well, what is that?" Adam asked.

Saul looked down at the treasured paper.

"It was a reminder," he said, and held it out for Adam to read the words.

The print was large and simply said, "The record of your debt has been canceled[282]."

Adam shrugged. "What's the big deal about that? I could get any number of programs or grants to cancel out debt."

Saul smiled at him. "But would they cancel *the record* of it[283]?"

Adam knew that they wouldn't. A record of debt was a powerful thing in the right hands. Mr. Specter used them all the time.

"I have to go," Saul said.

Before Adam could protest, Saul walked onto the piece of property adjacent to Adam's. He seemed to be looking for something.

Eventually, another form came from the direction of the city. Adam recognized Hyperon.

Hyperon met Saul, and they conversed. They began looking at some large rocks that were scattered beneath the trees on the property.

"Sir, my men and I will be back tomorrow," Dipsuchos said, quite close to Adam.

---

[282] Col. 2:14

[283] Lk. 7:42-43

Adam had been so preoccupied that he had not noticed the man's approach.

"Fine," he said. "Fine work today."

"Can we have our day's wages?" the foreman asked.

"I only pay when the job is completed," Adam said.

Dipsuchos took his hard hat off and wiped the sweat from his wide forehead.

"We have families, sir, that get their bread from the sweat of our brows," he replied.

"Isn't that a strange way to get bread?" Adam remarked and sent the laborers home without their pay.

He approached Hyperon and Saul who were straining to move a large stone with wooden levers.

"It appears that we are neighbors," Adam said.

The two men stopped their work.

"Is this where you are building the meeting house?" Hyperon asked forthrightly.

"Yes," Adam replied, "and what are you doing?"

"I am building a house for Wisdom," Hyperon answered, turning back to his work.

"With only two men?" Adam asked.

"For now," came the labored reply.

Adam determined to keep an eye on them. Tomorrow, he could survey whatever they had accomplished. For now, he decided not to worry about it and headed back into the city. It was time to relax after such a taxing day.

Chapter 49

Prudence knocked on the door and waited.

The dark circles under the eyes of the woman frightened her, but then, she felt sorrow for Sparrow's mother.

"Yes?" the woman said. She blinked unsteadily at the sunlight and shaded her eyes with her hand.

"Hello," Prudence said. "I've just come to check on you. Can I read to you for awhile?"

There was a flicker of recognition on the woman's face.

"I don't want to hear a long list of all the things I'm doing wrong," she said.

Prudence nodded. "I think you only hear that from yourself," she said.

The woman seemed confused by this.

She came out on the porch and sat in the chair that was in the shadow of the roof.

"I don't care if you read awhile," Rocky said, "but I might fall asleep."

Prudence smiled. She sat on the ground near Rocky's feet, and she took the green book from her bag.

"These were desperate times[284]," Prudence read.

Prudence almost knew the story by heart, but she still loved to look at the words. She loved telling that story.

"When the Shepherd counted his sheep that night, he found that one had gone missing[285]," Prudence read.

---

[284] Mk. 1:14-15; Rom. 1:16; 1 Thess. 1:4-5
[285] Lk. 15:1-5

Rocky sat still in her chair, staring straight ahead.

"He searched for his sheep, but it had wandered far away. He called, but it wouldn't answer. He cried, but it wouldn't come home. He traveled over many miles, searching many dark places. After all, these were desperate times, and he was a good shepherd.

"At last, he heard the faintest bleating. Through the mist, he finally saw his sheep on the opposite side of the ravine. The ravine was so deep, it had no bottom and so wide, it had no bridge. The shepherd set down his staff and gazed across the span.

"Then Wisdom whispered on the wind, 'You must rescue that sheep, the one you love.' And the shepherd knew what he must do."

Rocky stood up abruptly.

"What are you doing?" came a man's angry voice.

Prudence stood up too. She saw the man who worked for Specter hurrying up the road toward them.

"You'd better go," Rocky said quietly.

The man had crossed the distance and he grabbed Prudence's shoulder and shook her.

"What are you doing?" he repeated.

She met his eyes. "Reading," she said.

He looked confused for a moment[286].

"You leave this woman alone!" he shouted and shoved Prudence toward the road. She reached back and grabbed her bag.

Rocky shoved him. "Don't you shout at her," she said.

---

[286] 2 Cor. 2:14-17

Adam turned to her then and forced her back through the door. It slammed.

Prudence walked away slowly. She would let Wisdom do her work.

Chapter 50

While the other men laid out their tools for the day, Dipsuchos and Adam walked to Hyperon's building site to see the progress the men had made the night before.

Adam couldn't see a worksite. Footprints and stones were scattered everywhere, but there was nothing resembling a house. He crossed his arms smugly[287].

"Ooof," Dipsuchos gave a grunt as he tripped over something and landed on his face. The breath seemed knocked from his lungs, and he writhed on the ground holding his shin.

Adam looked on the ground to see what had tripped his foreman. Sunken into the earth was a large, rectangular stone the size of Adam's flatscreen TV. It had been chiseled and buried deliberately, but Adam could find no other signs of building.

Dipsuchos worked himself into a sitting position.

"I should have known to lookout for the cornerstone," he said, rubbing his shin.

"What's a cornerstone[288]?" Adam asked.

"It is the first part of the foundation from which you can make your building square," the foreman explained. "Without it, your whole building might be crooked and unstable[289]."

Adam had heard enough. "Let's get back to work," he said, giving his foreman a hand up.

Dipsuchos limped for the rest of the day.

---

[288] Ps. 118:22; Isa. 28:14-18

[289] Lk. 20:17; Acts 4:11; Eph. 2:20; 1 Pet. 2:6-8

At quitting time, Saul and Hyperon appeared on the road.

When they set to work, Adam approached them.

"I could sue you for harm to my foreman," Adam said angrily.

Hyperon turned and looked puzzled.

"I have not harmed anyone," he said.

"You buried that stone in the ground deliberately to trip people," Adam accused. "You wanted to warn us away from your place."

Hyperon shook his head.

"I did not know you'd be walking here, or I would have put a marker. I should think that a stone that large would be marker enough," he said calmly.

Adam spat at him and cursed.

"You should have it dug up before tomorrow, or I will notify authorities," he challenged.

"I will not dig it up," Hyperon said. "It is the cornerstone."

"Cops would side with me because of your murderous record," Adam said.

"I was cleared of that charge," Hyperon answered.

"We'll see," Adam felt he'd had the better of the exchange and turned on his heel to accompany his crew back to town.

Hyperon and Saul watched them go. Saul shook his head.

"He uses his eyes, but he doesn't really see[290]," Saul said.

Hyperon nodded. "Maybe he will come to see, in time," Hyperon said.

They put their shovels to use as they dug a footer. Hyperon had spent all of his month's pay on materials for the foundation. With a perfectly square cornerstone, he knew that the foundation would be solid and dependable. Sweat ran down his face, and he smiled as he wiped it away. He was finally building her house.

Hyperon kept a guarded watch on Adam's building throughout the next month. He saw when one of the framed walls blew over, and he heard Adam screaming at the men from the shade. He silently resolved within himself to warn Wisdom's people not to meet in such a building.

"One, two, three," Saul's voice became strained on the "three" as they lifted an eyebeam into place. Hyperon felt confident that they could place the trusses today and have the framing done by the next week. He was beginning to envision the rooms, and when he did, he also pictured the life that would be lived in them.

The evening glittered around them as they worked, and Hyperon knew that he was not building in vain[291].

---

[290] Mt. 13:14-15

[291] Prov. 24:3

Chapter 51

Prudence packed her things after school and tucked the green book under her arm.

Haste stuck his tongue out at her as he ran past on his way out of the school yard. Prudence watched him go, and then noticed a man leaning against a tree across the street. It was the man who had worked with Hyperon for Specter. She recognized him as the one who had chased her that night when she had been going to meet Saul on her bicycle.

Of all the days for him to be here! She hoped that he would leave her alone so that she could do the errands that Paddy had asked her to do.

She turned left out of the school's gate and walked a block. Traffic whizzed by, and when she turned to make sure it was safe to cross an intersection, she saw that the man was following her.

She went the long way around, through alleyways and across one very busy intersection, until she got to the house with the address Paddy had made her memorize.

When she skipped up the steps to ring the bell, the spy again leaned on a tree across the road.

The old man who answered the door seemed startled to see her.

"Hello," he said gruffly.

She smiled. "Hello, Mr. Cameron," she said. "I'm Prudence from the bakery. Can I come in?"

He nodded and made way for her to pass him into the front hallway. He shut the door.

"Could you lock the door, sir?" she asked. "I think there's someone following me."

He raised his white bushy eyebrows and reached back to turn the deadbolt lock. "Why in the world would someone follow you?"

"I have something they want," Prudence said simply, and took the green book out from under her arm. She held it tightly to her chest.

"Well, come in and have a mug of chocolate," Cameron told her, peering back out through the curtains. He shook his head and then turned away.

She followed him into a simple kitchen and sat in one of the two chairs. The old man put a kettle on and set out two mugs. Prudence watched him and thought with surprise that he kept a neater kitchen than her mother.

"So what brings you to my house? Did Paddy put you up to it?" he asked as he brought two cloth napkins to the table.

"Yes. You're lonely," she said.

He blinked.

"Is that really the reason?" he asked.

She nodded. "I came to invite you to a get together," she said.

He raised his eyebrows so high that they almost served as hair on his bald head.

"I don't like get togethers," he said.

Prudence bounced a little in her seat. "I know, but this one is different. This one is a get together for Wisdom's people."

He turned away from her to pour water from the now steaming kettle into the mugs.

"Well, I'm not one of Wisdom's people," he said.

"Why not?" she asked.

He was silent. He picked up a silver spoon to stir the mugs and stirred them thoughtfully. When he turned back to her, he had lost a little of his gruffness.

"What use is she if we are all headed to our deaths? We're all going to die sometime- both the wise and fools[292]," he said, taking the seat across from her and setting the mugs down.

She nodded.

"So, what happens then?" she asked.

He leaned forward like he hadn't heard her correctly.

"When?" he asked.

"When we die," she said.

His eyebrows frowned for him.

"How am I supposed to know?" he said.

Prudence smiled. "Perhaps you could answer that question with Wisdom," she suggested.

He chuckled. "Checkmate."

She slurped a little of the hot chocolate from her mug.

"Have you ever seen this book?" she asked, holding out the green book.

"Sure. I've seen you carrying it in the bakery," he said, "but what's a book got to do with life and death?"

In answer, she opened the book to the end and began to read.

" 'The shepherd knew what he must do,' " she read. Cameron stared into his empty mug.

" *'Suddenly, the Enemy appeared holding a black cup. 'Will you drink this cup?' the enemy asked the*

---

292 Eccl. 2:12-17

Shepherd. 'What is in it?' the Shepherd asked, knowing what He would do. 'This cup is full of the suffering of the sheep- loneliness, terror, pain, vulnerability, hunger, thirst, and death. But it also contains the folly of the sheep- the wandering, the stubbornness, the pride, the foolishness, and the heedlessness[293].'

" 'How well the Shepherd knew the folly of the sheep! How well He also knew their suffering! He could hear their death cries in his ears. He could hear the snarls of the wolves. He could see in His mind's eye the Enemy's laughing triumph, roasting each lamb on a spit. And there hovered the one lost sheep, teetering on the edge of the ravine, helpless to escape death's grasp[294].

'The Shepherd reached out His hand and took the cup. He drank the black contents and sank to His knees. Blood mixed with his sweat as he passed to the ground. A tremor wracked his body, and he died[295].'"

" 'The enemy bent to the ground and smiled grimly as he picked up the dark cup. As he straightened, he laughed at the sheep's desperate bleating. There was no one to save it now.'"

" 'Deathly pallor covered the Shepherd's face, and the enemy went his way. Just as the enemy's back was turned, a leafy golden-green shoot burst from the Shepherd's chest. It curled over him and leaves unfurled. It became a vine that inched its way to the great chasm that had no bottom and no bridge, and Wisdom's whisper in the wind became a shout of jubilee[296].'"

---

293 Lk. 22:42-44
294 Lk. 23:21
295 Lk. 23:46
296 Jn. 15:1-5

" 'The vine waited at the edge as it grew stronger and thicker. More and more of the leafy vine came from the dead Shepherd's chest. It began to braid itself and coil around the rocks. When it was strong enough, it began to braid across the expanse. It became longer and longer. It grew wider. Flowers began to bud. At first, the flowers that opened were small and red, like drops of blood, but as the vine leaned out over the chasm, the flowers grew lighter red, and then pink, until finally, they were large, white flowers, shining brighter than new snow at noonday[297].'"

Cameron snorted, but Prudence didn't stop reading.

" 'When the vine reached the lost sheep, it was braided so tightly, that the sheep didn't hesitate to step onto it. Slowly at first, and then more quickly, the sheep grazed on the flowers of the vine as it crossed the chasm to where the Shepherd lay. It nuzzled his shoulder and his side, but he was cold and lifeless. Finally, not knowing what else to do, the sheep lay down in the crook of his limp arm and rested its head next to the great vine growing from his chest.'"

Silence filled the kitchen.

"That's a stupid story," the old man said. "When people die, they stay dead. Shouldn't I know that? Everyone should know that!"

Prudence blinked back tears.

"Well, don't cry about it," he said irritably, rolling his eyes.

She said nothing.

---

[297] Isa. 1:18

"Why would that guy be following you to take such a silly book?" Cameron asked.

"He doesn't want the book," Prudence said.

The old man wagged his eyebrows questioningly.

"He wants the Life that came out of death," she said.

Cameron smirked. "A plant? That's the only life that came out of that guy. He died so that he could be a plant that would help a stupid sheep. Sounds like a waste to me. He should have just got on with his honest work and stayed with the other sheep."

Prudence's lips, which had been set in a thin line, turned up slightly now into a shadow of a smile.

"Would he have been honest to betray the one?" she asked.

"Bah," the old man threw his hands in the air and stood back from the table, letting his chair make a loud scraping noise on the floor[298].

"Is this why Paddy sent you? To ask me to believe some nonsense so that I would come to some kooky gathering so that I wouldn't be lonely? You can tell her I am plenty of company for myself here. Company won't change the finality of death."

Prudence nodded and tucked the book under her arm as she stood.

"May I please go out by your back door? Maybe then, I won't have to worry about the man across the street," she said.

---

[298] Jer. 33:11-16

“Now, that’s sensible. I wish you would do more sensible things. I will call the police and report the man while you slip out the back,” he said.

Prudence shook her head. “No. Sometimes, the police only make it worse,” she said, and slipped out the door.

Truth and Justice were standing there. Justice took her hand, and Truth trotted ahead of them as they wove through the city’s twisting alleyways. Prudence cringed when she saw the lifelike eyes of the owls watching her from their perch on the Megascops Theater, but when she looked back, she saw that she was no longer being followed.

Chapter 52

Adam rose earlier than usual so that he could meet with Specter before arriving at the job site. He kissed Rocky and explained that he wanted to get an early start. It was not a lie, but he didn't want to tell her the whole truth either[299].

He arrived at the office before Specter came in. The same secretary bid him to have a seat in the waiting area. Adam busied himself with a magazine, but his thoughts took precedence over the page before him. If he could just dupe Specter into funding this project, then he could be free of his master. Adam planned to work only for Adam in the future.

He was planning to make a visit to Paddy too. He needed to work around Hyperon to get Wisdom's fools to meet in his building. He knew now that Hyperon would not meet there. But, he felt that Paddy could be persuaded.

"Came to see me, my boy?" came the hissing voice by his ear. Adam jumped. He had not heard Specter come in, and he hoped the sly man had not discerned any of his private thoughts.

Adam followed him to his office. Today's yellow tie had brown speckles. It was hideous. Specter shut the door.

"How is the project proceeding?" Specter asked.

"Very well," Adam reported. "It will be done in a matter of days."

"Folly tells me you hired Dipsuchos," Specter said.

---

[299] 2 Tim. 3:6

Adam was somewhat surprised to learn that Specter knew this much.

"Yes," Adam replied coolly. "He's a dedicated crew leader."

"He's one of my best employees," Specter said.

Adam narrowed his eyes and grinned. "He's also very interested in working for Wisdom."

Specter laughed.

Adam tried to hide his confusion.

"My dear boy," Specter said, "working for Wisdom and following her are two different things, and I'm the fine line between them.

"Dipsuchos works for Wisdom without following her, which is the same as saying he works for me," Specter explained. "He could never work for her enough if he doesn't also follow her. That cursed Hyperon on the other hand, follows Wisdom and so works for her in the following. There's a difference."

Adam wasn't sure he understood the difference, but he nodded.

"So, tell me how my friend Rocky is doing," Specter said.

Adam told Specter about moving in with her and about the building process. Then, he told his boss about Wisdom's house that Hyperon was building. As he spoke, Specter's face began to match the yellow hue of his tie.

Without response, he pushed the intercom button on his desk.

"Call Horbah to my office," he said gruffly.

Adam hovered in the awkward silence while they waited for the other man.

The five minutes stretched into an infernal eternity. Adam had begun to sweat when Horbah finally let in a cool breath of air by opening the office door. Just as swiftly, he closed it again. Adam was surprised that the doorknob didn't come off in the guy's hand.

"What do you know about Hyperon?" Specter asked.

"I think he's planning a meeting with them," Horbah said.

"Who?" Specter questioned.

"All of the followers," came the reply, "even a few new ones."

"And have you been following your little girl?" Specter asked.

Horbah looked down at his shoes. "I did, but I lost her in the downtown area this afternoon," he said the words quickly.

Specter rolled his eyes and exaggerated a sigh.

"Horbah, have you ever heard of taking candy from a baby?" Specter said drily.

Horbah looked confused. "Well, I…" he was interrupted.

"You will not lose her again," Specter said. His words were calm and cool, but Adam felt the heat of them.

Specter sat in thoughtful silence.

"Do you know anything about this house Hyperon's building?" he asked.

Horbah shook his head. "Only from what Dipsuchos told me."

Specter pulled a notebook from his desk drawer and leafed through it. Adam wondered about its contents. Specter snapped it shut and replaced it.

"I am going to put a tidy sum of money into your account," he told Adam. "I want you and your crew to wait until Hyperon's structure is near completion. Then, Horbah will be at your disposal and together you will destroy it and kill Hyperon."

Adam blinked. He considered the repercussions of inflicting damage to such a degree on someone else's property and knew what happened to murderers. He hoped the police were still in Specter's pocket. He looked fleetingly at Horbah. The guy was a klutz, but certainly he would object to murder.

"I will take care of the ramifications," Specter said.

Adam had no love for Hyperon, but he knew that if Paddy discovered his intentions, he would be hard pressed to get any of Wisdom's people to meet in his building. Perhaps, though, with Hyperon out of the way, Paddy would be easier to convince. He also was tired of taking Specter's orders. However, he didn't voice any of this.

"Also," Specter said, turning to his computer screen, "I want you to make it look like Rocky did it."

Adam thought briefly about the kiss he'd given her on his way out the door. He cared little for her, and yet, the deception stretched farther even than his small amount of decency would allow.

"I can't do that," he said.

Specter turned to look at him. Horbah stared.

"I did not ask a question," Specter said. "I gave a command."

Adam hesitated.

"We all know you're just using her body and biding your time," Specter said crudely. "You wouldn't even have that half pleasure if it weren't for me. Don't forget where you came from, boy!"

Specter adjusted his glasses.

In a much calmer tone, he said, "What would you like as an incentive to take on this project?"

Adam considered this.

"Make me an equal partner in your company," he said, "with equal access to the assets."

Specter laughed.

"You're very ambitious," he said. Adam could not tell if he was mocking him. "But, if you do all that I have asked, I will give you everything that I have."

Adam reached across the desk and shook his hand.

"Don't wait too long, Adam," Specter said. "I'm ready to have that fool out of the way."

Due to the setbacks they'd had, Adam's crew was roofing at the same time as Hyperon. Adam found it hard to believe that Hyperon and Saul had accomplished so much in such a short span of time. Work disgusted him, but then he had been working more in the last few weeks than he ever had. He fingered the bank account statement in his pocket.

It was enough for him and Rocky to start someplace new and leave Opportunity behind. When he envisioned his future, though, he didn't really like her in the picture. She was aging rapidly, and she cried all the time. Perhaps he could use only a portion of the money to pull off this one last job for Specter. He'd be rid of Rocky and could leave it all behind him. He could move to a place where no one knew him and start over. Perhaps, he could find Wisdom someplace else, and then, he would amend his ways.

He decided to only include Haught in the plan. That way, he'd only have to pay one other man and there would be fewer witnesses.

He called to the younger man as the rest of the crew was leaving for the day.

"Haught, may I have a word?" Adam called.

He'd always been good at recruiting others. Isn't that the power he held over Hyperon? He'd recruited him too, once upon a time.

"What is it, boss?" Haught asked, jogging up.

"I have a delicate matter to discuss with you," Adam said confidentially. "Can you be trusted?"

"Sure," the boy said.

"I've heard that the building being built next door is going to be used to oppose Wisdom," Adam said seriously. "The man building it goes around persuading people that the works they do in Wisdom's name are no good." He shook his head for effect.

"If we were to destroy the building, we'd be offering Her a service," Adam suggested.

Haught backed up a step.

"Oh, sir," he said, "you can't mean to go that far! Just think of all the work they've poured into it. I haven't seen them do any harm."

"That's just it, Haught," he said, "they don't do harm. They speak harm. Why, just yesterday, the builder was watching you work and saying that your shingles were slanted. He said that though *you* thought you were doing it for Wisdom's sake, you really just had your own selfish ends in mind[300]."

Adam watched the scorn and derision dawn behind the young man's beard.

"I see how it could be good for the cause," Haught said, hesitatingly.

"Yes, that's it," Adam coaxed, "and I have it all arranged so that we won't have any trouble with the city authorities."

Haught still seemed to ride the fence[301].

"I will compensate you double what you are making building for me," Adam closed the cinch.

Haught held out his hand. "I would do anything to do the works of wisdom."

"So would I," Adam agreed. "Meet me here next week on the night of the full moon, about two hours after midnight."

300 Prov. 6:16-19
301 Rom. 1:28-31

Chapter 53

As Hyperon and Saul hung drywall, Hyperon contemplated the quickly depleting funds he had. Paddy compensated him generously for his work at the bakery, but with the expenses of fixing others' homes and furniture, he was not sure he could finish Wisdom's house anytime soon. Getting a loan was out of the question. No bank would loan him money because of his ancestry. Specter would influence them to deny him in any case.

Saul sensed his mood.

"Wisdom will provide for what she has asked you to do[302]," he said.

Hyperon smiled at him.

Working with Saul was almost as beneficial to his spirit as it was to his construction project. Tonight, they were all planning to meet together at Paddy's. Perhaps when the house was done, Wisdom's people could come and meet right here with her in safety. It was a beautiful hope in Hyperon's mind. He thought of how Sparrow would chat with Wisdom about dresses and flowers and her mama.

Hyperon had agreed to take Bene and Sparrow to see Rocky tonight. He hoped that it would be a good meeting. He thought it would be good to attempt it in the same night as a Wisdom gathering just in case the children needed support and assurance after seeing their mother.

Paddy agreed that this plan was best.

---

[302] Gen. 22:14

Hyperon and Saul quit work earlier than usual. Hyperon gazed across the street at the structure Adam was building. From the exterior, it looked magnificent. Pillars crossed the front, holding up the roof, and it had wide, welcoming double doors. This was no house, but a place for large gatherings and activities. He remembered what Adam purposed: to host Widom's meetings. Hyperon resolved to warn Paddy against it tonight.

Bene and Sparrow were ready to go when he arrived back at the bakery.

"Just let me wash up and change out of my work clothes," he told them laughingly when they met him at the door. He hurried up the steps and changed. He had long debated over whether to warn the children that they might also see Adam at their old home, but as he came back down the steps, he decided to keep the information to himself. Perhaps Adam wouldn't be there.

They went out and caught a passing trolley. It was now a familiar route to Hyperon. Sparrow chatted happily, and even Bene, who was slightly more sullen, pointed out a large dog and a speedy looking car as they rode along.

Hyperon hoped against reason that Adam would not be there. As soon as they rang the doorbell, Hyperon heard his footsteps and knew it was an unfounded hope.

Sparrow whimpered when the man opened the door. She buried her face in the side of Hyperon's hip and cried softly. Bene started forward, rolling up his sleeves.

"You better not have hurt my mother," he was saying.

Hyperon wondered if it had been wise not to prepare them for this, but then, he was taking the chance that Adam would not be at home. He also did not want to speak evil of their mother.

Rocky appeared from behind Adam and gathered her son in her arms.

"It's all right, son," she crooned. "It is all right."

Bene hugged his mother but kept an eye on Adam.

"He does not work for Specter anymore," she soothed. Her tired eyes feasted on the boy.

"Adam," she said softly, "would you mind giving us a chance to visit alone?"

Hyperon's gaze fell on Adam. He seemed nervous and shaky.

"Not at all," he coalesced. He disappeared into one of the back rooms, and Hyperon heard the TV come on.

Sparrow glanced shyly up at her mother.

"I have missed you," Rocky was saying.

She nudged them to the seats at the table Hyperon had mended and went to the kitchen to fix them a drink. Hyperon sat down, thankful at least that the chairs were still in one piece.

Hyperon saw when she opened the fridge that she didn't have beverages suited for children. She peeked inside, then shut it and opted to pour glasses of water instead.

"Sparrow, honey, why were you crying? You know, Adam was the man who saved you," Rocky admonished.

"He didn't save me," the little girl shook her head savagely. "He kept me in a cage at his house."

Rocky met Hyperon's gaze. She wordlessly questioned him.

"You should not let him in here, ma," Bene said. "He is an evil man."

Her former defensiveness fell over her again. "He is no more evil than Hyperon," she said. "Don't you remember how they both tortured us?"

Hyperon expected Bene to lash out in anger. Instead, the young boy got out of his seat and knelt before his mother. He wrapped his arms around her waist and laid his head in her lap.

"Can you not see the difference Wisdom has made in him, mama?" he pleaded. "Can you truly not remember the difference Wisdom made in you?"

Rocky stroked his hair. Her agitation was deep. Her expression revealed the war being fought between trusting herself and letting go to trust Wisdom.

"All I can remember is her betrayal, son," she wept softly.

The boy shook his head. "But that's not even a true memory, ma."

"Come back to Paddy's with us, mama," Sparrow was crying too. "We will take care of you there."

"What makes you think I'm not being taken care of?" the woman forced a smile and a pleasant tone.

The children looked at her.

"You are sick, ma," Bene said. "Come with us."

"I feel fine," she hardened herself against them, and Hyperon ached to see it. "I am happy here. But I am glad for you two to be with Paddy. You will have the opportunity to trust Wisdom if you choose to."

Adam emerged from the back bedroom and stood behind Rocky. He put his hand on her shoulder. Hyperon noticed that it was not a comforting gesture, but instead, a controlling one.

Sparrow hid behind Hyperon as he stood.

"You should go," Adam said.

"You should go," Hyperon countered.

Adam's face flushed, and Bene stood up and moved beside Hyperon.

"I have not been kind, but I am willing to make amends," Adam measured out his words. "I will ask you to kindly stay out of my personal life."

"I would be glad to make amends, but I will not stay out of your personal life when it involves your harm and the harm of everyone present," Hyperon's words were cautious yet firm.

Rocky crossed to the door and opened it.

"I'm glad you came, children, but it is time for you to go," she said. Hyperon ushered them past her. At the last moment, she swept them into her arms.

"Oh, children, it is better that you go away from here," she whispered.

"Please come with us[303]," Bene pleaded.

Adam crossed the room, pulled Rocky inside, and slammed the door.

"Do something," Bene pleaded with Hyperon. "Do something!" The boy pounded on the door.

---

[303] Gen. 19:15-17

"I cannot force her to come, son," Hyperon said. He heard no sign of struggle or violence from the other side of the door. Rocky had made her choice.

Hyperon lifted the weeping Sparrow and put a soft hand on Bene's shoulder.

Bene peered up into his face. "One day, there will be a beginning with no more ends."

The boy stared at the door. He raised one of his tanned hands and rested it there in the center of the door.

"Then I will not say good bye," he whispered, "I will only say, 'Until that day.'"

It was a solemn ride back to Paddy's. A weeping Sparrow was put to bed with the promise of being awakened for the gathering at midnight. Bene was wrapped in a warm woolen shawl and given a cup of soup. Paddy hummed and soothed their souls as if she had been applying bandages to the parts that were broken and bleeding.

Chapter 54

"Why are we here?" Prudence whispered to Justice.

His eyes followed hers to the owls' eyes. She looked at him, just a small, discarded boy, but she saw only courage. He pulled her at a run through the hot black alley on the north side and around the back of the theater. Truth ran behind them.

When they got to the back door, it opened. Prudence fought the urge to run and hide. The door hit Truth, who scuttled out of the way. An actress bundled in an overcoat said, "Ugh! Stay away from the door, you filthy brats!"

Prudence had no desire to go in that door, but Justice was insistent. She allowed herself to be pulled ahead, and Truth dogged their heels.

It seemed that every hallway was made of shadows. Every person they seemed to see was just a ghost. Somewhere, music was playing in a minor key, and Prudence wondered what she was doing in the hub of those who shy away from the light.

No one spoke to them or even seemed to see them, and Justice hurried along like he knew the place well.

"You shouldn't be coming in here," Prudence whispered to him.

He acted like he hadn't heard her.

Finally, they reached the end of a hall where a door was ajar to a storage closet. Light spilled out of that crack and revealed floating dust mites. Prudence crowded behind Justice as he approached that door.

Justice stopped. Prudence peered at the closet from over his shoulder.

"Prudence," said the voice she loved the most.

It was the Lady. Prudence leapt forward into the arms of her friend, and the Lady laughed.

"I never thought you would be here," Prudence said.

The Lady smiled. Justice and Truth huddled near her side, and she smiled at them as well.

"When you agreed to follow me, you didn't think it would only be in the nice, green places, did you? Didn't you know that I also often walk the valley of the shadow of death[304]?" the Lady asked.

Prudence considered this. "I suppose I never expected to find light in the dark," she said.

"We only have a few moments, Prudence, and I have some very important things to tell you," the Lady said.

Prudence listened attentively, studying the beautiful face.

"I know you will all gather soon at Paddy's, right?" she asked. Prudence nodded.

"And I know that a man named Horbah, who works for Mr. Specter, has been following you. Is that right?" the Lady questioned. Prudence nodded again.

"I am not going to allow him to harm you. You will need to be strong and courageous[305] in the coming days, my daughter," the Lady's voice wavered, and Prudence didn't feel strong or courageous.

---

304 Ps. 23:4

305 Josh. 1:7-9

"I have three tasks for you," the Lady sounded confident again.

"When you leave here, you will overhear a conversation that you must repeat to Hyperon. Do you understand?"

Prudence nodded.

"Second, your friends Sparrow and Bene have experienced a terrible day. When you see them at the meeting tonight, you must remind them of the Shepherd and the Book. You must remind them that I love them," the Lady said with a gentle smile.

Prudence tried to memorize every word. Her eyes strayed for a moment to Truth and Justice. Their eyes were fixed on the Lady as if they too were memorizing Prudence's tasks.

"Finally," the Lady said, "a week from now, all my followers must be together. You will need to convince them to meet again. I want them to meet at your house."

"All right," Prudence said.

The Lady's smile brightened.

"For this purpose I called you[306]," the Lady told her, lifting her chin. "Remember, don't be afraid. I will be with you, even when you can't see me. Be strong and courageous."

Prudence nodded. The little boys jumped up, and this time, Truth took Prudence by the hand.

"Justice is going to stay with me," the Lady said, at Prudence's inquiring glance. "I have work for him here."

---

306 Jer. 1:5

Truth pulled her back into the shadows, through the twisting passages of the Megascops. They entered a theater, but instead of taking a seat in the rows of chairs, Truth led her beneath them. They could barely see through the cracks of the ascending platforms that the chairs were on.

They waited.

Chapter 55

Paddy pushed all of her furniture to the wall to make more room for everyone to sit on the floor.

"This way," she was explaining to Bene, "even if someone tried to see in here through the window, all they would see is the silhouette of the back of an empty couch."

Hyperon half smiled. "I'm going to run up to my apartment, Paddy. I'll be right back," he said.

He took his stairs two at a time and left the door open behind him as he crossed the room to the desk.

He ignored the oven mitt now and picked up the spyglass. It was pleasantly warm, but not hot like before. He sat down in the chair and held the spyglass up to his right eye.

There sat Wisdom's Father. He looked as grave and glorious as He had the first time Hyperon had seen Him. Now, He held a large scale in His lap. Hyperon could see by the way His garment blew that He was holding a mighty wind on the scale[307]. After a moment, He let it go and reached for a container of water. This He also placed on His scale. Hyperon watched as the Father measured wind, water, rain, lightning, and thunder. Only after He had finished did His eyes meet Hyperon's. He gave a confident nod, one of a proud Father to a son who had done well[308].

Tears sprang to Hyperon's eyes and ran down his cheeks. What had he done well? And yet, he had always hungered for just that sort of nod from his earthly father.

---

[307] Job 28:23-28

[308] Isa. 55:6-13

Hyperon leapt up, keeping the spyglass to his eye. The warmth of it spread throughout his body. If Wisdom's Father could measure all those mighty things, then certainly He could measure hearts. Hyperon felt overwhelmed by awe, wonder, and love like he had never known. It was love emptied of selfishness.

Hyperon didn't want to set the spyglass down, but he heard voices in the courtyard below. The Father stretched out His hand, and a mighty wind blew through Hyperon's hair and around the room. Hyperon lowered the spyglass, but he took it with him as he went back to Paddy's wrapped in that wind[309].

Lovely was there, sitting quietly on the floor in front of the couch. Bene gazed into the fire as it burned low on the fireplace. Saul and his wife were talking to Paddy. Hyperon went into the back room and lifted Sparrow from where she was sleeping.

"Is it time already?" she said yawning.

"Yes," he said.

She rested her head on his shoulder. He wanted her to know the love of the Father. Her mother might not be able to give that sort of love. His own father certainly hadn't, but Wisdom's Father was abundantly able.

He set her on the floor by Bene and wrapped her blanket around her.

The room grew quiet, and they heard more footsteps approaching.

Obedience opened the door cautiously and searched the room with her eyes. Marv removed his hat as he followed her in.

---

[309] Jn. 3:8

"Where's Prudence?" Obedience asked.

Prudence huddled under the risers in the empty auditorium. Truth's eyes glittered, and he sat so still that she expected something to happen every moment.

Tap-click, tap-click, tap-click sounded louder in the empty dark than it should have. Prudence leaned closer to the crack in the floor, but couldn't see anything in the dark.

"Is that you, honey?" a man's tired voice asked. He seemed to be sitting in one of the seats close to where the children were hiding. Truth squeezed Prudence's hand in a needless caution to be silent. Prudence wondered how long the man had been sitting there in the dark and if he had heard them.

"Of course it is," a woman's voice said. "I'm the only one who knows you well enough to look for you here."

Prudence could tell that the woman was sitting down in one of the amphitheater chairs near the man from the halting click of her heels and the slight creak of groaning plastic.

"What has you down?" the woman said, and flicked a lighter to light a cigarette. Prudence could only see the faint outlines of the backs of their feet before the light went dim again.

"What else?" the man spat.

"My wretched twin," the woman said knowingly.

The man's chair groaned as he leaned forward. "I have this gnawing weakness, and I know she must be nearby. I wish I could destroy her," he said.

The woman exhaled slowly. “Why not take all that she loves, just as she took your loved ones from you, Alexander?” the woman suggested.

Prudence hardly dared to breathe. She remembered the Lady’s exhortation to be strong and courageous.

“Isn’t that what I’ve been doing all these years?” the man asked.

“Well, yes,” the woman hesitated, “but what if you took care of Hyperon? She loves him, and he is her trustiest tool these days. I’ve seen him working for her all over the city. What a fool he’s become!”

The man chuckled. “Oh, I already have a plan for Hyperon,” he said.

Truth started shaking. Prudence wondered if she was cold or afraid. She couldn’t see much of her face in the darkness.

“Oh? Do tell,” the woman said.

“Let’s just say that his latest work for Wisdom is going to go down in a blaze of glory,” he said.

“Intriguing,” the woman commented.

“And I am hoping that it will injure several of her other fiends in the process. I know that the woman called Rocky will be among them,” he said.

At this, Truth began to pull her hand. Prudence hardly dared to breathe, much less move, but she was so insistent that she began to edge away from the darkness and follow her back into the dim light of the hall. The man and woman continued talking, and Prudence was sorry not to hear more of their plans.

As Prudence crawled out from under the risers after Truth, her foot caught on a step, and she tripped.

She lost hold of Truth's hand, and her hands smacked the concrete floor hard, making a loud slapping sound.

"What was that?" the man's voice rose, and she could hear their plastic chairs springing up after them as they stood.

Truth grabbed her elbow and pulled her as she stumbled back to her feet. She ran back the way they had come.

"Wait!" the woman's voice caught up to them. She had seen them.

The hallway was clear except for one attendant. He looked at them in confusion and backed against the wall as they rushed by. Truth hit the door that spilled out into the black alley, and they burst through it.

She pulled Prudence into a side alley and swung up into a dumpster. She followed her without hesitation. The dumpster was only half full, so they hid below the rim, hoping that their pursuers would give up or rush by.

Truth grinned at her. Prudence didn't feel like smiling yet.

The din of confused conversation reached them, but no footsteps came down their side alley. They waited until the sky began to grow dark. Truth fell asleep.

Prudence shook the child. She woke up and smiled at her. She wished she had something to give her for her supper.

"I have to go to a meeting tonight. It's near the bakery. Want to come with me? I can get you something to eat," she told Truth.

She nodded happily and looked cautiously out of the dumpster. Satisfied that the coast was clear, she scrambled out and waited for Prudence to do the same.

They hurried to Paddy's.

One by one, the followers arrived as they had the last time. Hyperon sat over a mug of tea. The affecting scenes at Rocky's had zapped him of happiness, but Wisdom's joy bubbled up within him[310]. 'Until that day,' rang in his heart as no other battle cry could have stirred him. The vision of Her Father weighting the wind emboldened him for whatever he would be called on to do next.

Paddy handed Obedience a similar mug of tea, and she began her deep, throaty humming of the song that they all loved. Marv held Obedience's hand. It wasn't like Prudence to be late.

Sparrow jumped up and clasped her hands under her chin. "She's coming!" she said.

Hyperon thought at first that the little girl had heard her mother, but then, Prudence burst in the door. Her green eyes sought the room, but instead of her mother, she was looking for Hyperon.

"I've seen the Lady," she said breathlessly. Hyperon's eyes flicked to the doorway where a skinny child peeked in apprehensively.

Prudence turned and waved the little one in.

"This is Truth," she said.

When Hyperon opened his mouth to ask her one of his million questions, Paddy intervened by raising one calloused palm in his direction. He closed his mouth again. She took a few slow steps toward the child. She was filthy, with her hair stuck out in all directions. She

---

310 James 1:2-4

didn't come in at Prudence's insistent wave but instead hovered on the threshold.

Obedience and Marv rushed to Prudence and wrapped their arms around her. "I'm okay," she said.

"She's hungry, Paddy," Prudence said. "I told her you'd give her something to eat."

"Hmmm," Paddy agreed and walked toward him. The little girl scampered out of her way and came again to the doorway. She pointed straight at Hyperon.

"Hyperon," Prudence said, "someone is going to burn down your house."

Hyperon turned to look at her. Obedience stroked her braids. "Surely not, honey," Obedience said.

"The Lady told me that I was to tell you," and Prudence told them all what she had overheard. Hyperon listened and wondered. Of all the places for his Lady to be, he would have never imagined she'd go to the Megascops. He wondered if she had ever been there and seen his obsession with the hologram of Folly. Had she watched him as he memorized those despicable words? He shook his selfish thoughts from his mind and tried to concentrate on what Prudence had said about others being hurt. He couldn't let that happen.

Prudence crossed the room and hugged Sparrow. She smiled at Bene. "The Lady said you had had a hard day. She must care for you very much if she wants to comfort you when you are sad," Prudence said. Sparrow reached up and wrapped her arms around Prudence's neck[311].

---

[311] 2 Cor. 1:3-5

Hyperon turned to the child in the doorway. Paddy held out a few banana nut muffins. She smiled but backed away.

"Just set the basket down, Paddy," Prudence directed. "She will get them."

"Why doesn't she like people, honey?" Paddy was perplexed.

Prudence looked at Hyperon. "People have treated her shamefully and cast her out. She makes her own way," she said. "And the Lady sees to her needs."

They watched the child eat the muffins one by one as crumbs littered the ground around her. Prudence took a seat by Sparrow, but spoke to her father.

"Dad," she said, "we are all supposed to be together again in a week's time. On the night of the full moon, we are supposed to gather at our house."

He nodded slowly.

"All right," he said. Everyone gave silent agreement to this plan. They sat in silence, listening to Truth munch her last muffin. Hyperon passed the spyglass around. He wished that the Lady or her Father would tell them exactly what was coming and precisely what to do. He didn't want any of the beloved ones gathered in that place to be hurt by Specter.

He felt a hand on his shoulder. He looked up into the wizened eyes of Saul.

"Don't go back to trusting in yourself. The Lady will tell you what you need to know when you need to know it," he said.

Hyperon sighed. The older man clapped his shoulder.

When Paddy began humming again, they all began to sing. When the last note faded away, Hyperon looked back at the doorway, and the child was gone.

Chapter 56

They agreed to share the responsibility of keeping an eye on Hyperon's house. The children took turns before and after school. The men went when they could. Lovely took a book and sat boldly in the afternoon shade on the porch. Obedience took her knitting in the late mornings.

Hyperon worked in the bakery. Cameron remained punctual, but complained more than ever.

"I saw that shack you put on my land," he said. "Not much hand at carpentry, are ya? I thought you would build something great to honor the memory of my wife."

Hyperon listened and rubbed the countertop until it shone. Paddy's laugh spilled out of the kitchen.

Cameron was even sour to Prudence when she came before school. When his attention was fixed on his swamp muffin, Prudence leaned over the counter and said, "He's a little swampy himself." Hyperon chuckled.

Prudence hadn't told the whole group, but she told Hyperon that the man and woman she'd overheard intended to hurt Rocky. He hadn't even told Paddy about that detail, but he thought about it constantly. Surely the Lady wouldn't let something happen to her. Bene and Sparrow needed their mama.

Adam came in halfway through the week and asked for Paddy.

Hyperon tamped down his anger enough to feel pity. Adam was stuck in a game of his own making.

Hyperon listened closely to the murmur of their voices as they talked in the kitchen and was thankful that Bene and Sparrow were at school. He couldn't hear the words of what Paddy and Adam said, but the tone remained pleasant.

Soon enough, Adam emerged. He didn't make eye contact with Hyperon and acted as if he would just walk out the door.

"Wait," Hyperon said. A few customers looked his way and then resumed their own conversations. Adam turned and straightened the vest he was wearing.

"What?" he asked smugly.

Hyperon leaned on the counter, trying to appear casual.

"How is Rocky?" he asked.

Adam's eyes smoldered.

"None of your business," Adam said angrily. He turned to leave, but Hyperon crossed the room and stood in the doorway.

"Don't you think she'd be better off here with Paddy and her kids?" Hyperon kept his words quiet, but they still came out forcefully. "Don't you think she'd be safer?"

Adam's shoulders sunk. He looked every ounce the defeated villain he didn't have to be.

"She's made her choice," Adam finally said and dodged around Hyperon. He was back out on the sidewalk now, and Hyperon was holding on to the door of the *Banquet Bakery*.

"You can both make a different choice now," Hyperon said to his friend's retreating back. "You don't have to set fires to everything!"

Adam whirled. They locked eyes. Adam turned and ran.

When he got back to Rocky's duplex, Adam got a beer from the fridge and listened to the messages on her answering machine.

One was a marketing call. The other was from Mr. Fairbanks at the factory where she had worked. He inquired about her health, her children, and if she would be interested in getting her job back. Adam deleted it.

He walked down the hall to see if she had heard him or the message. She hadn't. She was asleep.

He switched the television on, but he couldn't sit still. His mind replayed Hyperon's words. Did Hyperon know what Adam was planning to do? How could he? For a moment, Adam considered taking the problem to Mr. Specter, but he hated being in the man's presence now as much as he had enjoyed it before.

He paced the kitchen, rummaging in the cupboards for anything to snack on. The TV droned, but it didn't have its usual calming effect. Adam couldn't think of anything except getting away from this place as soon as he finished his task.

Adam hadn't brought much when he had come to live at Rocky's. He really hadn't had much to bring. Now, he began to throw it all into a duffle bag. He put some clothes, his shoes from Specter, and a couple sundry items in the bag. He went to the corner of the kitchen counter where Rocky kept her cash in a red envelope. He took the whole thing. If she complained, he would explain that he had to use it for a surprise he was planning for her. She would go for that, and he needed to be ready to go at a moment's notice.

What if he skipped town without doing Specter's bidding? What if he could just walk away?

A knock interrupted his thoughts, and he began to perspire. He knew who was knocking.

Instead of the abhorrent yellow tie, however, Folly stood at the door with a conspiratorial glance over her shoulder.

"Quick," she said, "let me in before we're seen."

He stood aside, and her perfume emptied his mind of his troubles momentarily. He still couldn't put a finger on what the other elusive smell was, but he followed her into the kitchen, glancing at the doorway of the bedroom where Rocky was asleep[312].

"Listen," Folly said in a low voice, "when are you planning to pull off your job for Specter? This town is suffering. People are really in need, and Hyperon's nonsense is just making things worse."

"Well," he glanced down at the duffle bag.

She rolled her eyes.

"Really?" Sarcasm dripped from her tongue. "Do you really think you can elude Specter? Do you really care so little for the hoards of suffering people in this town? If Wisdom succeeds, who will take care of the single moms like Rocky? Wisdom would get rid of every grant and program. I've heard that she tells her people that if they don't work, they won't eat! I say we should rob the rich to feed the poor[313]."

Adam felt the old, familiar rise and fall of his emotions. He wanted to be a good person who cared well for the less privileged, but he wanted even more to be his own man and go where his own heart desired.

---

312 Prov. 7:21-23
313 2 Thess. 3:10

The fog in his mind lifted and revealed one inconsistency.

"Specter isn't taking care of Rocky in all this," Adam said. "He wants to off her."

Folly's wide eyes grew wider. She crossed the kitchen and covered his mouth with her hand. "She belongs to the other side," Folly said, "so we have to get rid of her. Besides, she knows too much of how we operate now that she's close with you[314]."

Folly crossed back to the front window and looked out the curtains. Adam supposed she was right. Rocky would go back to Wisdom and leave him in a heartbeat if her mind was clear.

"There are a few others we're going to have to get rid of," Folly said. Adam's dread surged.

"Two children snuck into the Megascops this week and overheard too much of Mr. Specter's innermost thoughts," Folly told him. "They may try to stop you."

Adam laughed. "Children?" he asked. "Now Specter thinks I am going to be derailed by children? You can take this message back to him: 'It's like taking candy from a baby.' That's what he told Horbah the other day."

"Listen, Adam, I care about you," she came closer to him. "I just want you to do this job and stay safe for the benefit of us all." She wrapped her arms around his neck.

"I can do it," he told her. It felt like a promise.

---

[314] Prov. 14:1

She smiled, and her blood red lips parted to reveal even, white teeth. "I believe you can," she said. She kissed him, and the memories of all the time he had spent at her house came rushing back.

At least he had an ally in all of this.

"Mr. Specter just wanted me to warn you about the children. It is a girl with brown braids and a little street urchin, about this tall," she held her hand out to indicate the size of a four or five year old.

Adam could picture the girl with brown braids.

"Isn't Horbah supposed to be taking care of that girl?" he asked.

Folly nodded.

"He is on her track, but you must be vigilant too. She may have told Hyperon and the others what she heard," Folly said.

Adam whistled.

"So that's how he knows!" he said.

Folly pulled back and looked up at him. "Knows what?" she asked.

Adam considered lying. "It's probably nothing significant," he told her, deciding to go with the truth, "but Hyperon seemed to know some of my plans."

"When did you see Hyperon?" she asked.

"This morning," he said.

She nodded. "Well, if he isn't trying to stop you, that's good. Watch out for the other kid too. Specter says it's elusive and dangerous."

Adam tried to imagine a dangerous kindergartener, but couldn't.

He heard stirring in the bedroom. "Hey," he whispered urgently, "you'd better go."

She rolled her eyes. “I know where I’m not appreciated! Come and see me sometime,” she said and left as quickly as she had come.

Folly believed he could do this. He knew he could. Just this one more job, and he would be his own master[315].

315 Prov. 1:11-18

Chapter 57

Hyperon walked to the edge of town at dusk. He enjoyed the cool evenings when he could work on Wisdom's house and imagine the life they would lead together.

Tonight, he was setting windows and doors. Paddy had surprised him by saying that she had arranged for them to be delivered the day before.

"That's funny," he had laughed with her. "I didn't even order any yet!"

She was triumphant in her joy. "Wisdom provides for her people," Paddy had said. He didn't even ask where the money had come from. Hyperon was simply thankful and exultant that Wisdom's people were united in wanting her with them.

He had tried to warn Paddy about Adam.

"I don't know what he said to you, Paddy, but you mustn't trust him," he said.

"Honey, I wouldn't trust him farther than I can throw him," she kept her hands busy snapping beans.

"What did he want?" Hyperon was curious.

"He wants us to meet in his building," she said.

Hyperon had plenty of protests, but Paddy held up her large hand.

"I didn't tell him as much, but I wouldn't set a toenail in there, and you can just stop your hollerin'," she said.

He smiled at the remembrance. "Hollerin'," indeed. He hadn't even uttered one word. He was glad that Paddy had good sense.

Cameron's grumblings came to mind as Hyperon stood on the road and surveyed Wisdom's house with the gloaming framing it. It definitely wasn't a shack, but it would look homelier with the windows and doors.

Saul had been here earlier, checking to make sure everything was secure. Hyperon was thankful for Wisdom's people who were willing to help keep an eye on the place. He noticed when he walked onto the porch that Saul had kept busy during his watch.

The back windows were hung in place neatly along with the back door. Everything smelled new, and Hyperon smiled at the sawdust on the concrete floor. He got to work right away.

Prudence sat at her desk, looking out on the street. It was hard to keep her mind on the puzzle she was working when she wanted to think about the Lady and Truth and Justice.

Horbah leaned on a fence post across the street. Prudence would have chuckled when it toppled over and he fell with it, but his presence was sobering. He stood up and straightened himself. He left the fence post where it was.

Prudence shut her eyes tightly. She could see the Lady bending over her in the alley. She remembered what it felt like to be lifted up and carried to safety.

That was the real difference. The enemy destroyed and left things as they lay. The Lady redeemed and picked up the pieces- no matter how many or how shattered- and patiently pieced them back together again[316].

---

[316] Lam. 3:55-60

Prudence opened her eyes, found the final puzzle piece, and popped it into its place.

Tonight they would meet at Marv and Obedience's home. It was risky, but Hyperon knew that it was worth the risk.

He hurried to finish work at the bakery. Cameron was taking his time with his soup, though most of the other customers had come and gone. Hyperon watched the old man out of the corner of his eye as he wiped down the counter and the other tables.

Bene ran in from Paddy's. "Need help?" he asked and didn't wait for an answer before he fetched the mop out of the utility closet.

"You're going to clean the table right out from under my bowl," Cameron complained. "What's the hurry, anyway?"

Hyperon knew what his hurry was. The boy was looking forward to the meeting. He planned to go see Rocky alone tonight and bring her to the meeting. Wisdom had told Prudence that they all should be gathered there. If he could just persuade Rocky to come, maybe it would save her from whatever terrible fate Specter had planned. He set aside his frustration and crossed the room. When Cameron peered up through his bushy white eyebrows, Hyperon slid into the booth seat across from him.

"You don't have to hurry," Hyperon said. "We have an important meeting tonight, so we are just cleaning as much as we can before closing time."

"Hmph," Cameron lifted his spoon slowly to his frowning mouth.

"Prudence told me that she visited you recently," Hyperon tried to remember what the girl had told him about the visit.

"I suppose you put stock in the book of fairy tales she carries?" Cameron asked. Then, without waiting for the reply, "A bunch of nonsense if you ask me."

Hyperon smiled wryly.

"You know, it does seem too good to be true, but what if it is?" Hyperon asked.

Cameron wrinkled his brow. "What?"

"What if the story is true? What if the Shepherd rescued the sheep? What if the fragrance from the blossoms of the vine really became the Lady Wisdom? What if her Father really is presiding over all- the living and the dead? What good would it do you to hold onto doubt? What good would it do your wife[317]?" Hyperon said.

Cameron chewed thoughtfully.

"It would be like trying to grab hold of water," Hyperon answered the question for him. "It would run right through your hand, leaving you holding nothing."

The complainer was silent for once. His soup bowl was empty. He plunked two coins down on the table, stood, and shuffled to the door. He turned back for a moment.

"Sounds like we're both empty-handed[318]," he said and left.

Bene leaned on the mop, admiring the shiny floor. "You're not empty-handed, Hyperon. You're like

---

317 1 Cor. 15:19-20
318 1 Cor. 15:50

someone who drinks really good water and is never thirsty again[319]," the boy said.

Hyperon stood and stretched and smiled. They finished the cleaning and crossed the alley to Paddy's.

While Bene and Sparrow ate their supper, Hyperon asked Paddy to come with him to the doorway. He spoke in a low voice.

"I've got to get Rocky," he said. "I'm going to go to her place and talk her into coming to Marv's."

Paddy crossed her arms. "What if your friend is there?" she asked

Hyperon shrugged. "Wouldn't the Shepherd go after the one sheep?" he asked.

Paddy smiled. "I suppose He would," she said.

He smiled and set off.

---

[319] Jn. 4:14

Chapter 58

Horbah hovered like a shadow nearby as Prudence walked home from school. Haste ran past her and pulled one of her braids.

"Slow poke," he called.

She kept her eye on the heavy set man who followed her. He didn't seem to mind that she knew he was there but kept a stone's throw between them. Just as she turned onto the street where her house was, she noticed that someone had stopped the man and was talking with him.

It was another man with an ugly yellow tie. Neither one of them was looking at her, so she circled around behind the house on the corner and crept up through the hedges. A dog whined in the fenced yard. She smiled at it, and it wagged its tail. She was glad it decided to be quiet.

"You've got to go now," the man in the yellow tie said. "We need to make sure this job gets done the right way," he said.

The man who had been shadowing her nodded glumly.

"What about the girl?" he asked.

"Forget about her for now, or if she causes any trouble, bring her along and cast her in with the others," the man in the yellow tie said.

The man grunted, and they parted ways. The man with the yellow tie walked away like he was walking home at the end of a busy workday in an office somewhere. Horbah walked as if he wanted to break up the concrete of the sidewalk with every step.

The dog yipped. Prudence backed through the hedges and reached a few fingers through the chain link. The dog licked her fingers.

"Being cast in doesn't sound promising[320]," she said to the dog.

Perhaps if she became the spy instead of the victim, she would be able to stop whatever it was that they were up to. She ran on light feet through the back yards of the houses on her street until she could see the man who usually followed her. He had already passed her house and was focused on the ground as he made his way out of town.

On a whim, she followed him.

Adam held a weeping Rocky in his arms. She had woken up and was an emotional disaster. He just wanted to get this job over with. Tonight was the night.

"I just don't know if I'm doing the right thing by staying away from my kids," she said.

"Hey," he said to her, "let's go out and get this off your mind."

She sniffled and nodded.

"I'll just get dressed up," she said.

He sat and waited a quarter of an hour for her to do whatever it was she did to attempt to make herself look like less of an old bag. When she was finally ready, he took a six pack from the fridge and put it into an old picnic basket.

Rocky started crying again.

"What is it now?" he asked.

---

[320] Dan. 3:15-18

"I used that basket once when I took the kids out into the country for a picnic," she said. "We had such a time that day! You should have seen how Sparrow…"

Adam interrupted her. "Look, this kind of sentimentality isn't going to help your mental health," he said. "Are you going to forget about it and come with me or should I look for other company?"

"I'm coming," she said, cowed.

They drank one beer on the trolley. Then, Adam slipped a pill into another bottle and passed it to her while they walked out of the city limits.

"I'm going to show you my building project," he said to distract her from the fact that he was attempting to drug her.

She began to wobble slightly, and he took her arm. Soon, they were beyond the reach of the city dwellers. The night surrounded them, and Adam felt his palms grow sweaty as he contemplated what he needed to do to finish this one last task for Specter. Haught had not yet appeared.

Adam showed Rocky around the building and then encouraged her to lie down beside him. She was snoring within minutes.

He crossed to Hyperon's house and tried the door. It was locked, so he went to the back and broke out a window. A noise arrested his attention. He glared into the woods all around but saw nothing. He gingerly climbed over the broken glass.

Inside, he found that Hyperon had completed the dry wall and was beginning to prepare the flooring. Luckily, all the flooring, cabinetry, and appliances were stored inside the building. Hyperon would lose it all.

Adam began making a pile of scraps of paper and other small chunks of wood at the base of a load bearing interior wall. He heard something and looked out to see Haught approaching.

He whistled from the window, and Haught's grin shone through the night.

"I'm going to go check on something," Adam explained. "You knock a hole in that wall and get all that trash inside so we can light a fire with it."

"Yes, sir," the boy said.

Adam crossed back to his building. Rocky was just as he'd left her. He grunted as he lifted her drugged form to haul her all the way back to Hyperon's.

Haught had completed his task by the time Adam returned.

"Who's this?" he asked.

"No matter," Adam told him, out of breath. "We're going to make it look like she's the guilty party, but she'll be dead when anyone comes to investigate."

Adam went and unlocked the front door. He laid Rocky across the threshold. She sprawled in her drugged sleep, and Adam realized anew how awful Rocky looked. She seemed a fitting offering to be given to Specter. What could Wisdom care about one who had forsaken her?

Footsteps on the road gave him pause, but when he looked out the door, he saw the jogging form of Horbah.

"Specter sent me to make sure it gets done," he explained.

"It's about to get done," Adam laughed, but he begrudged the fact that Specter was checking up on him.

"We won't leave one stone upon another[321]," Horbah said.

"Light the match," Adam commanded Haught.

"In the name of Wisdom," Haught said as he lit it and tossed it onto the pile of papers in the damaged wall.

Horbah produced two cans of lighter fluid. He gave one to Adam. They doused the adjoining walls, and the fire began to spread.

When it began to pinch his skin, Adam said, "All right. Let's go."

The three men ran out the front door into the night. Haught headed back into town.

"Shall we watch?" Horbah said. Adam didn't really desire to stick around, but he crouched behind a nearby tree with his accomplice. He might as well stay until he was sure that the job was done properly.

He didn't see the little girl inching away from the forest and running back toward town.

---

[321] Jer. 52:13; Mt. 24:2

Chapter 59

When Hyperon got to Rocky's, the sun was setting. The landscaping didn't look too good, but the roof was holding steady. At least some of his work was bearing fruit.

He knocked, but there was no answer. He didn't hear any sounds from within, and the lights were off. He went around the back of the building and tried the back door. It was locked.

There was nothing to do except go to Marv's house alone.

It wasn't too far from Rocky's. When Hyperon was about a block away from the house, he stopped and leaned against a tree. The sun had set, and the dusky twilight settled over the city like a blanket. Electric lights repulsed the quiet night and spurred vehicles, people, and sounds to keep awake. Hyperon thought about the long bus ride that had brought him to Opportunity. It seemed a lifetime ago. It was. He was a different man now.

When he was satisfied that he wasn't being watched or followed, he circled around behind Marv's house and knocked softly at the back door.

Obedience opened the door, and he slid inside. She closed it again quickly. Saul and his wife sat in the kitchen, along with Lovely and Marv. It was the only room in the house without windows. Hyperon leaned on one of the counters. Obedience shuffled some food around, but no one wanted to eat much.

"Everything seemed fine at the house," Saul said.

Hyperon smiled. "Thanks to your help!" he said.

"Where's Prudence?" Lovely asked.

Obedience exchanged glances with Marv as she cut up some fruit. "She hasn't come in from school yet," Obedience said. Hyperon instinctively looked out at the darkened sky.

"Does she normally take this long to get home?" he asked.

"Occasionally," Obedience replied, "when she goes to visit those children in the alleys. She calls them her 'Shadow Children.'"

Hyperon smiled. He hoped that was what was keeping her now. He pictured Truth and Prudence working together.

A knock sounded on the front door.

"Should I get it?" Hyperon asked quietly, and moved to open it without waiting for a reply.

When he opened the door, he was as surprised as the man who stood there. They looked into one another's shocked faces.

"I thought you said I'd be welcome," the old man said.

Hyperon smiled and stood back, leaving room for the man to enter.

"Of course you are," Hyperon said. "Come in."

Cameron stepped in and took off his top hat. He was dressed in a splendid striped suit, with shiny shoes and buckles. Obedience peeked out of the kitchen, closely followed by Paddy, who had just arrived through the back door with Bene and Sparrow.

"Well, Mr. Cameron!" Paddy exclaimed. "It's about time you joined in the fun!"

"Hmph," Cameron said, "I don't know about fun, but I have been thinking over what you people have told me."

Hyperon took his hat and led him into the kitchen where Obedience got him a cup of coffee.

"So, what made you decide to come?" Hyperon asked.

"I realized that it was always one of you people who spoke to me, and never anyone else. I guess if Wisdom's people are the ones who take the time, then I will take my time with them," he said.

"Wisdom makes time for everyone," Lovely said.

"You can sit by me," Sparrow said, patting the bench seat next to her, "and I will show you what to do."

The old man looked emotional as he slowly crossed the kitchen and took the seat next to the little girl.

A silence had settled on them when Prudence burst through the front door.

"Hyperon!" she gasped. "They've set your house on fire!"

Prudence gasped for breath.

"I followed Horbah," she said, "and he met two other men at your house."

"Honey, why would you do such a thing?" Paddy put her hands on her hips.

"While he was following me today, I saw him meet a man with a yellow tie. I heard them mention your name, Hyperon," the girl explained.

"But, Hyperon," she interrupted herself, "I don't have time for the rest. Go! They were setting your house on fire!"

Hyperon burst out the door with Saul on his heels. He calculated that it would take at least ten minutes to reach the outskirts of town. It was going to be too late.

He ran with all that was in him anyway. Saul trailed behind. Soon, it was the familiar city gate and then the dirt road beyond. Hyperon grew sick as he detected the red glow on the horizon.

Even in the darkness of night, he could see the blackness of the smoke rising, choking out the stars.

As he ascended a rise in the road, he could see that Wisdom's house was indeed on fire.

His anger and shock were replaced by grief as he approached. He had built in vain. A sob escaped him. He would not be able to put the fire out.

Part of the roof collapsed, and the burst of flame singed his skin. He shielded his eyes against it, and it was then that he saw the woman. She was lying in the front doorway in the only wall that still stood. He could not tell if she was dead or alive, but the flames would consume her soon.

Hyperon rushed forward. The fire reached for him and licked his skin. It burned. He knelt by the woman and saw to his horror that it was Rocky. Could she have set the fire?

He quickly lifted her in his arms. She moaned. She was alive. He slapped at the flame that had just started in several places on her clothing. The roar in his ears deafened him. He struggled to run away with her from the blaze.

The wall collapsed behind him, but he did not turn to watch it. He wasn't sure he was out of range yet.

He stumbled and they fell into the grass just out of the black ring spreading from the house. He realized absently that he had set her on a flowering vine.

Hyperon coughed. Rocky seemed to be still unconscious. He knelt over her and laid her carefully on her back. It was hard to tell how serious her burns were.

"Stand up," came a cold voice from behind him.

Hyperon whirled to see Horbah and Adam. Adam pointed a pistol at Hyperon's forehead.

"Is Specter so desperate to regain a following?" Hyperon demanded through clenched teeth.

"You're the desperate one now, Hyperon," Adam said. "You're back to no woman, no house, no money, and no hope."

Hyperon relaxed and stood to face them.

"I have a hope[322]," he said confidently, "and I would share it with you still, Adam."

The pistol lowered slightly, and Hyperon perceived a slight tremor to the hand.

"I know why you did it," Hyperon continued, staring down the barrel of the gun. "Specter controls you, but you could leave it all behind. Trust Wisdom!"

Adam's eyes shifted nervously to Horbah and back to Hyperon.

"Even though I destroyed everything of yours, you still want me to be on your side?" Adam asked incredulously.

"Just end him," Horbah crept closer.

"I want you to be on Wisdom's side," Hyperon said, "because in the end, hers will be the only side."

---

[322] Jer. 29:11-13; Heb. 12:1-3

Footsteps distracted them all. Saul came with Paddy. Prudence and Bene followed close behind.

"Hyperon, your house!" Paddy wailed.

"Stand back," Adam screeched.

Hyperon could see the terror in his eyes.

"Kill them, you dolt," Horbah shouted, "or you're going to have more witnesses to all that you've done."

Paddy shielded the two children and stepped back.

Just then, Specter emerged from the trees. All eyes seemed to be on him as the fire raged in the background. Hyperon's burns seared into his flesh.

Adam aimed the pistol at Rocky's unconscious form.

"Not her, you fool," Specter hissed, "the old woman."

Horbah lurched for the gun then, struggling to wrestle it from Adam's hand. Adam turned on him and fired. Hyperon heard Prudence scream.

Hyperon could see a spatter of blood, and then Horbah fell to the ground.

Adam's crazed eyes reflected the unbridled fire as he cocked the hammer again. Specter stood behind him.

Paddy pushed the children to the ground and took two courageous steps toward him.

It only took a second for Adam to aim the gun and squeeze the trigger, but to Hyperon, the moment the bullet shattered the end of the pistol lasted an eternity.

Hyperon leapt sideways and intercepted the bullet. He saw Adam stumble backwards and run for the cover of the woods. Flashing lights and sirens came from the city.

Hyperon was suddenly aware that Saul was kneeling over him.

"Hyperon!" he was calling, "Hyperon!"

Chapter 60

Adam watched from the cover of the trees as Saul desperately tried to help Hyperon.

He considered shooting but knew that Saul was out of range. Paddy and Specter stared at one another. Adam looked down at the gun still in his hand. When he looked back, Specter had melted away into the trees on the far side of the clearing. The fire crackled and choked.

Before Adam could decide what to do, the sirens reached the site. Emergency crews poured from the vehicles. They swarmed around Paddy, the girl, Rocky's boy, and the prostrate forms of Rocky, Hyperon, and Horbah.

The men helped Saul move Hyperon's form away from Rocky. The boy was kneeling beside his mother. One officer began to give chest compressions to Hyperon. Saul was motioning to the forest. Adam knew he should run back to the city, but he couldn't tear himself away from the scene unfolding before him.

The officer bent over Horbah and felt for a pulse. He let the man's arm drop, and Adam assumed that he was dead. Another siren approached. It was an ambulance. More paramedics emerged, only to be met by an officer. Two of them returned to the vehicle to exchange their medical bags for white sheets. The other hurried to Rocky's side and began to minister to her wounds.

The sheets were placed over the bodies of Horbah and Hyperon. The boy wept aloud and clung to the dead form of Hyperon.

Adam jumped at a tug on his sleeve. He recoiled as if he'd been burned, expecting to see Specter there.

Instead, the little waif from the alley stood gazing at him.

"What do you want?" Adam demanded.

The child turned his sorrowful eyes out onto the tragic scene in the clearing. He reached for Adam's hand.

"Don't touch me," Adam said angrily, taking two steps back. "You're filthy, and I hate you."

The little one started crying, and Adam turned fearfully to look at the people in case any of them heard the wailing.

Apparently, they couldn't hear it above the sirens. Adam decided it was now or never, and he went through the forest to take a different road back into the city.

He had many miles circling the city in the underbrush to consider that he could not go to his old apartment or to Rocky's home. They would search for him there. He had only one place to go: Specter's. He had to trust Specter to work out his difficulties for him.

It was dawn by the time he reached the office. The secretary had not even arrived yet. Adam waited in the alley until he saw her pull up.

He followed her in.

"It's urgent," he told her. "I need to see Mr. Specter right away." He almost screamed at her when she told him to take a seat in the waiting area. She dialed a number and mumbled into the receiver. He paced, nervously looking out of the window.

Specter came through the back door, and for the first time, Adam was not surprised by his appearance.

He didn't wait for an invitation to come in to Specter's office. He followed his boss in and pulled the door closed behind him. Specter sat while Adam paced in front of his desk.

"I presume you have an explanation for that embarrassing attempt?" Specter prompted.

"Horbah is dead," Adam said, "and so is Hyperon."

Specter grinned. "Never mind, my boy," he said.

"And now, Rocky will be a witness and so will Saul," Adam said. "I am a wanted man."

"Why, I am shocked that you consider yourself in any danger," Specter poured them each a glass of wine.

"I will take care of any repercussions you may have, but in the meantime, you should try to relax," Specter soothed.

He reached into his desk drawer. "I have just the thing," Specter said. "There is a symphony tonight at the Megascops. You remember it?"

Adam sipped his wine and nodded. He slowly lowered himself into one of Specter's chairs.

"Simply everyone is going to be there," Specter explained. "Folly has plans to go, and I can introduce you to so many others. I just happen to have a ticket here. Wouldn't you like to come along?"

Adam looked at the ticket. It was embossed with gold and the cost was evident. It would be good to take his mind off of his problems. He nodded.

"Wonderful," Specter said. "Why don't you get some sleep in the back room. I'll make sure no one disturbs you. In the meantime, I'll rustle up some clothes for you to wear to the Symphony, and we'll be on our way about six this evening. How does that sound?"

Adam nodded again, as one in a trance. He suddenly realized how sleepy he was. Specter herded him to the back room, and he lay down to sleep upon a cot. His last thought was that Specter had not seemed to care much about Horbah's death.

It seemed mere minutes later that Specter was rousing him. Adam had a crick in his neck as he looked up at his boss. Specter was holding up a tuxedo with a blue bow tie.

"Look what I found for you," he said proudly.

Adam dressed and washed his face and tried to wash the memory of the night before from his mind. He wondered at Hyperon's willingness to jump into a fire for a woman who hated him. He remembered the look of grim determination on Paddy's face as she came towards him[323]. He relived his own shock as Hyperon took the bullet for her. He wondered if Saul would report him to the police. He wondered what Rocky would do now. Perhaps he could blame it all on Haught. He wondered a lot of things, but he pushed them away.

Then, a startling thought hit him just as if it had been a bullet.

He would never be free now.

For the rest of his life, he would have to rely on Specter's generosity to keep him from being convicted of murder. Specter could use it as blackmail if Adam didn't do whatever he wished. What sense was there in

---

[323] Prov. 13:14

being an equal partner when the other guy held your life in the palm of his hand?

"The car is here," Specter called through the door.

Adam followed him to a luscious pearl colored limousine. Folly, draped in fur, held open the door. Rubies encased her throat. She laughed. Adam climbed in. The Megascops was not far.

A porter took their coats. It was an elegant evening party. The room was packed with well-to-do patrons who had all come to hear the symphony.

"Adam, come with me," Folly was saying as she took his arm. She led him through the halls to a circular ball room. He was conscious of her fine, gloved hand on his arm, the jingle of the bells worn around her ankle. Her auburn hair sparkled in the light of the great chandelier suspended above them[324].

The crowd pressed in and took their seats. Adam and Folly found theirs and sat to watch the symphony players ready their instruments.

Adam examined the room. The ceiling stretched up into shadows above them. A circular stair case ascended around the ball room, making it a sort of cylinder. He saw people sitting in balconies at every floor. There must have been seven floors that he could see.

The conductor tapped his baton on his music stand. The room went silent. Folly leaned closer to Adam. He thought of Rocky and felt sick. He looked up at the spiraling stairs and felt as though it might have

---

324 Prov. 5:5

been the gyres of a vulture. He could not hide his deeds. He could not change them. He was a slave to the demanding master he had hoped to elude. His future filled with images of the abuse he would suffer at the hands of Specter. This evening's treat tortured him. He now realized that it was just an enticement to forget that Specter ruled him.

The music began, a low thunderous wave of melancholy. The French horns seemed to pronounce his guilt while the violas frayed his nerves much as a busy bow will fray its strings. Even the harp held no soothing properties for his tormented mind but instead, each pluck felt as though it were a stinging slap on his cheek. Now, the words of Hyperon played louder than the music. Hyperon had wanted to forgive him, to include him. He did not understand it.

Adam excused himself to find some water.

"Oh, bring me some," Folly whispered. "I'm simply dying of thirst."

He exited through one of the sides. He spotted a refreshment table and made for it. He procured his ice water, but when he turned he saw something that made him forget about drinking it.

There, at the foot of the great spiral staircase stood Folly's mirror image. She had the same auburn hair, the same blue eyes. Adam saw Wisdom.

Everyone else in the room continued about his business, but Adam and Wisdom stared at one another. He considered running away. She frightened him. Her dress was simple, blue velvet. Her feet were bare and he wondered how she had been allowed in without proper attire. The music from the great room swelled. Adam noticed tears shining from her eyes.

She turned to ascend the staircase.

He set his water back on the table and followed her. He weaved through the men and women crowding the room and conversing on the staircase. Adam had a sudden thirst for her. It wasn't like his desire for Folly. Instead, it was like the arid parched throat of a man who has never known what water is[325].

He did not care who saw or heard him now.

"Wait!" he tried to call. There were so many things he didn't understand. He wondered if he'd even be able to hear her speak if he caught up to her.

She climbed without ceasing. Around and around the great room the stair wove. People adorned the balconies at the sides, all looking down on the orchestra. Velvet curtains partially screened them from the staircase.

At times, he almost caught up to her. Adam would look down to get his footing, and then she would be almost beyond sight again. It was like spinning on a swing and never being able to catch a clear view of anything.

At the very top, she stopped and entered a balcony. Its wall was short, allowing a view of the miniscule orchestra so far below.

He swallowed the air in great gulps as he followed her. She turned to face him and held up one slender arm.

---

[325] Ps. 63:1

"Will you confess[326]?" she said.

He heard her even above the crescendo of the music. Her voice quenched his thirst. He wondered how he could have lived without hearing it for so long.

"I cannot," he said. "I would have to die."

"Then you are dead while you live[327]," she replied. A boy slipped out of the shadows- older than the child he had seen at the scene of the fire- and stood by Wisdom's side. His young face had an uncanny look of grim determination.

Adam stared at the Lady and almost wished that he could confess if only to please her. But it was out of the question.

Specter emerged from the shadows.

"She is beautiful," he whispered to Adam.

"Yes," Adam agreed.

"But she is dangerous," hissed the master. "I've been working all my life to exact revenge from her and all she does is ruin my plans. Don't trust her."

Adam was very aware that he didn't trust Specter either.

"Confess and come to me, Adam," she said. "Your time is near, and you are in danger." Her hand stretched toward his. The little boy walked forward and held out both of his hands.

"I cannot confess, lady," he pleaded, "but I want to come with you."

"If you truly desired to come, confession would be a joyful task," she said.

---

326 1 Jn. 1:9

327 Rom. 6:20-21

"Listen to her," Specter said, "Speaking nonsense. Stay with me, and I will keep you from confession. No one will ever need to know."

"She knows," Adam said, motioning to Wisdom.

"I cannot save you if you are unwilling, Adam," she said, "but I desire that you would be saved[328]. Confess and turn to me!" The little boy was almost close enough to touch, but Adam didn't take his eyes from the Lady's face.

Adam did not care for either of his choices. He determined within himself to be free. He would not serve either master. He was master of himself, wasn't he[329]?

He began backing slowly toward the balcony wall. The symphony's music floated up and around him. He timed his steps to the low notes[330].

He could see Wisdom's beautiful mouth moving, but he could no longer hear her voice. The music drowned it out. The little boy looked back at her once, and then he stood still.

Specter, on the other hand, stepped toward him in time with the music.

"That's it, my boy," he coached. "Show her who your master is."

Adam's legs bumped the balcony's wall. He glanced over his shoulder into the shadowed recesses of the ceiling and the well lit orchestra below. He would find his own water. Wisdom held out her hand. He sneered at her, and then he jumped[331].

---

328 Ez. 18:21; 1 Tim. 2:3-4
329 Prov. 12:15
330 Prov. 28:26
331 Prov. 1:32

He fell into the air as the only place where he could be his own cruel master. His eyes focused upward on the grinning face of Specter as he heard screams from the crowd. He envisioned Wisdom weeping from the balcony over his dark purple blood spilled out on the enameled floor. He was his own master. As Specter's triumphant laughter drowned out the screaming, Adam recognized that the stifled smell hovering around Folly had been that of death.

Chapter 61

Trickling water roused Hyperon from a peaceful slumber. Someone was singing.

"Though you walk through the valley of the shadow of death, you will fear no evil. For I am with you. I have comforted you[332]."

He knew that voice.

As he sat up, he realized that he was outdoors. There was a stream just next to him. He began to hope that it wasn't just a dream.

Her singing faded, but the song hung all around him. Then, she was kneeling before him, bathing his feet.

"You should not be doing this for me," he said. "I have failed you[333]."

Her eyes smiled though her face remained serious.

"Tell me how you have failed," she said, continuing her task.

"I lost the compass, and I killed a man," he said. "I built in vain, and I am both too selfish and not brave enough to be a living sacrifice."

"May I tell you about your tasks?" she inquired.

He hesitated. "I am afraid to hear about them from your point of view," he admitted.

"You shouldn't be," she said. "In this place, there is no fear of that sort. Perfect love casts out fear."

"I will listen," he said, "and you're right. I am not afraid because you are here."

---

332 Ps. 23:5
333 Jn. 13:5-6

"Instead of returning to your evil ways, you ran from evil, and used the compass to prove your point!" she giggled.

He couldn't help smiling.

"In a time of true need, you used the sword hilt to defend yourself against a Deceiver who justly deserved his punishment. You could not defeat him with your strength or your wit. You relied on me, and I helped you," she continued. "Some enemies must be put to death."

"You did not build in vain when you helped Rocky and Saul and the others. You spent resources you had set aside for yourself for the good of your neighbors, even those who were unkind to you," she went on.

"You were a living sacrifice every time you set a swamp muffin in front of Cameron and showed him kindness. And finally, you embraced ultimate sacrifice when you dragged Rocky from the fire and shielded Paddy from the bullet that took your life," Wisdom grew solemn.

Realization seeped in.

"I do not have to go back," he whispered. "This is not a dream."

"Indeed, you cannot go back," she said, drying his feet.

He pulled her into his arms and kissed her. She laughed.

"I am only sorry that the others have not yet come to this place," he said, "but I cannot feel sad."

"It is like fear," she explained. "There is no sadness here. And as far as Paddy, and Sparrow, and Bene, it is like waiting on a baby to be born. The family huddles in great anticipation to see the new little one emerge and take its first breath. We wait here for them to be born into the beginning that has no end."

"Until that day," he said softly.

"Until that day," Wisdom said. Then excitedly, she pulled him to his feet. "Come and meet my Father."

Chapter 62

Rocky attended two funerals in one day, but they couldn't have been more dissimilar. Her burns had been minimal, and she had been released from the hospital that very morning.

Adam's had been held at the grave site on the hill overlooking Opportunity. His sister had made the arrangements and had never even heard about Rocky, so she had been excluded from the decisions. His casket was to be closed.

Rocky stood near the back, struggling with her emotions. She had not loved him. He had not loved her. He had used her, drugged her, and tried to kill her. She had barely escaped the relationship with her life. She had been wrong to trust him, and she realized, watching the dirt be piled on the casket, that she couldn't trust herself either.

A priest in a flowing black robe officiated. She barely listened to any of his words. A small crowd had gathered. She heard people offering comfort to Adam's sister.

"He was a good boy," one woman said.

"He's in a better place now," a former teacher encouraged.

"You have an angel in heaven watching over you," claimed a third.

Rocky rolled her eyes. What senseless babblings!

In the evening, she appeared late to Hyperon's funeral. It was to be held in the bakery, of all places. All the seats were filled when she arrived, so she tucked herself into the corner with the hat rack. Sparrow and

Bene sat near the counter on a makeshift bench with Paddy. Pastor addressed the crowd from the counter.

"At this moment, sadness fills this room because someone we loved deeply is gone," he said, "but in this very same moment, that someone is experiencing ultimate joy with Wisdom and her Father."

He began to sing the song- Wisdom's song- and many voices joined in. Rocky found herself whispering the words she hadn't uttered in many days.

The song died away, as he had. Rocky found that she was sadder about Hyperon's passing than she had been about Adam's.

"He died to protect someone else," Pastor was speaking again, "and gave the ultimate sacrifice of love. Let us not be embittered that he was taken too soon but rejoice that he walked worthy. Hyperon was Wisdom's man[334]."

The simple casket was closed but covered in wreathes of white flowers. Life seemed to be springing from death. Paddy, a hand on each of Rocky's children, approached the casket.

"Until that day, we will live as Wisdom's people," she told them, "and we will carry on the work that Hyperon was doing- her work."

Rocky saw Bene scrub at his eyes. Sparrow was openly crying.

"We will miss him, but we will grieve differently because we have a hope[335]," Paddy urged them.

Tears of grief spilled over onto Rocky's cheeks.

---

334 Heb. 11:37-38

335 1 Thess. 4:13-14

"Rocky," it was a whisper, like the fragrance from a blossom, "Rocky, come to me."

"I am here," Rocky whispered back. "Show me what I must do."

In that moment, Sparrow turned and saw her. "Mama!" she ran and threw her arms around Rocky's waist.

"Mama, are you okay?" Sparrow asked. Then, Bene was there too, hugging her. Rocky wept and knelt on the ground with their arms around her.

"I hope this means you're here to stay," Paddy said.

Rocky looked up at the smiling baker. "Yes," she answered. "I have tasks to do."

Chapter 63

Specter slammed his fist on Folly's table. The pitcher of water shook.

"His death has just given birth to a dozen more like him," he was saying. "They are all unpersuadable."

"We just need to recruit a dozen more of our own," Folly said nonchalantly.

"What do you know of this boy, Haught?" Specter asked.

"He's one of Dipsuchos' men," Folly mused, "and he's young."

Specter chuckled. "Not your type," he remarked.

She shrugged.

"I'll set him up in Adam's apartment," Specter said, "and I'm sure you wouldn't mind giving him an education."

"Or I'll find someone who will," she said noncommittally.

Specter spoke more to himself now. "We can still use Adam's building. Perhaps I can talk Rocky into being the hostess there," he said.

There was a short silence. Folly flipped the page of the magazine she was reading.

"Would you be able to get Haught here tonight?" Specter asked.

In answer, she picked up her phone. He answered immediately, as if he'd been waiting for her call.

"Come over tonight," she drawled into the phone. It was a short conversation. She hung up.

"He'll be here in less than ten minutes," she said.

Specter rubbed his hands together.

"I'll get out of your way then," he said, reaching over to dim the lights. "Show him a good time and then ask him to do you a favor."

"What favor is that, pray tell? And what favor are you doing me for this favor?"

"I'll double your pay for the month if you persuade him to break in to Hyperon's apartment and steal anything of value there," Specter said.

"He'll report to you in the morning," she promised.

Specter had hardly left her doorway when he saw the young man coming along the road[336]. He stopped dead in his tracks, though, when he also saw Wisdom.

Haught stopped to talk to her.

"I can't hear what you're saying, miss," Specter overheard the boy say.

"I'm sorry," he told her. "I'm in a hurry, and I don't know what you need."

Specter smiled as the boy rushed by and Folly greeted him at the doorway with a kiss. Specter turned toward Wisdom.

She shone. He hated her. He remembered the fiery car crash and the screams of his friends. He remembered her rejection. He remembered every sleepless night he'd spent since.

"Alexander," she called.

It was the first time he'd heard her voice in many years. It brought back his desire to conquer her and make her his own.

---

336 Prov. 7:6-9

"I have defeated you," he said, approaching her cautiously. "Hyperon is dead." Her beauty had not diminished in the many years since their youth. She still appeared youthful. Even Folly could not conceal her age so deftly.

" It's you who is dead, Alexander. Don't deceive yourself," she said softly. "To you, I am no longer Wisdom but Doom. Your days are numbered, but Hyperon's days are endless."

He ran from her and cowered in his home. A cough wracked his body and images of destruction disturbed his mind. He struggled to rid himself of the lingering scent of Folly.

Haught came to his office the next day carrying a large box.

"What's in it?" Specter asked after closing his door.

He opened the lid.

"You'll want to wear the mitt, sir," the boy said, holding up his burned palm in evidence.

Specter put on the mitt. Even so, he could feel the heat radiating from the spyglass as he picked it up.

"Did you look through it?" he asked the boy.

"No," was the simple reply, "It had burned enough of me."

Specter dismissed Haught, and the boy left the office hastily. Specter locked the door with his empty hand.

Careful not to hold it against the skin of his face, he held the spyglass up to look into it.

The light blinded his eye, but the image seared into his mind.

It was an image of Wisdom holding Hyperon's hand as they stood before a great throne where her Father reigned over all.

Specter flung the outdated tool from him and cursed. The blinding light not only blinded him but began burning his hand and arm. He clutched at his head with both hands as he fell to his knees. Wisdom had won.

Chapter 64

Marv had carried Prudence home, away from the sirens, the smoke, and the blood. She had wept through the night.

Obedience smoothed her hair and brought her snacks and drinks. Prudence was thankful for them, but she yearned for the Lady. She had so many questions and so much heartache.

She slept.

After two days, Obedience came into her room at dawn and pushed back the curtain.

"Prudence," she spoke her name softly. "Prudence, your shadow children are here."

Prudence opened her eyes and saw the filthy flurry of hair and the smudged smiles of Justice and Truth. She sat up.

"Is everything okay?" she asked. They smiled.

Truth crossed the room and grabbed her hand. She wanted Prudence to come.

"Did the Lady send you?" she asked. They both nodded.

"Well, just wait til I get dressed, and then I will come with you. I can, can't I, mom?" she said, turning to Obedience.

Obedience smiled. "Yes," she said, "I think the Lady has something for you to do."

Prudence dressed quickly and followed the children out into the brilliant sunshine. Justice stopped her, and motioned for her to bring the green book.

She retrieved it and hurried to keep up with them as they wove in and out of pedestrians and traffic through the city. She was surprised when they climbed the stairs leading to Cameron's door.

She knocked.

He answered promptly.

"I was hoping you'd come," he said, making way for her to enter the hall, "and I was hoping you'd read me the rest of that story. I have been missing Hyperon."

"I would be glad to read it," she said. "It makes Hyperon feel that much closer."

The old man led to the sitting room where Prudence, Truth, and Justice sat on a white couch. He cringed a little at the children's dirty hands on the furniture, but he said nothing. He took his seat across from them and ran a wrinkled hand across his eyes.

"Hyperon was always kind to me," he said, and his voice broke.

Prudence looked at him and saw her own grief personified. They wept together. Prudence took her handkerchief out and wiped her tears.

After she folded it neatly into her pocket, she opened the book and read.

Finally, not knowing what else to do, the sheep lay down in the crook of his limp arm and rested its head next to the great vine growing from his chest.

The fragrance from the blossoms and whisper on the wind united, and the sheep heard that it had become a song. The song filled all the air, and the green vine slowly turned golden.

The sheep realized that in addition to the song, it also heard the steady beating of the Shepherd's heart. It lifted its head and looked into the face that had been dead.

The Shepherd blinked, and then he smiled. He reached up one hand to move the golden vine from his chest and with the other, he patted the sheep on the head.

"Here I am," he told the sheep.

"Baaa," was the only reply the sheep could make, but the Shepherd knew its voice. He knew it was saying, "But you were dead!"

"Ah yes, but I am now alive. Whoever believes in Me, though he die, yet shall he live, and everyone who lives and believes in Me shall never die[337]*," the Shepherd said.*

He stood up, tall and strong.

"Now," he said to His beloved sheep, "come and follow Me[338]*."*

And the sheep did.

---

337 Jn. 11:25-26

338 Mk. 4:17

Recipes from *The Banquet Bakery*

Sparkleberry Muffins

From Paddy's Banquet Bakery

INGREDIENTS

1/3 c Butter
1 c Sugar
1 Egg
1 tsp vanilla
1/2 c sour cream or plain yogurt
3/4 c milk
1 tsp Baking Soda
2 c Flour
Blueberries, Strawberries, Sugar

DIRECTIONS

- Cream butter and sugar. Add egg and vanilla. Blend.
- Combine Flour and Baking Soda
- Alternate adding the flour mixture, milk, and sour cream to the creamed mixture. Beat well.
- Fold in the blueberries and chopped strawberries.
- Distribute to prepared muffin pans. Bake at 375 for 10 mins (15-18 mins for larger muffins).
- Dust with sanding sugar. Makes 12

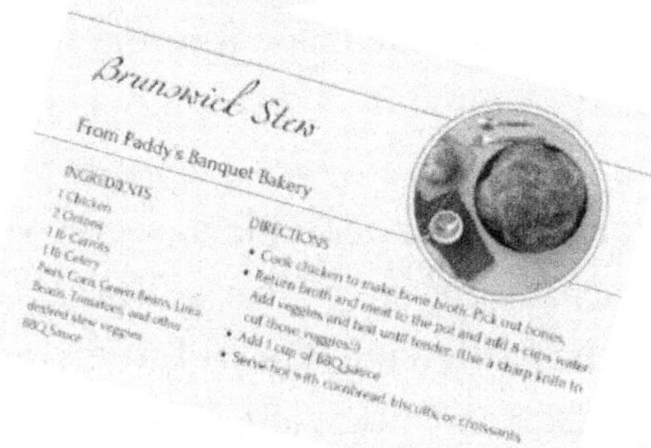

Brunswick Stew

From Paddy's Banquet Bakery

INGREDIENTS

1 Chicken
2 Onions
1 lb Carrots
1 lb Celery
Peas, Corn, Green Beans, Lima Beans, Tomatoes, and other desired stew veggies
BBQ Sauce

DIRECTIONS

- Cook chicken to make bone broth. Pick out bones.
- Return broth and meat to the pot and add 8 cups water. Add veggies and boil until tender. (Use a sharp knife to cut those veggies!)
- Add 1 cup of BBQ sauce
- Serve hot with cornbread, biscuits, or croissants

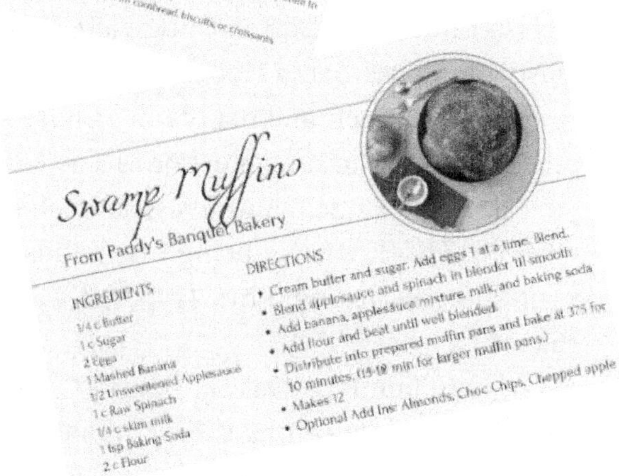

Swamp Muffins

From Paddy's Banquet Bakery

INGREDIENTS

1/4 c Butter
1 c Sugar
2 Eggs
1 Mashed Banana
1/2 Unsweetened Applesauce
1 c Raw Spinach
1/4 c skim milk
1 tsp Baking Soda
2 c Flour

DIRECTIONS

- Cream butter and sugar. Add eggs 1 at a time. Blend.
- Blend applesauce and spinach in blender 'til smooth
- Add banana, applesauce mixture, milk, and baking soda
- Add flour and beat until well blended.
- Distribute into prepared muffin pans and bake at 375 for 10 minutes. (15-18 min for larger muffin pans.)
- Makes 12
- Optional Add Ins: Almonds, Choc Chips, Chopped apple

Acknowledgements

Without the Incarnated Word, there would be no Great Story from which all good stories stem. I am thankful to Jesus for His Word, His Truth, His Justice, and His Wisdom.

Thank you to Incarnation Press, which puts flesh on Christ-exalting ideas. The world needs more good stories that point to the Greatest Story, and you make that possible.

I am deeply grateful to Megan Robertson for trudging through every detail of this manuscript with me. Without you, I would not have made it to the finish line. Thank you for every comment, every comma, and every prayer.

Sitting around the supper table at secret Wisdom meetings of our own, Julius Two Hearts, Darius Chaske, James Hunt, Natasha Littlewind, Dawn Littlewind, Alyssa Littlewind, Darren Littlewind, Kayla Robertson, Dusti Goodbird, Sarah Robertson DeLeon, Joy and Brandon Wegener, and many others have shared precious details of how our Lord Jesus has worked in your hearts, changed your lives, and helped you to have wisdom. Thank you for being my friends and for sharing your faith journey with me. Hyperon's journey was shaped by yours.

My family at Dakota Baptist Church prays for me, uplifts me, encourages me, and inspires me. Thank you especially to Jerry and Nancy Robertson and Rob and Carol Greywater for your love and for making me a part of your families.

Thank you, Nick and Colleen Geray, for your encouragement for this project and even more for serving the Lord through thick and thin. You shine His light, and it is evident every time we get together.

I consider myself one of the most blessed authors out there because of these folks who vie for the BIGGEST FAN position: Rick and Susie Dixon and Stephen and Linda Young. Your prayers, encouragement, and wisdom helped fill the pages of this book and also fill my sails each day.

Thank you to Anna, Judah, Maeve, and Othniel for giving your mom time to write. I pray that every word will be a blessing to you and lead you closer to the Lord Jesus.

Finally, 'thanks' seems an inadequate word for the help that my husband, Paul, has given me on this project through all the years of its development. From untangling plot knots to listening to hours of conversation about font size and on-demand-printing, your unselfish love has fulfilled Ephesians 5:25 over and over again. Thank you for encouraging me to keep writing. I love you.

And thanks to you, dear reader, for taking the time to read this story. I pray that it encourages, strengthens, and heartens you as you follow Jesus.

About the Author

Sarah Dixon Young uses stories every day to share the love of Jesus with her four children, her community, and the world. She is a home educator by day and a writer by night. When she isn't busy with those pursuits, Sarah loves snowshoeing, baking, gardening, or finding adventure in a book or in her real life as a pastor's wife on the Spirit Lake Reservation. Her favorite Scripture is Isaiah 12:2-3: "Behold, God is my salvation; I will trust, and will not be afraid; for the Lord God is my strength and my song, and He has become my Salvation. With joy you will draw water from the wells of salvation." You can follow her adventures at www.SarahDixonYoung.com

More Books by Sarah Dixon Young

In His Light: Opening the Window to the Transforming Love of Jesus (Devotional/Nonfiction)
God on a Shelf (Devotional/Nonfiction)
Advent 2020: Know (Seasonal devotion/Nonfiction)
Receive Him: A Disciple's Advent (Seasonal devotional/Nonfiction)
Gasparilla's Key and the Revenge of the Purple Mermaid (Fiction)

Other Works by Sarah Dixon Young

Weekly Column "Love Much" found in the Devils Lake *Journal*

First Person and Feature Articles at *Baptist Press*
Bible Lessons and Family Worship Ideas at
www.SarahDixonYoung.com

Made in United States
Orlando, FL
28 March 2023

31503024R00241